BLACK SUN ECLIPSE

BOOK TWO: PRAETORIAN SERIES

Praise for *BLACK SUN ECLIPSE*

Holy cow Don and Jeff did it again...I picked up *Black Sun Eclipse* for an expected fifteen minutes, but found myself glued to the pages for two hours. These guys are unparalleled in their technical expertise, realistic scenarios, and thrilling style. If you enjoy military geopolitical fiction, this is your next read. Hooyah!
—MARK DIVINE, NYT best selling author of *The Way of the SEAL*
and *Unbeatable Mind*; Founder, SEALFIT

Black Sun Eclipse is an intriguing glimpse behind the curtain of special operations and the unique professionals who do the deed every day around the globe. As a combat veteran and retired SEAL officer, I found myself convinced in the book's authenticity, following every twist, turn, and setback, while marveling at the professional accuracy and energy of the story. In my opinion, *Black Sun Eclipse* is on par with Tom Clancy's best novels, a whirlwind experience filled with action and suspense until the very last page!
—MARTY STRONG, Author, *In the Shadow of Evil* and *Kandahar Moon*; Twenty-year combat veteran United States Navy SEALs

A tale of authentically portrayed special ops action right down to the last double-tap. Tightly written, intricately layered, and suspensefully paced, *Black Sun Eclipse* has it all—foreign intrigue, ultimate danger, a wily, determined adversary, and an international team of close—combat pros who are as likeable as they are deadly. With accurate descriptions of all source intel collection, analysis, planning, and mission execution characterized by violence of action, this engrossing work of fiction could serve as a real-world guide for global counterterrorist operations. Highly recommended reading.
—DUANE EVANS, former CIA Operations Officer,
U.S. Army Special Forces, and Military Intelligence Officer;
Author, *Foxtrot in Kandahar* and *North From Calcutta*

Don Mann and Jeff Emde strike again with a fast-moving thriller. The Praetorians, a group of combat veterans with unique skills face down the threats of WMD to keep America, and the world, safe. Great character development and tense action will keep the reader's attention throughout the book. An excellent continuation of the Praetorian Series.
—DJ MALLMANN, Author, military/CIA thrillers
Shibboleth and the upcoming sequel *Terraglyph*

BLACK SUN ECLIPSE

BOOK TWO: PRAETORIÁN SERIES

JEFF EMDE and DON MANN

Published by Jeff Emde and BAR/MD Creative
Tucson, Arizona, USA

www.jeffemdebooks.com

Library of Congress Control Number: 2024919970

ISBN: 9798289014764 (Hardback)
ISBN: 9798281464208 (Paperback)

Cover design MD BAR/MD
Cover photographs © Adobe Stock

CONTENTS

FOREWORD

B*lack Sun Eclipse* is the second book in The Praetorian Series. The initial book, *Black Sun Rising*, introduces the reader to the Praetorians, a privately funded, independent team of international counterterrorist operators. While the books are intended to be read in order, it is not necessary. The following includes brief backgrounds on the team members introduced in the initial book.

The leader and sponsor of the Praetorians is Rusty Travis, a Texas tech billionaire whose wife, Cynthia, was killed in the 9/11 terrorist attacks. Despite his grief, he focused his time and fortune on helping the government track down the perpetrators. Frustrated with the bureaucratic inertia inherent in any government operation, he organized his own band of freelance special operators. Their targets are provided by the "steering committee," a group of representatives from the major western intelligence agencies who get plausible deniability and, more importantly, results. The Praetorians don't play by the rules. They don't take prisoners. Their job is simple—they kill terrorists—and they are good at it.

The first Praetorian was Gunny Medina, a grizzled old Marine with one eye and a bad attitude. A legend in the Special Ops community, "Mad Dog" Medina worked for the CIA before teaming up with Rusty. He used his experience and contacts to identify and hire the most experienced warriors from around the world. His first recruit was Alonzo "Lon" Oden, a Texas-born retired Delta Force Master Sergeant. He was followed by John Kernan, a former Navy SEAL Master Chief who retired rather than take a desk job. Next came Nigel Finch, a brash Chief Petty Officer who retired after twenty years with the SBS, the Special Boat Service—Britain's elite maritime commandos. He and Kernan are their maritime operations specialists. Hans Koenig, a German Fallschirjager (Free fall jumper) and specialist in High-Altitude-High-Opening (HAHO) parachute operations, is their jump master. He is also a language specialist who speaks eight languages and is proficient with computers.

When things get cold, the Praetorians look to Magne Berge, a former instructor at Norwegian Winter Warfare Training School. He is an expert in winter warfare, mountaineering, mountain ops, skiing, and all things cold. A former biathlon champion, he also serves as the team's lead sniper. While Berge prides himself on being handsome, he is not the prettiest. That honor falls to Sarah Rabin, a former undercover operator with Mista'avrim, Israel's feared counterterrorist unit. An exotic beauty, she is also an expert in street tradecraft, surveillance, hostage rescue, and interrogation. She is as ruthless and deadly as she is gorgeous, with expertise in Close Quarter Battle (CQB), hand to hand combat, and the use of edged weapons.

The newest members of the Praetorians are Alen Markovic and Steve Change. Marckovic was a Captain in the Serbian Special Brigade and, at 6'5" and 250 pounds, is an imposing figure. He was recruited for his language skills, his operational experience, and his expertise on Soviet era and Russian weapons systems. Chang became the newest member when he was a tapped to be the team's primary computer guy, but his utility goes beyond the keyboard. He was a US Air Force pararescue jumper and is a martial arts expert. Though less experienced than his comrades, he is a quick study and willing to do what must be done.

The Praetorians' most capable adversary to date has been Khalid ibn Mahfous Al-Maadi, a medical doctor and professor who teaches biology and genetics at the University of Cairo. Descended from Egyptian political royalty, Al-Maadi is also the cousin of Al-Qaeda leader Ayman Al-Zawahiri. Determined to make his mark on the world, he started his own terrorist group, Shams Sawda or Black Sun. His nom de guerre is Abu Almawt or Father of Death and his goal is the destruction of Israel. The Praetorians disrupted Al-Maadi's biological weapon attack and killed his Palestinian wife and co-leader, Nura. Al-Maadi managed to escape, hiding out with his cousin who was ultimately killed by an American drone strike. Al-Maadi has had two years to plot his revenge and it promises to be spectacular.

CHAPTER ONE
THE TIGER

The CASA CN-235 rolled to a stop in front of a commercial hangar at Taranto-Grottaglie Airport on the heal of the Italian boot. The CN-235 was a twin engine, turboprop cargo airplane that resembled the venerable C-130 Hercules, albeit about half the size. As the airplane powered down, it dropped its rear ramp and the pilot trudged down to inspect the freight he was to carry to his next destination. Arranged in a neat column just inside the hangar's large doors were three HCU-6/E aviation pallets. The first pallet contained a number of crates of electronic equipment, spools of wire, and toolboxes packed into a tight bundle by plastic shrink wrap. The second was loaded with about fifty small black pelican cases labeled SENSORI SISMICI—Italian for seismic sensors. The third pallet carried a single large wooden crate approximately eight feet long, six feet wide, and five feet tall. It was labeled POSTAZIONE DI LAVORO DEL SYSTEMA SISMICO—Seismic System Workstation. All three had large orange cardboard signs affixed which read PROPRIETÀ DELL'UNIVERSITÀ DI NAPOLI—Property of the University of Naples.

The pilot walked into the small office in the corner of the hangar and spoke to the man behind the desk. "Ciao. Do you speak English?" The man nodded. "I'm Gil Mitchell. I'm supposed to pick up some equipment from the University of Naples and fly it to Iraq." Motioning to the pallets, he added, "I assume that's my cargo over there?"

The man stood to shake Gil's hand. "Yes, it is. It arrived this morning by truck. I am Antonio Antonelli, the air cargo manager. Do you have some identification?"

"Sure. I also have my work order from the university, export authorization from the Ministry of Foreign Affairs, and the Italian customs forms." Gil handed the man his passport and an envelope containing the various forms.

Antonelli took the passport first before inspecting the documents. "American, eh? Couldn't find an Italian pilot to fly this thing?"

"None that was willing to fly to Mosul through the Turkish and Syrian air defense zones."

The man gulped. "Oh. So why are you doing it?"

"The money, of course. It's no big deal, really. I've flown into Mosul plenty of times before." He chuckled, "This time at least no one will be shooting at me...I hope!"

The man smiled. "Let's hope not. Former military?"

Gil laughed, "Aren't we all?"

"So it seems. Where is your copilot? I'll need to see his papers too."

"He's powering down the aircraft. He'll be over in a minute. Have my passengers arrived?"

"Passengers? I was only told about the freight."

"My work order says I'm to give a ride to the folks who'll be using all this crap." As he said this, a van pulled up to the hangar. Right on time. "Ah, speak of the devil." The air cargo manager turned as the van stopped and six people piled out pulling rolling suitcases. It was the rest of the Praetorian team.

Antonelli let out a heavy sigh. "Of course, no one told me. I'll call Customs and Immigration."

Hans Koenig and Sarah Rabin led the group toward the airplane. They were followed by Lon Oden, Magne Berg, Alen Markovic, and Steve Chang. All were traveling with backstopped alias documentation that would survive even the closest scrutiny. Almost anything is available if you're willing to pay for it and Rusty Travis, the head of the Praetorians, was more than willing to do just that. Approaching the air cargo manager, Hans said, "Ciao, I'm Professor Schultz from Berlin Polytechnic. This is Professora Maria Vanelli from the University of Naples."

Sarah took off her sunglasses and smiled. She was radiant as always. "Has our equipment been loaded yet? We need to get airborne as soon as possible. It's a very long flight."

The air cargo manager stared at Sarah. He gave a little bow and said, "Signora, your airplane only just arrived. The equipment is here and ready to load onto the aircraft as soon as I confirm the documentation." Wanting to extend his conversation with the beautiful "professora," he asked, "So, what is all this equipment?"

Motioning to the others to head to the plane, she explained. "This is seismographic equipment. It was designed to monitor volcanic activity, but we're going to install it in and around Mosul Dam to monitor its stability."

Feigning interest, the man asked, "Is there something wrong with the dam?"

"Yes. The Iraqis built the dam over a gypsum formation. Gypsum dissolves when in contact with water. The Iraqis have to constantly grout under the dam to ensure it does not collapse. The lake contains eleven billion cubic meters of water. If the dam fails, it will destroy everything downstream for hundreds of miles. So yes, there is something very wrong with the dam."

"Will your equipment fix it?"

"No, but it will provide advance warning if a problem starts to develop. So, you see it is very important we get our equipment installed as soon as possible."

"Of course, Professora. We will get your equipment loaded immediately."

The air cargo manager was true to his word. He quickly mustered his workers and they loaded the pallets onto the ramp of the CN-235. Gil used the airplane's winch to move them forward into position in the cargo bay. While Gil supervised the loading, Donny, his son and copilot, saw to it that all the required forms were filled out. After an Italian Customs and Immigration Official made sure all their passports were in order, the airplane was ready to depart. They'd been on the ground a little over an hour.

The twin engine CN-235 climbed into the Italian sky as the sun dipped below the western horizon. They vectored east across the Ionian Sea toward Greece. Their flight plan had them crossing into Turkish airspace near Izmir. A direct route to Mosul would take them over Syria which was still an active war zone with Turkish, Syrian, NATO, Russian, and even Israeli military aircraft zipping about. For that reason, commercial aircraft bound for Iraq stayed well north of Syria within Turkish airspace before turning south into Iraq. The Praetorians would do the same.

* * *

The Praetorians' target for this mission was Maksim Kotov, a Russian illegal arms broker working out of northern Syria. Kotov means "cat" in Russian, so he was known to his Russian suppliers as "The Tiger" and to his Arab, Persian, and Turkish customers by its Arabic equivalent— Al Namir. Kotov had been an officer within the Russian military's Main Intelligence Directorate, more commonly known by its Russian initials— the GRU. He served in Afghanistan, Chechnya, Nagorno-Karabakh, and Yemen before resigning to pursue more lucrative opportunities. Kotov was now in the business of selling anything to anyone. He sold to the Syrians, the Iraqis, the Iranians, the Turks, and any terrorist group that showed up on his doorstep with money in hand. A lot of countries wanted him dead, but regional politics made him the Praetorians' problem.

Kotov had the protection of both the Syrians and the Turks. He sold the Turks cluster bombs and other Russian weapons to use against the Kurds. To the Syrians, he sold chemical weapons and the infamous "butterfly" mines the GRU used in Afghanistan. These were explosives that resembled toys and attracted children. The Syrians used these against the Kurds. While the Turks and the Syrians were fighting each other, *both* hated the Kurds even more. When it came to the Kurds, the enemy of my enemy is truly my friend. Both the Turks and the Syrians had an interest in protecting Kotov and his operation.

Almost any weapon was available to Kotov. He had developed extensive contacts with corrupt generals in the Russian military. They would take the weapons out of inventory, mark them down as shipped to the forces in Ukraine or expended in training. The weapons were then shipped to the Syrian port of Latakia and then trucked overland to his compound located near Dayrik, a small Syrian city in the extreme northeast where Syria, Turkey, and Iraq met. While Dayrik was on the Syrian side of the border, the area was under Turkish control. From there he shipped weapons north to Turkey, south to Damascus or west to Iraq, Iran, and beyond.

While NATO was aware of this, Turkey denied its involvement and wouldn't even acknowledge Kotov's existence. What put Kotov on the Steering Committee's radar was information that he had recently acquired a significant amount of Novichok, an advanced Russian nerve agent that he intended to sell to the highest bidder. Under normal circumstances, the Americans or British would simply use the SEALs or the SAS to eliminate Kotov. However, this situation was different. Kotov lived in a compound close to the Turkish border. At the first sign of trouble, he simply slipped across the border into Turkey. The idea of the US or Britain launching a commando raid on the soil of another NATO member was unfathomable. Even if such a raid was successful, the Turks would likely kick the US Air Force out of Incirlik Air Base as they had threatened to do many times before. The loss of Incirlik would severely limit US military capabilities in the region just as Russian influence was on the rise. No, this case required deniability and finesse. It required the Praetorians.

* * *

About three hours into their flight, the white lights of the cargo bay snapped off and were replaced with a soft red glow to restore and preserve the team's night vision. This was their signal. The Praetorians opened the crate on the third pallet. While it did contain a workstation, what they wanted was hidden below it. The bottom half of the crate contained weapons, oxygen tanks, body armor, web gear, specialized cold weather clothing, and parachutes. Prior to joining the Praetorians, Hans Koenig had been a Fallschirmjager (free fall jumper) in the German Army's Kommando Spezialkräfte (Special Forces Command) where he was an Oberfeldwebel, or Master Sergeant. Due to his experience with High-Altitude High-Opening (HAHO) insertions, he would be in command of this mission. The strike team would consist of Hans, Lon Oden, Magne Berg, and Alen Markovic. Sarah and Steve would continue on to Iraq to maintain their cover and provide ground support as needed.

The men stripped off their civilian attire and retrieved khaki clothing from their luggage. Over these they put on knit polypropylene thermal outer garments. Before they jumped, they would add a windproof outer shell, knit ski mask, gloves, and goggles to protect from frostbite. They would be exiting the aircraft at twenty-five thousand feet where the outside air temperature was a balmy negative forty degrees Celsius.

Hans checked his watch—forty-five minutes to "go" time. "Okay, outer wind shells and chutes on." The men helped each other don their parachutes and double-checked all their connections. Each man had at his feet, a rucksack with Level Four body armor, web gear, ammunition, grenades, field medical kit, and any other equipment they might need. Each jumper also carried an individual oxygen tank for the descent. Hans connected his mask to the airplane's oxygen supply system and signaled to the rest of the Praetorians to do likewise.

They needed to breathe pure oxygen well before their exit from the aircraft to flush all the nitrogen from their blood. At lower altitudes, this was not necessary. However, at high altitude the reduced air pressure would cause nitrogen bubbles to form in their blood and they'd get the bends—like a deep-sea diver surfacing too fast. The air pressure in the cargo bay of the aircraft would be reduced gradually to allow the team to adjust so they'd also need the airplane's supplemental oxygen to simply breathe.

Sarah and Steve were wearing cold weather gear. The back of the airplane was frigid and got even colder as you neared the ramp. They were using supplemental oxygen as well since they'd be subject to the same decompression as the insertion team. They helped the jumpers by double-checking everyone's parachute straps but mostly stayed out of the way. The space between the pallets and the fuselage was already cramped enough. Ten minutes before their planned exit time, Gil contacted Hans on the aircraft's intercom. "We're further north than we originally planned, but it won't be a problem."

Hans was concerned. There was a limit to how much ground they covered once the chutes opened. He asked, "How is that not a problem?"

"Jet stream. The subtropical jet stream is unusually low today. We're in it now. You'll have a fifty-knot tailwind. It will also reduce the air blast when you clear our slipstream."

Hans grinned. "That will work!"

"I thought you'd like that. It'll take you a few more minutes to reach the target, but you'll jump further away from the air defense zone and this bird will look more like a pussy-ass commercial flight trying to stay away from the war zone."

Hans signaled to the other men. "We go in five. Disconnect from the aircraft oxygen and connect to your O2 bottles. Put on your gloves, head coverings, and eye protection. Clip on your rucks and secure your weapons."

Steve would be the jump master for this operation; he had experience from his Air Force Pararescue days. He clipped a heavy nylon safety strap from his harness to the fuselage near the back of the plane. Sarah also clipped in but closer to the cockpit. The four men were like alien turtles. They were hunched over from their combat loads. The parachutes on their backs coupled with the rucks strapped to their chests resembled shells.

Between the black head covering, eye protection, and helmets with NVGs attached, they no longer resembled humans.

Gil triggered a flashing yellow light from the cockpit. Seconds later the ramp started to open. A blast of arctic air flooded the cargo bay. The ramp stopped when it was horizontal to the floor of the cargo bay. A few seconds later, a green light flashed. Hans was the first in line. He walked off the back of the ramp and disappeared into the inky gloom. He was immediately followed by Lon, then Alen, and finally Magne. The whole process took less than five seconds. The airplane was suddenly empty.

Steve closed the ramp and the plane began to repressurize. After a couple of minutes, the cockpit door opened. Gil stepped out and asked. "Did everyone get out okay?"

"Yes. No problems."

Sarah commented, "It's in God's hands now."

Gil added, "Button up that crate. We'll be on the ground in about half an hour."

* * *

Though the four men exited the aircraft practically right on top of each other, the airplane was flying at over 400 kilometers per hour (kph) so they were quickly spaced out. Each jumper counted four seconds before deploying his chute to make sure they all opened at approximately the same altitude. Their parachutes were high-performance ram-air models. They were similar to the US military's HI-5 ram air tactical parachute system but had slightly larger canopies and a modified design which gave them a higher glide ratio and a maximum deployable altitude well over thirty thousand feet.

Hans immediately checked if he had a good canopy. It was fully deployed with no line twists; he was good to go. Within a few seconds, the other three jumpers confirmed good canopies. Prior to jumping, each man switched on a dim red beacon on the back of his helmet that revealed his position in the sky to the others. They flew silently southeast in the jet stream for the first several minutes; the lights of the villages below told them how quickly they were covering ground. Once they dropped out of the jet stream, their speed dropped, but they had plenty of altitude.

Hans checked his GPS; they were eight kilometers from their target—almost over Syria. The men were using encrypted tactical radios, keeping their conversations brief nonetheless. "Eight klicks out. Keep it tight." The responses were mere clicks. The target was a secure compound just northwest of Dayrik; it was not in the city itself. Maksim Kotov likely picked this for privacy and security. The Praetorians appreciated it but for other reasons—it would make their job easier while reducing the opportunity for civilian entanglements.

* * *

Maksim Kotov's compound was relatively new, about two hundred meters square and surrounded by a deep ditch outside a three-meter, chain link fence topped with razor wire. The Tiger lived in a large three-story house in the northwest corner of the compound. It had a flat roof and was surrounded by a four-meter-high concrete wall some ten meters from the house on all sides. Incorporated into the southern wall was a long, narrow building. From surveillance reports, they knew this housed Kotov's guards. There were two exits; a fortified gate on the west wall and a second to the south through the guard's barracks. This second gate opened directly onto the larger, fenced area. East and southeast of the house were two large, metal warehouses where Kotov stored his inventory. Directly south was an open area lit by streetlights where various vehicles were parked. These included cars, trucks, and even tractors. The compound was surrounded by fields and from the air appeared like the home of a wealthy farmer, not an arms dealer.

North of Kotov's compound was an open field of winter wheat. Lon and Magne would land here. Hans and Alen would land in the corn field to the south with a direct line of sight to the barracks door. A little after midnight, the team split up and began circling over their assigned drop zones. As they corkscrewed in, they flipped down their NVGs. When they did, each pair made out a small flashing infrared beacon and vectored in toward it. The men detached their rucksacks from their harnesses leaving them suspended some three meters below by a nylon strap. The rucks would land first and lessen the impact on the man to follow.

When Hans and Alen touched down, they immediately gathered up their parachutes to keep them from reinflating in the cool night breeze. As Alen was trying to unbuckle his parachute harness, a soft voice came from behind him. "Let me help you with that, laddie." It was Nigel Finch. "I was wondering when you lazy bastards were going to show up. Did you bring any beer with you?"

"Well, it was either beer or hand grenades. I opted for the grenades."

A kilometer to the north, the scene was being replayed only it was John Kernan who was meeting Lon and Magne. "Are you guys all saddled up for this rodeo?"

Lon shed his parachute and wind shell before collecting his rucksack. "We are. Let's check in with the boss. Alpha One, this is Alpha Four. Do you copy?"

The radio crackled in Lon's ear piece as Hans replied, "Good copy. We're down in one piece and have met up with Alpha Three. What's your status?"

Lon responded. "We're same. Have Alpha Six in tow. Give us five minutes to gear up and get a sitrep then we'll be ready to rumble."

"Copy that. Move out in five."

Nigel and John had been in country for five days reconnoitering Kotov's compound from afar. They'd been living on dirty water, eating MREs and sleeping in the dirt. They smelled like it too but no one complained. It was part of the job. The two men updated their colleagues on what they had learned.

As Hans and Alen put on their body armor and web gear, Nigel gave them the rundown. "We identified at least fourteen different guards—Russians from their appearance and the empty vodka bottles in the trash. Probably more in the main house."

Hans asked, "Spetznaz?"

"No. Too undisciplined. They look like ex-regular army."

"Locals?"

"Not this time of night. The domestic help leaves after dinner. No locals on site overnight."

Hans asked, "Security cameras?"

"Yes, there are security cameras but not long-range models. They primarily cover the compound and the warehouses. We're good out here."

Hans checked his watch. Five minutes. It was time to move out. As Hans was about to key the mic on his radio, Nigel stopped him. "You may want to hold off for a bit."

"Why?"

"They're about to change the sentries, twice as many eyes and ears. When they do, they'll talk and have a smoke for a few minutes before the new ones take their post and the old ones return to the barracks. After that, no one should come outside for another couple of hours. At least two of the guys on duty now have been drinking vodka for the last hour. When we hit the barracks, they'll be cold, hungry, and half drunk. That should be to our advantage."

"How long?"

Nigel checked his watch. "Should be any time now."

"Okay, I'll tell Alpha Three." Hans passed along the new information and waited. As Nigel predicted, within five minutes a new set of guards left the barracks. The old guards must have been extra cold and tired because they didn't even wait a minute before heading back. When the door to the barracks closed, Hans keyed his mic. "Alpha Team, execute. Tell me when you're in position and I'll turn out the lights."

Kotov's guards took up positions at the corners of the big compound. They didn't appear to have any NVGs but were armed with Russian AN-94 assault rifles—one of Russia's most modern rifles. Three of the men were actively smoking. What little night vision they had disappeared every time they lit a match. It was like shooting fish in a barrel.

The north side of the compound was darker with only one streetlight for the entire 200-meter length. The men spread out—Magne to the west, Lon in the middle, and John to the east by the warehouse. They crawled to within twenty meters of the guards and Lon keyed his mic twice to indicate they were in position. Hans shot out the transformer supplying power to the compound. All went dark. Magne and John dropped their sentries with a quick burst of 4.6mm rounds from their suppressed MP-7 submachine guns. The two men dropped to the ground with little noise. Lon immediately climbed down into the ditch below the fence and back up the other side to cut a hole in the chain link as John and Magne moved toward him.

As Lon's men were acting, Hans, Alen, and Nigel made short work of the sentries on the south. Once all were confirmed dead, Hans began cutting through the fence. As Hans was finishing, Alen and Nigel approached him running in a crouch. The three men darted through the opening to slip in among the vehicles parked south of the barracks. A minute or so passed until the door to the barracks opened. Two men with flashlights started walking toward the warehouse directly behind the house. Nigel whispered, "Generator. The power fails around here pretty regular."

Hans observed the two men approached the building. A few quick flashes from the dark north of them and the two men were dead. A shadowy figure ran out of the gloom and put two additional rounds into their heads. It was John Kernan. He was expecting them. Six bogeys down. Nigel grinned. "We anticipated this."

Hans pointed to the barracks door. "Do they secure it behind them?"

"As a rule? Yes. There's an external lock, but we've only seen it open from the inside. We've never seen a guard with keys to it."

"How heavy is that door?"

"Pretty fucking heavy. We can use a breaching charge but it would alert the guys in the house."

Hans mused, "I'd prefer not to announce our presence just yet. How else do we get it open?"

Alen chimed in. "We ask?"

"Funny."

"No, I'm serious. Two guys were sent to fire up the generator but the lights aren't back on yet. I approach the door and tell them I need help getting the generator started. We stack guys on either side. When they open it to find out what's wrong, we take them."

"They'll know you're not one of their guys, won't they?"

"I'll ask in Russian. With the lights out, it's not like they'll recognize me anyway. Once they open the door, it'll be too late. If they don't open it, we'll blow it and do this the hard way."

Hans shrugged. "Worth a shot but we need to be prepared to breach immediately if they don't open it."

Hans radioed Lon to advise him of what was happening. He and John immediately moved up toward the barracks leaving Magne to cover their flank. Alen and Hans met them near the door with Nigel covering them all from the car park. There were no windows facing out and the security cameras went down with the power. As Lon attached a platter charge to the door, the men lined up along the wall with their MP-7s at the ready. Alen took a deep breath and knocked on the door. From inside, a voice said, "V chem problema? (What's the problem?)"

Alen replied, "Generator. Ne mozhem yego zavesti. (The generator. We can't get it started.)"

There was a loud mechanical clack as the heavy bolt was pulled back. Opening the door, the irritated man said, "Iisus Khristos, neuzheli ty ne mozhesh'…(Jesus Christ, can't you do…)" Before he finished, Alen put three 4.6x30mm rounds into the man's chest. Alen burst through the open door with Hans, Lon, and John right on his tail. Alen and Hans went left while Lon and John went right. Directly ahead of them was a kitchen and common area with couches, chairs, and a large flat screen TV on the wall. There was only one other man in the room. He had a pen light in his hand which made him an easy target. Hans dropped him with a quick four-round burst. Lon Oden and John Kernan moved to the first room on the right. It was a bedroom with six bunks. Four were empty but two contained the sentries who just got off duty. They were smoking cigarettes and drinking vodka. The guards reacted to the noise and the last thing they saw were the muzzle flashes of the weapons that killed them.

Alen and Hans continued left. There was another sleeping room with eight bunks. Four were empty, three held sleeping guards and one was occupied by a man reading by the light of a small battery-powered lamp. He turned toward the opening door to find strange soldiers wearing NVGs. He called out to his comrades as he reached for the Makarov 9mm pistol on the table next to him. Hans quieted the man with a three-round burst before moving on to his next target. The other men, roused from their slumber, struggled to their feet and fumbled for their weapons in the dim light. Alen dropped two while Hans shot the other. They continued to the next door but found only an empty bathroom. Hans keyed his mic, "Alpha One, clear left."

Lon responded. "Alpha Four, clear right."

Magne and Nigel approached the door to the barracks. "Alpha Three and Five entering. Don't shoot us."

"Copy. We'll do our best."

The two groups returned to the kitchen/common room in the middle of the barracks. Hans asked, "Everyone good?" The men nodded or gave a thumbs up. "Nigel, set up at the door to the car park and cover our six. The rest of us are moving on to the primary target."

"Why do I have rear security?"

Hans smiled. "Because between you and John, you smell worse."

Nigel sniffed his underarm. "Yeah, I get that. But he's not exactly a bouquet of roses either."

"Believe me. We know." Motioning to the others, Hans said, "Let's move out. Alen, you and I will take the front door. Lon and Magne take the back. John, you keep eyes on that other gate on the west wall. If there's going to be any backup, it'll have to come through there or the barracks."

John gave a wink. "I know. I smell bad too. No one will get through that gate alive."

"Okay, let's move out."

The men slipped out the door connecting the barracks to the yard around the house. They panned their weapons in front of them from side to side and up and down searching for any threat. There were a few trees, a couple of bushes, and some construction debris but not much else for cover. John moved quickly toward the heavy gate to his left and set up behind some barrels. The four other men split up and headed for their prospective entry points.

Lon whispered into his mic, "Alpha Four and Five in position."

Hans replied, "Alpha One and Two in position. Execute." Hans crept up to the big front door, but it was locked.

To Lon's surprise, the back door was unlocked! "Alpha One, the back door is fuckin' open."

John interrupted, whispering, "Hold on a sec. We've never seen the guards with keys so they can't lock the doors behind them."

Lon said, "Shit. Do we have a bogey?"

"Maybe. Let me check the north side of the house." John crept out from behind his barrels and eased to the north focusing intently on the house. As the northern side came into view, a guard was standing next to the house pissing on the wall. *That's no way to treat your boss's house.* "Got a guard taking the pause that refreshes."

Hans said, "Drop him." Two quick flashes came from the dark.

"Bogey is down. North side is clear."

Hans tried the front door. It was locked without a keyhole. "Uh, we have a problem. This door is locked and only opens from the inside. We may have to breach it." Alen tapped him on the shoulder, made a knocking motion with his hand and shrugged as if to say, "Why not?" Hans shrugged back. "We're going to try something. When you hear a noise from up front, enter the house."

Lon looked at Magne quizzically but just shrugged. "Roger that Alpha One. We'll wait for your mark."

Alen approached the door and knocked. As he did, he said, "Problema s generatorom. Mne nuzhno soobshchit' ob etom bossu. (There is an issue with the generator. I need to let the boss know.)"

After a long minute, a voice from inside the house replied, "Da ni khrena. Kak budto ya ne mog skazat'. (No shit. Like I couldn't tell.)" A sleepy man opened the door only to be met by the butt of Alen's gun. The man fell to the floor in a heap. Alen zip tied the unconscious man's hands and feet as Hans whispered, "Alpha One and Two are inside."

Lon replied, "Alpha Three copies. We're going in." They quietly opened the door and slipped in, keeping low. It was a large kitchen with two sinks, a stove, an oven, a heavy wooden prep table in the middle of the floor, and two large pantries. It was unoccupied so they moved on to the next room. This was a fancy dining room with a heavy, dark table and chairs. They moved on deeper into the house. In the middle were stairwells leading up and down. Here they met up with Hans and Alen. Hans pointed to Magne and indicated he should stay there while the other three went down to the basement.

They moved quietly down the bare concrete steps. There was a soft glow coming from a room at the bottom of the stairs; it was some sort of control room. It had a large desk with several computers on it. Above it was a bank of monitors. While the equipment was on, there was only static on the monitors. Apparently, they were on some sort of battery backup but the cameras were not. Lon commented, "Backup power for the computers but not the cameras. Rookie mistake." There were three more rooms in the basement—a bedroom with four bunks, a toilet, and a large storage room; all were unoccupied.

Hans picked up a cup of coffee on the desk. It was still warm. "I suspect this is where the guy who answered the door was working. Let's go on up." Keying his mic, Hans whispered, "Basement is clear. We're coming up."

Magne replied, "Copy."

Once back on the ground floor, they formed a stack and moved up the stairs. Hans, Lon, and Alen aimed their weapons ahead of them while Magne kept his trained on the steps behind them. Once they reached the second floor, they paired off. Lon and Magne went left. Every room they encountered was empty except for the last. It was some sort of lounge or den overlooking the front of the house. Faint music wafted through the air. Near the window was a young guard sitting in an overstuffed chair listening to rock music. His eyes were closed but his foot was tapping with the beat of the music. The guard looked up just in time to witness the flashes from Magne's MP-7. Both bullets passed through his right eye. Lon keyed his mic, "Front half cleared, one bogey down."

Hans keyed his mic in acknowledgement. He and Alen were busy clearing rooms of their own. The first was a bedroom with no clothes in the closet, indicating a guest room. It was followed by a bathroom, and finally, an office. There was a computer on the desk but with the power out, it was dead. "Back half clear. Let's move on up. Intel says principal is on three."

The team reassembled at the staircase. Hans said, "There are three rooms to the left. Steve thinks one is a gym. There is an office, an unknown room, and then his bedroom. Steve said there is a large bed against the east wall and a bathroom beyond that."

Lon asked, "How the hell does Steve know that. There is nothing on imagery."

Hans smiled and explained, "Kotov's internet history included downloading an app for a robot vacuum, the kind that maps your house. Steve hacked Kotov's account and copied the map."

"Nice."

They moved up to the third floor in the same formation as before. Hans and Alen went right while Lon and Magne went left. This was clearly Kotov's personal residence. To the left, a small kitchen, a dining room, and a gym with weights, a treadmill, and a rowing machine. To the right was another office, a sauna, and what had to be his bedroom. All the other rooms were empty, leaving only his bedroom. Kotov was former GRU. He had served in Afghanistan and Chechnya. He wouldn't be a pushover.

The four men lined up outside the door—Hans, Alen, Lon, and finally Magne. Hans tried the handle, finding it locked. He raised his hand with fingers counting down—three, two, one...Alen's big boot kicked the door and it flew open. Hans dove thru the doorway and rolled to his right. Lon dove to the left just as gunshots rang out. The three rounds from a Glock 9mm slammed into Alen's chest as he moved to enter the room. He staggered back and Magne shot past him. The bedroom was large and dominated by an oversized bed on a raised platform. Kotov was on the opposite side of the bed firing blindly. A young woman, naked except for some panties, sat up in the bed screaming at the top of her lungs. Kotov fired three more shots before scurrying into the bathroom behind him and slamming the door. Hans grabbed the woman and dragged her from the bed. Pointing to an armoire, he shouted, "Otoydite ot etogo i derzhites' nizhe! (Get behind that and keep down!)" She scurried to the armoire and squeezed behind it.

She apparently was Russian, or at least understood the language. Their intel was proving reliable.

As the woman cowered, Alen staggered into the room. His body armor had saved him. He was winded but otherwise fine. He gave a thumbs up and followed Magne around the bed and toward the bathroom while Hans covered them from the right. Alen shouted to Kotov, "Ty v lovushke. Tebe stoit vybrat'sya. (You're trapped. You might as well come out.)"

Kotov's response was to send two rounds tearing through the door.

"U nas yest devushka. Vykhodite, i ona ne postradayet. (We have the girl. Come out and she won't be harmed.)"

From inside the bathroom, a deep voice said, "Vy mozhete poluchit'yeye, i den'gi tozhe. Den'gi v moyem kabinete. Prosto voz'mi yeye i eto i ukhodi. (You can have her, and the money too. The money is in my office. Just take her and it and leave.)"

The woman came out from behind the armoire and ran cursing toward the bathroom door. "Ty gryaznyy svinoy ublyudok! Yesli oni ne ub'yut tebya, eto sdelayu ya. (You filthy pig bastard! If they don't kill you, I will!)"

Lon hustled the woman from the room and threw her in the sauna. He took out his K-bar knife and jammed it into the door frame to keep it from opening.

Back in the bedroom, Alen turned to Hans and said, "And you thought chivalry was dead."

Hans spoke to Kotov through the door. "My zdes za Novichok. Gde eto nakhodit sya? (We're here for the Novichok. Where is it?)" Two more rounds came through the door in reply.

Turning to Magne, Alen said, "Well, I guess it's the hard way." Magne smiled and fired five rounds from his MP-7 through the door's lock plate. Alen kicked the door open and tossed in a flash/bang. "Fire in the hole!"

The blinding flash and deafening noise sent Kotov reeling backwards into his bathtub. Alen burst in and shot Kotov in the chest. The Russian feebly raised his pistol one last time before Alen put a second round through his hand. The gun clattered to the floor. "Clear!"

Alen grabbed Kotov's face. They were nose to nose. "Gde nakhodit sya Novichok? (Where is the Novichok?)"

Coughing up blood, Kotov smiled and spit out, "Ty opozdal, sukin syn. (You are too late, you son of a bitch.)"

Alen raised his MP-7 and shot Kotov in the forehead. "Shoot me, will ya. I may be a son of a bitch but at least I'm alive."

Lon retrieved the woman from the sauna. She had put on a robe. She was trembling; her rage had returned to fear. He used zip ties to secure her hands before leading her down the hall to the gym where he tied her to a large weight machine.

Alen dragged Kotov's body from the bathroom and laid him out on the floor. Hans retrieved a photo of Kotov taken in happier times, snapped on his flashlight, and compared it to the corpse at his feet. "Well, he isn't smiling but it's definitely him." He retrieved a camera from his vest and took several photos of the dead arms dealer. "Okay, let's get to that computer."

Lon correctly pointed out, "Uh, we have no electricity."

Hans got on the radio and said, "Alpha Three, this is Alpha One. Do you copy?"

Nigel replied, "This is Alpha Three. Good copy. What's up?"

"The house is secure. The target is down. We need power to exploit his computer or we have to take it with us. Can you help?"

Nigel replied, "I'll get the genny running. Give me a minute."

Hans and the others proceeded to Kotov's office to collect intelligence. In the bottom drawer was a large steel lockbox. One round from Lon's MP-7 and it was open. There was no intel but there was at least a hundred thousand Euros and US dollars as well as lesser amounts of rubles, Syrian pounds, and Turkish lira. There was relatively little in the way of paper files, but they took what they found. Hans sent Alen down the hall to deal with the Russian woman just as the power came back on. He turned on Kotov's computer and as it was booting up, retrieved his tactical laptop from his rucksack and connected it to Kotov's desktop. The laptop was loaded with the Praetorian's own software that allowed them to mirror the hard drive without having to actually log into it. The data was still password protected but that was something for Steve Chang to deal with; he was the computer geek. While the computer was grinding away, they searched the room taking pictures of everything that might even remotely be interesting. When finished with the hard drive, Hans went downstairs to the second-floor office to copy the hard drive of that computer.

In the gym, Alen approached the young woman and offered her a drink of water. The intimidating Serb tried to be calm and comforting. He spoke to her in Russian. He wanted her to assume this was a Russian-on-Russian thing. He wanted to plant the seed that Kotov had been killed by a rival Russian arms dealer or maybe even Russian intel angry that they hadn't received their piece of the action. When it was time to go, Hans collected Alen and said, "Pora idti. Moskva khochet otchet k utru. (Time to go. Moscow wants a report by morning.)"

Alen pulled Hans aside and whispered, "What about the girl? If we blow the warehouse, she might be killed. She's a noncombatant."

Hans pondered this a moment. "Put her in the basement. She should be safe there. And tell Lon to take the cash. What self-respecting rival arms dealer would just leave it behind?"

As they exited the house, Lon pointed to the man they'd left hogtied by the front door. "What about him? Do him or leave him?"

Hans replied, "Leave him but put him in the basement. Someone needs to see to the girl. He only heard Russian voices so he can't refute her story. I don't give him much life expectancy anyway. How would you like to explain why you were the only guy we didn't kill? Let's roll."

* * *

After starting the generator, Nigel Finch turned on the lights inside the warehouse. It was stacked to the rafters with crate after crate of Russian military equipment. Most of it was small arms—AK-74s and older AK-47s—but there were also RPK-74 light machine guns. Nigel identified at least three different types of anti-tank missiles—the AT-4 Spigot, the AT-5 Spandrel, and even a couple of the newest AT-14 Kornets. There were hundreds of the venerable RPG-7 rocket propelled grenade launchers but also the more modern RPG-29 Vampir and the RPG-22 Netto disposable anti-tank rockets. There was nothing that looked like nerve agent.

The rest of the Praetorians joined him in the search. Magne and John walked into the warehouse. Gaping at the mountain of rifle crates, John exclaimed, "That's a shitload of weapons."

Nigel snorted, "Most are AK-74s and 47s. Old stuff."

John asked, "No AN-94s? The guards were all carrying 94s."

Nigel chuckled. "Well, apparently ol' Kotov spared no expense when it came to protecting his own ass. This stuff is intended for the peasants."

Magne commented with a smile, "For all the good it did him. His men didn't get off a single round."

Hans, Alen and Lon started searching the other warehouse. This one was where he stored products for his more discerning customers. The first thing they encountered were at least twenty pallets stacked with Russian cluster bombs. Hans asked quizzically, "Well, what do we have here?"

Alen responded, "Cluster bombs. The little ones are RBK-250s, the ones in the middle are RBK-500s, and the big ones are RBK-750s. I even see a couple of PFM-1 dispensers. Those are air scatterable antipersonnel mines known as butterfly mines."

Hans gave him an irritated snarl, "I know that, you big oaf. The question was rhetorical."

Alen grinned. He'd done it just to irritate the German. "I didn't think you fallschirmjager types were well versed on modern weapons."

Hans snapped back, "Need I remind you that Germany invented cluster munitions?"

"You mean the Nazis? I assumed you guys didn't like talking about them?"

"Oh, shut up and find the damn nerve agent." Hans keyed his mic and said, "Alpha Team, we need to locate the nerve agent. Use the detection equipment. I doubt it's going to be labeled 'nerve agent.' And remember, Novichok is a binary agent. There should be two separate containers and they should be far apart. Kotov is smart enough not to store them next to each other."

Lon corrected, "You mean he *was* smart enough. Hell, I'd keep them in separate buildings. It's bad enough if your inventory goes up in smoke but to have it result in a cloud of deadly nerve gas? No thanks."

Hans rubbed his chin. "That's a good point. Tell Nigel and the others they may be looking for half of the weapon system."

They scoured the warehouses for almost thirty minutes to no avail. The Novichok nerve agent was not there. Hans checked his watch. "I don't think anyone outside this compound realizes we're here but we've been on target too long. Let's set this stuff to blow and get the hell out of here." He keyed his mic and said, "Alpha Three and Alpha Six, we need to go. What's the exit?"

Nigel replied, "A click southeast. We had a truck set up for us. Two in the cab; four in the back in a hidden compartment covered by bags of grain. We borrowed it from a local smuggler. It's only about thirty klicks to the Semalka Border Crossing and Iraq."

"Okay, we need to collect our chutes, gloves, altimeters, masks, outers, everything. If anyone investigates, we don't want anything that would suggest an aerial insertion."

"Let's be ready to roll out of here in twenty. Set the timers for an hour after departure. I don't want to be in the same zip code when this shit goes up." Hans checked the time—0110 hours. On the road by 0140. In Iraqi Kurdistan by 0300 hours with mission success and no casualties but also no nerve agent. *Was it ever even here in the first place? A high price for bad intel. What the fuck. Not going to lose sleep over it. Kotov was a massive asshole whether he had the Novichok or not.*

* * *

The Praetorians quickly policed up their parachutes and other equipment. Ordinarily they would have just burned them or buried them in a field but that risked them being discovered. They needed to keep up the business war illusion. With Nigel and John in the lead, they set off southeast to where they had prepositioned the truck. It was a moonless night. The six men trotted purposefully across the empty field unobserved. They approached a cluster of buildings near the road. Nigel put his fist in the air signaling the others to stop. He tapped John on the shoulder and pointed to the road. Without a word, he trotted off to the driveway connecting the buildings to the main road. After a minute, John got on the radio. "All clear."

The five men moved out in a crouch following Nigel. Next to one of the buildings was an old Kamaz cargo truck. Hans Koenig spoke the best Arabic and his Russian passed as native. He'd do the driving—and the talking. John Kernan would ride shotgun and navigate. Everyone, along with all their equipment, was relegated to the back. Hans and John stripped down to their khakis. Truck drivers didn't go tooling around northern Syria with MP-7s and body armor. Lon, Magne, Alen, and Nigel climbed into the hidden compartment in the back. Magne carped, "Why do I have to ride back here with Nigel? He smells like ass! He's worse than the damn Novichok!"

Hans smirked, "Because I'm in charge of this mission. You want to ride up front, you take command." Closing the door, Hans and John piled up a couple of bags of grain to disguise the access. To complete the ensemble, John attached two magnetic signs to the doors of the truck identifying it as belonging to an international aid agency. "This will explain why two gringos are driving a grain truck in Syria."

"Nice!"

"Steve gave them to me before we left. That kid is pretty handy at times." As Hans climbed into the driver's seat, John handed him the keys. "Let's blow this popsicle stand." Hans started the big diesel truck and slowly pulled forward. There was no sign of life anywhere. He eased onto the main road, turned on the headlights and headed for Dayrik.

The truck rumbled on through the quiet town and exited east on Hawler Street. Soon they were in the Syrian countryside, past the hamlet of Al Kazmiyah and approaching Zuhajrijja on the border. Turkey was just on the other side of the Tigris River but there was no bridge. They turned south and after five miles, they encountered their first road block outside Karbalaa. It was manned by Kurds, not Syrian government soldiers. Hans explained they were transporting grain to a refugee station across the border. Thanks to Steve, they came prepared with identification, paperwork, and a letter of introduction. Hans slipped the guard a handful of Euros to ensure the inspection was brief. They were about to leave when a series of low rumbles echoed from the west.

Hans peered back and in Arabic said, "Thunder. A storm is coming. We better get going."

The guard pointed to the sky. "No clouds, only stars. That is artillery."

Hans feigned surprise. "Then we *really* need to get going!"

The guard laughed. "No worries. It's miles away. Probably the Turks." Hans waved and continued on his way. Only four clicks to the Semalka Border Crossing and the relative safety of Iraq.

When they reached the river, they joined the queue of trucks waiting to cross the pontoon bridge spanning the Tigris River between Northeastern Syria and Iraq's Kurdistan Region. The crossing was controlled by Kurds— the Autonomous Administration of North and East Syria—on the west side and the Kurdistan Regional Government on the east. The border guards on the Syrian side simply waved them across. The problem that leaves is not a problem. Those on the Kurdish side inspected Hans's paper and lifted the canvas flap on the back of the truck to "inspect" the cargo. Again, with the exchange of a few Euros, they were on their way.

After they cleared the border crossing, John let out a sigh of relief. "I never imagined I'd be happy to be back in Iraq."

Hans just grinned. "The world is truly a strange place. Let's find somewhere to stop so the others can get out. They've been locked in a box with Nigel for over an hour. Let's just hope they're still alive."

About halfway to Dayrabun, Iraq, they found an isolated place to pull over. They opened up the hidden compartment and Magne, Lon, and Alen came crawling out coughing and gagging. Alen said, "Ten more minutes of that smell and we'd all be dead—except Nigel. He can stand the smell of his own shit."

Nigel followed and bellowed in his Scottish brogue, "You're all a bunch of pussies! John and I were out here for a week drinking camel piss and eating bugs while you were in Rome having wine with your pasta. Barely one hour of hardship and you're whining like little bitches."

Magne asked, "Nigel, did you change your underwear even once in the last week?"

"No, but I did turn them inside out—twice."

Hans just shook his head. "Okay, enough. Who has the satellite coms?"

Lon handed him a satellite phone. "Just hit send."

The phone rang twice and then a familiar voice answered. "Ciao?" It was Sarah.

"Hello. It's us. We're just outside Dayrabun heading your way."

"How did it go with the client?"

"The negotiations went very well. However, he did not have the merchandise on hand. It was nowhere to be found."

"What about our delegation?"

"All good. No issues at all. Where do you want to meet?"

"We'll meet you just east of Sumel, before Highway Two meets the Barzan Highway. Just past the American University of Kurdistan is the Family Mall Duhok. We'll meet you in the northeast corner of the parking lot. We have two black Mercedes vans."

"Copy. We're in a dirty, white Kamaz truck with a green canvas cargo cover."

Sarah said, "You should get there first. I'm about seventy-five clicks away. That's over an hour."

Hans motioned at Nigel and John. "That works. I need to find somewhere to hose two of these guys off. They smell like horseshit."

Sarah laughed. "We'd appreciate that."

* * *

The rest of the mission was uneventful. Hans stopped for fuel and took the opportunity to buy two large rolls of paper towels, a case of water, some liquid hand soap, and some new T-shirts. Nigel and John took makeshift baths in the back of the truck as they rumbled down the highway. When they arrived at the mall in Sumel, Sarah and Steve were waiting for them.

Steve tossed Magne and Lon some empty black duffle bags. "For your gear. We can't have you walking into the airport carrying MP-7s."

Lon said, "I figured we were going to ditch them."

"Turns out Gil has contacts at Mosul International Airport."

Lon shook his head. "Of course, he does. But what about Taranto?"

"He's going to drop us off in Cyprus first. We'll unload there. Gunny has it squared away."

Lon stretched his aching back. "That's great. I could use a cold one about now, and I'm sure Nigel and John could too."

Sarah laughed. "Then you guys need to ride with me. I have a sixer of Heineken in the back on ice."

"Shotgun!"

CHAPTER TWO
SCOPE OF WORK

Gil and Donny dropped the Praetorians off in Cyprus before returning the CN-235 to the company from which they had leased it in Italy. They offloaded their equipment in Larnaca as well. The Cypriot customs officials were aware of Praetorian Security Services and that they were licensed to possess and import weapons as part of their business. A couple of senior Cypriot banking and government officials were actually customers of the company so the customs officials never bothered to seriously inspect Praetorian cargo.

Upon returning to the villa, Alen, Magne, and Lon started in on cleaning and inspecting the weapons and communications equipment. Hans, with Sarah's assistance, scrutinized the parachutes for any damage, made repairs as necessary, and then meticulously repacked the parachutes so they'd be ready when next required. Steve took possession of the tactical laptop and set in on cracking Kotov's encryption. At everyone's insistence, John and Nigel were excused to take well-earned and desperately needed showers.

Down in the armory, Alen was disassembling and cleaning the MP-7s one by one. Lon approached and asked, "How do you like the MP-7? This was your first operational use of it, right?"

"Yes. We never got to use anything this high speed back in Special Brigade. We used mostly AKs. Maybe the odd submachine gun. Hell, when I started, we were still using the Czech Škorpian vz. 61. That 9x18mm Makarov round was all but useless against even the shittiest body armor. We got the CZ Scorpion EVO 3 about halfway through my career. While it was a better weapon, it's 9x19mm Parabellum was only a little better."

"So, what's your professional opinion of the MP-7?"

The big Serb grinned. "I really like it. It's short-stroke piston is a lot smoother than the Scorpion's blow back system. Makes it easier to keep on target. And that round. Jesus Christ, that's awesome! You get what? Five hundred joules of energy and over seven hundred fifty meters per second muzzle velocity with half the cross section of a 9mm?"

"Thereabouts. That's why it's better than the nine at penetrating level two and three body armor but it is still not as good as the 5.56mm round."

"I like it. Very handy for close quarters work or anything else that doesn't require a rifle."

Lon said, "Rusty buys only the best. But then he's only supplying just a handful of operators. I wouldn't want to have to buy enough to arm a battalion."

"That might cut into our beer budget."

After a few minutes, Nigel and John arrived in the armory. Both still had wet hair from their showers. Nigel bellowed, "Don't hog all the weapons. Leave some for the real warriors."

Lon ignored the dig. "Well, don't stand there looking stupid…jump in."

Nigel grabbed a weapon and racked its slide to make sure the chamber was clear. John asked, "Where's Hans?"

Alen replied, "Inspecting and repacking the chutes with Sara in the back."

"I'll see if they need a hand."

Before he left, Lon asked cautiously, "Uh, John, whatever happened to that cash we took from Kotov's office?"

"Hans and I invested most of it in the stock market. Also ordered a couple of hookers and some coke. They should be here any minute."

Lon shook his head, "Fucking asshole. What did you really do with it?"

"Well, we used some to bribe the guards at the check points and the Kurdish customs guys. A big chunk we gave to my smuggler, Abdul."

"You mean the guy you got the truck from?"

"Yeah. I called him from the shopping mall in Sumel to tell him where his truck was. He was pissed, too."

"Why is that?"

John grinned. "I told him I was going to leave it in Aleppo. If he ratted us out, I didn't want him sending the Syrians or the Turks in the right direction. Anyway, he was pretty torqued that he had to go to Iraq to get it back—until I told him there was thirty thousand Euros hidden in the smuggler's hold. He'll get over it."

"Well, what if he doesn't get across the border?"

John shrugged, "Then he ain't much of a smuggler and losing his truck will be a sign he needs a new profession."

Lon threw up his hands. "Can't argue with your logic. What about the rest of the cash?"

"I gave it to Gil."

"Gil? The pilot?"

"Yeah. He passed it to his contact at the Mosul airport to 'spread good will' by which he means payoff the officials to ignore us. He said it'll go a long way toward making new friends if we ever need them again. You never have enough friends in this line of work."

"You got that right, brother."

Gunny "Mad Dog" Medina walked into the armory. "So, this is where everyone is. Where are Hans and Sarah?"

Lon pointed behind him, "Parachute detail."

"Well, go fetch 'em. Mission brief with the boss in twenty minutes."

"Aye, aye, Gunny."

* * *

As the team descended on the conference room, Sarah went to the kitchen to grab extra cream. Gunny was there retrieving his ancient, stained KGB coffee mug. She stared at it with a mixture of distain, disgust, and fear. He didn't acknowledge her but anticipated what she was about to say. "No, I'm not going to wash it and you'd better not either."

She teased, "Nigel rinsed out his underwear in that thing this morning."

"Testosterone makes the caffeine stronger."

"You're sick."

The team took their seats in the conference room, only Rusty and Steve were missing. Rusty Travis, their billionaire boss and benefactor, came in a minute later and took his seat at the head of the table. "Just got off the horn with some of our clients. They're pleased with the outcome in Syria but concerned the nerve agent wasn't on site. Naturally, their first question was 'Where the hell is it?' I told them we'd figure that out so we sure as shit better." Looking around the table he asked, "Where's Steve?"

Gunny replied, "He'll be here in a minute. He's working on something."

"Then we'll save him for last. Okay, let's…"

Lon interrupted him. "Uh, boss. There is something we want to raise real quick. Should only take a second."

Rusty glared at him with a jaundiced eye. "Why do I feel like you guys want to unionize?"

Lon laughed, "It's nothing like that. It actually has to do with call signs."

Gunny snorted, "Call signs? Really?"

Lon continued. "We talked about it and we just want to simplify things, that's all. For every mission, we assign call signs based on who has operational command. For this last one, Hans was Alpha One. That made sense since it was a HAHO insertion and he is our HAHO guru. However, every time we switch it up, we have to remember who the hell is who. Is Alen Alpha Two or Alpha Five this time? We suggest that we just pick a permanent call sign and stick with it."

Gunny shook his head. "Are you to old to remember a one-digit number?"

Lon shrugged. "I remember mine but I am too old to remember the other seven."

Nigel nodded, "He's got a point. It gets confusing." Several others nodded in agreement.

Gunny leaned back in his chair and put his hands on his head. "Jesus Tapdancing Christ. Are you all as senile as Lon?"

In unison, they all responded, "Yes!"

Turning to Rusty, Gunny said, "Well, I guess the tribe has spoken." Turning to the rest of the team, he said, "Okay, who is going to be Alpha One? How do we decide? Fight for it?"

Alen quipped, "Then that would be Sarah." She gave him a quick smile and a nod to acknowledge the compliment. He was right.

Rusty said, "How about seniority? Gunny was the first Praetorian so he should be Alpha One."

The others nodded in agreement but Gunny objected. "No. It shouldn't be me. I'm not going on these missions. It should be the senior *operator*. That would be Mr. Oden."

Now it was Lon Oden who objected. "No, Gunny, you should be Alpha One."

"No, I'm going to be Bravo Two and Rusty will be Bravo One. That's Bravo, as in "B" for boss."

Lon smiled, "That works."

Gunny said, "I guess that makes John Alpha Two. Nigel is Alpha Three and Hans is Four. Magne and Sarah are Five and Six, and Alen and Steve are Alpha Seven and Alpha Eight. Any objections?"

Steve timidly raised his hand. "What about Gil and Donnie? I mean Gil flew the helo in Libya and both of them were involved in the Kotov op."

Gunny rubbed his chin. "Good point. They'll be Bravo Three and Four. Are we agreed?" Everyone nodded. "Can we get back to actual work now? The Kotov operation. I got the rundown from Hans. It went about as well as hoped—bad guys dead and no good guys hurt. The only hitch is the missing nerve agent. Initial satellite intel confirms both warehouses are a total loss."

Hans asked, "What about the house?"

"The east wall of the inner compound collapsed as did part of the third floor that wasn't shielded from the blast, but the rest of the house appears to be intact. The girl in the basement should have walked out unscathed, if that's what you're worried about." Hans just nodded. "Alright, so besides Nigel and John taking out everyone else's sense of smell, no one took rounds except Alen, right?"

Nigel quipped, "Well, it was his turn. I took them in Libya. His don't even really count since no actual blood was drawn."

Alen said sheepishly, "It still hurt, a lot."

Rusty interjected, "That brings me to the next topic. Alen took three in the chest. If he wasn't so damn big, he'd probably be dead. Those would have been head shots for a normal sized person."

Lon added, "Well, if it had been Gunny, they would have gone over his head—him being a broken down, hunched over, old man."

"Fuck you, Oden. I could be in a wheel chair and still kick your ass."

Rusty tapped his pen on the table like a gavel. "Okay, okay, children. We have work to do. My point is that we need better tactical headgear. The Kevlar brain pots we've been using are good but there is better, right Gunny?"

"With Rusty's help and business connections, I've been researching our options. There is a Swiss company developing a new helmet with a full three hundred sixty degrees of protection. The body of the helmet is a carbon fiber composite resin and includes an integrated Kevlar neck screen. The face shield is made of some new high-tech ballistic plastic the Japanese developed. It's not perfect but the pot will stop anything up to a 7.62 x 39

AK-47 round. The neck screen will stop a 9mm round but its gonna hurt like a son of a bitch and no guarantees on the blunt force trauma. The face shield will stop up to a .45 round but not more than one, maybe two. The other issue is whether it is compatible with our NVGs. We either cut out eye holes to fit or leave the eyes exposed. Thoughts? Comments?"

Magne asked, "Do we have the specs?"

Gunny replied, "We can get them."

John asked, "How much does it weigh?"

"Heavier than what you're using now—a little over two kilograms, but they have better ballistic protection."

John nodded. "Anything that keeps a bullet out of my brain is fine by me."

Nigel quipped, "You're a SEAL. How would you even tell the difference? Can't make you any dumber than you are now."

"Says the man who eats guts and oats mixed together with fat and then boiled in a sheep's stomach."

Nigel beamed, "That's the meal of a real man!"

Sarah added, "Yeah, caveman."

Gunny snorted, "Jesus Christ, I feel like a second-grade school teacher. Do we want the new helmets or not?"

They all nodded or said, "Yes."

"Good, because I already ordered them. We'll figure out the face shield/NVG issue later."

Magne asked, "If you already ordered them, why ask if we want them?"

Rusty chimed in, "Because he wanted to give you the illusion that he gives a shit about your opinions. Okay, next item on the agenda. Aircraft. This latest op raises a good question. Do we want to obtain a CN-235 of our own?"

Lon replied, "Well, it did come in handy. How much do they cost?"

"Not that much. They're $30 million new but the lead time is too long for our purposes. We can pick up a used one with relatively low hours for a few million."

Lon replied sarcastically, "Just a few million? Then what the hell, let's get two."

Rusty just smiled. "Gil said we can park it at the airport in Larnaca. There is room in the hangar for both it and the Bombardier 8000, so there'd be no additional hangar costs. In addition, Gil suggested we hire it out for legit commercial business. This would give Gil and Donny more experience flying the plane and provide cover for why it's here."

Gunny nodded. "We should do it. This last op would never have gone off if we hadn't been able to lease that bird when we needed it. I mean, even if we deployed from the Bombardier, there was no good cover for why it was flying into Mosul for less than 24 hours."

"Alright, it's settled. I'll tell Gil and Donny to start looking."

Gunny posited, "If they are going to be flying that bird out of Larnaca, they should probably live at the villa, don't you?"

"Well, at least one of them should for local runs. I'll talk to them and get their input."

Steve finally entered the conference room. "Sorry I'm late. I was testing out a theory."

Magne chuckled. "Professor Chang hard at work. What theory?"

"The 'No Chemical Weapons' theory. You guys didn't find anything in the warehouses but that got me to thinking, why not?"

John injected, "Because they weren't there?"

"Yeah, but they should've been. The Novichok wasn't the first CW agents Kotov dealt in. He has been selling the Assad regime chlorine, mustard gas, Lewisite, and even a little sarin for the last couple of years."

Rusty commented, "Maybe he was simply out of stock?"

"No, there'd still be traces."

Hans interjected, "The CW detectors we used detect vapors. Those warehouses were wide open, two large doors at either end. The wind blew straight through them. If the weapons were shipped a while ago any airborne traces of the CW agent would likely be below the detection threshold."

Steve said, "Exactly. So, I collected dirt samples from the boots you wore on the raid. All the soil samples tested positive for trace amounts of CW agents. I also identified what I assess are the two precursors of the binary Novichok weapon. Now here's the weird part. The shoes belonging to Hans, Alen, and Lon all tested positive for component A but not B, while Nigel, John, and Magne's shoes tested positive for component B but not A. That makes no sense, does it?"

Hans answered, "Yes, it does. Alen, Lon, and I searched the south warehouse. The other three searched the north warehouse. Kotov was keeping the two components separate, as in different buildings. Pretty smart if you think about it. I wouldn't want an accidental explosion rupturing both containers and creating a deadly nerve gas. If it were me, I'd bury that shit in two different holes a mile apart."

Steve continued, "Well, this proves Kotov did indeed have Novichok on site in the recent past."

Rusty asked, "When? How long ago?"

"Not sure. That shit is pretty persistent."

Rusty sighed, "Well, at least we waxed the right guy; we just did it too late. How do we find this crap?"

"I was able to break into his computer files. There is a lot to go through but I started on shipping records first. They list dates and destinations but nothing on contents or customers. There is no indication the Turks are using chemical weapons against the Kurds or the Syrians. All indications are their interest has been primarily cluster bombs. I doubt he'd sell it back to the Russians because, well, why? They invented the stuff. It's safe to assume the Russians could get their hands on some if they really wanted it. That leaves either the Syrians, Iran, or some non-state player like Al Qaeda, ISIS, or maybe even they Houthis in Yemen."

Gunny commented, "Scratch Iran. They make their own."

Rusty said, "That doesn't really narrow it down much."

Steve continued, "Of his most recent ten shipments, all went west to Latakia, Syria."

Gunny mused, "That would suggest they went out by boat."

"Yeah, but which boats and where were they going?"

"That's the sixty-four dollar question."

* * *

The Praetorians poured over the intel collected from Kotov's office and computers. His records were a mess. There was no rhyme or reason to his record keeping method. Some files were on the computer from the third-floor office while others were only on the second-floor office computer. Some were only on paper, others only on the computer, and still others a combination of the two. The papers were spread out over the floor in the gym downstairs. Documents were in Russian, Turkish, Arabic, Farsi, English, and Urdu. It was a tedious task to translate enough of each document to figure out which shipment—if any—it pertained to. It would take the combined language skills of the whole team to figure it all out.

Sarah stood and craned her neck. "Christ, this is going to kill me."

Alen smirked and said, "Christ? I thought you were Jewish?"

"Shut the fuck up and come rub my neck."

"Yes, ma'am." Alen walked up behind Sarah and started to massage her neck and shoulders.

"Don't be a pussy. Rub harder."

"Okay, you asked for it." He started kneading her neck and shoulder muscles with his big beefy hands. He was surprised how strong her muscles were. She appeared delicate and lithe but her deltoid and trapezius muscles were like iron. No wonder she bloodied his nose when he sparred with her. Sarah hung her head. "Too hard?"

"Hell, no. That's great." After a few minutes, she stopped him. "As much as I love that, we have work to do."

Alen smiled, "Anytime." *What man wouldn't take the opportunity to massage your neck and not get his ass kicked for the privilege?*

Just as they were getting back to work, Rusty Travis walked down the stairs. "Are we getting anywhere?"

Steve Chang answered for the group. "I think we are. It's turned into a bit of a briar patch. We're dealing with sloppy record keeping in at least six languages."

Hans interjected, "Make that seven. Just found one in Afrikaans."

Rusty shook his head. "Jesus Christ almighty! Do we need to subcontract some of this out to our stateside clients?"

"No sir! We got this." Steve was adamant. The others echoed his sentiment. "We'll crack this."

Magne stood and stretched his back. "Actually, we may have. We have an email from a Russian to Kotov."

Rusty was unimpressed. "Yeah. So. He's Russian."

"Yeah, but this email is in Turkish."

"Did it come from Turkey?"

"No, it didn't. What's interesting is it came from a guy named Grigor Semenov. Semenov is, or at least was, GRU."

"So was Kotov, old buddy. Not blowing my socks off with this."

Magne continued, "Semenov and Kotov both served together in Ankara back in the day. That might explain why they converse in Turkish."

Rusty was getting frustrated. "Still not impressed."

"Their message references something they call 'yeni gelen Hollandali folyo.' That made no sense to me so I played around with the translations. In Turkish, 'yeni gelen' means newcomer, 'Hollandali' means Hollander, and 'folyo' means folio—newcomer Hollander folio."

Gunny snorted, "Sounds like gibberish. Maybe some sort of code?"

Magne smiled, "Not a code, plain text. Just in multiple languages. The Dutch word for folio is foliant. Foliant was the codename of an old Soviet military program, the one that developed fourth generation nerve agents. Yeni gelen, or newcomer, in Russian is..."

Gunny finished the sentence, "Novichok. So that's how you talk about Novichok without the word Novichok showing up in any NSA keyword search."

"Exactly."

Rusty let out a long whistle. "Well holy shit. Okay, we have Kotov talking to this Semenov guy about Novichok. That still doesn't tell us where the hell it actually is."

"That email referenced an order number and a payment. This Semenov guy may be—or was—Kotov's supplier. Kotov was telling him he had sold the Novichok and was wiring Semenov his cut. From the date on the email, we know when Kotov sold it. So, we looked at all shipments after that date. There were only two. Both to Latakia."

"But how do we find the damn CW?"

Magne picked up a piece of paper from the floor. "This is a print out of an email Kotov sent to...someone. There's no name. I'll ask Steve what he can come up with on the email address. It's informing the buyer that his 'alwafid aljadid' was on its way. That's Arabic for..."

Rusty asked, "Novichok, right?" Magne nodded. "Jesus Tapdancing Christ. Okay, this shit is going to the Middle East—somewhere—but where?"

"Unknown, sir. It's probably in all this mess somewhere. We just need time to dig through it."

"Well keep at it. When you find it, I want to know ASAP. If not, we'll meet in the morning, compare notes and figure out where to put our resources."

* * *

While the Praetorians poured over the myriad of documents taken from The Tiger, their now deceased arms dealer, their future was being shaped by events 3,400 kilometers away. Karachi was Pakistan's primary seaport. Situated on the Arabian Sea, it was home to nearly 15 million people, making it the country's largest city. Between the Port of Karachi and the nearby Port of Qasim, the area handled 95 percent of the country's imports and exports. Virtually all the wealth of Pakistan transited Karachi.

Saman Kashani routinely cruised the docks at the Port of Karachi. He worked for a freight expediter. His job was to keep track of what ships were entering the port, where they were offloading their cargo, who picked it up, and when they left. He had to make sure the right truck got to the right pier to pick up or drop off cargo. Not all ships coming into the port were containerized cargo ships. Some were oil tankers that offloaded their oil at deep water offshore transfer stations or specialized petroleum handling docks. There were large bulk carriers filled with grain, cement, or scrap metal but also many smaller coastal freighters and old tramp steamers well past their prime. These small ships meant backbreaking work for the longshoremen and stevedores who had to endure long hours in the hot, poorly ventilated holds manhandling cargo manually. Saman did not envy those men.

Saman Kashani was not as he appeared. His name was an alias and his job was a front. His true name was Ibrahim Safra and his real job was that of a deep cover Mossad officer. He was a spy. As the only declared Muslim nuclear power on the planet, any materials imported to support Pakistan's nuclear program were brought in through Karachi. Because Pakistan had the only "Islamic Bomb," Israel followed developments pertaining to Pakistan's nuclear weapons and related delivery systems.

Safra was born to a Mizrahi family. They were Oriental Jews, the Edot Ha Mizrach, the Communities of the East. He appeared and spoke like a Pakistani, but his family was actually from eastern Iran. His parents were college professors that fled in 1979 to Israel—one step ahead of the anti-Jewish purges—when the Shah fell and the Islamic Republic of Iran was born. Ibrahim grew up speaking Farsi, Urdu, Arabic, English, and Hebrew. He easily passed as Persian, Pakistani, or Arab—which is exactly why Mossad sought him out.

Safra, AKA Kashani, monitored the Karachi docks seeking imports or exports that might be of interest to the State of Israel. Imports might be binders and propellants for Pakistan's missile program; or illicit uranium ore, parts for uranium enrichment centrifuges, and high-tech western equipment to sustain their nuclear weapons program. Exports of concern would be any of the above destined for any enemy of Israel.

Safra had been working the docks for over five years. He recognized most of the port officials on sight. He worked with the men in charge of the stevedores—both officially and unofficially. He knew which customs officials were honest and who took bribes. He was also acquainted with many of the captains of the ships that routinely visited Karachi. The smaller ships brought in products from all over the region—coffee from Kenya and Ethiopia, khat from Yemen, canned fish and bananas from Somalia, palm oil and cocoa from Malaysia, rubber and tea from Sri Lanka, and saffron, tobacco, raisins, and dates from Iran. If anyone was going to smuggle anything in or out of Pakistan, this would be the way to do it.

As a freight expediter, Safra had to keep a record of when ships arrived and who collected their cargos. As part of this, he took photographs of the ships and the trucks at the docks to send to customers to confirm arrival and pickup of their merchandise. He also made sure to include photos of the captains, crews, customs officials, and truck drivers. Over the years, he collected thousands of photographs which he dutifully sent back to Mossad in Israel. On this day, he took a photo that, unbeknownst to him, was the equivalent of rolling a grenade into a library.

* * *

Daniel Charon was at his desk inside Mossad headquarters in Tel Aviv when Rachel Dreyfus barged in. "Miss Dreyfus, do you no longer even pretend to knock?"

"I'm sorry, sir, but this is important."

Charon leaned back in his chair. "Isn't it always?"

"It really is this time."

"What do you have?"

"We just got a report from our man in Karachi. He dumped his latest collection of photos. We ran them through facial recognition and you'll never believe who we discovered."

He was used to Rachel's flair for the dramatic and wanted her to get to the point. "Josef Mengele? You realize he's already dead, right?"

An irritated Rachel replied tersely, "Yes, I am aware. This person is apparently very much alive."

"I'm busy, just tell me who the hell it is."

With a self-satisfied smirk, she said, "Dr. Khalid ibn Mahfous Al-Maadi—aka Abu Almawt."

Suddenly interested, Charon sat up in his chair. "Show me!"

Rachel dropped two photos on Daniel's desk. "This first one is the last known photo of Al-Maadi taken from the security cameras at the airport in Aqaba the day before we thwarted the Black Sun biological attack in the West Bank." Tapping the second photo with her finger, she said smugly, "Ibrahim Safra took this photo last week in Karachi."

Charon peered intently at the second photo and then back at the first. "Are we sure it's him? I mean, they're similar but there are differences. His hair is grayer, his beard is longer, and he's very old and haggard…but there's something else. Maybe the nose or through the eyes. He looks different."

"Facial recognition gives it a 63 percent certainty."

"From these photos? That is only slightly better than a coin toss. Not enough to act on."

Rachel presented a third photo and smiled, "Safra got a profile pic with a clear shot of his ear. We have lots of photos of Al-Maadi from his time at the University of Cairo and the ears are a dead-on match. Computer says it's a 97 percent match. You get old, wrinkled, and gray—or have plastic surgery—but unless you cut your ears off, they stay the same. That's how we debunked all those 'Hitler in Bolivia' photos back in the day."

"Okay, let's say it is Al-Maadi. What the hell is he doing in Karachi? He is one of the most wanted men in the world. After the Americans chopped up his cousin, he should be in a cave somewhere heating a tin of beans over a dung fire. Whatever it is, it must be important to get him out of the Hindu Kush. Was he traveling with an entourage? Bodyguards?"

"Unclear sir."

Studying the photograph, Charon asked, "Who is he talking to?"

"Also, unclear. We think he's a captain of a coastal freighter. We have no matches in our database—we're still looking. He may be new or this may be his first trip into Karachi."

"What vessel?"

"We don't know for certain. There were several at that dock."

"Match the time stamp on the photo with any port records. Also, ask if the Americans have any satellite images taken that day. They will deny they do, but they'll have some. Don't take no for an answer."

"Besides Safra, what assets do we have on the ground in Karachi?"

"None. And we don't know where Al-Maadi went after leaving the docks. Safra didn't realize he was a target of interest, so he didn't follow him to get a license plate number or anything."

"No, I wouldn't expect he would've. He doesn't look like the man in the wanted posters. Since we don't have the resources to pursue this, we may need to pass it on."

"To the Americans?"

"No, I have someone else in mind. Someone a little more flexible, and to be honest, a lot more effective."

"Who?"

Charon replied, "Sarah Rabin."

Rachel was taken aback. "Sarah Rabin? She quit. Works for some private company now."

"Yes, the Praetorians."

"I get she's a bit of a legend and all, but how do you expect her to do anything about Al-Maadi?"

Charon gave a slight smile and then asked, "Who do you believe discovered Black Sun in the first place?"

"Well, I assumed it was us, maybe with help from the Brits or the Americans."

"No. It was the Praetorians. They got a lead when they took out Mohammad al-Rafah and then ran it to ground."

"Wait. They killed al-Rafah? The Cobra?"

"Yes, and they discovered the bioweapon, took out the entire Black Sun cell in Libya, disrupted the terrorist attack, destroyed the bioweapon, and took out Al-Maadi's mistress, Nura Ostergaard nee Al-Doghmush."

"Hold on, it was one of our Eitan drones that took out the terrorists near the Rantis Checkpoint."

"Yes, that's true. But who do you think called in the airstrike and herded the terrorists into our kill box? And this was after they hunted down, killed, and burned all the other terrorists. So, you'd be hard pressed to find more capable hands than those of Sarah Rabin and her comrades."

"I had no idea."

"Nobody does and I want to keep it that way. This stays between us. Do you understand?"

"Yes, sir. Wow. Sarah Rabin. And all this time I assumed she had sold out like those Mossad and IDF guys who become bodyguards for movie stars."

"Not hardly."

* * *

Back in Cyprus, the Praetorians' hard work was slowly beginning to pay off. By cross referencing payment dates, shipping weights, handling instructions, customs forms, and signatures, they were able to determine which documents corresponded to which shipment. They first separated inbound from outbound, then started sorting by shipment size.

Gunny and Rusty came downstairs to check on them. The team had moved from the concrete floor to the sparring mats. Gunny asked, "Why are you doing this on the mats? Does it keep the papers from blowing around or something?"

Hans laughed, "No. It saves our knees. You try crawling around on a concrete floor for hours on end. None of us are as young as we used to be."

Rusty asked, "So, what do you have?"

Well, we've been able to separate the imports from the exports. The imports have customs forms. They're bogus, of course, but Kotov kept them. I assume he wanted to have some insurance in case the Syrian government raided his compound. He had the signatures of all the corrupt customs agents on the forms."

Rusty asked, "How would that help him? All the Syrians are corrupt as hell."

"Yeah, but if the kickbacks they sent to Damascus were less than you'd expect for a shipment of a particular size, the customs guy would expect an unpleasant visit from his boss."

"You mean if the corrupt customs guy was skimming from his boss."

"Yes, and they were. It's a bit of the old, 'I may go down, but I'm taking you with me.' Mutually assured destruction—Syrian style."

Gunny gazed upon the piles of paper. "Jesus. What a mess."

"You don't know the half of it. Like I said earlier, there are half a dozen languages on these documents. We are constantly having to stop to find someone to read it or have Steve scan it, run it through an optical character reader, and have the computer translate it. That is a hit or miss proposition at best."

Rusty commented, "Well, at least cull the imports from the pile. We're only interested in his exports."

Hans shook his head. "Not exactly. If we identify the Novichok on the way in—its weight, number of containers, etc.—it will help us identify it on its way out."

"Ah, got it." Rusty added, "Not to sound like a dick but how much longer will this take? We're kind of on the clock on this one."

"I understand, boss. We're going as fast as we can."

Gunny asked, "Where is Sarah?"

"She got an email from someone; probably Mossad. She needs to contact them using Signal but didn't want to do it near the villa. Even though no one can determine what she is saying, the cell tower data will say where she is when she says it. She's going to call them from Nicosia."

Rusty asked, "What is it about?"

"Not a clue. But if they are contacting her directly like this, I bet they aren't asking for Grandma's apple strudel recipe."

* * *

Sarah Rabin grabbed the keys to one of the Range Rovers and drove into Nicosia. She wanted a place with lots of people, and more importantly, lots of cellphones. She opted for the Cyprus Museum. All those tourists taking photos would be guaranteed to have their cellphones on.

She did not drive directly to the museum. She first drove to the Mall of Cyprus and made a small purchase. She then drove to the Greek Orthodox Church east of downtown and parked. She went into the church, lit a candle, and dropped some money into the collection box. Upon leaving, she set off on foot for downtown instead of returning to the Range Rover. She was running a surveillance detection route to make sure she wasn't being followed. It was an old habit but a good one. She'd do the same on the way home.

After taking a circuitous route through the twisted, illogical streets of the city, she arrived at the museum. It was only then that she turned on her burner cellphone. She took a few photos and texted them to a photo upload site to generate innocuous traffic for the phone. Then she opened the Signal app and contacted her former colleagues in Tel Aviv.

"Hello, Daniel. You rang?"

"Hi Sarah. How are things going? Keeping busy?"

"Always. While I'd love to chat and catch up, you didn't contact me to talk about the old days. What's up?"

"We recently came across an old friend of yours."

"Oh really? Who might that be?"

"Abu Almawt." Sarah stood in stunned silence for several seconds. Daniel asked, "Sarah, did you hear me?"

Recomposing herself, Sarah responded, "Yes. Where is he?"

"Pakistan."

Sarah was now mildly irritated. "We kind of knew that already. That isn't really news."

"Now Sarah, be patient. He was in Karachi, not the Hindu Kush."

"Karachi? With that big of a price on his head? Was he riding around in a tank?"

"Our man on the docks snapped a photo of him last week. I'm sending it to you now. Looks like he had some plastic surgery to alter his appearance but we're sure it's him. He was talking to someone we believe to be a ship captain, one of those rusty old coastal freighters."

Sarah's mind was racing. "Have you identified the captain? Or his ship?"

"No, not yet. But we're working on it."

"Send me everything you find on the captain. Get me his photo, the time it was taken, and geographic coordinates. We'll work this from our end too." She quipped, "The first one to figure it out gets to take him."

Daniel's mood was suddenly more subdued. "We'll pass you everything we find out but this one is yours."

Sarah was surprised. Daniel and Mossad were never ones to shy away from an operation, especially one involving a man who came so close to destroying Israel as a nation. "What to you mean it's ours?"

"We don't have the resources in place to pursue him. Not in Pakistan, not right now. We might over time but if he is up to something in the near term, the Praetorians are in a much better position to take advantage of it."

Sarah paused for a long minute. "Okay, I understand. We'll keep you posted."

Daniel said, "Do it through Mr. Travis, through the committee. This conversation never happened, understand?"

"What's the big deal? There's a standing kill order on Abu Almawt."

"I know but I've yet to get official approval to talk to you. You'll need as much time as possible so I reached out directly and very much 'off the record.' I'm afraid we've become very bureaucratic since you left."

"That's sad to hear. Thanks for the tip."

* * *

Sarah had to fight the urge to drive straight back to the villa. *Don't compromise security for expediency.* After making sure she was not under surveillance, she made her way back to Lakatamia. Running through the front door, she yelled out, "I have big news!"

Rusty and Gunny quickly emerged from Rusty's office. Rusty asked, "What news?"

Sarah smiled broadly. "This is for the whole group. They still downstairs?" She ran past the two men and to the basement stairs.

Gunny trotted after her pleading, "Wait for us!"

Sarah flew down the stairs. Steve was in the first office working on his computer. She slapped the door frame and said, "Chang, off your ass. I have big news." He jumped out of his chair and joined Rusty and Gunny in pursuit. Finding all the others hunched over Kotov's papers, she said, "Everyone, off your knees. I have great news." She had their undivided attention now. "Mossad found Al-Maadi. He was in Pakistan last week. They have a photo of him."

Everyone cheered but then Gunny threw cold water on their celebration. "Uh, Rabin, we kind of figured he's been in Pakistan ever since Zawahiri got pureed in Kabul, maybe even before. He's somewhere in the Hindu Kush with his cousin's people."

"The picture was taken in Karachi. He was at the port talking to a boat captain."

"Holy shit! That is big news. There's a massive price on his head. For him to surface in Karachi is dangerous as hell. There are about fifteen million people who would sell him out in a heartbeat for a tenth of the reward. How confident are they that it is really him?"

"He appears to have had some plastic surgery and their facial recog software gave it a 63 percent match. However, they got a good profile pic with a clear shot of his ear. That matches his university photos with a 97 percent certainty. They sent me the original photos to allow us to verify it ourselves."

Steve interjected, "I'm all over that. Give me the photos and I will have an ID in less than two minutes."

Magne asked, "Where is he now?"

Sarah answered, "Unknown. The Mossad agent didn't recognize him so he didn't tail him."

Alen asked, "This ship captain. Do we have a name on him? Or maybe the ship?"

"They're working on it but not yet. If we scrape the time and geocoords from the photo's metadata, we'll find out where he was standing when the picture was taken."

"If we figure out what ships were docked in the vicinity, that'd narrow down our search."

Gunny chimed in, "You get me a date and geocoords. I'll reach out and get satellite photos for that day. They're always snapping pics of Karachi. It's Pakistan's main naval base."

Hans rubbed his chin and asked, "Does anyone else think it is just a coincidence that Al-Maadi surfaces for the first time in over a year right after Kotov ships out an unknown amount of fucking nerve gas?" The room went silent.

Lon said, "Thanks for pissing on my campfire while I'm trying to make s'mores."

Magne asked, "What's a s'more?"

"I'll explain later."

Hans continued, "Seriously guys. We have an unknown quantity of Novichok somewhere out in the ether and a man determined to slaughter an entire race of people suddenly pops up on the radar? I mean, it might be just kismet but I don't think so."

Rusty said, "Our German friend has a point. We have two tasks on the table. We need to figure out what the hell happened to that nerve gas and figure out who Al-Maadi was talking to on the docks in Karachi. Let's pray the two are not connected."

* * *

The Praetorians now had two targets. Hans, being the best linguist, took most of the team to continue their deep dive into Kotov's records in an attempt to find the missing Novichok. Steve, Sarah, and Nigel retreated to

Steve's office to focus on exploiting what Mossad provided on Al-Maadi. Steve was able to quickly confirm the man in the photos was indeed Dr. Khalid Al-Maadi. He also pulled out the metadata from the photos and isolated the day, time, and location they were taken. Thankfully, the Mossad agent was using a smartphone and it captured a lot of metadata. Rusty reached out to the CIA representative on the steering committee to request satellite data from the National Reconnaissance Office (NRO). Once he learned of Al-Maadi's reappearance so close to the disappearance of the Novichok, the CIA man promised a week's worth of imagery of the Port of Karachi and the Port of Latakia, Syria within 24 hours.

Identifying the ship's captain was proving problematic. His face was not in any of their databases. Mossad found nothing either so they went back to Ibrahim Safra's written reports to get a list of all ships in port on the day in question. They were able to cull the list by eliminating the larger bulk carriers, oil tankers, and container ships that offloaded their cargos at specialized docks far from where the picture was taken. If the man talking to Al-Maadi was the captain of a ship, it was likely a fishing boat or a coastal freighter. They just had to figure out which one.

Coastal freighters, known as coasters or skoots, are smaller, shallow draft cargo vessels designed to navigate shallow waters and areas with reefs that would ground a deep draft, ocean-going vessel. They provide shipping to small ports, seaside villages, and small islands that larger ships either cannot or simply will not service. They were ubiquitous along the European, African and South Asian coastlines. They were not well-regulated and most were independently operated. Large ships are tracked anywhere in the world using commercial tracking services like Fleet Mon or Vessel Finder. Most smaller ships were not specifically identified by these services and were listed as only "cargo ship" or "fishing vessel" but it provided the larger, less nimble tankers and container ships a warning as to what other traffic was in their immediate area. Most of the smaller boats kept their transponders on so as not to get run over. Should they run into trouble at sea, those transponders would tell rescuers where to find them. However, if one didn't want to be found, turning off your transponder essentially made you disappear. This was the problem the Praetorians were facing. Anyone dealing with the most wanted man in the world probably didn't want to be found.

Hans and his group struck gold first. Based on sale dates, transportation records, and emails between Kotov and his underlings, they determined that if the Novichok left Syria by ship, it had to be on one of two vessels that departed Latakia, Syria within the timeframe. The first was a Panamanian flagged cargo ship, the *Sea Lion*. She was a 200-meter long general cargo vessel that docked at Latakia three weeks earlier. Her declaration when transiting the Suez Canal stated she was carrying oil processing equipment from Bandarabbas, Iran, but everyone assumed that included weapons for the Assad regime. According to satellite imagery, she was loaded with some unknown cargo for the return trip and had put to sea twelve days before the raid. According to the Israeli Navy, she was still riding high in the water before she ballasted up. She was mostly empty.

The second ship was the *Amuratu*, a Tanzanian flagged 800 metric ton coaster with a beam of 55 meters and a draft just under four meters. She was equipped with two cranes making her ideal for servicing the small ports with limited infrastructure. She had visited a number of minor ports along Western and Northern Africa before docking at Latakia. While the exact details of her cargo were unknown, she offloaded what appeared to be bulk agricultural products— palm oil and sacks of beans, rice, wheat, corn, and raw cocoa. She took on at least fifty 1250-liter bulk containers of Syrian olive oil along with several pallets of spices. She put to sea the day before the *Sea Lion*. While the *Sea Lion* headed for Egypt, the *Amuratu* turned west toward the Strait of Gibraltar.

* * *

Once he received the overhead imagery via a secure satellite downlink, Rusty called the group together in the basement. "Okay guys, we just got the imagery from our friends across the pond. I checked with MI-6, but they don't have anything more. Where do we stand on the two investigations?"

Sarah went first. "We've had no luck identifying the man talking to Al-Maadi. We have a good, clear photo but no hits in any of our terrorist player databases. Mossad found nothing either. It may be that Al-Maadi is purposely using some innocent civilian because he has never popped on anyone's radar. The guy could also be active but such a minor player, no one ever got his photo. Or we just missed him. Regardless, no one had him in the databases. After Mossad came up empty, they ran it by the CIA, MI6, DGSE and even the Egyptians. No one has anything on the guy."

Rusty pondered this for a minute. "Okay. Maybe we're too focused on intel databases. Do an internet-wide image search and use Wise Owl as the interface to compare our guy to every photo available online."

Steve was aghast. "That is literally trillions of photographs! Even if I had Dr. Williams' set up in College Station, it would take forever!"

"I realize that. Start with the top-level domains most common in the Middle East and expand out from there. He was in Pakistan so start with .PK sites. Even if this guy doesn't post a photo, he may have kids, nieces, or cousins that do. I'll send the photo to Dr. Williams and ask him to do the same. Maybe we'll get lucky. If we match a name to a boat in the harbor, that would give us a target. What about the nerve agent? Where to we stand on that?"

Hans spoke. "We identified the only two realistic candidates for transport by sea. The first is the *Sea Lion*, a 200-meter, Panamanian flagged freighter. She is currently at the Port of Alexandria loading cargo. We hacked the harbormaster's computer network. According to their records, she is taking on agricultural products—nuts, vegetable oil, spices, and cotton. She says her cargo is bound for India but we aren't buying it."

Rusty asked, "Why not?"

"She is owned by a Beirut holding company with deep ties to the Iranian Revolutionary Guard. There's a very good chance she's headed back to Iran."

"Her cargo is innocuous enough."

Nigel chimed in. "If that's really her cargo."

Hans replied, "We have no reason to doubt it. Egyptian trade with Iran is negligible. They backed Morsi and the Muslim Brotherhood when they ousted Mubarak. Then al-Sisi ousted Morsi and Iranian/Egyptian relations have been in the shitter ever since. There is a de facto embargo, but the Egyptians aren't too worried about cotton and soybean oil. Money is money, after all."

"Where is the *Sea Lion* now?"

"She has left Alexandria and is queuing up for the Suez Canal."

"How long does that take?"

As one of the Praetorians' maritime experts, Nigel answered, "It depends on congestion and paperwork. I checked Vessel Finder this morning. Southbound traffic is pretty clear. They still have to complete all the transit docs, line up a pilot, and pay the fees."

Gunny asked, "How much to transit?"

Nigel rubbed his beard. "Well, she's a 200-meter boat, displacing 35,000 tons, so it should cost about $250,000. That's with the pilot and the various bullshit fees they tack on."

Rusty asked, "Is there a way to screw up their paperwork? Maybe stall their payment?"

Steve nodded. "Oh, there might be a way."

"Good, let's slow them down. Would the Egyptians be willing to board her for an inspection?"

Gunny said, "Well, if one of our steering committee folks makes a formal complaint—say for illegally shipping proscribed materials to Iran. If we tell them the Iranians really own her and hint at a possible connection to Al-Maadi, I'd bet the Egyptians would board her if for no other reason than to piss off Tehran."

Nigel added, "If they do, we need to get someone on board with a CW detector. It's a big ship and that shit could be crammed into any nook or cranny."

John said, "If it were me, I'd hide it in the bilge or ballast tanks."

Nigel nodded. "Agreed. It's not going to be easy. We don't even know what we're searching for. I mean is it ten kilos or a hundred? Liquid or powder?"

Alen spoke for the first time. "It's a binary compound—both halves will be liquid. They were designed to be loaded into an artillery round in individual chambers separated by a bladder. When the shell is fired, the bladder ruptures and the spinning of the shell mixes the components."

Rusty shook his head. "Markovic, you are always full of surprises. Any idea on quantity?"

"No, sir. But they don't need a lot. There are several variants. The most lethal is A-230. The Russians claimed a lethal dose of less than 0.1 milligram, but that's likely hype. Probably more like 0.15 or 0.2 milligrams. You can still kill something like five to seven thousand people with a single gram of the stuff. Of course, there is still the distribution problem."

"Distribution problem?"

"It's like sperm. Technically one man is capable of impregnating every woman on Earth but there is a bit of a distribution problem. This is the same thing. You'll never ensure that each person gets a lethal dose and only a lethal dose. In a terrorist release scenario, much of the agent would end up on the ground or coating buildings, cars, or other inanimate objects. If there was wind, it would be blown all over. Many would get much more that a minimum lethal dose while others would get less. They'd still be affected, just not die."

Rusty added, "Unless you released it in a confined space like an office building or a subway tunnel."

"That would complicate matters."

Gunny now asked, "Okay, Alen. You're the expert on Russian weapons systems. How much does a single artillery shell hold?"

"Hmm. Well, I'd want maximum range to keep this crap from blowing back on my own troops so that'd be the 152-millimeter field gun or 122-millimeter rocket launcher. The artillery shells weigh 40 kilograms, the rocket warheads about half that. Most of the weight is steel, however, since you only need a dispersing charge and don't care about shrapnel, you make the casing thinner so you might have at least half of that nerve agent."

Gunny did some quick calculations. "From one rocket or round, anywhere from ten to twenty kilograms of Novichok which could kill anywhere from five to seven thousand people per gram." Scribbling out his math, he said, "That has the potential to kill 50 to 140 million people."

Alen said, "Well, technically, but like I said, there is the distribution problem." The room was quiet. Everyone was contemplating the ramifications of what was just said.

Finally, Rusty broke the silence. "Potentially millions of people dead from just twenty kilograms? We really need to find this shit."

CHAPTER THREE
A SHELL GAME AT SEA

Steve Chang was able to hack into the Suez Canal Authority's computer system and "lose" a couple of the required documents the *Sea Lion* needed on file before gaining access to the canal. He didn't delete the documents. The owners of the *Sea Lion* would have electronic receipts to prove they'd been submitted. Steve simply filed them into another ship's electronic folder and deleted the logs. It all took less than five minutes. Just to be certain, he also flagged the *Sea Lion*'s bank account for suspicious activity. It would take an additional three business days for any money to clear. The *Sea Lion* wasn't going anywhere.

At the urging of the American government, the Egyptians agreed to board and inspect the *Sea Lion*. It didn't take a lot of prodding. President Abdel Fattah al-Sisi had no love for the Iranians. They had supported President Mohamed Morsi, an Islamist who took over after Hosni Mubarak resigned in the wake of mass protests. A year later, it was Morsi who was ousted after another round of nationwide protests called for his resignation. When he refused to resign, he was ousted in a military coup and ultimately replaced by his Minister of Defense—Abdel Fattah al-Sisi. The Iranians let it be known they were none too happy their man, Morsi, was replaced which only secured the new leader's animas. Not only did al-Sisi approve the operation against the *Sea Lion*, he also agreed to have two American and British "technical consultants" assigned to the inspection party. These two men remarkably resembled John Kernan and Nigel Finch.

After its paperwork glitch had been cleared up and its payment processed, the *Sea Lion* entered the Suez Canal at Port Said. The passage was uneventful. The captain and crew of the *Sea Lion* had made this trek several times before. There was little for them to do. Mr. Assam, the pilot provided by the Canal Authority, was in charge of the vessel. After some 75 kilometers, they passed the city of Ismailia, the unofficial halfway point. Twenty kilometers more and they entered the Great Bitter Lake, a large salt water lake midway between the Mediterranean and Red Sea. Here the routine trip came to a halt.

The pilot, Mr. Assam, received a telephone call. Summoning the captain, he explained. "We have been ordered to pull out of the channel and heel to."

The captain was shocked, "Ordered? By whom? The Canal Authority? I was told our payment was processed."

The pilot replied, "No, sir. The order comes from the Egyptian Navy."

The captain turned to starboard. A ship was approaching; it was the ENS *Shabab Misr*, a South Korean made Pohang-class corvette. The pilot wasn't joking. He ordered his helmsman to reverse the screws and stop the ship. Turning to the pilot, he asked, "What is this all about?"

"I have no idea."

* * *

The man talking to Dr. Khalid Al-Maadi on the docks in Karachi was not a well-known or particularly engaged terrorist supporter. He was Zihad Haq, a man in his mid-30s who was the captain of the trawler *Baadbani Machhli*; *Sailfish* in Urdu. Originally his uncle's boat, Haq started as a deckhand in his teens. His uncle had no male offspring and treated Zihad as his son. When his uncle died of a heart attack, he left the boat to his nephew with the condition that Zihad supported his widowed aunt. Haq lived on Baba Island—close to the Karachi Fisheries Market where he sold his catch. The day he was talking to Al-Maadi, he was at the freighter docks to pick up a new net winch. Ibrahim Safra AKA Saman Kashani, the Mossad agent at the Port of Karachi, didn't recognize him because he had never been there before.

About the time the *Sea Lion* was being stopped in the Suez Canal, Haq eased his trawler into the nightmare that was the Karachi fish harbor. Fishing boats of all sizes were crammed together maneuvering into any crevice along the pier where they offloaded their catch and got paid. Across from the pier were a string of jetties protruding into the harbor where the local boats were tied up between sorties into the Arabian Sea. Hundreds of boats were lashed to the jetties and each other in a haphazard way. Haq shook his head questioning how any of them put to sea. It was the epitome of chaos but somehow it worked—albeit not efficiently.

Zihad Haq was lucky to find a slot on the south end of the pier. While his senior deckhand oversaw the crew loading the catch into large plastic bins and swinging them over to the pier, Haq contacted his buyer. He had a good catch and the buyer was eager to lock it in rather than haggle and risk Haq taking it to auction where the price might be driven up. Pakistan was a country of over 240 million hungry souls. When it came to food, it was a seller's market.

After agreeing on a price, Haq left the pier to take his sales slip to the buyer's seafood company office one street over. Once his catch was weighed, he got paid. It was his normal routine. He next checked in with the Marine Fisheries Department for any updates on catch limits, weather, military maneuvers, or anything else than might impact his next voyage. All this was his normal routine. What he did next was a break. Rather than returning to the *Sailfish*, he walked north and then east toward Dockyard Road. He crossed the street and continued north to the Quetta Chaman Hotel, a rather seedy place but exactly what one would expect for a cheap hotel on the docks.

Haq approached the front desk and said, "Alfaar?" The scruffy clerk glanced up from his newspaper and took a long drag from his cigarette but said nothing. He just slid Haq a key and pointed to the stairs at the back of the lobby. There was a metal circle attached to the key with the number "210" stamped on it. Haq took the key and nodded. At the top of the stairs was a dark, dingy corridor. The air was heavy with the smell of sweat, fish, and tobacco smoke. No pleasant aromas of chai tea or spices in this place. This is where working men stayed. When he found room 210, he knocked.

A voice came from behind the door, "Yes?"

Zihad Haq replied, "Alfaar." The door opened and before him stood Dr. Khalid ibn Mahfous Al-Maadi—Abu Almawt, the Father of Death, the head of Black Sun, and, since the death of his notorious cousin, the most wanted man in the world. "Please, come in."

Haq was taken aback. He almost didn't recognize him. "Brother, you have changed since we last met. You have shaved your beard and cut your hair. You could pass as an infidel."

"I thought it prudent after what happened to my dear cousin Ayman."

Zihad added solemnly, "May peace be upon him. What a tragedy."

"Yes, it was. I have been reading reports in the Western press regarding his murder. They say the British and Americans had spies watching him and his family. That's how they were able to direct the missiles from the drone so accurately. If they saw him, they probably saw me as well. I was lucky I wasn't killed alongside him."

Haq was surprised. "You were with him in Kabul the day they…?"

"Yes. I had been staying with him when he was in Pakistan. I warned him about going to Afghanistan but he insisted it was safe. After the Americans left and our Taliban brothers once again took control of the country, he was eager to go to Kabul. I warned him that the Americans undoubtedly would leave behind a network of spies. He insisted the Taliban would root out any spies and keep him safe. After a few months without incident, I too was convinced. I had joined him in Kabul only the week before. Several times he and I would stroll along the roof together in the very spot the American missiles struck."

"Were you there when…?"

"No, thankfully. I was down in the kitchen getting a coffee. Maybe if I had, he would still…"

Haq interrupted him, "No. It would have made no difference except you would be dead along with your cousin. I read about these devilish weapons they used to murder him. There is no way to guard against such an evil machine."

"Objectively, that is true, but I can't help but wonder. Poor Cousin Ayman. May he and Osama rest at the feet of Allah for eternity." Haq nodded solemnly. "Well, after that, I assumed they had photographs of me and that they would identify me eventually, so I decided to change my appearance. They're hunting for a man living in the wilderness, so I gave them a modern businessman. I shaved my beard, cut my hair, and dyed it a light brown. I also had surgery to alter my appearance—different nose, eyes, and mouth. What do you think?"

"You could pass as a European. Maybe not a Brit or an Irishman but certainly French or German."

"I'm glad."

Zihad stood erect. "What do you require of me, Abu Almawt?"

"Is your boat here?"

"Yes, sir. At the dock unloading our catch."

"Are you sure you are still willing to help me take my revenge?"

"Our revenge. And yes, I am sure. Uncle Ahmed made me promise to not get involved in matters of Jihad. He was worried it would bring down trouble on me, and by extension, him. But he is gone now. I consider my obligations regarding that matter fulfilled. I am ready to follow the path of righteousness wherever it may lead."

"Good. In a few days' time, I will need you to give your crew some time off. Tell them you need to make repairs on the boat or something."

Zihad nodded. "They won't question me. I'll give them their bonus a little early. There will be no complaints."

"Good, because you and I need to take a little trip."

* * *

As the *Sea Lion* slowed to a stop, the captain ordered the crew to power down the main engine and drop anchor. It wasn't like he had a choice. He was in the middle of a lake in the middle of a desert. Where was he going to go? The ENS *Shabab Misr* drew alongside the big freighter about a hundred meters off her port side and prepared to lower a rigid-keel, inflatable boat into the water for the boarding party. As she did, her two forward mounted OTO Melara 76 mm compact naval guns swung around and zeroed in on the bridge of the *Sea Lion*. The Egyptians were not messing around.

The *Sea Lion* was hailed by the Egyptians. "*Sea Lion, Sea Lion*. This is Egyptian Navy corvette ENS *Shabab Misr*. Lower your ladder and prepare to be boarded and inspected."

Captain Behzadi of the *Sea Lion* responded, "Egyptian Navy corvette, what is this about? We have permission to transit the canal from the Suez Canal Authority."

The captain of the *Shabab Misr* ignored his protestations. "Have your crew assemble at the muster station. You may keep one man in the engineering spaces to monitor the ship's generator. The canal pilot will remain on the bridge." This was not a discussion. It was an order.

Captain Behzadi walked out along the port bridge wing as the boat with the boarding party pulled away from the Egyptian warship. He turned to his first officer and said, "Lower the ladder and have the crew assemble on the upper deck at the aft muster station. Let's get this over with quickly."

"Aye, captain."

Captain Behzadi was standing on the deck of the ship when the first Egyptian sailor scrambled over the railing. He was armed with an AK-74 which he kept at the ready. He was followed by an Egyptian officer in his early thirties. "I am Lieutenant Hamza. I have orders to search this ship for contraband. Your men are to assemble on the aft deck where my men will guard them while we do this. Do not interfere or otherwise resist. You will be held accountable for the behavior of your men. I also require two of your officers to accompany my men to provide access to any spaces on the ship. Do you understand?"

"Yes, of course, Lieutenant Hamza but what is this about? I'm sure if you told me what you were seeking I could…"

Hamza cut him off with a wave of his hand. "Which officers will accompany us?"

Captain Behzadi waved over his first officer. "This is Mr. Hassanzadeh. He and my chief engineer, Mr. Bahrami will do it."

"Behzadi? Hassanzadeh? Bahrami? There are a lot of Iranians running this *Panamanian* ship."

Behzadi said defiantly, "Most of the crew are from the Philippines." He now understood what this was about…politics.

While the captain was talking to Hamza, the rest of the boarding party clambered aboard the ship. Among the Egyptian sailors were two European men—John Kernan and Nigel Finch. Once everyone was on board, Hamza told Behzadi, "I will need your bill of lading, ship's manifest, crew list, and your log book."

As Hamza and the captain headed for the ship's office, the rest of the team had the crew kneel down on the deck. Two sailors trained their weapons on the crew while two more secured their hands with zip ties. The rest of the 15-man boarding party spread out to search the ship. John and Nigel would each take four Egyptian sailors and start searching. John would take the cargo hold and forecastle, and Nigel the crew quarters and engine room. As they split up, John said, "Nigel, it's been a while since I did a Visit Board Search and Seizure."

The big Scot laughed, "I didn't dream I'd ever be doing a VBSS after taking this gig. I may be a little rusty. Most of the stuff we find we just kill or blow up."

"Well don't blow anything up until I'm far, far away."

Nigel snorted, "No promises."

The two teams started combing the ship. John's men started with the cargo hold. The Egyptian sailors were unaware they were searching for chemical weapons so they sought out anything that didn't belong—guns, munitions, drugs, or any other contraband. John accompanied them but he was only interested in finding the Novichok. The Egyptian sailors were efficient and uninhibited. They broke up pallets loaded with bags of grains and nuts, randomly cutting open some in search of proscribed items. While they did, John subtly monitored his CW detector for any activity. Once they were done with the cargo hold, they moved on to the forecastle and bow.

Nigel's team started with the officer and crew quarters on C and D decks. There they found a number of minor violations—some marijuana, illegal alcohol, pornography, and even a fairly large stash of MDMA. One of the sailors brought it to John. "Sir, we found this."

John estimated the weight of the bag. It was about two kilograms. "Ecstasy?"

"Yes, sir. MDMA."

"Where did you find it? Whose cabin?"

"I wrote it down. His name is…"

"Save it for Lieutenant Hamza. Anything else?"

"No, sir."

"Okay, carry on, sailor."

The search of the engine room took longer but still yielded nothing. After searching for four hours, John, Nigel, and Lieutenant Hamza met in the ship's conference room on the upper deck. Hamza asked, "Well? Anything?"

Nigel replied, "No. Just some drugs and other minor contraband but not what we're looking for."

Hamza said, "I've been ordered to extend any courtesy you require. We will start over and open every bag, barrel, and crate if necessary."

It was a waste of time and manpower. Their CW detectors were extremely sensitive. If anything was there, they would have chirped. "No, Lieutenant. While I admire your enthusiasm, that won't be necessary." Turning to John he asked, "What have we missed?"

Hamza interjected, "I found blueprints of the vessel here in the ship's office. Might that help?"

John chuckled, "Now you tell us. Let's see them."

Hamza went to the office, opened a drawer along the back wall and pulled out a thick roll of blueprints. He spread them out on the conference room table and the three men poured over them. John pointed to the various compartments forward of the bridge—the cargo holds, anchor winches, and spaces within the forecastle and bow. "We checked all these spaces. We found nothing. Most of this ship is the hold."

Nigel went through the crew spaces. "The bridge and C Deck were clean. Found drugs, booze, and porn in the crew cabins on B deck. To be expected, actually. Never met a sailor to stay completely sober for an entire voyage. Mess rooms, kitchen, and ship's laundry were all clear. Engine room was messy, but we found nothing. We spent a lot of time down there. No extra noise." He gave John a sideways glance. By "noise" he meant a response from his CW detector.

Lieutenant Hamza asked, "Well, what's left?"

John replied, "The bilge."

Hamza recoiled at the idea of crawling through the filthy, dank, oily bilge—quite literally the bowels of the ship.

John said, "Rock, paper, scissors. Loser goes."

Nigel nodded but Hamza was confused. "What's that?"

Without explaining, the two men made fists with their right hands and shook them—one, two, three. Nigel picked paper. John picked rock. Nigel beamed. "I'll explain it, Lieutenant Hamza, while my friend goes hunting."

The three men walked down to the engine room. The main engine was off, but it was still loud. At the very bottom of the compartment was the bilge pump room. Adjacent to the pump was a metal hatch about three by four feet secured by four door dogs. John flipped the dogs and gave the door a pull. It groaned loudly as it swung open. He had to put his back into it to get the door open wide enough for him to crawl in. "Well, I guess I don't have to worry about it slamming shut on me." John strapped on a helmet and, picking up a flashlight, crawled through the hatch. While they waited for him, Nigel explained to Hamza the intricacies of "rock, paper, scissors."

It was another hour before John crawled out of the hatch. He was sweating, soaking wet, and covered with oily grime. Nigel handed him a bottle of water. As John chugged it down, Nigel asked, "Well? Anything?" John just shook his head. "I could have told you that before you went in."

"What?"

"Yeah. The way you struggled to get that hatch open? That thing hadn't been opened in months. Maybe even a year."

John scowled. "Why the hell didn't you say that before I went in?"

"You didn't ask."

The boarding party had searched for over five hours. There was no Novichok. Before departing, Lieutenant Hamza pulled Captain Behzadi aside. "Thank you for your cooperation, Captain. We found some contraband but most doesn't warrant further detaining or confiscating your vessel."

"Most?"

"Yes. There was this, however." Hamza produced the bag of Ecstasy. "We found this in one of the crew's quarters."

Behzadi blanched. Drug smuggling was seriously punished in Egypt but even more so in Iran. "Who? Which crew member?"

"Ali Gul. A machinist, I believe."

The captain asked, "What are you going to do?"

Hamza replied coldly, "Either you handle it or I do."

To Hamza's surprise, Captain Behzadi said, "Take Gul with you."

"Really?"

"I am obligated to report him. If I do, given the amount of drugs, they will most likely hang him. He will fare better in Egypt."

Hamza was taken aback. He had given Behzadi the choice hoping he would take the man with him and punish him administratively. Hamza didn't want to do the paperwork that accompanied an arrest, but he had painted himself into a corner. "Alright. We'll take him with us."

The Egyptian sailors and the two "consultants" departed the ship with the offending crewman in handcuffs. On the way back to the ENS *Shabab Misr*, Nigel apologized to Lieutenant Hamza. "Sorry, mate. That was an unexpected turn. Didn't mean to make extra work for you."

Lieutenant Hamza shrugged. "Not a problem. I was expecting to make a big seizure. By comparison, this paperwork will be quick. I'll fill out a couple of forms and pass him on to the police."

Nigel slipped a couple hundred Euro notes into his pocket. "We appreciate all you did. Have a nice dinner on us."

Hamza tried to give the money back. "I cannot accept this. I was doing my duty as an Egyptian sailor."

John smiled and said, "We understand. That's exactly why we want you to have it. As two former sailors to a current one."

* * *

After releasing the *Sea Lion* to continue on her journey, John and Nigel returned to the villa on Cyprus to brief the rest of the Praetorians on what happened. It was already late, but John was allowed to take a shower to wash off the bilge gunk before they got started.

Gunny called the meeting to order. "Alright, as you all have figured out by now, the VBSS on the *Sea Lion* went down this morning. The guys are back so I'll turn it over to them."

Nigel took the lead. "We boarded the vessel with the Egyptian Navy boys. They did a banner job boarding the vessel and securing the crew. They were right intimidating so there was very little push back. Though she's Panamanian flagged, Steve's info on the actual ownership was spot on—the captain, first officer, chief engineer, and the rest of the officers were all Iranian. The crew was a mishmash of other people—Filipinos, Pakis, Indonesians, and the like. We searched the vessel from forecastle to stern, bridge to bilge and found no weapons of any kind."

Rusty commented, "I suspect if she'd been boarded sailing to Damascus instead of from, the story would have been different."

John nodded. "I suspect so but it wasn't due to a lack of effort. The Egyptians were very thorough. They made a mess of the cargo hold. They did find contraband including a fairly large stash of Ecstasy but nothing of interest to us. The Egyptians took one sailor into custody for the drugs. The captain was given the opportunity to handle it himself but gave the crewman over to the Egyptians. He said they would likely hang the guy in Iran if he took him back."

Rusty shook his head. "They're pretty harsh over there. He's lucky—if you can even say that. What else?"

"Nothing. Nigel and I had our CW detectors going the entire time. Not a peep out of them."

Gunny asked, "Could they have malfunctioned? You did check the batteries, right?" Nigel just flipped him off.

Steve chimed in, "No, I checked them both when they got back. Both units are working fine, although John's was pretty dirty." Turning to the ex-SEAL he said, "Next time you take one in a bilge, take better care of it. Maybe tie it around your neck or something."

It was now John's turn to flip the bird. "Fuck you, computer boy."

Rusty got everyone back on point. "Okay, okay. Back to the matter at hand. Where the hell is this Novichok shit?"

Sarah said, "It has to be on the other ship; that coastal freighter, the *Amuratu*."

"Agreed. Where the hell is she now?"

Steve shrugged. "We don't know. Last we saw, she was heading west toward Gibraltar. Her past pattern of activity, as best we determined it, would suggest she is going to head south along the west coast of Africa. That appears to be her stomping grounds; the smaller Atlantic and river ports."

"Can we track her?"

"That's going to be tough. Her transponder activity is spotty. She is not signed up with any of the fleet tracking companies so even if she pops up, she'd only be listed as an unidentified freighter and that only for traffic control purposes."

"How the hell do we find her then?"

Steve replied, "Well, if she turned north toward Europe, there will be harbor master records, maritime radar traces, fuel sales records, and NATO shipping updates we can access. We should find that out quickly. Alert the coastal patrols and they'd board her. If she turned south, we're going to have a bigger problem. There is no unified system used by the various ports and harbors. Each country has a different logging system—if they have one at all. I'll start looking at Morocco, Mauritania, and Senegal, and work my way south. She has a top speed of what? Ten knots? She couldn't have gotten too far. Even less if she made any port calls. Also, even if we find her, who's going to stop and board her? The Togolese?"

Rusty pondered this for a moment. "Okay. Get on finding where she is, or at least where she isn't. Draft whoever you need to help."

Steve nodded. "Hans and I will get on it right away."

Gunny jumped in. "The rest of you, find out everything about this boat—how big it is, blueprints, details on the captain and crew, who she hauls freight for, where she buys her fuel, radio frequencies she uses, transponder ID, anything."

"Yes, Gunny."

Rusty interjected. "Get me what you have already and I'll reach out to the steering committee and ask if they have anything of use."

Gunny turned to Nigel and John. "You had a long day, but we need you two to start planning for a takedown of this boat. Start with what you know. Everyone will feed you more info as it becomes available."

John replied, "Yes, Gunny. We'll start immediately. How are we going to get on target? They have a big head start and we don't have the assets to leapfrog them."

"I'm still figuring that out. If they're headed south, they are probably going to sail around the Cape and back up to the Middle East."

Magne asked, "If they are going back to the Middle East, why go all the way around Africa? With the canal fees, the money is probably a wash but that adds a lot of time."

Gunny mused, "Maybe they don't want to break their pattern and draw attention to themselves. More likely, they didn't want to subject themselves to what the *Sea Lion* just went through. Anyone calling on a Syrian port is going to automatically be suspect. The fact that they'd have to sail right past Israel to get to the Suez may have been another factor. Regardless of why, we must consider all contingencies. Nigel, what's the status on *Mother Goose* and the Diver Delivery Vehicle?"

"Mother is fine. The supercavitating DDV is in her well deck. I can swap it out for the older one if you need me to."

"No. If we need one, we'll need the speed. Make sure Mother is fueled up and ready to put to sea on no notice." Nigel nodded. "Now everyone, get to work."

* * *

Khalid Al-Maadi sat quietly in the dark, second-floor office of the safe house in northern Karachi. The house was like many in the area, a simple concrete structure inside a small, walled compound. It had been rented through a trusted cutout. He was safe, at least for a little while. Through the French doors on the south side of the room he gazed upon the megalopolis of Karachi splayed out before him for miles. He sat on the battered couch along the opposite wall far from the doors. He longed to stand out on the balcony in the sunshine but after what happened to his cousin, Ayman al-Zawahiri, he dared not put himself in a position to be observed by anyone outside the walls of the residential compound.

The image of his uncle's mutilated body splashed across the second-floor study of his Kabul residence was burned into Khalid's brain. As a medical doctor, he had experienced plenty of blood and gore. He dissected human cadavers in medical school. He had amputated gangrenous limbs in filthy Gaza Strip hospitals and operated on young Palestinian fighters who'd been gut shot by anti-armor rounds fired from Israeli helicopters. But the slaughter of his cousin was different. This was a man he admired, a family member, a de facto father to him for the last few years. The scene was fresh in his mind—the crash of the missile's impact, the mist of blood that still hung in the air as he rushed to his cousin's room, and the smell. The smell was of blood, the acrid smoke of the missile's smoldering solid rocket engine, and contents of his cousin's bowels sprayed all over the room. Say what you will about killing a person using a regular Hellfire missile, the explosion and fire of the warhead had a cleansing effect. The six blades of the R9X Ninja warhead made for a sloppy, wet death scene. The Americans said they used it to minimize "collateral damage." Khalid didn't really believe this, although the number of victims of the R9X were certainly more limited. Khalid himself had been only a couple of rooms away and was unscathed. Had they used a regular Hellfire, he would likely be dead too. However, the condition of an R9X victim was frightening. The amount of blood and gore made a wholly terrible impression on the survivors.

His thoughts turned to his failed attack on Israel. Had he delegated too much of the planning and execution to others so as to continue his comfortable life as a respected college professor? Andreas Ostergaard, AKA Kalib Kabir, had been brilliant but weak. Al-Maadi had to assign Nura, his own wife and lover, to babysit Ostergaard and to keep him focused on their mission. The mental picture of the pasty Ostergaard having sex with Nura made his blood run cold. Then there was the Libyan, Omar Trabelsi. His arrogance and sloppy security were their undoing. Even before him, there was Mohammad al-Rafah AKA Alkawbra. Though he was instrumental in the tactical design of their plot, didn't all their woes begin when he was assassinated? While Nura insisted al-Rafah would never talk, did he betray them before he was killed? How else were the Israelis or Americans or whoever it was tipped to the plan? And Nura, poor Nura. She was as lovely as she was dedicated. Ruthless and cold when necessary but also passionate and beautiful. She was to be the Roxelana to his Sulieman the Magnificent. Oh how he missed her. How had she died? Was it at least painless? And who killed her? He had no idea. He just hoped he would get his revenge, and soon.

As Khalid sat in the dark with tears welling up in his eyes, there was a knock at the door. Wiping his eyes, he answered, "Come in."

A young man entered the room. "Sir, I have a message from one of our contacts in Syria."

"What is it?"

"It's about the Tiger."

"Al Namir? My broker?"

"Yes. He's dead. He was killed in some sort of military action. They killed him and destroyed his compound."

Khalid sat up. "What? When? Who did this?"

"It happened some ten days ago, they think. As to who, they don't know. There was no reported military activity in the area—no tanks or helicopters. It may have been the Kurds, the Syrians, the Turks, or even the Russians. He had lots of enemies."

"The Russians? Why would they…?"

"What if he cheated them like he tried to cheat you? They're not famous for their understanding and patience."

"How does this affect us?"

"That is unclear, sir. I learned that the *Sea Lion* was boarded and inspected yesterday while transiting the Suez Canal. The Egyptian Navy stopped her in the middle of the Great Bitter Lake and boarded her. They searched the ship for over five hours. The captain reported they found nothing except one crewman smuggling drugs."

Khalid was confused. "The *Sea Lion*? What ship is this and why would we care if the Egyptians stopped her?"

"She left Latakia the same day as the *Amuratu*. The captain of the *Sea Lion* reported that there were two English-speaking Europeans among the boarding party—Americans or British. Very unusual."

Khalid recognized the seriousness of the situation. "What of the *Amaratu*? Have they been boarded?"

The man smiled, "No, sir. I've been in contact with Captain Qadir. There have been no problems. They are on schedule."

"Well, thank Allah for that. Regardless, we need to alter our plan and move up the rendezvous. We will meet with Haq and pick a location. We won't tell Qadir where until just before. I don't want him changing his schedule."

The man protested, "Qadir is trustworthy. Your cousin and Sheik Osama himself trusted him with their lives."

"I understand that, but we cannot take any chances. My cousin trusted the Taliban with his security. How did that end? Besides, it is not Qadir I mistrust. I don't know his crew and will not put the fate of us or our mission in their hands. Just make sure he follows the plan. Understood?"

"Yes, Abu Almawt."

As soon as the man left, Al-Maadi retrieved a burner phone from his desk and called Zihad Haq. "It's me."

It took Haq a second to recognize the voice. "Oh, yes. What do you need of me?"

"There have been some developments. Nothing serious but we need to move up our timetable just to be safe."

"Okay. I will tell the crew the boat is going in for some repairs. I paid them for the last catch so they have money in their pockets. They won't argue. How long will this take?"

"How long will it take you to go to Madagascar?"

"Madagascar? That is beyond my range. We'll need to stop for fuel."

"No, no stopping. Load additional fuel if you need to. I will pay for everything, of course."

Haq mulled this over. "Well, the weight will not be an issue since we won't have ice or fish. I will need to figure out how much additional fuel we'll need and arrange for barrels to be loaded on board."

"Do it today."

"I will also need a couple of men to help me with the ship since we will be sailing all day and night."

"Pick your most trusted deckhand. I'll bring my man, Mohammad. Secure enough provisions for four men for two or three weeks. I'll have money sent to you by courier. Just tell me how much you need. How fast is your boat?"

"Without a load, like this, maybe twenty knots in good weather."

"That will have to do."

* * *

Back in Cyprus, the Praetorians were uneasy. They had yet to find the *Amuratu* or even determine if it went north or south at Gibraltar. They had been checking harbor records in Spain, Portugal, and France but found nothing. The absence of a "no" was not the same thing as a "yes." She might have sailed straight to Ireland or changed her name and transponder to disguise who she really was. It wasn't beyond the scope of reality that she sailed into the Atlantic. She wasn't designed for the open ocean but that didn't mean she wouldn't handle it. After several days, Rusty called a meeting.

"Anything on the *Amuratu*? Do we have any clue where this bucket of bolts actually is?"

Gunny answered for the team. "No, sir, we don't. There is no record of her putting in at any harbor along the European coast."

"What about West Africa?"

"Nothing yet. Their record keeping ain't exactly the best and there are a shit ton of little coastal towns and river ports where she could stop."

Rusty pondered this. "What's your best guess?"

Gunny took a deep breath. "If I were to bet, I'd say she turned south. That appears to be where she works. She reportedly loaded up with olive oil in Syria. She may have a single buyer somewhere in Africa or the Middle East. If that's the case, she may head directly to the customer."

Nigel chimed in. "That all makes sense, but she wasn't fully laden. Why avoid all the ports? She's a tramp steamer. Why not pick up additional cargo along the way to offset your costs?"

Rusty answered, "Because someone is paying you to avoid any authorities. When you come to dock, the harbor master has the authority to inspect your vessel. If you are carrying contraband that is not on your manifest, he's authorized to seize the cargo or impound the ship, right?"

"Yes, sir. But from what Alen said, the Novichok is relatively small and unlikely to draw attention. It might be disguised as cooking oil or engine oil. Some backwater harbormaster is not going to have the latest and greatest CW detector."

Gunny said, "True but why risk it? We have to assume whoever bought the Novichok is paying top dollar for it. Why risk losing it to save a few bucks on shipping costs?"

Sarah interjected, "What if the *Amuratu* is carrying other contraband? Something not so easily concealed?"

Rusty asked, "Like what?"

"Guns, drugs, maybe even people."

"Expand the search to the south. Assume she made no port calls. Figure out how far she might possibly have sailed and check everything from there north."

* * *

Later that afternoon, Steve was hunched over his computer when he got a hit. He called out, "Found her!"

Everyone within earshot rushed to his office. Hans asked, "Where is she?"

"Angola. Get Rusty and Gunny down here."

In a few minutes, the old Marine and the Texas billionaire walked in. Rusty asked, "What do we have?"

Steve replied, "Your hunch paid off. Nigel and John figured out her likely speed, fuel, and time at sea since she left Syria. They came up with a maximum range of about 12,000 kilometers and that is right where I found her. She refueled in Benguela, Angola."

"Where the hell is that?"

"Yeah, I had to google that one too. It's a port city about 400 kilometers south of Luanda and about 12,000 klicks from Latakia, Syria. She left this morning and continued south."

Rusty grinned broadly and said, "That's damn good work, kid. We may have to keep you around."

"Just doing my job, sir."

"Knock off that 'sir' crap. We're all on the same team here." Turning to Gunny, Rusty asked, "Next steps?"

"We definitely need to stop and board her. Assuming the buyer of the Novichok is not some Angolan warlord, this boat will keep going. South Africa is next, but I think this ship is going around the cape and into the Indian Ocean."

"Agreed. Where and how do we stop her?"

Hans suggested, "Well, the sooner and further south the better. If we assume she's headed for Pakistan or the Persian Gulf and we just wait for her to come to us, we run the risk of this stuff being offloaded in Somalia or Yemen. *Mother Goose* is ready to go. Kismayo is the southernmost Somali port—if we put to sea immediately, we should intercept her before she gets there."

Sarah, playing devil's advocate, said, "What if she stops in Tanzania or Kenya and offloads the stuff there...before we get to her?"

"Well, not much we can do about that. If they do, then we'll find out after we stop the ship and you convince the captain to tell you who they gave it to."

Sarah smiled, "It'd be my pleasure."

Nigel asked, "How are we going to track her? She's not running a transponder, right?"

Steve answered, "That's true. However, she does have an INMARSAT. I detected it when she left Benguela. The ship received an incoming call, but I didn't get the chance to intercept it. I'll ping it periodically to get a loose fix on her location. When we're ready to hit her, I'll up the frequency to get a tighter fix."

Magne added, "Once we get within a couple hundred kilometers, we use a long-range drone to track her. They'll never see it, especially at night."

Rusty faced the group and said, "Okay. Let's do this. Nigel, you and John have your ops plan ready? We're going to be limited in our resources—no air-dropped fast boats."

The big Scot grinned. "Aye, we have a nasty surprise for the lads. We'll get her."

"Okay, everyone be ready to ship out in an hour. Steve, get with the Suez Canal Authority and grease our passage through. Front of the line."

Steve added, "Not a problem. I'll get us a naval escort if you want. Oh, I almost forgot. I got the name of the *Amuratu*'s captain. I hacked the fuel company's billing system. His name is Imran Qadir. I'll see what I can find out about him before we leave."

* * *

To Captain Imran Qadir of the *Amuratu*, his name was very fitting. Qadir means "servant of the powerful" and he had been such a servant for decades. Now in his sixties, Qadir was one of the rarest breeds of Islamic extremists, both active and old. He met Ayman Al-Zawahiri in an Egyptian prison in 1981 when both were among the hundreds arrested after a plot against Egyptian President Anwar Sadat was uncovered. Qadir was recruited by Al-Zawahiri into Egyptian Islamic Jihad (EIJ) which later merged with Al-Qaeda. Luckily for Qadir, Ayman envisioned him as a support asset rather than a fighter. Because he was a sailor, they fronted him money to buy a ship for logistical support when needed.

When not helping Al-Qaeda, Qadir was free to pursue his own business interests and he was quite successful. He briefly popped up on the radar of international intelligence agencies in May 1996 when Sudan expelled

Al-Qaeda from the country in the face of Western pressure. Qadir's vessel was contracted to move much of Bin Laden's possessions—including the bulk of Al-Qaeda's weapons cache—from Port Sudan to Karachi. Once Bin Laden got established in Jalalabad under the protection of Taliban leader Mullah Mohammed Omar, Qadir again fell off the radar; yet he remained a committed, albeit cautious, jihadi.

In the ensuing years, most of his old EIJ comrades met untimely deaths. Some of his oldest friends died at the hands of the Egyptian Mukhabarat after the assassination of Anwar Sadat in October 1981. Qadir was suspected but since he was at sea when Sadat was killed, he was able to avoid arrest. Mossad agents killed a few more in Sudan as they helped Osama Bin Laden evacuate. Still others died fighting in Pakistan, Iran, and Yemen. The majority, however, were wiped out in Afghanistan; killed by American soldiers, bombs, or Northern Alliance soldiers seeking revenge for abuse suffered when Al Qaeda and the Taliban ran the country. Through it all, Imran Qadir continued to captain his ship and sail the waters of the Mediterranean, Atlantic, and Indian Oceans. On the surface, he was just one of many, nameless seafarers; a man above suspicion. Beneath it, however, he continued to support jihadist causes by smuggling people, money, guns—and more recently—advanced chemical weapons.

Qadir was a stickler for operational security. That was how he survived. When he got a message using a codeword known only to Ayman Al-Zawahiri, he had to response. Though Ayman was most definitely and publicly dead, whoever was contacting him must be a close associate. He was pleased to discover it was none other than Khalid Al-Maadi—Abu Almawt—the man who came within a hair's breadth of destroying Israel and now, with the death of Al-Zawahiri, the most wanted man on Earth. He was honored. He pledged to help in any way possible.

As the *Amuratu* weighed anchor to leave Benguela, Imran Qadir retrieved a burner phone from his cabin. He powered it on and after a few seconds, it pinged. He had a text message. It had a date some twelve days hence, a time and coordinates—10°27'0" South, 43°37'0" East. It was signed only "AA." Qadir charted the coordinates. They corresponded to an empty hole in the Indian Ocean north of the Comoros. It would be tight but they'd make it. He responded with only "OK Q." The rendezvous was set. He snapped the phone in two pieces, walked out onto the bridge wing, and dropped them in the ocean.

* * *

Mother Goose weighed anchor in Larnaca and set a course for Port Said, the northern entrance of the Suez Canal. Nigel was at the helm with John acting as his first officer. Alen, Hans, and Lon were the "crew." Having a salvage tug carrying passengers did not jibe with their cover story. They would pick up the others along the way. Their passage through the canal was prearranged. Steve even got them moved to the front of the queue. In case anyone questioned this, he added a notation to her file that she was being given expedited passage to the Red Sea to assist on a classified Egyptian Navy salvage operation.

When they reached the canal, a small boat pulled alongside to transfer the canal pilot. By pure coincidence, it was Mr. Assam, the man piloting the *Sea Lion* when she had been boarded. When John welcomed him aboard, Assam took a double take. He recognized John but from where? When he encountered Nigel on the bridge, the light came on. Nigel led the party of Egyptian navy sailors when they searched the bridge of the *Sea Lion* where Assam remained for the entire five-hour inspection. Nigel nodded his acknowledgement but said nothing. Assam double-checked his paperwork, "classified salvage operation." He recalled the deference Lieutenant Hamza had shown these two "enlisted" sailors. He asked no questions and their journey was wholly uneventful. As they passed through the Great Bitter Lake, Mr. Assam gazed out to where the *Sea Lion* had been inspected. He turned to Nigel and John, gave a little salute, and smiled. They were all on the same side.

At the southern exit of the canal, a boat came out to collect Mr. Assam. Nigel put his finger to his lips, slipped a wad of hundred Euro notes in Assam's pocket and said, "We and Lieutenant Hamza appreciate your discretion."

As he got on the boat, Assam turned to the men and said, "Good luck, gentlemen. Happy hunting."

As his boat pulled away, Nigel turned to John and said, "I kinda like that guy."

"Me too. He knows. Knows we know he knows. Still says nothing. A good man."

Mother Goose headed down the Gulf of Suez at a moderate speed. They were not in a big hurry. They had already selected an interdiction point off the southern coast of Somalia and they were a full 2,000 kilometers closer to it than the *Amuratu*. Their next stop was about 300 kilometers to the southeast where the Gulf of Suez meets the Red Sea. On the eastern shore at the tip of the Sinai Peninsula was the resort town of Sharm el-Sheikh. Here they would pick up the rest of the team.

As they rounded the point at the Ras Mohamed Nature Reserve, they spotted a large speedboat approaching. John checked his watch. "Right on time."

Nigel slowed *Mother Goose* as the speedboat circled them and pulled along the port side. The rest of the Praetorians scrambled aboard. Gil, their pilot, was at the helm of the speedboat and held her steady while his son, Donny, tossed the bags of gear up to Alen and Hans. As Rusty climbed aboard, he asked Nigel. "Any problems at the canal?"

Nigel shook his head. "No, but we did run into an old friend."

"Oh?"

"Our pilot was the same guy who was piloting the *Sea Lion* when we stopped her."

"Any issues?"

"No. He recognized us but didn't say a word. I'd bet Steve's little entry regarding the classified navy salvage reaffirmed we were not people he should fuck with. I don't think he would've anyway. He's a squared away guy."

John added, "I concur."

"Well, that's good. Shit, talk about a small world. Let's get moving."

Nigel and Gil exchanged waves. Nigel shouted down to him, "So, trying your hand at piloting something a bit more challenging, eh?"

"Challenging? This is a snap. You only have to think in two dimensions. Explains how you Neanderthals manage to do it. Good luck."

"Aye, you too. Don't get a sunburn on the beach."

"Not a worry. We're going scuba diving. Great reefs around here." Nigel just flipped him off as the speedboat tore away.

The voyage down the Red Sea was routine. The weather was great and the seas calm. At their current speed, it would take them four days to travel the almost 2,000 kilometers to Bab el-Mandeb, the strait where the Red Sea meets the Gulf of Aden. From there it was east to the Indian Ocean and south to their target.

Mother Goose didn't exactly offer five-star accommodations and with ten people on board, things were tight. Since someone had to be at the helm at all times, they took turns but always kept Nigel, John, or Gunny—their experienced sailors—close at hand. Lon assumed the role of ship's cook. Hans volunteered to help him, not because he was being helpful but rather to make sure Lon didn't kill anyone by over-spicing the food. Steve monitored the *Amuratu's* progress via the INMARSAT and, using *Mother Goose's* satellite link, tried to learn more about the *Amuratu's* captain and crew. As for the others, they continued to prep for their mission.

While Gunny drove the boat, Nigel and John prepared for the *Amuratu.* Laid out across the stern deck were long lengths of cables and ropes interspersed with odd black buoys. Alen was bored so he jumped in to help. "What's all this?"

Nigel explained. "Normally, when you are going to take down a moving vessel, you fast rope down from a helo. The other option is to use four fast boats with about ten men per boat. You drop them at night from a C-130 well out in front and to the side of the target ship. You parachute in after them. When you get to your boat, you cut away the parachutes, sink the pallets, and get on board. As the target passes, you slip in behind her, staying in her wake. You then move closer and split up—port, starboard, port, starboard. You ease up on the ship and, using a hook on a pole, attach a caving ladder to the ship. If the ladder drops for any reason, the first boat peels off and the second moves up. You go up the ladder, take the bridge, and secure the crew."

"Yeah, but we don't have any of that; let alone forty guys."

John smirked, "No shit. Nigel has a plan for that."

Alen asked sarcastically, "What are you going to do? Torpedo them from the sub or call in a friendly air strike?"

Nigel snorted, "She's not a sub, she's a DDV, a Diver Delivery Vessel. And no, she doesn't have torpedoes. Well not yet anyway. I need to talk to Rusty about that."

Alen scoffed, "If it goes underwater, it's a submarine to me."

Nigel shook his head. "Amateurs."

John chuckled and explained. "She may not have torpedoes, but she'll have an octopus."

Alen asked, "What the hell is an octopus?"

"All this on the deck."

"Okay, I'll bite. How does it work?"

Picking up a section of thick steel cable, John said, "This is the main cable. Hanging off of it are ten-meter lengths of industrial nylon rope. The sections are separated by these black buoys. They are designed to float just under the surface so the target won't see them. We drag this across the path of the target ship. The *Amuratu* doesn't have a bulbous bow so when she runs over the main cable, she'll drag it under her keel and into her screws. The screws suck up the main cable and the tentacles foul the screw."

"What if the screw just cuts the cable?"

Nigel said, "Well, first it's a bloody thick cable but there are two added features. The tentacles are designed to stretch rather than break and they will wrap around the screws and the shafts. The friction will cause them to melt and completely gum up the bearings. They'll assume they're fouled on some rogue fishing net lost from a factory ship. It happens more times than you think."

Alen nodded, "Okay, what's the other feature? You said there were two."

Nigel grinned an evil grin. "There are five kilos of C4 and a transponder in each buoy. We monitor where each buoy is along the ship and command detonate them from the DDV either individually or all at once. The later situation would be like getting hit with ten small torpedoes at the same time. That's a last resort, actually."

"How are we going to deploy this thing? It's got to be heavy as hell."

"Aye, it weighs a fair bit but thankfully we have a strapping big Serb to help us."

John explained. "We're going to tow it out on a raft. Pull it off in a straight line and then tow it with the DDV. When we're in position, we'll pull it across the *Amuratu's* bow using the DDV. The last buoy is motorized to keep tension from the rear make sure it doesn't drift too far and overshoot the target. Once it gets tangled in their screws, they'll have to stop for repairs. That's when we board her. We'll go over the bow while they're focused on the stern."

Alen was skeptical. "The torpedo idea makes more sense. It'll be pitch black, it's a big ocean and this is what? A hundred meters long? What if you miss?"

"Aye, but that's what the drone is for. Steve will be tracking the ship from above. We'll know exactly where she is at all times. GPS is a wonderful thing."

"Well, I hope this works. I'd prefer they didn't realize we were coming until it's too late."

Nigel grinned, "Oh, it'll work. I'd bet my life on it."

Alen quipped, "You may be doing just that."

* * *

Khalid Al-Maadi was at sea again. It was the first time since the Praetorians disrupted his biological attack on Israel and he was forced to flee to Pakistan via Iraq. Of course, he didn't actually understand it was the Praetorians or who they were. All he knew was *they* destroyed his life's work and probably killed the love of his life. He would take his revenge. If not against them specifically, then against the society they represented.

Khalid never liked the ocean, if even to splash on a beach on holiday. His previous experience only confirmed his bias. He had been a slave on a filthy rust bucket eating wormy food and drinking brackish water that smelled and tasted of fuel oil. Now he was on Zihad Haq's fishing trawler, the *Sailfish*. While the accommodations were a little better, the whole boat smelled of old fish and diesel oil. As much as he had hated the disgusting old freighter, it offered a smooth ride. The *Sailfish* was a much smaller boat and pitched with every wave. Khalid was seasick most of the time so the mediocre food he ate ended up as chum for the fish more times than not.

Khalid leaned over the rail and vomited into the water. As he stood, Zihad handed him a bottle of water. "Here, drink this. You're going to dehydrate if you keep this up. You can last a long time without food, but you need to keep hydrated. I really assumed you'd be used to it by now."

Taking the water, Khalid said, "It seems not. Apparently, mine are a desert people meant to stay on dry land."

Zihad suppressed a smile. "You're not the first man to discover he was not meant for the sea. Stay on deck and keep your focus on the horizon. That and the fresh air will help you. Didn't you bring motion sickness pills like I suggested?"

"Yes, but I have taken them all."

"Well, it won't be much longer. When we rendezvous with the *Amuratu*, we will get some from Captain Qadir."

Khalid wiped the vomit from his mouth. "Let's pray to Allah that he has some."

"If he transports the brothers, I'm sure he does. If not, he will at least have some ginger. No captain wants a bunch of men puking all over his ship."

* * *

It had been seven days since *Mother Goose* picked up the rest of the Praetorians near Sharm el-Sheikh. They were traveling south paralleling the Somali coast but slowed as they approached Kenya. They were where they wanted to be. They were now like a spider on a web waiting for a fly. Steve had learned more about the *Amuratu*'s captain and wanted to share it with the team so Rusty called an all-hands meeting on the fantail of the ship. "Steve has some info on the captain of the target ship."

Steve stepped up. "Okay, when they refueled in Angola, we learned the captain of the *Amuratu* is Captain Imran Qadir. He is Egyptian. Unsure of his exact age, but he appears to be in his early sixties. He has one arrest in 1981 but no indication of a trial or conviction. This is where it gets interesting. He was arrested in a round-up of fifteen hundred suspect extremists after Egyptian security uncovered a plot to kill Anwar Sadat."

Lon quipped. "Uncovered a plot? They shot the man on national television. Not exactly ace detective work required for that."

Steve said, "Qadir was arrested in February in connection with an earlier plot. Sadat was assassinated in October. Do you know who else was arrested in February 1981?"

Nigel answered sarcastically, "About one thousand four hundred and ninety-nine other guys?" The team laughed.

"Ayman al-Zawahiri." The laughter stopped. "It took me a while to dig it out. Those records are not digitized. I was able to access Egyptian Ministry of Justice archives. Some of the documents were scanned so it was tedious as hell. They were in Arabic so Sarah and Hans helped me. The records are incomplete, but Qadir and al-Zawahiri were in the same prison."

Gunny chimed in, "Not to sound like an asshole, but there was a shitload of people arrested. Do we have any indication they ever even met?"

"Not directly."

Rusty commented, "That's pretty fuckin' thin, kid." Steve just smiled. "What aren't you telling us?"

"The next time Qadir shows up is in Port Sudan in 1996. After Egyptian Islamic Jihad, al-Zawahiri's old group, tried to kill Egyptian President Hosni Mubarak in 1995, they wore out their welcome in Sudan. Bin Laden, al-Zawahiri and the gang were kicked out in May 1996. They set up shop in Jalalabad under the protection of Mullah Omar. Bin Laden and al-Zawahiri left on a chartered jet but Bin Laden had left a bunch of stuff behind, stuff he wanted, including his prized horses. Who carried all that shit out of Sudan?"

Rusty asked, "Qadir?"

"Qadir. Bin Laden and al-Zawahiri trusted our good Captain Qadir enough to have him transport their most prized possessions to Karachi. Reports at the time said this included a bunch of Al-Qaeda fighters and the organization's entire weapons stash. I'd bet Captain Qadir has been their logistics guy for decades. From all appearances, he is just the captain of a small coastal freighter but what better cover for moving men, weapons, money, or anything else between Europe, Africa, the Middle East, and Asia?"

Rusty smiled and said, "Jesus Christ, kid, that's good work."

"Sarah and Hans helped. It was a team effort."

"Regardless, I'm going to send Williams at Texas A&M a case of scotch for recommending you."

Steve actually blushed a bit. "Thank you, sir."

"Enough praise. Back to the task at hand. What's the status of the target?"

"Still on course. She's tracking just north of the Comoros, about nine hundred klicks due south. Taking into account her current speed and heading, as well as ours, we'll intercept them in twelve to thirteen hours."

Gunny said, "Nigel, you and John figure out when you want to interdict the *Amuratu* and adjust our course and speed accordingly. I want *Mother Goose* out of their visual range when it happens. The last thing I want is them radioing out any intel on us. Not a ship size, direction of travel, nothing. Understand?"

"Yes, Gunny."

Turning to Magne, he asked, "How long before the drone is up on her?"

Magne replied, "The drone is good to go at any time. She has plenty of loiter time but I suggest we hold off for a few hours, reduce her fuel load a bit, and add some armament—just in case."

Rusty smiled. "I like that idea." Turning to Steve he asked, "Can you keep track of her via the INMARSAT for a few more hours without them getting wise to ya?"

Steve nodded. "Not a problem."

Gunny asked, "Magne, what armament did you have in mind? She's rigged for several." The drone was a modified version of the RQ-7 Shadow unmanned aerial vehicle. One of Rusty's companies had modified it with larger "wet" wings to increase fuel capacity and lift. The increase lift meant air launched weapons were now an option.

"I had something non-attributable in mind, maybe Turkish? That Roketsan OMTAS antitank missile has a tandem-charge HEAT round. It only weighs thirty-five kilos but will take out their steering box or bridge if necessary."

Gunny shrugged. "That should do the trick. Wouldn't hurt to have an insurance policy. Let's do it." Clapping his hands together, he shouted, "Alright folks, let's get to work. Apparently we have terrorists to kill."

As the sun raced to the west and night began to fall, the team was almost ready. A loud pneumatic "whoosh" signaled the launch of the armed drone off the bow of the ship. It flew straight as it gained altitude then banked south in search of the *Amuratu*. This was Nigel and John's cue. The DDV was loaded with all the gear they'd need. Using the ship's crane, they lowered the inflatable raft holding the octopus into the water off the stern of the ship and directly behind the opening of the well deck. The octopus was laid out in a serpentine pattern so it slipped off the raft without tangling. The raft was attached to the ship, but the end of the octopus was connected by a thick nylon rope to the DDV and secured by a retractable bolt that allowed them to disconnect the octopus from inside the DDV without having to surface.

Steve and Gunny were flying the drone and it took them over an hour to acquire the *Amuratu*. She was further south than they expected. Steve pinged the *Amuratu*'s INMARSAT terminal one last time to make sure he had not locked onto the wrong ship in the fading light. Gunny asked, "Is that her?"

"Yes, Gunny. Her SATCOM puts her at 2°43'55.14" South, 43°01'29.55" East. That's the same location as the drone. No other ships for several miles."

Gunny beamed. "Good work, kid. I'll take it from here. Go get ready."

Steve sprang from his chair. He was excited. This was his first real combat since the car chase in Ramallah.

John was at the helm of *Mother Goose* heading south. As they neared the designated launch point, he slowed the ship. Using his tactical radio, he reached out to Nigel and said, "We are a go for octopus deployment."

"Roger. Unleashing the kraken." Inside *Mother Goose*'s well deck, Nigel clambered onto the DDV. The vessel was a 2/3 scale prototype of a supercavitating hybrid design that one of Rusty Travis's companies developed for the US Navy. It was more conical in shape rather than tubular like a traditional submarine. In the center of the flat aft end of the craft was a hydrodynamic drive for low-speed performance but on either side were chemical rockets for high speeds. In the nose of the DDV was a cavitator, a device that created a huge bubble through which the vessel traveled with almost no drag. With the rocket motors pushing the DDV through the bubble, it was capable of traveling a hundred kilometers per hour while fully submerged.

Nigel walked down the length of the DDV and, at the stern, double-checked the nylon cable connecting the octopus before climbing inside the small submarine. From the fantail, Alen jumped onto the raft carrying the octopus. He untied the last buoy and kicked it into the water. As the wake of *Mother Goose* grabbed it, the buoy pulled a length of cable and "tentacles" after it. The buoy bobbed just under the surface with only a one-meter antenna visible. The next buoy slid to the edge where Alen gave it a nudge and it too plopped into the water. Another section of cable and tentacles followed. The next buoy and cable went more quickly. As the weight of cable being dragged behind increased, the remaining buoys slid off the raft quicker and quicker. In a few minutes, the entire one-hundred-meter length of the octopus was stretched out behind the ship attached only to the DDV. There was a tug on the DDV as the last octopus section hit the water and pulled the line taut. Alen said, "The octopus is in the water."

Nigel replied, "Everything is nominal here. Hoist the raft onto the deck."

"Roger that." Alen Markovic used the ship's crane to pluck the raft from the water and lower it onto the deck where Lon and Steve lashed it down.

Lon said, "Your beastie is in the water and he looks hungry."

"Well, let's feed him."

The assault team assembled in the well deck of the ship. Gunny went down for one last inspection. "Okay, are we clear on the mission plan?" Everyone nodded. "Alright, once you separate from *Mother Goose*, we will take her several miles west. I'll feed you location data on the target. This octopus thing is Nigel's baby, so he'll guide it into position." Turning to Nigel, he said, "Make sure you detach the octopus *before* the *Amuratu* hits it. She's a big boat and won't be stopping on a dime. I don't want the DDV yanked by the tow rope and dragged into her screws as she goes by. After its deployed, stay ahead of her to the east. Once she's entangled and they shut her engines down, wait until they are fully engaged at the stern before you approach the bow. This is not a naval vessel. I doubt they'll be posting sentries, but you never know. Take them down quickly." Staring directly at Steve, he added, "Anyone fires on you, take them out. Understood?" Steve nodded. "Okay. Let's go."

Led by Nigel, one by one the Praetorians climbed down the hatch into the vessel. Only John remained on the deck. The main compartment was designed to transport up to twelve swimmers, their weapons, and scuba gear so there was plenty of room for the assault team. Forward of this area in a separate water-tight compartment was the bridge. The batteries were under the deck, the engines in the stern, and the supercavitation bubble generator, the cavitator, in the nose. At the aft end of the main compartment was the lockout trunk through which divers exited the vessel while underwater. They wouldn't be needing that on this trip.

As soon as everyone was on board, the interior lights went to red to protect everyone's night vision. On the bridge, Nigel keyed the mic. Bravo Two, this is Alpha Three. How do you copy?"

Gunny replied, "This is Bravo Two. Read you Lima Charlie."

"Roger. We're ready to launch."

Gunny pumped sea water into *Mother Goose*'s ballast tanks lowering her another meter in the water. This provided positive buoyancy for the DDV and it bobbed gently as it lifted off the steel bottom of the well deck. John said, "Casting off," as he untied the line affixing the DDV to *Mother Goose*. The converted salvage tug eased forward and the DDV slid slowly through the opening in the ship's transom pulled only by the drag of the octopus in the ship's wake. When she was well clear, John Kernan scrambled down the hatch and closed it behind him. "We're away." Nigel powered up the main hydrodynamic drive and steered the DDV to port and then due south, away from *Mother Goose* and on a collision course with the *Amuratu*.

It was another two hours before they intercepted the coastal freighter. Gunny had been giving them regular updates on her location. The DDV was operating just above the surface to allow her onboard radar to scan the ocean around them. When they finally detected the *Amuratu*, Nigel retracted the small radar antenna and used the vessel's sonar to track her progress. Over the intercom he said, "Okay folks. It's show time. Deploying the octopus."

Nigel steered the DDV across the bow of the oncoming freighter dragging the octopus behind. John Kernan was on the control of the small thruster attached to the rearmost buoy. Nigel said, "Launching the octopus in three, two, one…launch." He hit the switch and there was an audible "clunk" as the bolt holding the tow cable was released. John and Nigel peered at the screen which showed their position relative to the *Amuratu*. The eleven buoys of the octopus showed up as a string of green dots on the screen. "Johnny Boy, a little reverse thrust on the aft buoy if you would. She's still moving with our momentum."

"Gotcha. One third back thrust."

After a few minutes, the octopus's movement had stopped, "That'll do it. Contact with target in three minutes." They waited patiently as the large triangle representing the *Amuratu* inched closer to the string of green dots. Finally, the triangle intersected the line almost dead center. "Bullseye!"

The string of dots representing the octopus curved and wrapped around the triangle. At first Nigel was afraid the octopus had hung up on the bow. If that happened, the *Amuratu* was large enough that the ends of the cables wouldn't reach the screws. That would mean using the C4 charges. They would stop the ship but take longer—the element of surprise would be gone. Nigel breathed a sigh of relief a few seconds later as the octopus started to slide under the keel. When it reached the stern, the thick cable and nylon tentacles were sucked into the propellers. A terrible screeching noise pierced the sonar hydrophones followed by a loud mechanical knocking. Finally, through the hull of the DDV, they all heard a loud bang followed by silence. The propellers had stopped. John turned to Nigel. "Good work, for a drunken Scotsman."

Nigel got on the encrypted radio. "Bravo Two, this is Alpha Three. Deployment was a success. She's dead in the water."

Gunny replied. "Damn good work, Alpha Three. Give them at least fifteen minutes to get to work and then take her."

"Copy that."

In the main compartment, Lon reacted to the loud bang. "Well, that didn't sound good—for them. Okay team, saddle up."

* * *

On board the *Amuratu*, Captain Imran Qadir was lying in his bunk, drinking tea and reading a book before turning in for the night. He had turned the helm over to Mohammad, his first officer, only twenty minutes earlier when the terrible noise caused by the cable and lines of the octopus ensnaring the screws reverberated through the ship. *Oh shit. That doesn't sound good.* He raced to the bridge in his stocking feet. "Mohammad, what the hell happened?"

"Not sure, sir. We may have broken a propeller shaft."

Qadir checked the control panel. "No. Both shafts have stopped." He got on the ship's intercom and said, "Engine room. What is going on?"

After a few long moments, the engineer came on and said, "Captain. We hit something. Maybe a reef? The engines made a terrible screaming noise and then just stopped."

Qadir was an experienced captain and this didn't make sense. He checked the charts. The water below them was over three thousand meters deep. There were no sea mounts or reefs in this area. He turned the rudder. There was no response. "Engine room. The rudder is not responding. Are hydraulics down?"

"No sir. The hydraulics are functional. The rudder must be jammed."

Qadir pondered this for a second. "It must be an entanglement. Don't try to restart the engines. Keep auxiliary power functioning. We're going to need it. I suspect we ran over a large fishing net from a purse seiner or long line factory ship. We're going to have to clear it."

Turning to his first officer, he asked. "What's the weather like?"

"Radar shows no storms in the area. Winds are calm."

"Well, thank Allah for that, but we're close to Somalia'

Mohammad asked cautiously. "Pirates?"

"Are there other boats in the area?"

"Nothing on radar within twenty miles. The closest vessel is moving away from us."

"Pirates would probably be in smaller open boats. They may not show up on radar. I doubt they did this, but they'll certainly take advantage if possible. Break out some weapons. I want three armed sentries—one near the bow and the other two at the stern, just in case."

"Aye, Captain."

"Get the portable lights and bring them to the stern. And wake everyone up. It's going to be a long night."

Qadir grabbed a large flashlight and trudged down the companionways from the bridge to the deck. He walked to the stern of his ship and peered over the side at the inky blackness. He snapped on his flashlight and shined it down at the water. While he didn't see a lot, he did make out a mass of bright yellow nylon lines floating below. *Fucking fishing net.*

The entire crew of the *Amuratu*, all twenty-one men, were roused from their bunks and put to work. They rigged harnesses and two of the engineers were lowered over the stern to make an inspection. They reported back that there was a large steel cable and a multitude of thick nylon lines completely tangled around both screws and the rudder. It was going to take torches, knives and a lot of time to clear the mess. Qadir took the news stoically. "Get started. There is nothing else to do but fix it." He returned to his cabin to put on some shoes. *On the bright side, if this had happened yesterday it would have been a disaster.*

* * *

While the crew's attention was focused on the stern of the ship, a black shape slid across the water toward the bow. Normally, one boarded a ship from the port or starboard sides—preferably both at the same time. Tonight, the only real blind spot was under the bow. The DDV slowly eased up to the *Amuratu*. On its deck, John Kernan and Lon Oden stood, each with a long fiberglass pole. At the end of each pole was a large iron magnet encased in rubber. Each man swung his magnet over to the hull of the freighter where it attached with a quiet "clunk." They then pulled the DDV closer to the hull and attached the other ends of the poles to rings in the DDV's deck. This would keep them firmly attached to the larger ship but also keep the waves from beating the smaller vessel against its hull.

John softly called down into the DDV. "Ladder."

Out of the hatch came another long pole but this one telescoped out to about thirty feet. Attached to the end was a large hook and a cable caving ladder. John extended the pole up to the deck of the freighter and hooked it over the railing. He gave it several strong tugs before starting his climb. As he did, Lon moved a few meters away and trained his MP-7 up toward the deck.

Up on the *Amuratu*, the forward sentry smoked a cigarette. He was grinding it out when he heard a strange scraping noise. He walked to the point of the bow. A strange piece of metal was hooked to a rung of the railing. Just before John reached the top, the head of the sentry peeked over the rail. He was shocked to find a man climbing up just a few feet below. It was, however, the last thing he saw as two rounds from Lon's suppressed MP-7 tore through his chin and out the top of his head. Reaching the top, John checked the dead sentry. He had an AK-47. "Good shooting Alpha One. One Tango down. Be advised, he was armed with an AK. These guys are more than they appear." He cautiously peered through his NVGs down the deck of the ship. There was no one else on the forward section of the deck but several people milling around toward the stern bathed in the harsh light of several halogen work lamps. *They won't see shit.* No one was visible on the bridge.

Lon keyed his mic. "What ya got, Alpha Two?"

"Bow and main deck are clear. No one visible on the bridge. Only activity is at the stern. Lots of bright lights. They'll be blind to us. I'm moving down to the anchor winch. Start coming up."

"Copy."

As John jumped over the railing, Lon came up after him. Below, the rest of the Praetorian team was climbing up on the deck of the DDV for their turn at the ladder. It only took a couple of minutes for the eight commandos to board the ship. They split into two teams. Lon, John, Magne, and Sarah moved down the starboard side of the ship while Nigel, Hans, Alen, and Steve moved down the port. Each was armed with a suppressed MP-7 and equipped with NVGs.

John and Lon moved silently up the companionways to the bridge. There they found only one person—Mohammad, the first officer. He was sitting in the captain's chair monitoring the ship's radar. When he glanced up at the two soldiers, he was surprised but didn't panic. He immediately reached for the pistol on the console in front of him. He swung toward his intruders but was struck down by six rounds from the MP-7s. The weapons were almost silent. The tinkling of the empty brass shell casings hitting the deck was louder that the shots that spawned them. John keyed his mic. "Alpha Three, this is Alpha Two. Bridge secured. One crewman down. Be advised, he also had a weapon."

Nigel said, "Alpha Three copies. Crew is armed. Another Tango down."

While Magne, Sarah, Alen, and Steve kept an eye on the bulk of the crew working near the stern, the rest of the Praetorians continued to systematically clear the ship. The officer and crew quarters on C and B deck were deserted. On A deck, the ship's cook was in the galley making coffee and sandwiches for the crew. When Nigel entered, the man was startled but got over it quick enough to send a large carving knife whizzing past Nigel's ear. That earned him two in the chest and a third in the forehead. Nigel reported, "This is Alpha Three. Decks A, B, and C are secure. Another Tango down. Heading down to the engine room."

Nigel and Hans moved down the stairs to the engine room. They weren't sure how many men to expect down there. Despite the main engines being shut down, the loud din of the hydraulic pumps and electrical generator drowned out any competing noise. In the mechanic's workshop, they found two sweaty men using an acetylene torch and a grinder to fashion large hooked knives almost a meter long to cut the nylon ropes. Hans yelled in Arabic, "Hands up." The man with the torch slapped his buddy to get his attention as he threw a hammer at the intruders. Hans shot the man in the chest while the other grabbed one of the hooked blades and chucked it at Nigel. The blade glanced off Nigel's helmet and imbedded itself in a thick piece of insulation protecting a steam pipe. Hans immediately dropped the man with two rounds in the face. "Jesus! Thanks, mate. That was close. Damn near took my head off! How come I'm always the bloody target?"

Hans replied, "I'm beginning to feel unwanted. Maybe we should shoot first and ask questions later?"

"Aye." In the next room, the ship's engineer was monitoring the generator. He had an AK-47 next to him. Nigel shot the man where he stood. Nigel reported, "This is Alpha Three. Engine room secure. Three more dead Tangos. I'm not saying these guys were expecting us but they're certainly prepared for uninvited guests so be on your toes. Heading back up."

John came on the radio. "This is Alpha Two. We have secured the radio room and ship's office. All that's left is the hold."

"Copy. Let's deal with the crew first."

At the stern of the ship, Captain Qadir was overseeing the repairs. One of his engineers working over the side was brought up to give him a status report. "Captain, something isn't right here. This is no fishing net. The cable is at least three centimeters thick. I've worked on fishing boats and I've never seen two-centimeter-thick nylon ropes attached like this. And the line buoys, they're black. Buoys are white, yellow, or orange. They're meant to be visible."

"What are you saying?"

"Sir, I think this is some sort of…weapon."

Qadir instantly grasped the importance of what his young engineer was saying. "Everyone, arm yourselves. Prepare to be boarded!" He called the bridge on the intercom. "Mohammad! Mohammad! Are there any other ships in the area?" There was no response. Shouting into the microphone he repeated, "Mohammad! Mohammad?" Still nothing. He then punched the button for the engine room. "Abdul. Break out the weapons. Abdul?" Again, only silence.

Turning to his men, Qadir said, "I fear the infidels are here. You men, come with me to the weapons locker. The rest of you go to the cargo hold and get to the Yemenis' guns."

Qadir, followed by five crewmen, raced through a nearby hatch and sprinted toward the ship's weapons cache in the laundry room. The other ten split up and moved forward along the deck—an armed sentry and four crewmen on either side of the superstructure. These were the first to encounter the Praetorians.

Alen was close enough to overhear what the captain said. "This is Alpha Seven. The alarm has been raised. The crew knows something is wrong. The captain and at least five men entered the superstructure. We have five tangos moving forward along the port side. That leaves five more unaccounted for. Alpha Five and Six, keep your eyes peeled. They may be coming your way."

Nigel broke in. "Everyone, weapons free. These guys are not fucking about. Alpha One and Alpha Two, follow me into the hold. I don't want them getting behind us. Alpha Four, you back up the others and make sure no one shoots down on us from the superstructure."

No sooner than Nigel had said this, the five crewmen on the port deck came charging at Alen and Steve. The man with the AK was in front firing blindly and the others followed armed with hammers, wrenches, and knives. Coming from the brightly lit stern to the darkness of the cargo deck left them compromised. Steve and Alen opened fire and dropped all five within a matter of seconds. On the starboard side of the ship, Magne and Sarah encountered another five crewmen similarly armed. They quickly dropped four of the attackers but the fifth dove through an open hatch into the superstructure. Sarah said, "Damn it!" She keyed her mic and said, "This is Alpha Six. Four Tangos down on the starboard side but one got inside. Repeat, one Tango running free on the starboard side, first deck."

Nigel responded, "Alpha Three copies. Four Tangos down, one in the wind on starboard side."

Captain Qadir and his five crewmen sprinted through the narrow passageway to the laundry. There they encountered the crewman who had escaped Sarah and Magne. He had caught a round in his right arm but was ambulatory. The seven men burst through the door to the ship's laundry and straight to a large cabinet on the far wall. Qadir slid the cabinet along the wall to reveal a hidden closet behind. The room was filled with AK-47s, pistols, ammunition, and even a couple of RPG-7s. Qadir passed AKs to his men and took pistols for himself and the wounded crewman.

"Okay, we need to get to the hold and the Yemeni weapons. If we do that, we should have them outgunned."

The wounded man said, "Captain, they're on the main deck. How do we get there?"

Qadir paused for a moment before replying, "The service hatch off the main companionway on the engineering deck. Let's go."

The men followed their captain down the stairs. At the end of the corridor was a large hatch secured with dogs. The rusty hinges groaned as they pulled the hatch open. Just outside the door was a small catwalk with metal stairs leading down into the dark hold of the ship. There were a few dim lights high in the middle of the hold and the men just made out the hatch covers above them. On the floor of the hold were pallets holding more than fifty 1250-liter bulk containers labeled as Syrian olive oil. Toward the bow were several pallets of spices and other crates.

Qadir motioned for his men to move up along the starboard side. Two of the men climbed atop the bulk containers and moved forward in a crouch while the others navigated among the pallets. Unbeknownst to them, Nigel, John, and Lon had already slipped into the hold from a deck hatch at the forecastle. Using their NVGs, they calmly observed the seven men approach them. John raised his weapon but Lon stopped him. He whispered. "Wait. Let's see if they lead us to the chemical weapons."

About halfway through the cargo hold, Qadir stopped. "You men on top, keep your eyes open and cover us." Below them, the other crewmen and the captain started to open the top of one of the bulk containers. This one had an unusually large lid. They unscrewed the lid but instead of olive oil, it exposed Russian RPK light machine guns stacked inside. Pointing to the next container, Qadir said, "Open that one. It has the ammunition and magazines." As soon as they cracked open the second container, the sailors fitted two of the RPKs with seventy-five round drum magazines.

Observing this, Nigel said, "I've seen enough. We need to waste these guys. Try to leave a couple alive for interrogation."

Lon smiled, "It's your mission, boss. I got the two motherfuckers up top."

John nodded, "We got the ones on the deck."

Nigel said, "On my mark. Three, two, one…" The big Scot and his colleagues cut loose with bursts from their MP-7s. Lon immediately dropped the two men on top of the pallets. John and Nigel cut down the men with the machine guns. Captain Qadir was hit but was able to duck behind a pallet. The wounded sailor took another round in the chest and fell at his feet. He was alive but just barely.

The Praetorians stopped to assess. Lon turned to John and said, "I'm going up. Cover me." Lon climbed up a pallet containing bags of spices and from there, jumped on top of the closest bulk container. With his weapon at the ready, he crept forward. The sailor on the port side was clearly dead but the other was still alive. He started to feebly raise his AK until Lon put a round into his head. He keyed his mic and whispered, "Top clear. Two Tangos down."

Nigel replied, "Copy. Cover us. Moving up."

John and Nigel moved forward cautiously. When they reached the location where the *Amuratu*'s crewmen had recovered the machine guns, they paused. The two men with the RPKs were dead. A third one, wounded, tried to crawl away. John shot him. Nigel keyed his mic. "We're in the hold. Five Tangos down. Two unaccounted for."

Alen replied, "Roger. Main deck is secure. Nine Tangos down."

Nigel gave a hand signal to Lon directing him to move forward. As he stepped across to the next bulk container, two pistol shots rang out. From the muzzle flash, he determined they came from the space between the container he was standing on and the adjacent stack. "Cover your eyes. Dropping a flash bang in three, two, one…" Lon took two steps back and tossed the flash bang in the crevice. There was a deafening bang and blinding flash. He moved forward and aimed his MP-7 down at Captain Qadir. In Arabic he shouted for him to drop his weapon. Qadir tossed his pistol aside and then tossed out the pistol of the wounded sailor at his feet.

Nigel rushed into the crevice, grabbed Qadir by the scruff of his neck and dragged him into the space between the pallets and the hull. John dragged out the wounded man. After a quick examination, he dragged his finger across his throat. The man was dead.

Qadir was still disoriented from the flash bang. It went off right next to him and burned his arms. Being in the tight space between stacks of pallets only amplified the blast. His ears were ringing and he was blinking his eyes in an effort to force them to focus. He finally said, "What's the meaning of this? You have no right to board my ship and attack my crew!"

Nigel picked up one of the RPKs and said, "This gives me the right, asshole. We have some questions for you."

"About what?"

"The Novichok."

Qadir blanched initially but then a smile spread slowly across his face and he started to laugh. This was not the reaction they were expecting. "You are wasting your time. I will tell you nothing."

Nigel and John smiled at each other. "Our friend Sarah may have something to say about that."

* * *

With the crew dead and the captain tied up in the ship's office, the Praetorians began their search of the *Amuratu*. Their chemical weapons detectors started chirping as soon as they turned them on. The Novichok was on board, but where? When their initial search turned up nothing, Nigel called in Sarah. Nigel and Sarah walked into the office. Grabbing Qadir by his face, Nigel said, "Captain Qadir, we know who you are. We know your history. We know you were friends with Ayman al-Zawahiri, at least until the Americans hit him with that flying food processor. We know you picked up chemical weapons in Syria. We need to know where they are."

"I don't know what you're talking about. Even if I did, I wouldn't tell you."

"Mate, we do this the easy way or the hard way. Either you tell us now, or my friend Sarah here, will make you tell us later after much pain."

Qadir gawped at Sarah and laughed. "A woman? What is she going to do? Fuck me until I talk?"

Nigel shook his head. "Oh, you're going to be fucked, all right, but not in the good way. Sarah, he's all yours."

Sarah shook her head. "Stupid misogynists. They only learn through pain."

Nigel shrugged. "Well, don't say I didn't warn you." He left the room and shut the door behind him. As he walked down the corridor, Captain

Qadir cursed aloud and then screamed. *Well Captain, who's getting fucked now?*

While Sarah worked on the captain, the rest of the team searched the ship. From their CW detectors, they were confident the Novichok had been on board. They found two distinct hotspots in the hold among the sacks of spices. Steve conducted a rapid assay and determined that the two components of the binary agent had both been there, and were stored separately, but they weren't there now.

Nigel and Lon waited outside the ship's office. The screaming turned to cursing, then whimpering, and finally silence. They were curious but didn't want to interrupt Sarah's work. This kind of interrogation used pain and fear on one side, and comfort and soothing on the other. Finally, after two hours, the door opened and Sarah exited. She was sweating from exertion and was splattered with blood on her clothes and face. Nigel asked, "Well?"

Sarah wiped the blood and sweat from her face. "It was here. He was initially hired by Kotov to deliver a few thousand guns to the Houthis in Yemen. The other packages were to be delivered separately to another customer but he didn't have a final destination. He described two sealed metal containers weighing about fifty kilos apiece. He was told to store them separately and not let them leak. That has to be the Novichok, right?"

"Sounds like it. Where is it?"

Sarah continued, "The captain said he got a message about a week and a half ago with only a date and geocoords, someplace in the middle of the ocean south of here. Someone was practicing good ops sec. They transferred the Novichok to a fishing trawler yesterday. That's why they were late to the rendezvous."

Nigel erupted, "Goddamnit! We missed it by twenty-four hours?"

"It would appear so."

"This trawler, where was it going?"

Sarah replied, "He doesn't know. It continued south after they split up but that means nothing. It could have gone anywhere."

"This boat, does he have a description? A name?"

"It was a trawler, about twenty or twenty-five meters. White. The name was '*Badbani Machly*' or something. It isn't Arabic. I'm not sure what it means."

"Does he have anything else? Transponder ID? Captain's name?"

"No. He received the date and location via a text on a cellphone at his last port call in Angola. He'd never seen the boat or its captain before. The captain was young, late twenties or early thirties."

Nigel rubbed his chin. "Who else was on board?"

"Three other men, all Middle Eastern or Pakistani." Sarah smiled.

Nigel looked at her askance. "What? What aren't you telling me?"

Sarah grinned. "He identified two of the men from a photo. It was the photo we got from Mossad. It was Khalid Al-Maadi."

"Are you sure? Was it him?"

"Captain Qadir didn't know his name. I showed him four photos. He identified two of them as being on the trawler."

"Who was the other?"

"The unidentified ship captain Al-Maadi was talking to on the docks in Karachi."

Lon groused, "Motherfucker! And we missed them!"

Sarah shrugged. "Well, at least we know for certain who we're hunting."

"That's cold comfort."

Sarah asked Nigel, "What are we going to do with the ship?"

"Well, she's full of guns that don't need to reach their intended destination. If we leave her adrift, there is a good chance she'll be boarded by the Kenyans who will ask a lot of questions, or be captured by Somali pirates who will have a lot of weapons to sell. Given those two possibilities, I say we scuttle her."

Lon nodded. "I agree. Uh, what about the captain?"

Sarah said, "This guy has been dealing death and transporting terrorists for decades. Shouldn't a captain go down with his ship?"

Nigel replied, "Aye, he should. It's going to be light in a couple of hours. We need to scuttle this tub and get back to *Mother Goose* before anyone finds her. Gather up the dead Tangos and put them where they won't float away. We don't want any bodies washing up on a beach somewhere. Once that's done, get everyone onto the DDV. John and I will open the seacocks to start flooding the ship. Open every hatch, porthole and valve you find. We have some shape charges in the DDV to open holes in the hull. We'll also use the charges on the octopus. They're all tangled around the screws. They'll open a big hole in the stern."

Sarah replied, "I'm on it."

Lon said, "I'll get the shape charges."

Most of the corpses were on the main deck. They dragged these into the ship's laundry. The ones in the engine room, galley, and bridge were crammed into lockers. The six in the hold were stuffed into a large locker in the forecastle.

As the rest of the team climbed down the caving ladder to the DDV, John and Nigel were in the engineering spaces opening every valve that let in sea water. John turned on the ballast pumps to add sea water to the ballast tanks. Nigel opened the bilge hatch to vent the air inside and broke the line feeding seawater for the engine cooling system. The engine room was quickly filling with water that poured into the bilge. It wasn't long before the *Amuratu* started to settle at her stern. In the cargo hold, they placed two large shape charges on the hull below the water line on the port side close to the stern. After setting the timers, John and Nigel climbed the ladder from the bottom of the cargo hold to the deck. They removed the dogs on three of the large deck hatches on the port side. Once the ship listed enough for the deck to be awash, the water pouring in through these hatches would take her quickly to the bottom. After one last glance around, they climbed down the caving ladder to the DDV, disconnected the vessel from the *Amuratu,* and climbed inside. Nigel eased the DDV away from the freighter and headed northeast to rendezvous with *Mother Goose.*

"Bravo Two, this is Alpha Three. Mission complete. We're heading home."

"Copy that Alpha Three. Good job."

Rusty and Gunny followed the action via the live drone feed as it continued to circle over the *Amuratu.* There was no outward sign of the explosions when the shape charges went off. However, there was a large fountain of water thrown up when the C4 charges in the buoys were detonated, ripping gaping holes in the stern tubes holding the propeller shafts. Within minutes the *Amuratu* was listing heavily to port with her stern underwater and her bow rising above the waves. After ten minutes, her deck was awash. As the list angle increased, the deck hatches broke loose and sea water poured into the open hold. Two minutes later she capsized. A steam-like plume blasted from the hatches on the bow as the last of the air in the vessel was forced out. Seconds later the bow slid beneath the waves. The *Amuratu* was no more.

* * *

Back on the *Mother Goose*, Rusty and Gunny were trying to accept their pyrrhic victory. The mission had gone off without a hitch. The Praetorians took the ship without sustaining any casualties of their own. However, they failed to achieve their objective; they missed the Novichok. The only bright side was now they knew who had it.

Gunny instructed the drone's autopilot to return to *Mother Goose* and circle. They needed more people to recover it so they'd have to wait for the DDV to return. Gunny got out paper charts of the region. The trawler with the chemical weapon wasn't a speedboat; it couldn't have gone too far. If it came from the north, would it return that way too? Probably. He needed to figure out how far it might have traveled since its rendezvous with the *Amuratu*. As Gunny poured over the charts, Rusty scanned the horizon with binoculars. "Uh, Gunny? Our guys are coming from the south, right?"

"Yeah, but you won't be able to see them. They're too low in the water."

"Well, then what's this coming from the west?"

Gunny snatched the binoculars from Rusty and peered out over the water. It was still dark but he made out three open boats a few miles away and moving east toward the sun as it was just beginning to crack the horizon. "Fuck. Goddamn pirates."

"Pirates? Seriously? We're not exactly a Spanish treasure galleon."

"They don't care. The Somali pirates are mostly after ransom."

"Can we outrun them?"

"Maybe, but our guys are heading here. I can radio them and tell them to move further east, but these pirates are persistent. They'll track ships for days."

Rusty turned at him for guidance. "Well, tell me what to do?"

Gunny paused for a minute. "I got an idea." He got on the radio to Nigel on the DDV. "Alpha Three, this is Bravo Two. Do you copy?"

"Aye. What's up?"

"We have three open boats closing on us from the west, moving fast. I suspect they're pirates."

Nigel chuckled, "You *bosses* might need to get your hands dirty after all."

An irritated Gunny replied, "I'm not laughing. It's just the two of us."

Nigel replied, "Three if you count the drone. It's still carrying that anti-tank missile. That should even the odds a bit."

Gunny grinned, "I forgot about that. You may be right."

"Meanwhile, I'll put the DDV in supercav mode. We'll be there shortly."

"Roger that."

When Nigel told the others what was happening, they strapped in and gave a thumbs up. Nigel engaged the cavitator in the nose of the vessel. There was a loud noise that was a cross between gurgling and a rush of air. He then warmed up the chemical rockets. "Going hot in three, two, one ..." There was a roar from the back of the DDV as the two large rockets ignited. The ship lurched forward as the team held on for dear life. Within seconds the DDV was moving about twenty kilometers per hour (kph). As the bubble from the cavitator began to envelop the little submarine, its speed increased. When the bubble reached the aft end, the DDV was already up to 50 kph and picking up speed. The ride was remarkably smooth as the bubble provided an almost zero drag envelope through which to fly. As the DDV passed 90 kph, Nigel backed off on the throttles. They would cover the thirty kilometers to *Mother Goose* in a little less than twenty minutes.

Back on the ship, Gunny calmly watched the three boats approach. The drone was now overhead and circling above the speeding boats. From the camera feed, Rusty counted the armed men on board—twelve on the larger middle boat and eight each on the other two. A man on the bow of the middle boat had an RPG-7 on his shoulder. Rusty commented, "These guys don't look friendly to me. They have an RPG. When are they going to be in range to use that thing?"

"Not for bit. It only has a range of about seven hundred meters. He'll have to get a lot closer if he wants any chance of actually hitting anything. One shot won't take us out, but they might get lucky and hit the bridge. I suggest we take them out first. Time for us to visit the weapons locker."

The men trotted to the fantail and down the companionway to the well deck below. Along the forward wall were a number of lockers. Each was about two meters across and held tools, coveralls, torches, and dive gear—everything one would expect to find on a salvage tug. Gunny opened the middle locker and reached up on the roof and hit a concealed switch. When he did the back of the locker swung inwards to reveal a hidden room containing the Praetorians' weapons stash. Turning to Rusty, he said, I'm getting the Barrett sniper rifle. Grab a couple M72s. If they get within a couple hundred meters, we'll need them."

"What's an M72?"

Gunny stared at him incredulously. "It's a Light Antitank Weapon."

"Oh, you mean an LAW. Why didn't you just say so? I'm on it."

Gunny grumbled, "Have you forgotten everything they taught you in the army?"

Rusty slung an M-4 over his shoulder along with a bag of magazines and grabbed two LAWs before trotting back to the bridge. As Gunny followed carrying the big rifle and a box of ammo, Rusty peered out at the three boats. "They're getting pretty damn close."

"Yeah, time for us to say hello." Gunny put down the rifle, moved to the drone's control console and turned on the fire control system. A large green set of crosshairs appeared on the monitor. Using a joystick, he lined the crosshairs up on the lead boat. "Going hot!" He armed the rocket and hit the launch button. High above them and to the north, a line of smoke appeared as if out of nowhere. The rocket flew straight for a moment before arcing down toward the oncoming boats. A second later, the middle boat exploded into flames.

Rusty hollered, "Well, hot damn! Bullseye!"

Gunny was focusing on the other two boats. They both veered away from the flaming hulk of their comrades' boat, but they kept coming. In fact, they picked up speed. "These guys are slow learners. Take the wheel." Gunny grabbed the rifle and walked to the bow of the ship. The Barrett M107A1 is a semi-automatic sniper rifle that fires the massive 12.7x99 NATO cartridge, the official name of the .50 caliber Browning Machine Gun cartridge that has been in use since 1921. It was capable of launching a 50-gram slug at nearly 900 meters per second and hit a target 1,800 meters away with accuracy.

Gunny unfolded the front bipod of the rifle and laid it on the deck. Lying behind it, he peered through the telescopic sight and located the boat to the north. It was coming straight for them. Four men were at the bow blindly firing AK-47s. Most of the rounds fell harmlessly into the ocean but there were a couple of "pings" as lucky rounds bounced off *Mother Goose*'s hull. When the boat was about a thousand meters away, he lined up the driver in his crosshairs and fired. The huge bullet ripped through the man's chest sending him flying toward the rear of the boat where he landed in a bloody heap. Another Somali pirate sprang up and took the wheel. Gunny groused, "Jesus, these guys are stupid! Don't they see they're outmatched?" He lined up for another shot. This time he aimed lower, where he assessed the ship's wheel would be. He squeezed the trigger and the boat's helm practically exploded, shattering the wheel and eviscerating the man behind it. The boat immediately slowed and turned to the north. It was out of action.

Rusty yelled down to him. "That's two down, one to go."

The last pirate boat, witnessing what transpired, tracked south to get into Mother Goose's wake and avoid the gunfire coming from the bow. Gunny repositioned on the deck to get a better angle. As he did, the port side of the pirate boat came into view. Instead of shooting the man driving the boat, he fired where he assessed the boat's inboard motor must be. He fired three rounds in quick succession and after the third round, black smoke started billowing out just forward of the stern. The boat slowed and started to peel off to the south. From the bridge, Rusty made out flames among the black smoke. He yelled down, "She's on fire. She's done." As he said this, an RPG-7 round emerged from the smoking boat, arced up, and exploded in the water just off their port side. "Motherfucker!" Rusty picked up his M-4 and fired at the burning boat through the bridge window.

Gunny spotted a man in the nose of the boat loading another rocket into his launcher. "Well, they are persistent." He fired two quick shots from the big rifle and the man went down in a red mist of his own blood. Seconds later, a fireball erupted from the back of the boat as its ruptured fuel tank exploded. A handful of pirates jumped into the water. "I'd say that's all we'll hear from them. Tell the team they missed the party."

Rusty got on the radio. "Alpha Three, this is Bravo One. Pirates neutralized. You can quit hiding." Rusty stopped Mother Goose in the water and focused on the three pirate boats. The survivors from the two on fire were clinging to debris and making their way slowly to the boat with the shattered helm. As Gunny entered the bridge, Rusty said, "The second boat is still afloat so they won't drown. Should we pick them up?"

Gunny snorted, "Fuck those guys. They'd have slit our throats if they'd had the chance. If they make it, they make it. If they don't? It's God's will. Sharks need food too."

A few minutes later, the DDV surfaced behind the ship. "Bravo Two, this is Alpha Three. We're ready to dock."

Gunny replied, "Roger. Meet you at the well deck."

* * *

While John, Nigel, and Alen secured the DDV in the well deck, the rest of the team prepared to recover the drone. They erected two ten-meter poles about midway between the stern and the bridge. Stretched between them was a large net with a large red circle in the middle. A strong nylon rope was strung from the bridge, over the top of the poles and down to the stern. Two shorter poles were attached in a similar manner closer to the stern to keep the net about two meters off the deck. When all was ready, Magne Berg gave Steve Chang a thumbs up. The Praetorians on the deck moved off the fantail and waited. Steve maneuvered the drone until it was coming in directly behind *Mother Goose*. Steve said to Gunny, "Increase ship's speed to maximum."

"Copy that." Gunny pushed the ship's throttles to their maximum. Far behind them, a small dot appeared in the sky as the drone moved to catch the ship. As the small aircraft got closer, Steve cut its airspeed. He was trying to make the differential speed between the ship and the aircraft as low as possible without the drone stalling and crashing into the sea. The drone continued its slow approach. It was flying low over the water. Steve was aiming for the big red circle about fifteen meters above the deck. The drone started its final descent. Just before it crossed over the stern of the ship, he cut the engine. The four-bladed pusher prop required centrifugal force to keep its blades extended so when the engine stopped, they snapped shut just before the drone hit the net. The net sprang first forward and then back. The drone bucked up and down like a cowboy riding a bronc but after a few seconds, it settled. The recovery was less violent than it appeared. Besides, the drone was designed for this.

Steve called out, "Recovery complete. The drone is on board."

Gunny smiled. "Good job kid. Once she cools down, check her out and refuel her. We don't know what we'll run into next."

"Yes, sir."

Magne, Hans, and Sarah started taking the drone apart. It had a modular design. Its wings and tail assembly came off easily. They were constructed of carbon fiber which made them both strong and light. Without ordinance and most of its fuel expended, the fuselage weighed less than eighty kilos. She would be refueled and rearmed within the hour.

CHAPTER FOUR
SEA OF NEEDLES

The day before the Praetorians interdicted the *Amuratu*, Zihad Haq had guided his trawler to the exact spot in the ocean where Al-Maadi had instructed Captain Qadir to meet them. The location, about a hundred nautical miles north of the Comorian capital of Moroni, was well selected. It was essentially a hole in the ocean with no nearby shipping lanes or fishing grounds. The *Sailfish* was there first but within a couple of hours a coastal freighter appeared on the southern horizon. They waited patiently for the ship to close the gap. Al-Maadi stared at the ship through his binoculars. He was almost giddy with anticipation. "Remember, Zihad, no radio, no satellite communications. That led to my undoing before."

"Yes, Abu Almawt." They moved slowly toward the freighter. When they were within a thousand meters, Haq signaled the ship using a handheld signal lamp. Dot dash, dot dash—Morse code for AA, as in Abu Almawt. Haq flashed his signal to the ship three times before he received a reply. Dot dot, dash dash dot dash—Morse for IQ, as in Imran Qadir. It was the *Amuratu*.

The *Amuratu* cut her engines and slowly drifted to a stop. Haq sailed past and then circled back so both ships were pointing north. The wind was from the west so he pulled the *Sailfish* alongside the larger ship's leeward starboard side so the *Amuratu* would keep the wind from buffeting the smaller *Sailfish*. As she neared the *Amuratu*, he cut his engine; his deckhand, Hamid, placed rubber bumpers along her port side. Crewmen on the *Amuratu* tossed down two lines, one at the bow and one at the stern, and Hamid lashed the two vessels together. It was awkward since the deck of the *Amuratu* was quite a bit higher, but it would do.

Al-Maadi and Zihad Haq gazed up at the deck of the freighter. A moment later, a rope ladder came rolling down from above. Imran Qadir's head appeared over the railing. He shouted, "Abu Almawt, right on time."

Al-Maadi shouted back. "Greetings Captain. I'm so glad you made it." Motioning to Haq he said, "This is…"

Qadir cut him off. "No names. A wise man once told me you never say what you don't need to say."

"Yes, of course. It's just that my cousin always trusted you implicitly."

"Who do you think that wise man was? Come on up. We'll discuss the transfer."

Al-Maadi and Haq climbed up the rope ladder and when they reached the top, a couple of sailors helped them on board. Qadir said, "First, we have the barrels of diesel fuel as you requested. My men will start lowering them down to your vessel immediately."

Haq said, "My men will show your men where to put them."

"Excellent." Turning to Al-Maadi, Qadir said, "Now, let me show you your prize." He led them to a hatch near the bow and then down a ladder into the cargo bay. It took a couple of minutes for their eyes to adjust to the dim light in the hold. When they reached the bottom, Qadir led them to some pallets containing bags of spices and nuts. Removing a bag on top of the first pallet, he shined his flashlight into the space beneath it illuminating a large metal container. It was a cube about forty centimeters on a side; on top was a large round metal lid held on by clamps. Between the lid and the metal ring below it was a thick, red rubber gasket. "According to the Russian, this is one half of the weapon." He pointed across the hold. "The other is over there."

"Let me see it."

Qadir led them to another pallet on the opposite side. He slid off a bag of sesame seeds to reveal another, identical metal container. The only difference was the lid on this one had a black rubber gasket instead of red. "This is it. The Russian was adamant that the two be separated at all times. Should they leak and their contents come in contact…" He dragged his finger across his throat.

Al-Maadi nodded. "I understand. It is very, very dangerous. This is exactly why we bought it." He turned to Haq and said, "We will have to store them as far apart as possible. Will that be a problem?"

"No. There is a compartment in the bow where I keep spare nets and line. We'll put one there and the other in the aft catch tank. How dangerous is this stuff? I mean, each component individually? If one leaks, will it ruin my next catch?"

Captain Qadir just shrugged. "I have no idea about such things. I only transport per my instructions."

Al-Maadi answered, "Neither component is considered a chemical weapon in its own right, but they are toxic. The best thing would be to not allow them to leak in the first place."

Haq was not satisfied with his answer. "How do we guarantee they don't leak?"

Qadir snapped his fingers. "I have some of those blue plastic barrels with lids. We'll put the cans inside a couple of those. They are very tough. If the cans leak, the barrels will contain them."

Haq nodded. "Yes, that should work. I have similar barrels on board with fuel. I doubt even my own crew would notice the difference. Oh, I'm a little embarrassed to ask but we've had a bit of a problem with mal de mer."

Qadir was taken aback. "Sea sickness? On a fishing boat?"

"Well, not everyone on board is a sailor." Al-Maadi started to squirm with embarrassment. "Abu Almawt's comrade has been sick since we left port."

Qadir chuckled, "Ah, I see. Yes, I have some Dramamine and some ginger. Which do you prefer?"

"Can we get some of both in case the Dramamine doesn't work for him?"

"Certainly. I'll have one of my men fetch it."

While Captain Qadir saw to the medicine, two of his crewmen carefully removed the first metal canister and placed it gingerly into a plastic drum. They snapped on the lid and tightened its locking ring securely. They had no idea what was in the drum, but if their captain—who had been hauling deadly munitions for years—was scared of it, so were they. Using the ship's crane, the crewmen lifted the barrel out of the hold and lowered it into the catch tank in the fantail of the trawler. Only after the first barrel was clear of the ship, did they load the second container. The crane swung the second barrel out over the ship and onto the *Sailfish* where Hamid and Al-Maadi's man, Mohammad, wrestled it into the compartment near the bow.

As Haq returned to his trawler to make sure his cargo was secured, Al-Maadi was led to Qadir's cabin. "Captain, I cannot thank you enough for your help. I hope you found the compensation adequate?"

"I did, but it wasn't necessary. Were it not for your cousin and Sheik Osama, I wouldn't even have a ship. Please accept my condolences for your cousin's death. He was a great, great man."

"Thank you, Captain. It was terrible. I was one of the first people there after... The Americans and their allies are barbarians. But I will avenge him and what you brought me is key to that."

"I would like to know what you have planned but I know better than to ask. Strange things happen every day. I do not want to be in a position to betray you, if even by accident. I am sure I'll hear about it when it happens."

Al-Maadi smirked. "Oh, you will most definitely hear about it, I assure you."

"Well then, that will be all the satisfaction I need. Best of luck, brother."

Al-Maadi shook the captain's hand. "And for you as well."

Captain Qadir handed Al-Maadi a bottle of Dramamine and another bottle of ginger root. "Try the ginger...I mean, have your man try the ginger first. Take it from an old sailor, the Dramamine will make him groggy and should only be used if the ginger fails."

"Thank you, Captain Qadir."

When Al-Maadi climbed down the ladder to the *Sailfish*, Zihad Haq was at the helm. As soon as Hamid and Mohammad cast off the lines, the *Sailfish* pulled away from the freighter. Al-Maadi waved goodbye to Captain Qadir who was peering down from the railing of the *Amuratu*. Haq asked, "Back to Karachi?"

"No, head southeast. I don't want them to see which way we are headed."

Confused, Haq said, "You don't trust Qadir?"

"I do, but I don't trust his crew. Besides, any man can be compelled to talk. If a man is so compelled, he only reveals what he believes to be true. If someone compels Captain Qadir, I want him to tell them we went south."

"Are our enemies aware of him?"

"I'm not sure. The *Sea Lion* being boarded bothers me. If it was not just a coincidence..."

"I understand. So, we go southeast and then once out of their sight we continue on our original course."

"Yes."

Haq asked, "May I make a suggestion?"

"Of course."

"Instead of heading straight to Yemen, we should go northeast to the fishing grounds. We then go west with the other fishing boats. If someone is trying to find us, we will be but one of dozens of fishing boats."

Al-Maadi mulled this over. "Do we have enough food, water, and fuel?"

"Yes, Abu Almawt. Plenty."

Patting the bottle of Dramamine in his pocket, Al-Maadi said, "This makes sense. Let's do it. We'll hide in plain sight. What to the Westerners say? A needle in a haystack?"

* * *

While the *Sailfish* motored northeast to the fishing grounds of the mid-Indian Ocean, the Praetorians on *Mother Goose* were trying to figure out what to do next. After the DDV was tucked away and the drone prepped for its next mission, Rusty called a group meeting. "Okay, sports fans, we had a good drive but no touchdown."

Sarah turned to Lon with an expression that said *What the fuck?* He whispered to her, "It's a sports metaphor. Football. American football. It means we did a lot of good work but didn't score."

"Ah. Got it…I think."

Rusty continued. "The Novichok was on that ship but it was transferred to another boat before we caught up to them. Our old friend, Khalid Al-Maadi was on the second boat along with the guy Mossad saw him jawing with on the dock in Karachi a while back. The captain of the freighter said the second boat headed south but that doesn't mean shit. Al-Maadi has used misdirection before. Remember Cairo? So, the big question is, what next? Anyone?"

Steve volunteered, "I may have something."

"Well, shoot. Ain't no one interrupting."

"Okay, according to Sarah, the captain of the Amutaru said the boat they transferred the CW to was called the *Badbani Machly* or something like that, right?"

Sarah nodded, "Yeah, but that isn't Arabic. At least not any Arabic I ever heard before."

Steve continued. "I ran that name *Badbani Machly* through the translation program and got nothing. Then I thought, we're a long way from anywhere. Maybe he hired a local boat? Since we're sitting off the coast of East Africa, I told the computer to try variations on the name phonetically to come up with alternate spellings that correspond to regional languages.

I ran it against French, English, Portuguese, Bantu, Swahili, Dhivehi, and Comorian. Since the captain said they went south and given our proximity to South Africa and Madagascar, I added Zulu, Xhosa, Afrikaans, and Malagasy. Still got nothing."

Rusty was getting impatient. "I don't care what you didn't find, I only care about what you did."

"I'm getting there. The Mossad agent photographed the captain and Al-Maadi on the dock in Karachi. I initially discounted Pakistan because it is four thousand kilometers away and we're talking about a fishing trawler with limited range. But running out of alternatives, I gave it a shot and added Urdu, Hindi, and Persian to the search and got a hit."

Rusty perked up. "Okay, now you have me. What hit?"

"The captain's *Badbani Machly* in Arabic was actually *Baadbani Machhli, Sailfish* in Urdu."

Sarah asked, "I'm no sailor but how does a coastal fishing boat travel 4,000 kilometers, actually 8,000 kilometers round trip."

Nigel chimed in. "Well, I am a sailor and it's a problem. Trawlers actually have a pretty good range. They have to travel from the port to the fishing grounds, pull their nets, and then head back on one tank of fuel. They can sail quite a way, but 8,000 kilometers? That's a stretch. No gas stations in the ocean."

John Kernan interjected, "But what if there was? What if the *Amuratu* transferred fuel as well as the CW? If the trawler filled up on fuel and brought extra diesel in barrels, she'd get here no problem. She'd be sailing in a straight line and not dragging nets. Once she meets up with the *Amuratu*, the freighter tops off her tanks or gives her barrels of fuel or both. She'd make it back as long as the food and water lasted. The captain said there were four men on that trawler. The standard crew would be bigger. Besides, if you're going to give them fuel, why not food and water too? They could do it."

Steve reasserted himself. "Well, they could do it and they did do it. The *Sailfish* is a Pakistan registered fishing boat operating out of Karachi. It was registered to Aman Haq, a long-time fisherman from the area. No criminal activity. No record of extremist ties."

Gunny said, "*Was* registered?"

Steve smiled, "Aman Haq died three years ago. He transferred his fishing permits and ownership of the boat to his nephew, Zihad Haq."

"What's his story?"

"I hacked the Ministry of Interior's criminal database. Zihad Haq was arrested as a teen for participating in riots fomented by Tehrik-i-Taliban."

Gunny said, "Those are some nasty motherfuckers."

"Our guy was released due to his age and turned over to his uncle Aman. No record of him getting in any trouble since."

Gunny rubbed his chin. "Maybe the uncle kept him on the straight and narrow. When the uncle bought the farm, the kid returned to his old extremist buddies."

Steve nodded. "That appears to be what happened. I found a photo of Zihad from his captain's license and national ID card. Wise Owl says it's a 99% match with the photo Mossad provided of the guy on the dock with Al-Maadi."

Lon shook his head, "Well I'll be goddamned. That asshole drove 4,000 kliks, picked up his shit, and now has to drive back another 4,000 kliks. Why the hell didn't he just wait for the *Amuratu* to get closer to Yemen? She was headed there anyway."

Sarah said, "To avoid us. If he'd done that, he'd be dead and we'd be done. Our life just isn't destined to be that easy."

Rusty brought them back on point. "Okay, the trawler is the *Sailfish*. The *Sailfish* is from Karachi and is captained by a guy with extremist ties and is providing water-taxi service for the biggest asshole on the planet. How do we catch him before he kills a shitload of people?"

Nigel said, "Well, the shortest distance between two points is a straight line. If he's taking the shit back to Pakistan, he's headed due north as fast as his boat will take him. He has a day's head start on us at least. That would put him about five hundred nautical miles north of their rendezvous point."

Steve opened up his laptop and brought up Google Earth. "Okay, that would put them east of Mogadishu somewhere."

His recent encounter still fresh on his mind, Rusty asked, "What about pirates? I mean, wouldn't they be worried they'd be attacked too?"

Steve clicked on another open tab on the computer. It was a commercial ship tracking website. Pointing to the screen he said, "This is us, just east of the border of Kenya and Somalia. All these little triangles represent ships at sea. They're color-coded, yellow for cargo ships, orange for tankers, blue for fishing boats, and gray for 'unknown.' Notice anything?"

Nigel chuckled, "Yeah, they're all avoiding the Somali coast and the fucking pirates."

"Yeah. I'd say so. If this Haq character is an experienced captain, we're safe to assume the *Sailfish* did the same."

Gunny pointed at the screen. "Okay, so they went further east to avoid pirates. We do the same. We push *Mother Goose* to flank speed to close the gap. How accurate is this ship tracker?"

"It's updated via satellite regularly, every ten to fifteen minutes. Some of the larger vessels have additional data like the name, tonnage, size, speed, and course. Unfortunately, you don't get that for most of the ships, especially the small ones. If we find him, we should be able to track him."

Gunny grumbled, "Well, at least we can see where he isn't. That's something, I guess."

John said, "Check out the traffic north of us. It's all freighters and tankers. No fishing boats. This program is based on satellite data so it's not like he faked that. He's not there. Now look further east at this mass of fishing boats midway between the tip of India and Somalia. Those are the Indian Ocean fishing grounds. If you're in a trawler, where better to hide than among hundreds of similar boats? I'll bet he went that way and intends to slip in among boats returning to port. It's like a movie when the hero running from the bad guys slips into a parade."

Rusty poured over the screen. "That makes sense, but how do we find the *Sailfish*. She's a needle in a haystack. Hell, she's a needle in a sea of needles!"

John asked Steve, "Can you set up a program to track those fishing boats?"

"Well, sure. I guess so. But what am I looking for?"

"A fishing boat that ain't fishing. All those boats will be setting nets, seining, and collecting their catches—all except one. One of those boats should have a different pattern of activity. Can you go back in time on this program?"

Steve understood where he was going. "Yeah, if I access the archived data."

"Let's identify all ships joining the fleet from the south in the last twenty-four hours. Then we separate those who are fishing from those who aren't. Nigel and I will show you what to look for. I have a sneaking suspicion there's only one boat out there on a pleasure cruise."

Rusty smiled. "I like it! You guys get on it right away. Gunny, let's get *Mother Goose* closer to the action."

Gunny grinned. "You got it, boss."

* * *

For two days, Steve, Nigel, and John sifted through the data. The target trawler wasn't fishing. The *Sailfish* only had four men on board, one of them was Al-Maadi, and Al-Maadi was no fisherman. They probably weren't even carrying nets. That was just extra weight. Using the ship tracking program, they discovered a couple of boats moving northeast from the Comoros. Both were north of the Seychelles sailing directly for the fishing grounds. Steve marked their positions using a series of red and yellow dots. After another two days, the boat represented by the yellow dots slowed and started sailing in a long, straight line due east before stopping and turning back to the west. Nigel said, "That one is trawling. Where is the other?"

Steve tapped a key and a line of red dots appeared. "Right here. She's just motoring through the middle of the fleet."

"Click on the icon. Is there any data? Maybe they turned on their transponder once they joined the fleet."

Steve replied, "No. It still just says 'Unidentified vessel.'" He clicked on a couple of other icons but got the same response. "None of these boats have any data associated with them."

"With this many boats and only periodic updates, there is a good chance we'll lose her in this mess."

Steve said, "The tracking program is limited by the frequency of satellite updates. Our best bet is for us to keep eyeballs on her 24/7. It's tedious as hell, but it may be the only way."

Nigel scratched his head, "Aye, it may indeed."

* * *

The next morning, Rusty walked up to the bridge with a cup of coffee for Nigel. The big Scot had been staring at the screen for hours hitting the "refresh" button every couple of minutes. He was bleary eyed. "Oh, thank you, Rusty. I needed this."

"What's the status on our pigeon?"

"He's moved across the fishing grounds and now is on the extreme northern edge. If he's leaving, he'll have to commit to a direction soon. My money is on north-northeast toward Pakistan."

"Need me to spell ya?"

"No, thanks. John should be here in a minute."

Two hours later, John called the Praetorians to the bridge. It was crowded as everyone tried to squeeze in around the laptop. John said, "He's committed. About twenty minutes ago two tankers and a cargo ship sailed west and he slipped in behind them."

Gunny asked, "West? That gives them a lot of options."

"One of the tankers is a Chinese ship, the *Yan Tai*. According to the ship tracker, it's headed for the Suez Canal. Our trawler is staying with them. If she was headed for Pakistan, she would have continued north, right Nigel?"

Nigel grumbled, took out his wallet and peeled off a hundred euro note. "Okay, you win. I would have sworn she was headed back to Karachi."

John snapped the note from Nigel's hand and tucked it into his shirt pocket. "Anyway, if the *Sailfish* stays with these larger vessels, she'll be easier to track. Their transponders are on and providing speed and heading. We only need to make sure the trawler is with them."

Rusty beamed. "Great work guys. Let's set a course to intercept them, preferably before they reach Yemen."

* * *

While they kept track of the *Sailfish* and its escort of three massive ships, the Praetorians moved *Mother Goose* into a parallel heading south of them. The two tankers made the little convoy easier to follow, but they occasionally lost track of the small trawler when clouds interfered with the satellite coverage. The little trawler had no transponder, or at least didn't have it on, so they relied on commercial satellite data. As they neared Socotra, the Yemeni island off the Horn of Africa which is the unofficial entrance to the Gulf of Aden and the Red Sea beyond, they had to make a decision. Where and when would they take the *Sailfish*? All the canal traffic stayed north of the island to avoid shallow water, reefs, and pirates. This was a very busy part of the ocean. Pulling off an attack would not necessarily be difficult but stealth would be all but impossible.

The Praetorians met to strategize. Gunny pulled up a large electronic chart of the area. "Okay folks. We need to pick a time and place for the take down." Turning to Nigel and John, he said, "You two are our most qualified maritime ops specialists, as scary as that sounds. What's your assessment?"

John retorted, "Thanks for the vote of confidence, Grandpa. This area is pretty congested by ocean standards, but there will still be miles between vessels. If we peel the *Sailfish* away from her three escorts, we take her out with little effort and no witnesses. Even if she raises the alarm, people will assume it's Somali pirates. They won't suspect a well-maintained salvage tug. If we put the drone up armed with a light weapon like a LAW or 70mm rocket, we might disable her with no one on the bigger ships getting wise."

Nigel nodded in agreement. "That might work. We drive right up to her under the guise of rendering assistance. To any other ship that happens along we're a salvage tug helping a smaller boat in trouble. If they hail us, we just say we were called in to help them get to Djibouti or one of the Yemeni ports."

Rusty laughed, "Hell, we might even offer them a tow to a more secluded part of the ocean!"

Gunny shook his head. "Oh, hell no! If they have Novichok on board, I want that thing on the bottom of the ocean as fast as possible. I don't care how many people are watching."

Lon asked, "Why even use the drone? If they get hit with a rocket, they'll realize they've been compromised. They could set the Novichok adrift or mix it right there on the boat. Sure, they'd kill themselves, but they'd put up a cloud of that shit which could drift anywhere. Also, what would it do to the water? I'm not exactly a tree hugger but what would releasing a ton of some of the most toxic shit in the world do to the fish? The locals eat them, ya know."

Magne said, "Lon's got a point. The less time we give them to react, the better. The components were packaged separately, but who's to say they still are. They might have put that shit in an RPG round, hung it under a cheap drone, or tied it to a damn dolphin for all we know. We need to be close enough to kill them all—the quicker the better."

Hans asked, "What about an EMP round? If we hit them with an electromagnetic pulse, the engine quits and they're dead in the water. It'll look like the engine took a shit. We roll up as good Samaritans and then wipe them out."

Alen nodded. "I like that idea."

Nigel interjected, "Nope. No guarantee. According to the Pakistani registration, that boat is old and diesel powered. That means it probably has analog controls like cables and linkages. The older diesel engines have mechanical, not electronic, fuel injection systems. They only need electricity to start 'em. An EMP would take out their radios and navigation systems, but the engine would keep running."

"Well, what do you suggest?"

"Brute force. We come up from the south like we're just crossing their heading. The bigger ships are maintaining a distance of about a mile. The trawler is closer but they're staying pretty far back from the last tanker to avoid the chop of his wake, maybe a thousand meters. We move like we're going to cross in front of them but then turn to starboard and ram the bitch. *Mother's* steel hull is plenty strong enough. If the *Sailfish* doesn't go down immediately, she'll be crippled. We board her and take out the crew before they have time to react."

Rusty mulled this over. "Well, it does have simplicity on its side. I just want to make sure we aren't taking out the wrong trawler. We haven't put eyes on her yet. We're depending on analysis of vessel tracking services and the word of a dead terrorist sea captain. No slight to Sarah's interrogation skills but what if the guy was lying…about, well, everything?"

Sarah snorted, "Not likely, but I'll concede it's a possibility…although a slim one."

Gunny said, "No, Rusty is right. We don't want to take out civilians based on some incorrect assessments. We'll plan on Nigel's brute force approach but before we execute it, we'll use the drone to confirm we have the right boat. Agreed?" Everyone nodded. "Okay, let's make it happen."

The next morning, they launched the drone before dawn. It flew an intercept course to the *Sailfish*. While it orbited high above, they used its long-range cameras to get their first view of the trawler. It was as Captain Qadir described. They clearly made out the name on its stern, *Baadbani Machhli*. Under it in English was painted the word "*Sailfish*." John chuckled, "Nice of them to provide a translation for us. It is definitely the right boat."

There were only two men in sight. Gunny zoomed in on the helm. "Can't see through the glass, but I'll bet that's Haq, the captain." He panned back to the stern of the boat. Someone was leaning over the side puking. He laughed. "Seasick. What do you bet that's our college professor turned terrorist?" The man stood up and wiped his mouth. When he leaned back to drink a bottle of water, he was practically facing the drone. "Smile for the camera!"

Sarah peered intently at the image. "That's Al-Maadi. I'd bet my paycheck on it. This is definitely the right boat."

Rusty asked, "What's with all the barrels on the deck?"

Nigel replied, "Fuel. Those are fuel drums. That explains how she made it all the way to the Comoros from Karachi. They converted her into a floating gas can. Still, I bet they had to take on additional fuel from the *Amuratu*. That's a lot of diesel. She probably won't have to stop before returning to Karachi, that's assuming she's even going that way. She could be going to Yemen, Egypt, Qatar, Iran, or anywhere else within a couple thousand kilometers."

Rusty took a deep breath. "Well, we need to stop her before she goes anywhere."

Gunny nodded, "Agree. Nigel, John? What do ya think?"

John said, "We hit her tomorrow morning about this time. At their current course and speed, it should put them a couple hundred klicks past Socotra. The water there is over four thousand meters deep. A good place to sink the boat. No one will try to recover it. Also, this morning there were only two men on deck." He turned to Sarah and winked, "If Qadir was telling Sarah the truth, and having sparred with her, I expect he was, there are two more below deck. They probably had the late shift and are sleeping. Likely will be tomorrow as well. The other ships in the area will have a light watch on duty that early in the morning."

Gunny turned to Magne and Steve. "Grab these yahoos and recover the drone. It needs to be airborne and over the target at least an hour before we hit it. I want to keep an eye out for pirates or patrol ships. That means you guys need to be up early."

Magne smiled, "No problem, Gunny. Not like I need as much beauty sleep as these trolls."

"Yeah, yeah. We know, you're the most handsome."

As Magne smiled, Lon interjected, "You mean pretty, don't you? Handsome usually refers to a man."

Magne shot back, "Jealous Oden? I shit prettier than you."

Gunny just shook his head. "It's like I'm babysitting a bunch of twelve-year-old kids with machine guns."

* * *

As the drone returned to *Mother Goose*, things were happening on board the *Sailfish*. Al-Maadi walked up to the bridge and asked, "Where are we?"

"About two hundred and fifty kilometers from Socotra, the island that marks the entrance to the Gulf of Aden and the Red Sea beyond. That is where we turn north. Until then, we are just another trawler headed for market."

The *Sailfish* continued its trek to the west in line with its three larger unofficial escort ships. As it neared Socotra, Haq was scanning the seas around him. Something to the south caught his attention. It was another ship. Not a big tanker or even a coastal freighter like the *Amuratu* but rather another fishing boat. As it came closer, he recognized it as a long line fishing boat. He pointed it out to Al-Maadi. "Abu Almawt. You see that boat?"

Taking the binoculars, Al-Maadi turned his gaze to the spot on the horizon where Haq was pointing. "Uh, yes. I see it. What is it?"

"Another fishing boat. Probably a long liner going after tuna or sailfish. From her heading, she appears to be returning to port in Oman. When she crosses our path, I'll slip in behind her. If anyone looks at us, we'll look like half of a fishing tandem."

Al-Maadi smiled. "Good idea. While my cousin trusted Qadir, he had been betrayed before, as have I. If for some reason he alerted the authorities or just spoke out of school, they'll be searching for a single boat, not two."

It took the other fishing boat almost an hour to catch the *Sailfish*. When it did, instead of continuing north, it dropped in behind the *Sailfish* and turned west. Al-Maadi asked, "Now what?"

Haq shrugged. "Well, so much for that idea. We still need to turn north. We might as well do it here. If coastal patrol aircraft fly over, there will still be a fishing boat behind the tanker. It just won't be us." Haq cut the wheel of the *Sailfish* to starboard and moved away from the other ships heading into the Gulf of Aden. "You haven't told me yet and I understand why, but where are we going?"

"We're going to meet more of our brothers near Al Ghaydah. Do you know where that is?"

"Eastern Yemen. I'll set the course."

* * *

The pre-dawn pneumatic blast of the drone launcher served as an alarm clock for the Praetorians, not that many were asleep anyway. Steve and Magne had been up for about an hour prepping the drone for launch. Once the drone was airborne and sent on its way to intercept the *Sailfish*, they headed down to the galley for coffee. Gunny was cooking breakfast. "These are the last of the fresh eggs so get 'em while they're hot."

Alen, Lon, Hans, and Rusty were already seated. Sarah wandered in, poured a cup of coffee, picked out a Danish but waived off the bacon and eggs. She took a seat at the table and craned her neck. "I can hardly wait to get back to my own bed. I don't want to sound like a prima donna bitch, but we really should upgrade the mattresses on this ship."

Nigel snorted, "You're just spoiled. In the old days, sailors only had hammocks slung between the canon."

She asked incredulously, "Have you ever slept in a hammock when you weren't drunk on a beach somewhere?"

He replied sheepishly, "No."

"Then shut the fuck up."

"Yes, ma'am."

Gunny came over with a large bowl of scrambled eggs and a platter of bacon. "This is it for the fresh eggs. We do have cartons of that prefab shit in the freezer, but it's not the same."

Lon asked, "Got any salsa?"

"Who do I look like? Your abuela? Get it yourself, lazy ass."

Lon feigned indignation, "Are you calling me a lazy Mexican?"

Gunny Medina shot back, "You're what? A quarter Mexican? I'm full-blooded, so I'll call you whatever the hell I want."

Steve was the last to sit. Rusty asked him, "What's the status of the drone? How long before it's on target?"

Steve checked his watch. "Should be over the trawler in about twenty minutes if she kept the same bearing and speed. We'll check on her as soon as we eat."

The Praetorians kept up the banter as they ate. They were prepared for action but no one was overly concerned about this operation. There were only four men in a relatively small vessel and they expected two of them to be in their bunks when they struck. After breakfast, Gunny, Rusty, and Nigel followed Steve to the bridge where the drone's operating console was located. Steve checked the drone's coordinates and the tanker's last position on the ship tracker website. "The tanker is right where she's supposed to be. The drone is over the target. The sun is starting to come up so we should get a good visual in a few minutes." The drone's camera was still in infrared mode, so the picture was in varying shades of gray. On the monitor, the tanker took up most of the screen. "I had it tracking the tanker since she was easier to lock in on. Steve zoomed out and pointed to the smaller fishing boat traveling behind it. "They're still staying about a kilometer behind the bigger ship." Zooming in on the trawler, Steve said, "There she is." Staring at the grainy image, he asked, "Is there something different about her?"

Nigel said, "The barrels. The barrels on the fantail are gone. Is there a better picture?"

"The drone is moving away. Let me turn it around and have it orbit over the trawler." In a few minutes, the drone was directly over the *Sailfish*. "Yeah, those barrels are gone now."

Rusty said, "Maybe they stashed them below deck? If they transferred all the diesel to the boat's fuel tanks, they'd be empty and easy to handle. Hell, they may have even tossed them over the side."

Lon said, "Yeah, but why? They've had them on deck all this time. Why toss them now?"

"How the hell should I know? I'm not the sailor in this group."

Nigel shook his head. "No, that doesn't make much sense. There's no reason for it." He peered intently at the image on the screen. "Steve ol' buddy, zoom in on the bow section. That's the front to you fly boys."

Steve huffed, "I know what the bow is, asshole. At least I can spell it." Steve adjusted the camera and zoomed in. "There. Anything else missing?"

"Not missing, lad, something there that wasn't before."

Rusty and Gunny leaned in. "What?"

"Fishing gear." Pointing to the screen Nigel said, "These are long line reels. They weren't there yesterday. Why bring them out now?"

"Maybe they want to look like they've been fishing," Rusty posited.

"No. This is something else. When can we lose the infrared?"

Steve answered, "Any minute now. Why?"

"Just do it."

Steve hit a button and the screen briefly went black. After a few seconds, the image reappeared in color, albeit dim. "There it is…oh fuck!"

Rusty asked anxiously, "What? What's the matter?"

Gunny picked up on it too. "The color. *Sailfish* is white. This boat is blue. So, unless they painted the motherfucker in the middle of the night, this is the wrong boat."

Rusty barked, "Goddamnit! How the fuck did this asshole figure out we were onto him? Did he detect the drone yesterday?"

Steve shook his head. "I doubt it. We were too high and had the sun behind us. Besides, if he suspected we were there, I doubt Al-Maadi would have posed for the camera. This has to be something else."

Gunny interjected. "This is just a FUBAR situation. I doubt he had another trawler waiting in the wings to slip in and take his place. Even if he was that clever, wouldn't you pick a boat that's the same damn color? No, this was just bad fucking luck. Is there anything on this new boat? You got a name or anything?"

Steve checked the ship tracking website. "Goddamn. It's running with a transponder. It is the *Allaadigha*, which apparently means 'stingray' in Arabic. It's part of a commercial fleet out of Djibouti."

Nigel added, "She's a long liner, probably has a hold full of tuna, mackerel, and sailfish. She's just returning to port."

Rusty asked, "So, speaking of sailfish, where *is* the *Sailfish*?"

Gunny scratched his head. "That's the question. Steve, figure out when this *Stingray* joined our little convoy."

"I've been recording all the ship tracker data. Let me run it backward." Steve furiously tapped the "page up" key until he found it. "Okay. It joined the convoy yesterday morning around 0900 hours. That's not too long after we broke off from them. As it came in, our 'unidentified vessel' which *was* the *Sailfish,* turned north on a heading of 340 degrees."

Gunny asked, "Where will that take them?"

"Yemen."

"Fuck me." Turning to Nigel, he asked, "Can we intercept them?"

"We can try. But they might change course at any point along the way."

Steve interjected, "Use the drone. If we push it to its maximum speed and plot an intercept course, assuming they're still on the same heading, we should catch up to them in the afternoon."

Rusty said, "Do it."

"I'm not sure we'll have enough fuel to get it back. We may lose it."

"I don't care. I'll buy another one. Just do it. Nigel, push *Mother* to her red line and go after them."

"Aye, Rusty. If we close the gap fast enough, we might save the drone too."

"Alright, Lon, tell the others the intercept is aborted, but tell them to be prepared to engage. Got it?"

"Yes, Gunny."

* * *

The drone sped north in search of the *Sailfish*. Steve tried to locate the errant trawler using the ship tracker program but lost it about an hour after it changed course. He was archiving what appeared on the monitor, but tightened the coverage area of the program to give him better detail of the part of the ocean the trawler and the tankers were transiting. Once the *Sailfish* moved out of that coverage area, it was no longer being recorded. Steve took the last recorded location, calculated its speed and heading, and sent the drone to the location where he hoped the trawler would be. While the drone would get there, *Mother Goose* was too far away and too slow to catch up.

At about 1300 hours, the drone was at the estimated intercept point. Using the ship tracker, he found a number of unidentified vessels in the area. He had no idea which was the *Sailfish*, so he would have to visually inspect each one. To conserve fuel, he programed the drone's autopilot to fly from ship to ship to ship using the most efficient route. Steve studied the monitor with the drone's camera feed. He stared at the screen as each vessel came into view. He zoomed in on the boats hoping to find his quarry, only to be disappointed each time. He was about to intercept his fifth bogey when Nigel and John came onto the bridge.

Nigel asked, "How's it going?"

"I'm about to check out my fifth possible." The two men moved in behind him and peered at the screen. A few seconds later, a fishing boat appeared at the top of the screen. It moved steadily toward the middle and as it did, Steve increased the magnification on the camera. "Okay, let's see who we're dealing with here." Steve maneuvered the drone to approach the boat from the stern to get a shot of its name. It was in Arabic. "I can't quite make that out, but it isn't the *Sailfish*."

John said, "I could have told you that. That boat has twin booms on the rear fantail." Tapping the screen, he said, "See that? Those are nets. This is an active purse seiner. The *Sailfish* had no gear on deck. Plus, no fuel barrels."

Steve sat back in his chair. "Yeah, I saw that but had to make certain. Well, off to the next one." Steve tapped a couple of keys and the autopilot directed the drone to the next target.

"How long to the next boat?" Nigel asked.

"About four minutes." The three men waited patiently. In three and a half minutes, there was a "ping" from the console. Steve leaned in squinting at the screen. "Okay, there it is. Should catch up in a few seconds."

As the ship on the screen grew steadily larger, Nigel quipped, "Well, it's white instead of blue. That's something at least." A few seconds later there was something else. "What is that on the other side of the boat? Is that a sailboat?"

John and Nigel instinctively moved closer to the screen trying to get a better view, crushing Steve between them. He pushed them back. "Jesus guys, I can just zoom in."

Nigel barked, "Well do it then!"

Using the joystick, Steve kept the crosshairs on the boat while he increased the magnification. John pointed to the screen. "What the fuck? It is a sailboat...or at least I think it is. That's a mast, right?"

Nigel snorted, "It's a dhow with its sail down."

John studied the map and asked, "How far off the coast are they?"

Steve checked the drone's coordinates. "About a hundred and fifteen klicks."

"A dhow is a coastal boat meant for shallow waters, not open ocean. What the hell is it doing out there?"

Steve added, "And meeting a trawler?" The drone flew closer to the boats. Steve maneuvered it to get an image of the stern of the trawler.

Nigel pointed to the screen. "Are those blue barrels?"

John grinned "Sure looks like it."

The drone angled around the trawler and Steve zoomed in on the stern. It was the *Sailfish*. "Bingo!"

John gave Nigel a high five. "I'll go get Gunny and Rusty."

Steve guided the drone away from the *Sailfish* and the dhow. Nigel said, "What the hell are you doing?"

"The drone is too low. They'll see it. I'm going to fly east and gain altitude. Don't worry, they aren't going anywhere. I just want to make sure they don't spot us. We've had enough bad luck on this op."

Several minutes and a couple of thousand feet later, he turned the drone back toward the two boats. Gunny and Rusty, with John in tow, arrived at the bridge as they were getting their first view from directly above the *Sailfish*. "There she is boss. And she has a visitor."

Rusty asked, "What's that other boat?"

Gunny answered, "It's a dhow, a local trading vessel. They're traditionally one or two masted sailing boats. Most of the newer ones have diesel engines too. They're unique to this region. They're a cheap and efficient way to carry goods between coastal towns. He's a bit far offshore though."

The men below ran a line through a pulley on the mast of the dhow to the fantail of the *Sailfish*. After the line was attached to a blue barrel in a net, two men on the dhow pulled the rope lifting the barrel off the deck while a man on the *Sailfish* kept tension from the back. The men expertly guided the barrel gently over to the dhow landing it softly on its bow deck. Rusty asked, "Is that the Novichok?"

Gunny shrugged, "Can't tell from here."

A minute later they repeated the process with a second barrel only this one was placed at the stern of the sail boat. Nigel said, "They put the first one at the bow and the second one at the stern. Keeping them separate. That's got to be the Novichok. Otherwise, why not put both barrels in the center cargo hold?"

"I think you're right." The men loaded three more barrels in the net and swung them over to the dhow amidships. Gunny grunted, "Three? Must be empty."

Nigel replied, "Either that or Hercules is on the rope."

Gunny squinted at the screen. "Can we see the people on board?"

"I'm on it," Steve replied. As the rest of the Praetorians crowded onto the bridge, Steve zoomed in on the dhow. He counted six men on board. The were all dressed in thobes and keffiyehs. There were five men on the *Sailfish*, four wearing loose slacks and one in a thobe. After a couple of minutes, the one in the thobe swung over to the dhow. They cast off the lines tying the two boats together and the dhow started moving away. Two of the men on the *Sailfish* clapped each other on the back and hugged.

Rusty snorted, "They're sure happy. Like they just killed a couple million infidels or something." Steve kept the camera on the two men as they separated. He got a great shot of their smiling faces. It was Al-Maadi and Haq.

Gunny growled, "Fuckin' Al-Maadi."

Nigel asked, "Now what? Follow the CW or Al-Maadi."

Rusty pondered this for a minute. "Can we do both?"

Steve said, "Now that I know where the *Sailfish* is, I can probably keep tabs on it using the ship tracker software, so long as they don't slip in with a bunch of other fishing boats. If they do, we're in trouble because the slow refresh rate will screw us up. That dhow is pretty small and I don't see a transponder on the ship tracker. If we don't use the drone, they're gone."

"Okay, Al-Maadi is a target but not necessarily an immediate threat. The CW is. Keep the drone on the dhow. We need to find out where it goes. We'll track the *Sailfish* as best we're able with the ship tracker. Let's pray we keep our eyes on both. If the dhow goes straight north, can we intercept it before it makes the coast?"

Steve checked the screen and shook his head. "I don't think so. It's motorized, and while we're certainly faster, we're too far away. Now, if it sails up or down the coast we probably could."

Gunny mulled this over. "Okay, we need to stay on the Novichok. We'll continue north and cover the Yemeni coast."

Hans asked, "What if they go to Oman?"

Rusty replied, "If the dhow heads to Oman, we ask their government to intercept it. If it heads to Yemen, well, there isn't any government there, not really. That's where I'd go if I were them. If they do, we're pretty much fucked. We have no airlift options to catch up with them and the drone will run out of gas before too long."

Steve said, "Okay, I'll stay with the dhow but someone else is going to have to keep tabs on the *Sailfish*. I can't do both."

John raised his hand. "Nigel and I will monitor the *Sailfish*."

Sarah stepped forward. "Hans and I will help as well. There are several ship tracking services that use different satellites. By monitoring both at the same time, we should be able to track Al-Maadi."

Gunny nodded and said, "Good thinking. I leave it to you four to figure out who does what. Magne, you help Steve track that dhow. Alen and I will drive the boat."

Alen was surprised. "Uh, I've never driven a boat that didn't use paddles or an outboard motor."

Gunny grinned. "It's easy. I'll show you."

* * *

The dhow took a heading of north-northwest, straight for the Yemeni coast. The *Sailfish* motored northeast toward Pakistan. The Praetorians' primary target was the dhow and the chemical weapon. For another couple of hours, the dhow plodded along until it changed its heading. "Okay, we have a course change on the dhow," Steve called out. "She has turned fifteen degrees to the west. She's headed straight for Al Ghaydah, Yemen."

Gunny turned the wheel over to Alen and walked over to Steve's monitor. "Fuck! I was afraid of that. That's the worst-case scenario. They're going to be docking in Yemen and will be gone before we can do anything about it."

Magne peered at the screen. "Well, we could always crash the drone into it and hope it sinks."

Rusty shrugged. "It'd be money well spent. We just buy another one."

Gunny shook his head. "No guarantees it'd sink the dhow. The drone is only what? A hundred kilos? And she's almost out of gas so a secondary explosion is not a forgone conclusion. Modern dhow's have steel hulls. We might mess it up but I doubt we'd stop it."

Steve said, "Okay, we wait for them to unload and crash the drone into whatever they use to carry it away be it a truck or a donkey cart."

Gunny scratched his head. "That's more realistic, but we can't do it in the town. We might end up mixing the precursors in the explosion and killing a few thousand innocents. Kind of defeats the whole purpose."

Magne said, "Okay, they're not going to use it in Al Ghaydah. I doubt Yemeni fishermen are in their target package. It'll have to be moved somewhere else. If they were going to do that via a boat, why not keep it on the *Sailfish*? While we can't disregard the possibility, it would make more sense to move it by air or ground. The Saudis, CIA, and JSOC all have drones in the sky and combat aircraft available. Flying it out would be risky. Either they drive it out or put it on another boat."

Sarah asked, "Drive it where? Sana? Aden? They aren't going to go overland to Saudi Arabia. That's a great way to catch a Hellfire up your ass."

Lon said, "I guess that leaves Oman." Lon pulled a large paper map from a rack and spread it out on the ship's chart table. "Okay, unless they pack it out on a camel, that leaves them with two options—the Coast Highway or up the middle of the country on Highway 31. The Coast Highway has more towns if you need fuel, food, or water but Highway 31 is a couple hundred kilometers shorter."

Gunny snorted, "I guess we just have to wait and see what they do. How much longer can the drone stay up?"

Steve said, "If we go all kamikaze on them, maybe two or three hours. If we want to recover it, maybe an hour and a half."

Gunny muttered to himself, "Shit."

Rusty said, "Don't worry about the drone. If we take out the Novichok, I'll buy ya ten more drones."

Gunny stared at the map. "If they go to ground in Al Ghaydah, we can't attack them in the town. I don't want to lose the drone if we don't have to. We may need it to go after Al-Maadi."

Rusty mused, "We should've brought two. Well, next time."

Gunny stood up. "Okay. All of this is academic until we know what these motherfuckers do. Keep the drone on them and let's see what happens."

The dhow continued to the beach near Muhayifif, the small fishing town between Al Ghaydah and the Arabian Sea. There were no docks or even a jetty or breakwater. Dhows and other small boats sailed as close to the beach as possible and transferred their cargo to small skiffs and dinghies for the last forty meters to the shore. As the drone circled, the tactical picture became clear—it was a nightmare. There were dhows and dinghies everywhere. The beach was crowded with fishermen unloading their haul. There were scores of women and children just off the beach sorting through the day's catch. A hundred meters beyond them was a major road, businesses, groceries, boatyards, and fields. Any accidental release of the Novichok would kill hundreds if not thousands of innocent people.

The dhow dropped anchor and the crew started to unload cargo. Two blue drums were rolled onto the large flat deck amidships. Nigel said, "There they are."

A moment later, another blue barrel was rolled out, then another, and another—five in all. John grumbled, "We're fucked. This is another goddamn shell game. Which barrels are the ones we want?"

Gunny sat back with his arms crossed. "Patience. We're not screwed yet."

The Praetorians studied the screen in silence as the drums were lowered over the side into waiting skiffs and rowed ashore. On the beach, a group of men unloaded the barrels onto the sand. Each rolled a barrel inland over planks. When they got to the last two barrels, Gunny pointed excitedly to the screen. "See that!"

Nigel shrugged, "What?"

"With the first three barrels, one guy was able to lift one out of the skiff by himself."

"Yeah, because they're empty."

Gunny grinned, "So why did these last two require two guys?" Turning to Sarah he asked, "How much did the captain of the *Amuratu* say each precursor weighed?"

She replied, "About fifty kilos."

"Okay, a hundred pounds of CW and another twenty or twenty-five pounds for the barrel. A lot of weight for one skinny longshoreman; strong back or not." As he said this, the men handling the barrel dropped it into the water.

Nigel laughed, "Well, apparently too much for two strong backs."

Gunny tapped the screen. "No, I was right. That barrel. It's floating too high in the water to be full of olive oil but too low to be empty. Either that's our Novichok or these guys are smuggling Styrofoam."

The men rolled the barrel up onto the planks and off the beach. The skiff with the last barrel beached itself, the men returned and repeated the process. The first three barrels were tossed onto a couple of waiting donkey carts and driven away. The two suspect barrels were sitting together near the road while one of the men who unloaded them sat on top. Nigel said, "Apparently this longshoreman has only one task today, babysitting these barrels." A few minutes later, a van pulled up at the curve in the road and stopped. It was a newer Mercedes Sprinter van with some Arabic writing and a logo on the side. The driver and the longshoreman lifted the barrels into the van. As the drone circled around, the two men strapped the barrels to the side of the van's cargo compartment. When that was done, they both climbed into the van and drove away.

Lon quipped, "Our longshoremen just joined the Teamsters Union." The van drove only a few hundred meters before stopping at a commercial facility. "What the hell is that place?"

Steve pulled up a Google Earth image of the area. "That is the Egrahit Fish Port."

Rusty asked, "Can we take them out there?"

Gunny shook his head. "There's a hell of a lot of civilians in there. Besides check this out." He pointed to the screen. "See those trucks? Those are technicals. They have Russian 12.3mm heavy machine guns mounted on them. That means plenty of soldiers nearby. Even if we got ashore, we'd be at a severe tactical disadvantage."

Lon sighed. "A Blackhawk Down situation."

"Except without any air evac."

Rusty said, "Well, that's a non-starter."

Sarah pointed to the back of the van. "It has a license plate so maybe we can figure out who it belongs to."

Lon mused, "Could be stolen. Probably is."

Sarah leaned back in her chair. "They aren't going to use that shit in Yemen. Driving it to Saudi would be a suicide mission. That leaves Oman. I doubt they'd risk crossing the border in a stolen vehicle."

Gunny interjected, "This is a dead end, at least right now. One thing we learned from last time is that Al-Maadi is the key. He and Nura were the only ones who were privy to all the details. He likes the control; he needs to be the hero of his story. He maintained control of the BW agent until he turned it over to that Palestinian doctor in Jordan for deployment. The only reason he didn't inject those mopes himself was he was compromised. He'll want the same level of control now."

Magne asked, "So what next?"

"We cut off the head of the snake. If he dies, his plan dies."

Magne said, "Works for me."

CHAPTER FIVE
INTO THE LABYRINTH

Aboard the *Sailfish*, Khalid Al-Maadi and Zihad Haq sailed northeast back toward Karachi. Al-Maadi was experiencing anxiety about his plan. He'd spent a fortune securing the Novichok from Kotov and just turned it over to men he'd never even met before. If he was wrong about them, and his Pakistani contacts who vouched for them, he just squandered his opportunity to avenge the death of his wife and the destruction of his very life.

As Al-Maadi stared out at the horizon ahead of the trawler, Haq approached him with a bottle of water and some ginger. "Here, take this. It will calm your stomach."

Al-Maadi shook his head. "No, thank you. I'm okay today. I'm getting used to life at sea."

Haq put the pills in his hand. "Take them. The sea is calm right now but there's a storm ahead. It'll get worse." Al-Maadi took the pills and chased them down with water. "I'm actually surprised you're still with us, Abu Almawt. I really expected you to get on the dhow and go with the weapon."

"That was my original plan."

"What made you change it?"

"The drone."

"What drone?"

"Back when we were transferring the chemical weapon, there was a drone flying over us."

Haq was taken aback. "There was? Why didn't you say anything?"

"I didn't want you, Hamid, or Mohammad to do anything that would alert them that we knew they were there. I'm not sure who was operating it, but I wanted us to appear as nonthreatening as possible. Just two boats transferring cargo."

Haq immediately stared up at the sky. "Is it still here?"

Al-Maadi smiled. "That's exactly what I was trying to prevent."

Haq blushed with embarrassment. "I'm sorry, Abu Almawt. I didn't mean to…"

"That's alright, Zihad. Its human nature. Besides, the drone didn't follow us. It tracked the dhow toward the shore."

"Who do you think it was?"

Al-Maadi shrugged. "Maybe the Saudis spying on the Houthis or the Omanis searching for smugglers. Maybe even the Americans hunting for someone like Ayman to kill. By acting calmly, we showed whoever was watching that we had nothing to hide and they went about their business."

"But what if they intercepted the dhow? What if they seized the weapon?"

"I don't think so. If they knew about the weapon, they'd have simply sunk the *Sailfish* with a Hellfire missile. It must have just been some routine surveillance drone. In a few hours, steer close enough to the coast for me to get a cellular signal. I'll contact our comrades to make sure they made it safely to Oman. But for now, we just relax and enjoy the sea air."

Haq again scanned the heavens in search of the drone. "How are you so calm?"

"A wise person once told me that panicking never improved your situation."

"Your cousin?"

"No, Nura. My wife."

* * *

Mother Goose sailed in pursuit of the *Sailfish*. They were even farther behind than when they started. To recover the drone, they had to actually sail toward the Yemeni coast and away from the *Sailfish*. The drone's fuel was running dangerously low and they had to close the gap to ensure the drone reached *Mother Goose* before it crashed into the sea. The Praetorians erected the recovery net amidships and prayed the drone would make it. They let out a collective sigh of relief when the small aircraft fell into the net. When they disassembled it, they found how close they came to losing it. It'd been flying on fumes. They immediately pointed the bow north-northeast and pushed the throttles to full speed. *Mother Goose* was faster than the *Sailfish* but the trawler had a big head start.

John approached Rusty, Gunny, and Nigel on the bridge. "We may have a problem coming our way. There's a tropical storm in the Arabian Sea. We're going to miss the worst of it, but we're going to hit some of the outer bands. The cloud cover is going to make tracking the *Sailfish* a hell of a lot harder if not impossible."

Rusty groaned, "Jesus Christ! Of course, there's a tropical storm! What else can go wrong?"

John said, "We're going to assume they're going back to Karachi and push *Mother Goose* to her max to close the gap. Unless you want to call the Pakis and ask for their help."

Gunny scoffed at this. "Fuck that. I don't trust those bastards as far as I can throw Finch's fat ass."

Nigel protested, "Hey!"

"Sorry. No Pakis, not after Abbottabad. You'll never convince me those fuckers didn't know Bin Laden was there the whole time. Our best chance to catch Al-Maadi is to *not* call the Pakis."

Rusty said, "Okay, you guys do some digging. Find out where and how to lease a chopper. I'll contact Gil and get him in the air to Karachi. It might get real sticky over there. We'll be hanging out in the breeze. If anyone has concerns, speak up. I'll not force anyone to go on this one." The Praetorians were silent. He expected as much. They wanted Al-Maadi as badly as he did. "Okay, let's get to work."

* * *

Zihad Haq guided the *Sailfish* closer to the Omani coast. Khalid Al-Maadi held a burner cellular phone waiting for bars to appear. Haq asked, "Anything yet?"

"No. I had a bar but it disappeared. This phone is a piece of crap."

"Yeah, well, you get what you pay for. That's why they cost less than 5,000 rupees. Not like you get a top-of-the-line Samsung for that. I'll bring us closer to shore. I want to avoid that storm to our east."

Al-Maadi rubbed his stomach and smiled. "I appreciate that."

"The port town of Duqm is up ahead. It is an oil town. It'll have good cellular service."

"How far?"

"An hour or two. It's also a fishing port so we won't be out of place. Hide in plain sight."

"Tell me when we're close."

The *Sailfish* sailed north and the voyage was uneventful, although the seas were getting rougher. Al-Maadi was thankful Haq had forced him to take the ginger. Al-Maadi was sitting on the bow, forcing himself to keep his eyes on the horizon to fight his nausea, when Haq approached. Gesturing to the northwest, he pointed out a large tanker steaming out into the Arabian Sea. "From Duqm. We're close enough for your phone."

Al-Maadi pulled the cheap LG flip phone from his pocket and turned it on. Two bars. Good enough. He removed a slip of paper from his pocket and punched the numbers into the phone. After a few seconds, it rang. A man answered suspiciously, "Hello?"

"Is this Odai?"

"Who is this?"

"I am the man who provided your cargo."

The man was not convinced. "What cargo?"

"The two blue plastic drums you picked up near Al Ghaydah."

Odai was still leery. "I don't know what you're talking about."

Al-Maadi let out an audible sigh, "From the *Baadbani Machhli*."

With the name of Haq's boat, the man relented. "The *Baadbani Machhli*. Okay, right. Who is this?"

"Abu Almawt."

Odai was instantly cowered. "I'm so sorry, Abu Almawt! I didn't know it was you. I mean, we weren't expecting to hear from you until…"

"Not on the phone. Did you pick up the cargo?"

"Yes, sir. It is with us now."

"Did you make it over the border okay? Any issues?"

Odai said, "No, sir. No issues at all. They hardly noticed us. I told them we had serviced refrigeration equipment at the fish market. They just waved us through."

Al-Maadi asked, "So, everything is on schedule?"

"Yes. We are currently…"

Al-Maadi cut him off. "That's enough. Say nothing else. I just wanted to make sure everything is going as planned."

Odai asked, "Do you want us to move up the timetable? We would save a couple of days if we cancelled some stops."

"No! Stick to the plan. If you miss appointments, there will be questions. Your company may even come searching for you. Everything must appear perfectly normal. Do you understand?"

"Yes, sir. Inshallah, we will be at the rendezvous at the appointed time."

"Very good. Safe travels."

"And you as well, sir."

Al-Maadi ended the call and then broke the phone in two before tossing the pieces over the side. Haq chuckled, "I hope you have more of those."

"Plenty, but I'll pick up more in Karachi."

Haq asked, "Why didn't you tell him about the drone?"

"He didn't need to know. There's nothing he could do about it. If I told him, he'd look for it, just as you did. It's human nature. I want him acting as if everything is fine. If it is fine, he won't draw attention to himself. If it isn't fine, it won't matter. I didn't want to give him any excuse to deviate from the plan. Now let's go to Karachi."

* * *

Rusty and Gunny stood on the bridge of *Mother Goose* peering at the sea and darkening sky in front of them. The outer bands of the tropical storm were already upon them and slowing their progress. Gunny studied the radar and grumbled, "We may be fucked, boss. We're getting slammed by this storm."

"Well, so are they, so it's a wash."

The old Marine rubbed his chin. "Well, maybe not. If John and Nigel's projection is right, this last band of weather slipped in behind them. We're in it. They aren't. They're on calmer seas and better winds. We may not catch them before they make port."

Rusty groused, "Goddamnit! What is with this asshole and his luck?" Moments later, John and Nigel appeared on the bridge, smiling. "What are you two grinning about?"

Nigel said, "We may have a solution. If we …"

Gunny cut him off, "I already told you; I don't trust the Pakis. The most I'm willing to do is reach out to the Israelis and ask their man on the docks to keep an eye on them."

"No. We have a better plan."

Rusty perked up. "I'm all ears."

Nigel continued, "We might leap frog ahead of them and be on shore when they get there."

Rusty asked, "How the hell do we do that? Did you find a wormhole or something?"

John said, "We use Gil. Nigel, Hans, and I figured if Gil and Donnie fly into Karachi and rent a chopper, they meet us at sea and ferry the team ashore. There's a lot of details to work out but it may be our only shot."

"Get on it."

* * *

The rest of the *Sailfish*'s journey was uneventful. While *Mother Goose* was in hot pursuit and sailing faster, the trawler's head start was simply too great. The *Sailfish* would make the port in Karachi two hours before the salvage tug. The trawler paralleled the shoreline before turning northeast at Masirah Island off Oman's east coast. From that point on, the *Sailfish* held a steady heading of 50° for several hours until the outer bands of the tropical storm in the Arabian Sea swept over the trawler and the commercial ship tracking services lost contact. Nigel and John projected where the *Sailfish* would be, assuming she maintained the same heading and speed. Once *Mother Goose* was out of the weather, they launched the drone and began searching for their quarry. In order to maximize the drone's fuel load, it was sent aloft unarmed. Their first concern was finding the trawler, not sinking it. They had other options for that.

As they approached the Pakistani coast and Karachi, Al-Maadi and Haq were unaware of the drone flying high above them. Once Steve confirmed they had reacquired the *Sailfish*, he flew the drone higher than before. They didn't need to identify the people on board, they just needed to track them. Nigel and John walked onto the bridge. Gunny was at the helm with Rusty at his side. "Chang, you ready to roll?"

"Yeah, just a second. I want to set the auto-track on the drone." Turning to Gunny and Rusty, he asked, "You guys ready to take over here?"

Rusty replied, "We got it. You get going."

"Okay. The drone should hold the contact but monitor it anyway. The closer we get to port, the more clutter there's going to be."

Gunny added, "We can't get too close. Karachi is Pakistan's main navy base. If they spot our bird, they'll assume it's an Indian drone and shoot it down. The drone is stealthy but I don't trust that. When we get close, I'm going to fly her lower and further back to stay out of their radar footprint as long as possible. We won't follow the *Sailfish* into port. The fish harbor is on the other side of the navy base. Once she gets past the Manora breakwater, you guys will be on your own."

As he finished, the "whomp, whomp, whomp" of a helicopter became audible. Nigel said, "Our ride is here. Alpha Eight, you ready to rock and roll?"

Steve Chang smiled, "I'm ready."

The Bell 412 helicopter landed on the fantail. "Right on time."

Gunny smiled, "You're damn right he's on time. Bravo Three was the best damn chopper pilot in the division."

Nigel, John, and Steve made their way to the helicopter. Sarah, Magne, Hans, Lon, and Alen were already on board waiting. They were all traveling light, dressed in civilian clothes and carrying only small arms. If they ran into serious trouble, they'd be outgunned. Steve was last and handed Alen a backpack as he scrambled onto the aircraft. Lon, sitting in the copilot's seat, clapped Gil on the back and the helicopter immediately lifted off vectoring north toward Pakistan.

Lon asked Gil, "I didn't get a chance to talk to you before you took off. Any problem getting the helo?"

"Not after the wire transfer went through. I told them I needed it to fly some VIP investors to checkout real estate on the outskirts of the city. All your alias IDs are in the black bag under your seat. Pass them out. You're a delegation of European industrial investors."

"Great." Lon retrieved the bag, found his packet and passed the rest to the team in the back. "What's our insertion point?"

"JPMC. That's the Jennah Postgraduate Medical Center. It's a large medical complex with a helipad about seven klicks east-northeast of the fish harbor. It's as close as we can safely get. I'm going to approach from the southeast over the Indus River delta and fly low over the city squawking like a medical transport flight. If they ask, I'll say some rich guy was in the delta and crashed his Range Rover."

"Nowhere closer?"

Gil grinned and added, "Sure. I considered the dockyard heliport but figured inserting eight armed people next to six navy destroyers was a bridge too far."

"Yeah, I get your point."

"Donny, er, Bravo Four will meet you there with ground transport. He rented a shuttle bus with dark windows in keeping with our VIP cover. He'll drive you to the fish harbor."

Lon said, "Haq, the captain of the boat, lives on Baba Island according to his registration. I'm worried they may stop there first. I wanted to keep me, Alen, and Hans with you so, if necessary, we insert nearby, find them and take them out. That's just a precaution, mind you. I assume they'll stop somewhere near the docks first. The boat needs to refuel and I don't see Al-Maadi hiding on an island with no ready escape path."

Gil shook his head. "No, that's a non-starter. Karachi is a mess of restricted airspace. Beside the naval base you have Masroor Air Base less than ten klicks north. They have F-16s, Mirages, and Chinese JF-17s, so we have to steer well clear of that place. They'd blow this flying truck out of the sky in a second. To the northeast you have Jinnah International Airport and their air traffic control zone. South and east of the navy base you have the Pak naval academy, their marine cadet college, and a navy heliport. If we try to get to Baba Island, we'd be dead before they figure out we aren't Indian spies."

"Shit. That fucks things up."

Gil said, "How about we plan on all of you getting off at the hospital. Gunny and Rusty are tracking these mopes, right?" Lon nodded. "If they put in at Baba Island, they aren't going anywhere, at least not right away. You'll have some time to figure a way to get there that doesn't involve surface-to-air missiles. Maybe something radical like, I don't know, a boat? There is a ferry service."

Lon said, "I just hate making this shit up on the fly."

"I hear ya, but until that trawler ties up somewhere, all your planning is theoretical anyway."

"That's true."

Gil smiled, "Don't worry. They're doing twenty knots and we're doing one forty. We'll be there first. What did Confederate General Nathan Bedford Forest say—firstest with the mostest?"

"Yeah, but his side lost the war."

Lon relayed the change of plan to the rest of the team in the back. There was some grousing but they all recognized the situation was fluid. John came up with a suggestion. "How about we send someone down to the mouth of the Baba Channel. It leads into the port. We put someone near the oil pier. They keep eyes on the *Sailfish* to see if it heads for Baba Island or the fish harbor."

Nigel chimed in. "That isn't a bad idea. But set up further in the port. There's a cruise terminal and a yacht club pier near the harbor master's office. That should provide cover for action for a westerner hanging around."

John asked, "What if they stop at Manora, that area across from the cargo terminal?"

Nigel shook his head. "Not likely. It's occupied by a ton of government facilities. Al-Maadi is still the most wanted man in the world. I don't see him risking it. No, he'll head for the fish harbor or Baba or Bhitt Islands, someplace he can disappear. Since the only way on or off the islands is by ferry, I'm leaning toward the fish harbor. From there he catches a boat or takes a taxi to anywhere in the city."

John nodded. "Makes sense. Either you or I should stake out the channel. These other mopes couldn't tell a trawler from a tanker." In unison, the rest of the team flipped them off.

Nigel grinned and said, "I agree. You or me?"

"Me. It was my idea. I'll grab a taxi at the hospital."

Hans asked, "What about exfil afterward?"

John shrugged, "We'll figure that out when the time comes."

* * *

The helicopter flew to the town of Gharo some fifty kilometers east of the hospital before turning west. As they neared Karachi, air traffic control contacted them. "Unidentified aircraft, what is your purpose and identification."

Gil responded, "This is helo AP-47483 requesting clearance to JPMC with an accident victim."

There was a long pause. "AP-47483, I have nothing in the system. Your clearance is not approved. You are a leased commercial aircraft, not a medevac aircraft."

Gil groused to Lon, "Fuckers looked up my tail number." He keyed his mic and said, "Karachi tower. You are correct, but it's an emergency. We're flying an automobile accident victim to the hospital. He's a VIP."

"I don't care who he is. You're not a medevac flight and don't have clearance," the controller responded tersely.

"Well, someone is going to have to break the bad news to Mayor Akhtar since it's his brother we're carrying. He flipped his Range Rover while visiting a power plant." There was another long pause. "Karachi tower? You copy?"

"Clearance granted."

"Roger. Thank you, Karachi tower."

Lon said, "That was close."

Gil grinned. "Hey, I always do my homework." They continued on across the city. Lon shook his head. "Jesus, I don't look forward to operating in this environment. It's a tactical nightmare. There are fifteen million people, half of whom would kill us as soon as look at us. It is surrounded by Pak military bases. Despite the British, the road system is shit, no offense, Nigel."

Nigel shrugged, "None taken. I'm a Scot."

Peering down on the city, Lon sighed. "This place is the world's biggest maze."

Magne took on a lofty tone and said, "Behold the labyrinth of King Minos. Designed by Daedalus to contain the mighty Minotaur. But alas, instead of an empty maze, we have a city of millions and instead of a beast—half man, half bull—we have a terrorist mastermind. Oh, that the Greek warrior Theseus had the easier task."

John glared at Magne with a mix of envy and distain. "Where do you come up with this shit?"

"As I have said, I'm not just the most handsome and the mightiest warrior among us, I am also the most learned. I am a renaissance man."

Nigel snorted, "You're also full of shit. Translate that into Greek, ya Nordic poof." The rest of the team howled with laughter.

Magne just smiled. "You all wear your jealousy with such style."

"Well, we'll all be dropping into the labyrinth in a few minutes so keep your eyes peeled for monsters."

When they neared the hospital, Gil circled the complex before gently landing on the large red H painted on the helipad across the street from the main building. About thirty meters away, a young man wearing a suit and aviator sunglasses was kneeling down behind the van. It was Donny, Bravo Four. The team piled out and walked toward him. Gil turned to Lon and said, "Donny will take it from here. I'm going to top off our fuel. I'll only be a few minutes away. Call me on my cell if you need me."

"Roger that," Lon said, as he shut the cockpit door. As soon as he cleared the aircraft, it lifted off and flew north.

Lon trotted over to join the rest of the group. Donny said, "I have transport. That white mini bus over there."

"What were you doing behind the van?"

Donny held up a can of spray paint. "New toy from the labs of Praetorian Security Services. This applies a clear lacquer impregnated with finely ground mica crystals. It acts sort of like a stealth coating but instead of reflecting radar waves, it reflects light. Keeps cameras from getting a usable image."

"Cameras like those on license plate readers?"

Donny smiled, "Exactly."

"Let's hope it works. Oh, we need to drop Alpha Two near a taxi stand on our way out."

"No problem."

John jumped out of the van near the hospital's main entrance and flagged a taxi. The rest of the team drove west toward the fish harbor. Karachi's traffic was terrible, but they were at least an hour ahead of the *Sailfish*. John Kernan's cab driver was efficient and aggressive. He dropped John off at the Karachi Yacht Club pier a good twenty minutes before the rest of the team was even close. He used his encrypted satellite phone to contact *Mother Goose*.

"Bravo Two, its Alpha Two. We had to make some changes due to a shitload of restricted airspace near the fish harbor. I'm down by the Karachi Yacht Club pier so I'll have eyes on the target when it enters Baba Channel. Copy?"

Gunny pulled up a large map of Karachi. "Okay, copy. I see your pier. Are you going to cover the channel from there?"

"Yeah, Oil Pier Three is currently unoccupied. I also picked up a pair of cheap binoculars on the way over. What's the status of our target?"

Gunny checked the drone feed and replied, "Uh, he's getting pretty close. Fifteen, maybe twenty minutes out."

"Roger. Do they still have all those blue barrels on the aft deck?"

"Yeah. They're still there. Should make it easy to spot."

John peered up as a Pakistani navy helicopter flew over him on its way to the navy base. "Bravo Two, you may want to be careful with that drone.

There's a lot of military air activity around here. If they see that thing, they'll splash it. I'm not so much worried about the drone but I don't want them out searching for its operators."

"Copy that. We'll stay on the target until he commits to the Baba Channel. He may still go to Korangi Creek instead."

"Okay. Copy that. Tell me when he commits."

"Roger."

John waited patiently. He scanned the waterway with his binoculars for the *Sailfish*. After about ten minutes, his phone chirped. It was a text from Gunny. "Committed to B. Coming your way." *Showtime!* John focused on the channel. Large ships unloading at the oil piers obstructed his view of the harbor's mouth some two and a half kilometers south of him, but he saw about a kilometer by squatting and peeking under the thick bundle of pipes that connected the oil pier to the tank farms on shore. Another five or six minutes and there it was. A lone trawler motoring up the channel, only this one had no nets or tackle visible. As it got closer, he made out the blue drums tied to its aft deck. *Bingo.* He called Lon and reported. "Alpha One, this is Alpha Two. Target is passing my location." He pressed the binoculars to his face and studied the boat as it passed. There were four men clearly visible. All were dirty and haggard with long beards. Despite this, he easily recognized Al-Maadi and Haq. "Two tangos confirmed. Repeat, I have visual confirmation on our two tangos. Copy?"

Lon said, "Alpha One copies. Maintain visual contact and tell us what they do at the point."

"Copy." The *Sailfish* motored up the channel. Haq guided her past Bhitt Island on his left. This was expected since Haq lived on Baba Island which was another half kilometer up the channel. The trawler continued past the opening to China Creek on his right which led to the container ship docks. Just beyond was a finger of land pointing south into the channel. It was lined on both sides by about two dozen Pakistani Navy warships. This was the country's primary navy base and beyond it was the fish port. John had to be more discreet now. A big, burly Western man with binoculars peering intently at a military facility was all but guaranteed to draw unwanted attention. He kept his eye on the *Sailfish* until it rounded the point heading north. In case anyone was paying attention, he turned his focus back to the tankers to the south. "Target has turned north past the navy base. He's heading your way."

"Copy that. Get up here."

"I'll flag a taxi and head your way." John walked off the pier into the deserted yacht club parking lot. *Shit.* He turned left on Asim Road toward the harbor master's office. There was surprisingly little traffic and certainly no taxis to be had. He was starting to get worried. As he walked in front of the cruise line office, a box truck pulled up and stopped. The driver with a clipboard in his hand, got out and walked into the building. He left the engine running. As soon as the man went inside, John jumped in the truck, made a U-turn and headed north. He called Lon and asked, "Uh, where are you guys? I'm on my way."

"That was quick. We're at the Baywest Container Terminal."

"Text me the address. I'll be there in a few."

"Copy. Sending now."

As John guided his stolen truck across the Native Jetty Bridge, Nigel and Alen walked two blocks south to an eight-story hotel. They took the elevator to the eighth floor and walked to the stairwell on the west side of the building. The door to the roof was locked but one kick from Alen's massive right foot opened it. From their new vantage point, they observed every boat approaching the fish harbor. Keying his encrypted communication unit, Nigel said, "Alpha Three and Alpha Seven in position."

Lon replied, "Copy. Advise when you see it."

The minutes ground on. They were beginning to fear they'd lost them when Alen tapped Nigel on the shoulder and pointed. "There. I see the barrels."

Nigel peered intently down the channel. "You've better eyes than me, mate." Then it appeared—the white fishing trawler with no nets, no gear, and blue barrels on its aft deck. "That's her. Let's move." As the two men flew down the stairs, Nigel called it in between breaths, "Target heading north up the channel toward the fish harbor. We're moving to your location."

"Copy Alpha Three."

Now the only question was which side of the fish harbor? John parked the stolen truck on the street behind the group's van and walked casually toward his comrades. When he ambled up, Magne said, "Nice taxi."

Hans quipped, "Did you tip your driver to wait for you?"

"Hey, there were no damn taxis. I had to improvise. Besides, I'm here, aren't I?"

Sarah said, "Nice ride!" Steve Chang just shook his head.

Lon reported, "Okay, they're headed this way, up the channel. Nigel and Alen are on their way back." Seeing the truck, he asked, "A box truck? Really?"

John said, "I wanted to blend into my environment."

"Well, blend your ass over to the water and tell us where they're headed."

John left the group and walked west to the piers. He stepped behind a pile of empty crates as the *Sailfish* motored slowly among the confused jumble of boats. When the trawler finally committed, John spit, "Goddamnit." He keyed his mic and said, "They're pulling up to the first jetty on the west side. Repeat *west* side." The Praetorians were on the east side.

Lon grumbled, "Fucking figures. Okay, saddle up. We're moving."

John asked, "You want me to drive the truck?"

"Isn't it stolen?"

"I doubt it has even been reported yet. I'll tear off the license plate. Half these trucks don't have them anyway."

Lon pointed to the truck. Donny was spraying his magic paint on its license plates. "That won't be necessary." John was confused. "I'll explain later. Take the truck. We can ditch it where we end up just as easily as over here."

* * *

Zihad Haq expertly guided his trawler through the jumble of fishing boats. To the uninitiated, it was a manifestation of pure chaos, but Haq had been doing it for years. He steered clear of the large concrete pad near the mouth of the fish harbor where the other trawlers were unloading their catches. He squeezed past four long piers jutting eastward into the cramped harbor and eased up to the fifth. His deck hand, Hamid, slung bumpers over the side of the trawler as it bulled its way to the dock between other boats. Hamid jumped from the bow with a rope and lashed the trawler to the dock. They had arrived.

Al-Maadi was eager to get off his floating prison. While he had gotten somewhat used to life at sea, he longed to have dry land under his feet. As Haq powered down the engines, Al-Maadi said, "I'm getting off. I need to get back to the safe house. I need to start the next phase. Do you need me here?"

Haq had to suppress a laugh. As a sailor, Al-Maadi was just slightly above useless. "No. We'll be fine. You and your man should go. The other captains are familiar with me and Hamid, but you and Mohammad may stand out. You're obviously not sailors. No offense, Abu Almawt."

Al-Maadi chuckled, "None taken. I recognize my limitations. We'll leave immediately."

Mohammad walked up with the two duffle bags they had started the trip with. He also had a cellphone in his hand. "Abu Almawt, it's one of our people. He is at the Al Sadat hotel with a car. He'll come get us."

"The hotel, is it far?"

"Less than a kilometer."

"Tell him we'll meet him there. I need to walk on something that isn't moving."

Mohammad smiled, "Yes, sir." He relayed the message to their driver before helping Al-Maadi off the boat. Al-Maadi walked to the end of the pier and started to turn north to walk along Fish Harbor Road when Mohammad stopped him. "No, sir. We'll take the path behind the beached boats. You'll be less visible. We can't be too careful."

Al-Maadi motioned for Mohammad to take the lead. "You're right. Thank you."

* * *

Across the harbor, John Kernan was observing through his binoculars. "Okay, two men got off the boat and are walking west along the pier. One of them is definitely Al-Maadi." He paused. "Okay, at the end of the pier, they started to turn north but then continued west into that mess of beached boats. They're continuing west…wait. Now turning north through the boatyard. Out of my visual."

Lon checked the mapping software on his tablet. "That dirt road continues north before turning back east. Any chance he gets on another boat over there, Alpha Two?"

"Doubt it. They're all wrecks."

"Copy. We have to assume he's moving into the city and that means heading east eventually. Get back here, ASAP."

"On my way, Alpha One."

Most of the Praetorians had loaded into the van with John and Nigel following in the stolen truck. Donny steered the van north past the Marine

Fisheries Department and promptly found himself stuck behind a couple of semis stopped in the street to unload cargo. Donny honked but the drivers and forklift operators ignored him. He yelled out of his window, "Get out of the way!"

Lon tried to remain calm. "Let me see if I can get them to move." Lon hopped out of the van and approached the man he assessed to be in charge. There was a heated discussion, but in the end, the trucks stayed put. Lon stormed back. "If it wouldn't draw attention, I'd have shot the son of a bitch. He won't move until he's unloaded." Traffic was beginning to build up behind them. He keyed his mic. "Alpha Two and Three, we're stuck here. Can you back up, parallel us, and take point?"

John replied, "Yeah, we'll get to an east parallel. Give us a minute." John and Nigel were boxed in too but only by a small pickup truck.

Nigel jumped out and approached the vehicle to find the driver gone and the pickup locked. He ran back and said, "The driver abandoned his wee truck and it's locked."

John grinned and said, "Well, that's his problem, not mine." He put the box truck in reverse, gunned the engine and slammed it into the little truck. The pickup's tires scuffed on the ground as the box truck muscled it off the street pushing it into the car parked next to it. One more push and they were free. John cut the wheels to his left backing up on the perpendicular road behind them. He then drove forward to turn left onto the first street east of the stranded van. As he did, a Pakistani man chased them, screaming for them to stop. "Oops. Must be the driver of that pickup."

Nigel laughed, "Car theft, hit and run, criminal mischief. You're building quite the resumé."

John drove the truck north but was limited by traffic. He and Nigel kept their focus to the left where they expected Al-Maadi and his companion would have to emerge. Nigel asked, "What were they wearing?"

"Dirty white thobes and red keffiyehs."

"Oh, that'll narrow it down. According to the map, all those roads back there come out on Fish Harbor Road. If we set up on the southern end, they'll have to pop out in front of us somewhere."

John said, "Just tell me where to go."

"We need to get to the northeast corner of the boat basin. Turn left up here and then a right parallel to the water."

John guided the truck through the confused traffic surrounding the cramped harbor and managed to squeeze into a spot facing north opposite the boat basin. Nigel focused his attention ahead of them while John occasionally used his side mirrors in case Al-Maadi—or the police—slipped in behind them. Nigel keyed his mic. "Alpha One, what's your status? We're at the northeast corner of the boat basin facing north. If they leave the area on foot, this is the only way."

Lon replied, "We're still stuck three blocks behind you. We may have movement soon. The truck blocking us is almost empty."

Just then, something caught John's eye. He slapped Nigel's shoulder and pointed ahead. "There! Three streets up on the left. Those two guys walking north. That's them!"

Nigel said, "Alpha One. We have visual on the two tangos who left the boat. They're moving north toward that dumpy hotel, the Al Sadat. We're moving to intercept."

"Roger Alpha Three. We copy. If you get a shot, take it. Don't wait on us."

Nigel replied, "Roger that," and then added, "Sorry Alpha Six, I know you wanted to do this guy personally."

Sarah replied, "That's okay. Just take him out."

Nigel and John placed their suppressed Sigs in their laps. John eased the truck into traffic and moved slowly north. Al-Maadi and Mohammad crossed the street about a block ahead of them and were now walking north on the east side of the street. John pointed to them and said, "On your right. They're yours, Nigel."

Nigel rolled down his window and leaned halfway out. "Ready, mate. Let's finish this." Just as he said this, the two men got in a red SUV parked on the street. "Shit!"

John keyed his mic. "Tangos just got in a waiting vehicle. Repeat, tangos are mobile. It's a…red Toyota Hilux. They've just turned right, east, at the hotel. Now tuning left, north, onto…wait, just turned east again. Jesus, they're all over the fucking place. Okay, they're northbound on Boat Building Yard Road. Repeat northbound on Boat Building Yard Road!"

Nigel groused, "Couldn't they name it something easy, like Elm Street or Abbey Lane?"

Lon replied, "Copy that. North on Boat Building. We're free now. Moving into the number two position behind you. Don't lose them."

John snapped back, "We'll try, but this thing isn't exactly a Corvette."

The Toyota drove north where the majority of the boatyards were located. Since the new passenger van stood out, Lon instructed Donny to hang back. John and Nigel's beat up old delivery truck definitely blended with the neighborhood. Lon hated being out of the action. "Alpha Two, this is Alpha One. What's their status?"

"Okay One, they just turned east toward Gullam Ali, but the two roads don't connect."

Lon was studying his mapping software. "They don't. If he doesn't move to eastbound on Mohammadi Colony Road, he'll be stuck in that huge freight yard to the north."

Nigel answered, "You're a damn fine prognosticator, One. The Tangos just turned east on Mohammadi Colony Road." There was a pause for several seconds. "Okay, they're northbound on Mauripur Road. Repeat, northbound on Mauripur."

John turned to Nigel and said, "There are easier ways to get to Mauripur. He's looking for a tail. Did he make us?"

Nigel shrugged. "We'll find out soon enough."

In the van, Donny sped to catch up. "Hold on everyone, this is going to get bumpy!" The truckers in the area must have been surprised by the fancy Mercedes van flying down the dirt road bouncing over the myriad of pot holes. When they reached Mauripur Road, he guided the van north and hit the accelerator. "Alpha Two, this is Bravo Four. We're in the two and will be with you in a minute."

John replied, "Good. I'm feeling rather crispy back here. There's more traffic on this road and we have a two-car screen, but I don't want to get burned. We're passing the football stadium. Tell me when you can take over the one position. The Hilux has a long whip antenna and an oversized spare tire on the roof rack. That will help distinguish it from the other vehicles on the road."

Donny replied, "Copy that. Moving up. Give me a minute."

The van quickly caught up and slipped in about a hundred meters behind the Toyota. As they did, John and Nigel dropped back behind a semi a few hundred meters back to keep out of sight. The red Toyota turned east onto Lyari Expressway and then north on Manghopir Road. Lon studied his map. "Where in the hell are these guys going?"

Donny interjected, "Right turn ahead."

"What's the road?"

"Uh, Altaf Ali Barelvi Road. Jesus, these guys need shorter street names."

Lon nodded. "No shit." He keyed his mic and said, "Alpha Two. We are east on Altaf Ali Barelvi Road. Repeat, east on Barelvi. After the turn, move up and take over the one. You should be sufficiently cooled off."

"Alpha Two copies. East on Barelvi. Moving into the one." John pushed his truck to catch up. As soon as he did, the red Toyota turned left. "Left, north, on Nawab Saddique Ali Khan Road. That's a mouthful."

"Copy. North on Ali Khan." After a few minutes, they turned again. "Okay, northeast on Shah Suri."

"Copy, northeast on Shah Suri. We're going to run out of city before too long."

"Don't lose them. We'll tighten up, just in case."

A few minutes later, the red Toyota slowed and turned left on Shahjahan Avenue. A moment later, John broke in, "We have something. He is left, west, on a side street. No name. Just before the Kashmiri Market. This must be his end point. There's nowhere to go once he gets in there."

Lon replied, "Good work, One. Be ready for action. We're right behind you. Give him some room. We don't want to spook him."

The red Toyota took two quick turns and was briefly out of sight. John followed but after the second turn, he found only an empty street. "Oh fuck. Where did he go?" In front of them was a street several hundred meters long lined with two and three-story concrete houses. "Every house has a vehicle entrance. They must have pulled into a garage somewhere."

Nigel said, "Yeah, but where?"

John keyed his mic. "Houston, we have a problem. Target vehicle appears to have gone to ground but hell if I know where. He didn't keep going. We'd have seen him ahead of us. He's in one of these houses."

Lon replied, "Copy that. Give us a second." He hit the dash of the van. "Goddamnit! This fucking close and we lose him? Not again."

Steve was in the back and chimed in, "Hold on a second. I got the imagery for this area on my phone. Most of these houses have inner courtyards. If the Toyota is in there, it's visible from above."

Magne shot back, "Well, in case you haven't noticed, we're in a van, not a chopper."

Steve smiled. "The lord provides, or in this case, Steve provides."

Sarah grinned. "What the hell did you bring in your backpack, computer boy?"

"A drone."

* * *

A mere fifty meters from where John's stolen box truck was stopped, the red Toyota Hilux came to a stop in the courtyard of the safe house. Al-Maadi and his man Mohammad climbed out of the Toyota and stretched. Their driver, Aslam, grabbed their duffle bags and led them into the house. Khalid Al-Maadi was happy to be home. Well, not home. Not really, but the closest thing to it of late.

"Aslam, show Mohammad to one of the guest rooms. I'm going to take a shower. I fear I smell horrible." Khalid walked up to his third-floor bedroom, stripping off his foul-smelling clothes as he went. He turned the water on in the shower and stepped in before giving it a chance to warm up. He shivered at first but within a minute, it began to warm. He lathered his hair and entire body before using a coarse sponge to scrub himself from head to toe. He had weeks of grime, sweat, and stink to get rid of.

* * *

Out on the street, the Praetorians were trying to salvage their operation. It wasn't like they could go house-to-house kicking in doors. Well, they could, but not for very long before the police or military showed up. They'd have to be more subtle. John opened the hood of the van and turned on the flashers. To the casual observer, it was just another disabled vehicle.

The van stopped before turning onto the street where the red Toyota Hilux disappeared. Steve opened his backpack to retrieve a large, gray pouch made of thick plastic. Lon said, "If this doesn't work, we're going to have to set up in this neighborhood and hope to God he leaves before the neighbors dime us out to the cops."

"I know." Steve took a knife and carefully slit open the bag to reveal its contents. He slid out a large model airplane with the wings folded along its sides. He held it by the fuselage as he carefully snapped the wings into place. He then attached a small propeller to the thin black shaft protruding from the nose. He turned it over and removed a piece of plastic covering the camera aperture on the belly. Picking up the small controller, he said, "Okay, she should be ready."

This type of drone was new to Lon. "Is this electric or gas? It's pretty light to be battery powered, but I don't see an engine."

Steve explained, "It's kind of both. It is electrically powered but not by batteries."

"What does it use? Solar?"

Steve chuckled, "No. A fuel cell." Hans overheard the conversation and turned around to investigate. Soon the other Praetorians were listening as well. "Okay, quick explanation. This is a single-use, disposable, self-destructing optical drone. It is powered by a fuel cell and has an extremely long loiter time for a drone this size. It has a unique configuration, to say the least."

Hans asked, "Looks like a million other drones. What makes this one so special?"

"The drone is its own fuel. The fuselage of the drone is made of a unique, hydrocarbon-based polymer. When exposed to ultraviolet or UV rays, the material sublimates into a gas which then feeds a high energy density fuel cell powering the motor."

Sarah asked quizzically, "Sublimates? Like melts?"

Steven replied, "Yes. Sublimation is when a material goes from a solid directly to a gas. It's like dry ice, only instead of fog, this makes fuel. The fuselage is hollow and doubles as the fuel tank for the sublimating fuel vapor. It only does this when exposed to UV rays. That's why it's stored in that thick bag. It stops the UV from destroying it in storage."

Hans said, "Wow, that's pretty slick. But what keeps the outside part of the fuselage sublimating itself into oblivion?"

"The outside of the fuselage is treated with a very thin resin that inhibits the UV reaction and keeps it airtight. The disintegration still occurs, just at a much slower rate than on the inside."

Always the skeptic, Magne asked, "Okay, if the body of the drone deteriorates to provide the fuel, wouldn't it weaken it? What keeps it from breaking in two once it has used enough fuel?"

"That's the beauty of the design. As the fuselage sublimates and the fuel is consumed, it does weaken but it also becomes lighter so it doesn't need to be as strong. The UV inhibitor resin applied to the outside also provides strength. The drone is still able to fly, even when much of the fuselage is so sublimated that the aircraft is actually translucent. Once it finally does consume all its available fuel and crashes, what's left of the outside fuselage crumbles into dust. All that is left is a small electric motor, some simple actuators, a model airplane circuit board, and a cheap cellphone camera."

Lon checked his watch and interrupted, "Okay Mr. Science, the lesson is over. Let's get this bitch in the air."

* * *

Inside his safe house, Al-Maadi let the warm water pour over his body washing away the dirt, grit, and filth of the weeks at sea. While he appreciated the fresh sea air, especially compared to Karachi's smoggy miasma, he was happy to be back in civilization. He had survived with his cousin in the mountains of Pakistan, and later in Kabul, but he was a man of the city and enjoyed all the creature comforts civilization had to offer.

Stepping out of the shower his eyes fell on his old thobe and keffiyeh. He picked them up to place them in the hamper but recoiled at their rank odor. It was a mixture of sweat, body odor, diesel oil, and fish. *Is that what I smelled like?* He tossed them into the trash. *I need to remember to have Mohammad burn these.*

He put on some clean clothes—trousers, a shirt, a light jacket, and some casual shoes—before walking downstairs. Still drying his hair with a towel, Al-Maadi said, "Aslam, please tell me we have some fruit in the kitchen."

Aslam smiled. "Yes, sir. We have fresh fruit, bread, vegetables, and chicken. I was going to have my mother make us a curry for dinner." Tossing Al-Maadi an apple, he added, "It'll be a while before we eat. I'm going to check the street."

"Good." Al-Maadi took a bite of the apple before walking out onto the second-floor balcony overlooking the courtyard. The sun was high but it wasn't too warm. Despite being surrounded by buildings, there was a cool breeze blowing. Below him Mohammad was by the Hilux. He was removing the old license plates and replacing them with new ones. He then walked over and double-checked the heavy vehicle door leading to the street to ensure it was secured. *Ah Mohammad. Always cautious, or even a little paranoid.* While he had a view of the city from his third-floor office, no other buildings were visible from the second-floor; but then he wasn't visible to them either. He was just enjoying being on *terra firma* when Aslam hurried back into the room and onto the balcony with Al-Maadi.

"We may have a problem."

From below, Mohammad heard this and immediately ran into the house. "I'll be right there, Abu Almawt." Within seconds, he had sprinted up the stairs and joined the other two men. "What is it?"

Aslam replied, "It's probably nothing, but there is a box truck parked on the street. It appears to be a normal delivery vehicle, but the driver isn't there."

"Is it blocking the street?" Aslam nodded. Mohammad grabbed him by the arm and demanded, "Show me!"

Aslam led Mohammad to a curtained window overlooking the street. Pointing down, he said, "There. Maybe it's broken down."

Mohammad peered down at the truck. "It looks like the truck that was behind us at the docks."

Aslam shrugged. "It looks like every truck down at the docks."

"But it isn't. I recognize it. I recognize that piece of paper caught in the grill."

Aslam studied the truck intently. He wasn't sure whether to believe Mohammad or call bullshit. "I hadn't noticed that. You have good eyes. But this is Karachi, most trucks have trash in their grills. That doesn't mean anything."

"That's why you are a driver and I am Abu Almawt's chief of security," Mohammad said condescendingly. "The other men I asked for, where are they?"

"There are six. Downstairs and in the cellar."

"Get them all. I need them armed."

Aslam replied, "Yes, sir. Right away, sir."

Mohammad walked quickly back to Al-Maadi. The expression on his face said it all. Al-Maadi now assessed his dismissal of Mohammad's caution was both ill-conceived and ominously prophetic. "I take it we are leaving?"

"Yes. The truck on the street is the same one I saw down by the docks."

"Are you sure?"

"Yes, I am. We need to go."

"How? They're right outside our door!"

"I don't believe they're certain where we are. We'll leave through the rear of the compound."

"What makes you sure they don't know?"

"They're not shooting at us," Mohammad replied coldly.

"I need to go to my office. There are some papers I must have."

Mohammad shook his head. "No. There is no time. If I'm wrong, we come back for them. If I'm right, well…remember what happened to your cousin."

A wave of anxiety washed over Al-Maadi. "Yes, you're right. Lead the way."

* * *

Back in the van, Steve Chang fired up the drone. The little airplane was rather loud inside the vehicle but once he tossed it into the air and it took off, it became almost impossible to detect. "The camera feed will show up on my iPad. Someone needs to monitor it while I get this thing high enough not to fly into a wall or something."

Sarah grabbed the tablet. "I got it." She tapped on the app and the wobbly image from the drone appeared on the screen. "Okay, it's transmitting, but the image is a little shaky."

Without taking his eyes off the drone flying over the street, Steve replied, "In the lower right-hand corner there should be a little 'S' icon. Hit it. It's the image stabilizer."

Sarah tapped on the icon and the picture became much clearer. "That did it."

Steve flew the little drone over an adjacent street until it had gained enough altitude to clear all the houses. He then brought it back and aimed it north over the east side of the street on which their target was hiding. "Okay, starting a run over the east side. Keep your eyes peeled for the red Hilux." The drone flew slowly over the houses while peering down into the enclosed courtyards below.

Magne asked, "What if they covered the Toyota with a tarp or parked it in a garage?"

Lon replied, "Then we're pretty much screwed. We'll have to set up at either end of this street and hope they leave before the cops come and run us off. Our covers won't hold up. This isn't exactly an industrial area."

After a few minutes, the drone reached the end of the street. Steve said, "That's all there is on this side. I'm going to flip a U-turn and come back over the other side." He guided the little drone into a wide arcing turn and lined it up over the houses on the west side of the street. They studied every courtyard below. Once they spotted a red car and circled back, only to discover it was a Kia sedan. As the drone approached the end of the street above them, Steve had almost lost hope until he caught a flash of red. "Hey. Wait a sec. What was that?"

Lon replied, "Yeah, I saw something too. It was partially obscured by a tree or something. Swing back around."

Steve turned the drone around and once over the house, set it to orbit. "Okay, is that your vehicle?"

"Can ya zoom in?"

"Yes, but just a bit more. I'll bring it down. They won't hear it." The drone bled altitude until it was only about fifteen feet above the tallest house. "That's as good as we get with that damn tree in the way."

John tapped the screen. "Doesn't matter now. That's the fucking car. Spare tire on top and that whip antenna. That's our tango's ride."

Lon peered at the screen and then up at the drone. "Second house on the left. It's three stories in the back, two on the street side. Probably a basement as well. All the windows except those on the front all look down on the courtyard. Ground floor windows facing the street have bars. Balconies above the courtyard on the second and third floors, west side only. Am I missing anything?"

Steve added, "That's what I'm seeing." He studied the screen more intently. "Uh, oh. What's that?"

Everyone gathered around the little tablet trying to see. Alen said, "Men, at least four...with weapons. AKs by the look of it."

Steve quipped, "Well, I guess it's the right house. Now, what do we do about it?"

Alen said, "They can't make out the van from there, but they can see the truck. I'd suggest we drive the van around the block and block off the other end of the street. That way if they try to make a run for it in the Toyota, they're hemmed in."

Lon nodded. "Good idea." He scrutinized the screen as the drone circled. "Does anyone see a back door to this place?"

Magne shook his head. "Doesn't appear to be one. It's built right next to the house behind it. No alley. That means they have to exit through the front, either the front door or the vehicle entrance since the windows on either side of the front door have bars."

Lon rubbed his chin. "That also means we only have those ingress points. Easier for them to protect."

Hans pointed to the tablet. "So far, at least, they have no guards on the roof. We come in from the top. There's a drain pipe on the house on the corner that leads to the roof. From there a couple guys jump over and enter the target residence through that third-floor balcony."

Lon said, "You'll be sitting ducks if they see you."

Hans grinned. "That's why I was going to suggest you do it."

Sarah chimed in. "Then we'll need a diversion, but not one that will alert them right away."

Magne said, "What are you going to do? Knock on the door?"

Sarah shrugged. "Why not?"

"Because they'll shoot you?"

"Not if I shoot them first."

Magne smiled, "Fair enough."

Lon interjected. "Who's going to knock on the door?"

An exasperated Sarah huffed. "Me, of course. I'm the only one here who'll pass as a local."

Alen volunteered. "I'll do it."

Lon replied, "No. When the guy finds a Serbian giant outside his door, he might suspect you're not from the neighborhood."

Sarah snapped, "Quit trying to protect me, damn it! I can kick all of your sorry asses. I'll do it."

Lon smiled, "It's just that if you get killed, we have to find another girl to replace you and women like you don't exactly grow on trees."

Sarah was accustomed to the guys being overprotective. She found it irritating but also a little endearing. "Don't worry. I have a sister. And she's the pretty one."

Alen choked and mumbled to Magne, "The pretty one?"

Lon sighed. It was a losing battle arguing with Sarah. She was both stubborn and, in this case, right. "Okay, that's our plan. Sarah, Hans, and Alen go in the van with Donny. Approach from the north walking along the west side of the street so they don't see you. Steve, John, and I will go over the roof. Nigel and Magne will contain on the south and cover Sarah. Once she breaches, you follow. I hate to do this shit on the fly, but we don't have much of a choice. From the footage, they're better armed, so make every shot count. We good?" They all nodded.

* * *

Inside the house, Aslam directed his men. Despite his bluster, he had little actual fighting experience and now wished Mohammad had stayed to take charge. He glanced out the window onto the street. The box truck was still there with its emergency flashers on and its hood up. *Maybe it just broke down. Maybe Mohammad was overreacting. There haven't been any helicopters. If the police were going to raid the house, wouldn't there be helicopters?*

The six men he had in the house were all armed with AKs. He positioned one at the front door, three by the vehicle gate, and one each covering the two barred windows on the ground floor facing the street. There were no windows on any of the other sides and only the secret door accessing the basement of the house behind them. He locked and barricaded this after Al-Maadi and Mohammad fled. What he hadn't considered was the roof.

* * *

As Donny drove Sarah, Hans, and Alen around to the north end of the street, Lon, John, and Steve prepared to climb up to the roof. Lon and John stretched their backs and shook out their arms in preparation for the climb up the cast iron drain pipe on the side of the corner building. Lon double checked his weapon and said, "Okay. Let's do this."

Steve grabbed the pipe and scurried up the wall as John gaped in amazement. Within seconds, he was on the roof. Steve scanned the rooftops and called down softly, "It's all clear. Come on up."

John mumbled, "What is he? A goddamn monkey?"

Lon groused, "I could have done that too, when I was his age."

"You were never his age."

Lon grabbed the pipe and began scaling the wall—albeit at a much slower pace. John followed behind him. When they reached the top, Steve was kneeling down. "Okay, there's an access panel to the house below us, but I jammed it shut with my knife. I checked out the target house. The roof is slightly lower than this one, maybe half a meter. No one was up there. There is a roof access door on the south side, but it's locked. We're going to have to swing down to the balcony. Come on, follow me."

John was incredulous. "He did all that while we were climbing up? How slow are we?"

The three men scurried across the rooftop in a crouch to keep from being visible from the third-floor windows. The balcony was only on the backside of the building opposite the street and above the courtyard. It was their way in.

Steven and John stopped midway along the western edge of the house, dropped to their bellies, and crawled to the edge. In the courtyard below, they made out three armed men at the vehicle gate. Their attention was focused outside with two of the men peeping through the cracks between the gate and the walls. Lon stayed on the south side of the roof and crawled out to the edge where he snuck a peek at the third-floor balcony directly below his comrades. It was empty but there was a man on the second-floor balcony. It was Aslam. Lon keyed his mic and whispered, "This is Alpha One. We're in position. Third-floor balcony is clear. One tango on the second-floor balcony, but he is standing back from the edge. Alpha Two and Eight should be able to enter the third-floor balcony without being compromised. We have three additional tangos in the courtyard at the vehicle gate. No visual on the others."

Sarah replied, "This is Alpha Six. Copy. We're ready for the breech on your word."

Nigel said, "Alpha Three and Five ready."

Donny added, "This is Bravo Four. I'm monitoring the drone feed. Will advise any changes."

Lon replied, "Good to hear, Bravo Four. I guess it shouldn't be too hard to fly compared to an F-18. Alpha Six, you're on."

Sarah crossed the street to the east side. Nigel got on the radio and asked, "Alpha Six, what are you doing? They'll see you."

"I want them too. If they know I'm a woman before I knock, they'll be less concerned. To these guys, all women wear burkas and work in the kitchen. They won't see me as a threat."

Sarah walked about sixty meters before crossing back over the street. She paused in front of one of the windows and took a slip of paper from her purse. She wanted to be noticed. She glanced at the paper, then up at the address above the door, then back at the paper. To the casual observer, she was lost. She approached the front door and knocked.

Inside the house, there was confusion. They were expecting the police or paramilitaries, not a glamorous woman. One of the men walked out into the courtyard and yelled up to Aslam. "There is some woman at the front door. What should I do?" As Aslam spoke, there was more knocking from the door.

"I will be right there. Don't let her in." Aslam scurried down the stairs and across the courtyard. Once out of sight, Steve Chang grabbed the gutter along the roof eave, slipped over the side, and swung onto the balcony before landing cat-like on the concrete floor.

Lon said, "Alpha Eight is in. Alpha Two, your turn."

"On it." John slid over the side, grabbed the wrought iron railing, and climbed down after Steve.

Lon followed him. "This is Alpha One. Roof team is in."

At the front door, Aslam peered out the peep hole. He was shocked to encounter a beautiful woman standing there. He opened the door a crack and said, "What do you want?"

"I am looking for my cousin's house but I think I'm on the wrong street. Is this the Khan residence?"

"No. You have the wrong address."

She batted her eyelashes and smiled, "Could you look at this address and point me in the right direction?"

Normally, he would have sent her on her way, but he wanted to extend his interaction with this woman. "Sure, I guess." He leaned his AK against the wall, opened the door about a foot and reached for the scrap of paper.

Sarah handed it to him and said, "Thank you. You're too kind." As he took it, she raised her suppressed 9mm Sig and shot him through the forehead. The man next to him froze for a brief second which was all it took for her to shoot him too. As she walked into the house sweeping the area in front of her with her weapon, she said, "This is Alpha Six, two tangos down. Front door open."

Nigel and Hans swept in behind her. Nigel eased up to her and moved to the left while she moved to the right. To be sure, Hans put two more rounds into each of the two men Sarah had just shot before moving forward toward the courtyard. Magne entered the house while Alen moved up to cover the street and the vehicle gate. Alen was promptly met by an unaimed burst of AK fire from the barred window to the right of the front door that sent him diving for the wall. Magne asked, "Alpha Seven, are you okay?"

Alen shot through the window before replying. "Roger. I'm good."

The men in the rooms either side of the front door were initially surprised but quickly recovered. While the one on the right had shot at Alen, the other moved quickly toward the front door. Almost simultaneously, Magne and Nigel shot him as he entered the foyer. The man on the right, fleeing Alen's return fire, dove behind a sofa where Sarah found him. Two quick shots to the chest and a third to the head turned his lights out forever. This left the three men at the vehicle gate.

Hans started to move out onto the courtyard only to be met by a blast of AK-47 fire from his right. He dove behind the red Hilux as a barrage of small arms fire came from above. It was John and Lon. They were firing down on the terrorists from the third-floor balcony. They immediately downed the terrorist who fired at Hans while the other two ducked through a small door into the house. John said, "Damn it! I didn't see that door."

Lon keyed his mic and said, "Another tango down in the courtyard but the other two are inside the house. Repeat, the courtyard is clear but two tangos running free. Not certain how many more we're dealing with."

In the courtyard, Hans checked on the downed terrorist. The man was still alive. Hans said, "Sorry buddy. Can't have you on my six." He put two rounds into his brain pan.

Turning to John and Steve, Lon said, "We need to clear the rest of this floor, I'll take the south. John, you take the north. Steve, you cover the stairs so no one gets behind us."

Steve made his way to the stairs and crept silently to the second-floor kitchen. Men were scurrying below. The two remaining terrorists were in a panic. One of the men fired a wild AK burst behind him to hinder any pursuers. He didn't aim, he was just shooting. As he did, the second man sprinted past him and up the stairs directly toward Steve.

When the man reached the top of the stairs, he was surprised to find Steve standing in the kitchen. The surprise didn't last long as Steve dropped him with two rounds in the chest. The man immediately dropped his AK and fell to the floor gurgling. A large pool of blood began spreading across the floor at the top the stairs. Steve grabbed the man by his collar and dragged him a few feet away so as not to be visible from below.

The last terrorist came charging up the stairs. "Ahmed! Ahmed! Where are you?" When he reached the top, he slipped on the slick blood and fell awkwardly to the floor. He struggled to regain his footing on the slippery floor only to be hit in the head with a cast iron skillet. The man staggered forward and slammed into a wall. Before he gathered himself, Steve slipped in behind him and broke his neck. The Praetorians were unaware they'd killed all the men defending the house, so they cleared the structure room by room. There was no one else. Al-Maadi had gotten away—again.

On the third floor, Lon had discovered Al-Maadi's office. He gathered up every piece of paper, every thumb drive, and every piece of computer equipment he found and shoved them into pillow cases. In the basement, Magne discovered the secret door leading to the house behind them. He and Hans entered the house and, though the house was obviously lived in, their searched turned up no one. "Whoever lives here is probably at work and will be home soon. We need to get the hell out of here."

"Copy that." He got on the radio, "There was a backdoor connecting the house to the west. The house is empty. The target is gone."

Lon replied, "Copy that, Alpha Four. Take quick snaps of the dead tangos and get back here. We need to blow this place before the police show up."

"Copy, on our way."

Donny got on the radio. "This is Bravo Four. We have police approaching from the south. Everyone needs to get their ass to the van, now! We need to blow this popsicle stand."

Lon said, "You heard him folks. Move!"

Magne interjected, "I suggest we exit through the basement door to the house behind us just like Al-Maaid did. That way we're not on the street where all the shooting just happened."

Lon immediately concurred. "He's got a point. Everyone to the basement. Bravo Four, pull up to the next block."

"Bravo Four copies."

The team gathered up as much intel as possible and ran through the secret basement door to the residence behind Al-Maadi's safe house. Lon checked the street before turning right and walking toward the van. The rest of the team followed. As Sarah was walking, a door to one of the houses opened and a middle-aged woman stuck her head out. Before the woman spoke, Sarah asked, "Did you hear that noise? What was it?"

The woman shrugged and replied in heavily accented English, "I was going to ask you!"

Sarah replied, "Well, whatever it was, it wasn't good. I already called the police, but we're getting out of here. If I were you, I'd go back inside, lock the door, and stay away from the windows."

They piled into the van and Donny pulled away moments before the first police car arrived on the scene from the south. It could go no further as it was stuck behind the abandoned box truck. John crowed, "I told you that piece of junk would come in handy."

Steve asked, "Where's the drone controller?" Donny handed it back to him. Steve circled the drone above the house. "The police are setting up a perimeter, blocking both ends of the street."

Lon added, "They're probably waiting for reinforcements before entering the house. They don't know what they have yet. If they're focused on the house, they're not looking for us—at least not yet."

Steve said, "None coming after us." They turned south on Manghopir Road and soon encountered two wailing police cars approaching from the opposite direction. There was a long minute of tension until the two police cars screamed past them, turned into the neighborhood and sped toward the house.

"Steve, does that thing archive footage?"

"Yeah, why?"

"It was orbiting the whole time on autopilot. Check if it picked up any vehicles leaving the house we left through. That's how Al-Maadi got away."

"On it, Lon." Steve dug through the footage, speeding it up and then slowing it down. After a few minutes, he said, "I got it. Right before we hit the place, a blue Mercedes sedan left the residence directly behind our target house. It drove north before turning right and out of view."

Donny yelled from the front, "A blue Mercedes? I saw that car! The fucker drove right past me when Sarah, Hans, and Alen were getting out. Motherfucker!"

Lon shook his head. "That's our modus operandi with this guy. I swear to God, the son of a bitch is just fuckin' with us."

Sarah snorted, "He can fuck with us all he wants, but we only have to catch him once."

John replied with a grin, "True dat."

CHAPTER SIX
MISSION FAILURE

After the assault on Al-Maadi's safe house, the team returned to the Karachi hospital where Gil picked them up in the helicopter and flew them back to *Mother Goose*. While Gil and Donny returned the van and helicopter, the Praetorians set sail for Muscat, Oman. As soon as the ship docked in Muscat, the team disembarked and were replaced by a crew from Praetorian Security Services who'd refuel *Mother Goose* and sail her back to Cyprus. The team headed straight for the airport where Gil and Donny were waiting with the Bombardier 8000 to fly them immediately back to Larnaca. There would be no down time. The team had too much work to do.

The flight back was quiet. The Praetorians were mentally and physically exhausted. They didn't take failure well and their latest mission, by any objective measure, had been a failure. Rusty's people were down and he tried to cheer them up. "Come on gang, chins up. We had some setbacks, but it wasn't all bad."

Lon said, "The Novichok is still in the hands of terrorists and the mastermind of the plot remains on the loose. To make matters worse, we have no clue what the plot actually entails but knowing Al-Maadi, it will be deadly and spectacular."

"Okay, I'll grant you that. It didn't go the way we wanted but it wasn't a total waste. Let's look at what we accomplished, starting with information gleaned from the Kotov raid. We discovered our old friend, Al-Maadi purchased the Novichok. We figured out how it was transported and where it was going. Thanks to Steve, we identified and tracked the *Amuratu*, a terrorist support ship. Thanks to Nigel's ingenuity with that octopus thing, we stopped it on the high seas where John and Lon led a boarding party that seized the ship and eliminated the crew. Sarah then obtained vital intel from the captain before we scuttled the ship without anyone anywhere being any the wiser. We identified the trawler and followed it to Yemen. Then we tracked Al-Maadi to his safe house in Karachi, eliminated his men, cleaned out his office, and blew town without anyone catching a bullet."

Gunny chimed in. "Hell, even Rusty and I got into the action by fighting three boatloads of pirates! I haven't had that much fun in years."

Lon groused, "Yeah, but we didn't get Al-Maadi and we didn't recover the Novichok."

Gunny nodded. "True, but we weren't aware Al-Maadi was even involved. As for the guys with the Novichok, I'm sure we'll ID them when we get back. Now, everyone get some rest and be ready to hit the ground running. We have to do a forensic deep dive on the guys in Yemen and the take from Al-Maadi's office."

* * *

Khalid Al-Maadi and his bodyguard, Mohammad, drove northeast on the M-9 toward Hyderabad, Pakistan. After two hours, they reached the city and stopped to stretch their legs. Per Mohammad's security protocols, they hadn't turned on their cellphones. As Mohammad topped the Mercedes off with fuel, Al-Maadi used a payphone to call Aslam to ask what happened with the strangers outside the safe house. There was no answer at either the home or Aslam's cellphone. He returned to the car to inform Mohammad. "I used that pay phone to call Aslam. No answer at either the house or on his cell."

Mohammad pondered this for a brief second. "The house I understand. If it was the police and they had to abandon it...but his cell? That doesn't make sense." Mohammad opened the trunk of the car and retrieved a burner phone from his bag. As it powered up, he opened a small notebook of phone numbers. He found the one he wanted and dialed. A middle-aged woman answered. "Hello, Mrs. Khara?"

"Yes." She asked warily, "Who is this?"

"I'm a friend of your son. I'm one of the men he wanted you to cook dinner for tonight."

There was recognition in her voice. "Ah, yes. He called me about it this morning. Are you one of the...travelers?" She was familiar enough with her son's activities not to ask for specifics.

"Yes, I am. I was trying to reach Aslam, but he isn't answering his cellphone. Do you know where he is?"

"No. He was supposed to call me over an hour ago. I haven't been able to reach him since this morning. Have you heard from him?"

"No, ma'am, I've been on the road. I'm sure he's fine. Probably out shopping for groceries and left his phone in his car. I'll try him again later."

The woman was now concerned. "It isn't like Aslam to not call me. Are you certain he is fine?"

Mohammad tried to reassure her. "Yes, I am sure of it. I'd wager he'll be calling you any minute. Sorry to bother you." Before she answered, he ended the call.

Al-Maadi asked, "Well?"

Mohammad was stone-faced. "Aslam and the others are dead."

Al-Maadi was stunned. "Did she tell you that?"

"No. She didn't have to. Aslam would have contacted me to provide an update."

"But your phone was off."

"There would've been a missed call. We have to assume he is dead and the safe house was breached. We need to keep moving. Fortunately, none of the men knew of your plan so we shouldn't be compromised."

Al-Maadi said, "The men wouldn't talk."

"Men always talk...eventually." Mohammad took a deep breath. "Sadly, casualties were expected. Where to now, Abu Almawt?"

Al-Maadi replied, "Multan. We need to meet a couple of our Shams Sawda' brothers there."

"That's half a day from here! We've been traveling for many hours already. We need sleep. I have family in Gambat. We'll be safe there for a few days while things cool off."

Al-Maadi shook his head. "No. We spend the night and continue tomorrow at first light."

Mohammad asked, "Abu Almawt, if you don't mind me asking, what's in Multan?"

"The road to Chashma."

Mohammad was genuinely surprised. "The nuclear power plant?"

"Yes, but that isn't why we're going there. Let's go. We have a long drive ahead of us."

* * *

Once back at the villa, the team dove into the new data; half on drone video from Yemen and half on what Lon gathered from Al-Maadi's office at the safe house. Steve loaded the drone footage onto his image processor and worked to clean up the video. There was nothing new from the footage of the *Sailfish*. He was able to confirm that it was crewed by the same four men and one was definitely Al-Maadi but that was it. There was no identifying information on the dhow that took the Novichok to shore and none of the sailors on board were in their databases. He next turned his attention to the truck that hauled it away.

Sarah entered the room carrying two cups of coffee. "Here. Thought you might need this. Find anything yet?"

"Thanks, and no. No new info on the trawler or the dhow. Looking at the truck now."

Sarah sat next to him and peered intently at the screen. "There's a logo or some writing on the door of the truck, but it's too dirty to read it. What about the tag?"

"I was just getting to that. It's an Omani license plate. I'm hacking their Ministry of Transportation." His fingers flew across the keyboard. "Okay, they have a 32-bit encryption. I've seen this before. Should be a snap." He navigated into a folder on the screen and selected a file. "Okay. Shouldn't be long."

Steve sipped his coffee, leaned back in his chair, and stretched. Sarah smiled and said, "Feels good to sleep in your own bed again, doesn't it?"

"You can say that again. At the risk of sounding like a whiner, the bunks on the ship reminded me of my Air Force rack, and not in a good way." As he spoke, the computer chimed. "And here we go. We're in."

Hans walked in the room and rolled up a chair. "Good morning, folks. What do we have?"

"Steve just hacked the Omani Ministry of Transportation. About to run the tag of that van."

Steve entered the license plate number and read the results. "Okay, the vehicle belongs to the Al-Rashid Environmental Engineering Company."

Hans added, "It might be a stolen van or just a stolen tag."

Sarah asked Steve, "Any way to dig into that logo on the side of the van? It's covered by dirt but…"

"Give me a sec. The image processor has some filters that should help." He isolated the image of the van and started flipping through the various filters. When he hit on the right one, the logo popped out as if from the ether. "Here we go. The van is definitely Al-Rashid."

Sarah scooted over to another computer and searched the company's name. What she found was alarming. "Uh, Houston, we have another problem." Hans and Steve read the screen over her shoulder as she navigated through the company's website. The deeper they dug, the more concerned they became. "We need to tell Mad Dog and Rusty about this, ASAP."

After they gave Gunny and Rusty a quick rundown, the bosses immediately called the Praetorians together to discuss it. As the last person sat down, Gunny said, "Okay, Rabin, show us what you and Chang found out."

"Steve hacked the Omani Ministry of Transportation website and learned that the van belongs to the Al-Rashid Environmental Engineering Company. We then researched the company and it's not good news." She tapped on her laptop and the Al-Rashid website popped up on the conference room screen. "They're based in Muscat but have offices all along the Persian Gulf in Dubai, Abu Dhabi, Doha, Manama, and Dharan. They install and maintain industrial HVAC systems in hospitals, hotels, large office buildings, you name it. From their website, their design engineers are a mix of Middle Eastern and Western folks from Egypt, Britain, Germany, Australia, the US, and Korea. The techs appear to be almost exclusively Middle Eastern or from South Asia—Pakistan, Malaysia, and the Philippines. I suspect they need Arabic and Urdu speakers to interface with their customer's technical staff."

Nigel asked, "On their home page, in the corner, was that a football pitch?"

Steve replied, "Yeah, we noticed that too. That's the new Rashid bin Saeed Al Maktoum Stadium in Dubai. The current sheikh built it to honor his late father. It reportedly cost $6 billion to build and seats over 110,000 people. It's to host the World Cup Regionals next year. It's supposed to be the largest air-conditioned space in the world. Al-Rashid Environmental didn't have the contract for the HVAC system, that went to a Korean company, but they were a major subcontractor. They have the contract to maintain and operate the system, and are the warranty contractor for the Korean prime so they have complete access to the stadium's HVAC system."

Gunny interjected, "As well as countless other potential targets. Who owns this outfit? Any history of extremist connections?"

Sarah replied, "No. The Al-Rashid family is quite wealthy with ties to both the Saudi and Omani royal families."

Lon quipped, "And the Bin Ladens were tight with the House of Saud. So what?"

Sarah continued. "The rumor is that they got the stadium contract due to their close ties to the Omani Crown Prince who happens to also be the Minister of Culture, Sports, and Youth. It's a bit of a family tradition. His father, the Sultan, was the first head of the Oman Football Association. The Crown Prince and the oldest Al-Rashid son, Issa, attended Oxford together."

Nigel said, "That doesn't mean they aren't still extremists."

Sarah said, "The Crown Prince also attended Sandhurst while Al-Rashid got his masters in mechanical engineering at City College of London. The Sultan's family are friends of the British Royal family and Al-Rashid is married to a British expat with familial ties to the British Royal Family."

Nigel fidgeted awkwardly. "Okay, not likely to be at the top of anyone's potential terrorist list. But why is an Al-Rashid van picking up chemical weapons in Yemen?"

"Al-Rashid Environmental is a big company. All you need are one or two bad apples. Al-Maadi may have easily sent someone to apply at the company just because they have access to a lot of potential targets. If a Shams Sawda terrorist gets a job at Dunkin' Donuts, it doesn't mean Dunkin' Donuts is a terrorist organization."

Rusty rubbed his chin. "Actually, this is a positive development. This all but assures us that Al-Rashid Environmental will be cooperative when the time comes. They have a lot at stake—like pretty much everything. Keep digging. We need to figure out where that van went."

Steve chimed in. "I have an idea with regard to that. We have a license plate on the van. I want to hack Al-Rashid's network to find an inventory of their vehicles. A company that big and that international must have one. If they have an electronic log of who has what vehicle, I might identify the driver, or at least who the vehicle is assigned to. I'm also going to determine if Oman has a traffic camera system with license plate readers. I'm pretty sure they do in Muscat but I don't know about the highway network."

Rusty said, "Get on it. Hans, you're our second-best Arabic speaker and computer guy so help Steve and Sarah. The rest of you, find Al-Maadi. I'd really like to wax this son of a bitch before he kills a hundred thousand people."

* * *

Khalid Al-Maadi was physically and emotionally exhausted when he arrived at Mohammad's cousin's house in Gambat. The family was told nothing about Al-Maadi. He was introduced simply as Mohammad's friend Khalid—but from Mohammad's deference, they assumed he was important. Mohammad had contacted them during the last stop for gas and a large Pakistani meal was waiting when they arrived. Khalid and Mohammad ate ravenously. They'd been at sea for weeks and since returning to Pakistan, had only eaten an apple at the safe house and gas station food. Khalid thanked the family for their hospitality and gave them 40,000 rupees—a little less than $200—for their trouble. Though they provided him with a comfortable bed, he slept fitfully. The stress of the day trumped his exhaustion. *What happened at the safe house? Was it the Pakistani police or someone else? Did the Israelis have the resources to pull off an operation that big? In Karachi? Probably not. The Israelis were good but they weren't supermen.* Finally, he drifted off to a fitful sleep.

Al-Maadi felt he'd only been asleep for a few minutes when Mohammad roused him from his imperfect slumber. "Abu Almawt, it's time to get up."

Rubbing the sleep from his eyes, he asked, "What time is it? I said wake me at six o'clock."

Handing him a cup of strong coffee, Mohammad replied, "It *is* six o'clock. Just like you ordered."

"Yes, of course. It's just like…"

"…you didn't sleep at all. I feel the same way." He chuckled, "When we've delivered a blow to the infidels and blasphemers, we will sleep for a month while Allah guards us as a reward for our devotion."

Khalid stretched and there were audible pops as he twisted his back. "You assume I'll live that long. I feel like I'm a hundred years old."

"You just need a decent night's sleep. Take your time. I'll be outside in the car."

Mohammad's statement meant the exact opposite of "take your time."

He was ready to go and only waiting on his boss. Khalid sipped his coffee. Since it was not too hot, he chugged it down. He quickly dressed and after using the toilet, headed down to the kitchen where his hostess was cooking breakfast for her family. She asked, "Let me fix you something for breakfast. Mohammad has already eaten."

"No, ma'am, but thank you. That won't be necessary. We have long travels ahead of us. I want to thank you and your husband for allowing us to stay the night."

"No thanks are needed. Hospitality is what Islam requires. Besides, Mohammad is my family, so his friends are my family as well."

Khalid nodded, "You are too kind."

"At least take some food for the trip." She laid out a thin towel and began piling on parathas, a traditional bread baked in ghee. "Some of these are plain and some are filled with potatoes, chili, and garlic. They'll sustain you." She whispered to him, almost conspiratorially, "The two on the bottom have honey in them in case you crave something sweet."

Khalid gave her a little bow, "Thank you. May Allah bless you and your family."

"He already has." She wrapped up the parathas and put them in a plastic bag along with a couple bottles of water. "Safe travels."

Khalid slid into the front passenger seat of the Mercedes and put his parcel in the back seat. Mohammad sniffed the air. "Parathas?"

"Yes. Plain, potato, and honey."

Mohammad beamed widely. "I love my cousin. She always takes care of me and my stomach."

The drive to Multan took about six hours. They followed Highway Five northeast as it paralleled the Rohri Canal, past the city of Khairpur and then the Sukkur Barrage, a low dam which diverts water from the Indus River into canals that irrigate nearly eight million acres of land. They reached Multan around noon. While Mohammad topped off their gas tank, Al-Maadi made two quick telephone calls. Within fifteen minutes, a man arrived at the gas station. He passed Al-Maadi a note. Few words were exchanged. After the man left, Al-Maadi and Mohammad took the MM Road due north; straight to Chashma.

Chashma Colony was a city on the left bank of the Indus River and named for the Chashma Barrage, another large dam feeding water to irrigation canals and generating electricity. But Al-Maadi wasn't interested in the dam, he was there for Chashma's other claim to fame—the Chashma Nuclear Complex.

The heart of the complex was the Chashma Nuclear Power Plant or CHASNUPP. It was a large commercial nuclear power plant with four 300 megawatt reactors running on low enriched uranium. Although started with technical assistance from the French, the units were ultimately based on a Chinese design and completed with Chinese cooperation. These reactors, however, were strictly monitored by the International Atomic Energy Agency (IAEA), so gaining any kind of access to them would be very difficult. Khalid's real interest lay a short distance south of the reactors— the plutonium separation plant.

* * *

Back in his office, Steve Chang made relatively quick work of the network security at Al-Rashid Environmental. Once inside the system with Sarah and Hans' help, he found the technician dispatching subnetwork. Using the license plate number from the van, he was able to zero in on the driver who had checked it out.

"Our lucky lottery winner appears to be...Aziz Uddin."

Hans wrote the name on a notepad. "I'll see what Human Resources has on him."

Steve navigated through the dispatching subnet to learn more. "Okay, our guy is based out of Salalah, the capital of Dhofar Governorate in the south. That makes sense since it's the closest city to Yemen. If he has commercial customers in Yemen, he knows how to get across the border. According to the mileage records, our guy drives a lot but then again, there isn't much down there and what *is* there is scattered all over the place. He's like a door-to-door salesman in West Texas."

Sarah asked, "Any identifying information on him?"

"Nope. Just his employee number and I already gave that to Hans." Steve clicked on a hotlink on the page and beamed broadly. "Well holy shit! I love technology!"

"What is it?"

"Al-Rashid has a commercial fleet monitoring system on all their company trucks, including Mr. Uddin's van."

"You can track him?"

"If I had supervisor access."

Sarah smirked. "You mean you don't?"

Steve scoffed at her comment. "No, but I will in about five minutes." Steve's fingers danced across the keyboard while Sarah stared at her watch. A few minutes later he said, "Presto! I'm a manager."

Sarah announced, "Four minutes forty-seven seconds. That's cutting it close, don't ya think?"

"Not really. I stopped for coffee."

"Okay, smart ass. What ya got?"

Steve typed in a couple of commands and hit enter. "Okay, Mr. Uddin, or at least his van, is currently approaching Haima from the southwest on Highway 31."

Gunny had just walked into the room from the kitchen. "What did you guys find?"

Sarah replied, "Steve hacked the company's network. Our target van is assigned to a Mr. Aziz Uddin. He's an HVAC technician based out of Salalah. Uddin is currently just outside Haima, about midway between the Yemeni border and Muscat."

Gunny added, "That's assuming this Uddin guy is actually driving the van. They may have stolen it, paid him to take it, or killed him and left his corpse in a ditch somewhere. If you're about to kill a hundred thousand people, capping an AC repairman isn't going to slow you down much."

Hans spoke up. "Okay, I'm into Al-Rashid's personnel info. Aziz Uddin is thirty-four years old. Born in Charsadda, Pakistan. Went to trade school in Lahore. Has worked for Al-Rashid for three and a half years. Employment record is spotless. He appears to be single. Mom is listed as next of kin."

Gunny processed the new information. "Okay. No attachments other than mommy. Where does mom live? Is it in his file?"

Hans studied his screen. "Okay, here it is. Mom lives in Peshawar."

"Pesh! That's the middle of Indian country." Hans's expression was one of confusion so Gunny clarified. "Feathers, not dots."

Hans nodded. "Oh, American Indians. I get it. Another 'Old West' American colloquialism."

"That town he was born in, where is it? It's familiar."

Hans pulled up mapping software and typed in "Charsadda." "That town is just north of Peshawar." He pointed to the town on the map. "Still Indian country?"

"You betcha. Now this doesn't prove Uddin is a bad guy but if you wanted to find one, it'd be a damn good place to start. Do we have a photo of this mope?"

Hans navigated back to Uddin's personnel page. "Yeah. I got a picture of his company badge." Hans clicked on the badge and enlarged it. A picture of a young Pakistani man with a thick mustache and a keffiyeh filled the screen. "Just another Paki dude."

Gunny turned to Steve and said, "Pull up the drone feed from when they were loading the barrels into the van."

"Yes, Gunny." Steve opened the drone footage and fast forwarded to when the dhow was unloading cargo near the beach. When he got to the men loading the drums into the van, he stopped. "Let me zoom in and clean up the image." Thirty seconds later, he had a clear shot of the two men. "The guy on the left is balding but the guy on the right looks like a match."

Hans turned his monitor toward Steve's, so the two images were side-by-side. Hans said, "Send me that photo. I'll run it through visual recognition." Steve took a screen shot, cropped it, and sent it to Hans' computer. Hans entered it and the photo from Uddin's badge into Wise Owl. A few seconds later there was an audible "ping." "They're a match."

Gunny rubbed his chin. "Okay, we know Uddin is one of our perps. But who's the other guy?" Hans shrugged. "Run baldie through Wise Owl."

Hans ran the second image but it came back negative. Hans said, "Maybe he works for Al-Rashid too? I'll download all the employee photos from their personnel database into a separate file, run baldie's photo against it and see if we get a hit."

"While you do that, I'll get the others. They need to hear this."

It only took Hans a few minutes to download all the photos from the Al-Rashid companies employee files. As he did, the rest of the Praetorians crammed into the room. Once the download was complete, Hans entered the photo and started the program. "Okay, let's see what we get."

After a few minutes, Lon carped, "Why is it taking so long?"

An annoyed Hans replied, "Al-Rashid is a big company and the drone photo quality isn't the best." Patting his computer like a loyal dog, Hans whispered, "Don't listen to him *mein Schatzi*." Seconds later, there was the familiar "ping." "We got a hit."

Gunny asked, "Who's the lucky winner this time?"

Hans read from the screen. "Odai Safi. Let me pull up his file." He hit a few keys and read from the screen while translating from Arabic to English. "Mr. Odai Safi. Age thirty-two. Born in Lahore, Pakistan. Attended the same trade school as Uddin. Has worked for Al-Rashid for less than a year. Works out of the Sharjah support facility."

Rusty asked, "What the hell is he doing in the middle of Bum Fuck, Yemen?"

Hans replied, "Good question. He's off the reservation, that's for sure."

Gunny smiled. "Nice American Indian reference, for a kraut."

"Thanks." Hans navigated through the personnel database like he had written it. "Okay, here we go. Mr. Safi is currently on holiday. He has the week off. Strange, I don't recall any Yemeni locations in the most recent Club Med brochure," he added sarcastically.

Rusty shook his head and said, "He wasn't in Yemen to work on his tan."

Steve went back to the fleet monitoring software and interjected. "Heads up. Our guy pulled off the highway a few minutes ago. He's at a Shell station in Haima. Probably just gassing up."

Magne peered over his shoulder. "Our guy is the green box, right?"

"Yeah."

Pointing to the screen he asked, "What's this red box over here?"

Steve replied, "Another vehicle but that doesn't make sense. Another company's trucks shouldn't show up on Al-Rashid's fleet monitoring account."

"Maybe it isn't another company's truck. Can you identify it?"

Steve rolled the cursor over the red box and clicked. To the side an information box opened on the screen with details. "It's another Al-Rashid truck, all right."

"Who's the driver?"

"Currently unassigned. It's not a service vehicle. It's a cargo truck. An Isuzu box truck."

Hans said, "You have the vehicle ID number. Search for it on their database."

Steve slapped his forehead, "Duh." He entered the ID number and hit enter. "Oh shit. It said it's supposed to carry spare parts and refrigerant from Muscat to Dubai on Monday morning. Guess who the driver is…"

Sarah replied, "Odai Safi?"

Steve nodded. "Give the pretty lady a cigar. The note says Safi is in

Muscat on holiday and will drive the truck to Dubai rather than fly back."

Rusty snorted, "Helpful little shit, isn't he. How fucking convenient."

* * *

Al-Maadi and Mohammad reached the area around CHASNUPP in the late afternoon. The countryside was dominated by small fields arrayed haphazardly and dotted periodically with small villages, gas stations, and other small businesses. About five miles to the west, the lights from the Chashma Nuclear Power Plant dominated the horizon. The day was starting to fade as the sun slipped toward the mountains to the west. As the MM Road approached the Chashma-Jhelum canal, Mohammad asked, "Where to, boss?"

"Keep going straight, across the bridge."

"But the nuclear power plant is to the left."

"The man we're seeking lives north a short distance; in Kundian. We'll meet him tonight."

"Yes, sir. Just tell me where to go."

They crossed the canal and continued north for almost ten miles before Al-Maadi motioned to the west. "Here. Turn left here. On Der Ismael Khan Road. Follow it into town. It will turn into Kundian Road. Continue on it until I tell you."

"Yes, Abu Almawt."

Mohammad and Al-Maadi drove on in silence for over half an hour. The fields gave way to scattered houses, gas stations, restaurants, and schools. Once in the town, the main road turned left but Al-Maadi guided Mohammad straight onto what was now Kundian Road. A few more twists and turns and they found themselves in the heart of the dusty city of Kundian. The street was rough and strewn with trash. The houses were very similar; simple concrete structures of one or two stories built almost up to the road itself. Each had a passage leading from the road to a courtyard beyond. Finally, Al-Maadi signaled Mohammad to pull over and stop. The road was narrow and he had to park halfway onto the sidewalk. As a precaution, he placed his 9mm pistol in his lap. Al-Maadi peered intently at a house across the street. Mohammad asked, "Now what?"

"We wait."

"For what?"

"Not what, for whom. Nawaz, my contact at the plutonium reprocessing facility south of the nuclear power plant."

Mohammad frowned. "I am not technical, by any means, but I thought the power plant, and everything in it, was under Western safeguards?"

Al-Maadi smiled, "It is. The International Atomic Energy Agency monitors all that is there to make sure none is diverted for weapons or other nefarious purposes."

"Then what does the plant reprocess?"

"Spent fuel from Pakistan's weapons reactors located at the Khushab Nuclear Complex east of here. Their reactors only produce plutonium for atomic weapons but it must be separated from the rest of the spent fuel which is highly toxic and radioactive. That is what this plant does."

"Are we going to get plutonium?"

Al-Maadi shook his head. "No. The Pakistani military has plans for every gram of that. We are obtaining something else, something just as valuable, to us at least."

As the two men waited, the street was getting darker. Mohammad, exhausted from the long day, nodded off while Al-Maadi surveilled the house. An hour or so later, an old yellow Toyota approached. It slowed and stopped in front of a house a few dozen meters away on the opposite side of the street. The driver got out, unlocked a large wooden gate and swung the doors open. He drove the Toyota through the opening before returning to close the gate behind him. As he did, he scanned the street. His eyes fell briefly on the blue Mercedes parked just down from his house. He gave a brief nod before disappearing inside. While the gate was closed, it was still ajar. He didn't lock it.

Al-Maadi shook Mohammad to rouse him. "He's here. Let's go."

Groggy from his nap, Mohammad wiped the sleep from his eyes. "He's here? I didn't...you should have wakened me."

"You needed the rest and we have a lot of work ahead of us."

The two men exited the Mercedes and walked toward the gate. Khalid Al-Maadi took a deep breath and pushed the gate open. He wasn't exactly sure what he'd find inside. He hadn't met Nawaz in person. He was recommended by his late cousin. Normally, that would be all the vetting he needed but his cousin was now dead. Did Nawaz's loyalty die with him? How many men had sold their fealty to the Americans for a lot less than the reward currently on Al-Maadi's head?

Inside the gate, a man stood silently in the shadows. Al-Maadi just made out the pistol in his hand. The man asked, "Are you the cousin of... the doctor?" On its surface, it was an innocent question intended to evoke a confirmation without revealing any information.

Al-Maadi replied, "That depends. Are you the...chemist?"

"I am the chemist, yes."

"Then I am the doctor."

The man stepped forward and Mohammad stepped between him and Al-Maadi. The man paused, and held up his gun before putting it in his pocket. "Just a precaution. Certainly, you understand, Abu Almawt."

Khalid nodded. "I do. You must be Nawaz."

"I am." The man was Nawaz Zaman, a chemical engineer at the plutonium reprocessing plant located south of the Chashma Nuclear Power Plant. "Welcome to my home. Please come in. I wasn't sure when to expect you. My wife should have dinner prepared. I'll tell her we work together. She won't ask questions."

"Thank you. We'll need to find accommodations before it gets too late."

"Nonsense, you'll stay here. Allah demands it."

Mohammad interjected, "That will not make sense given your story."

"I'll tell her you're from Islamabad. She won't question it."

Al-Maadi mulled this over for a moment. "Okay. That would be good, thank you. What about our car? Is it safe on the street?"

Nawaz chuckled. "A Mercedes? I should say not! Park it in the courtyard next to mine. It will add credence to the story that you're from Islamabad. My wife thinks everyone there is rich."

Mohammad parked their car in the courtyard and Nawaz locked the gate behind him. The three men walked into the house where Nawaz's wife was setting the table for dinner. She was a rather round, plain woman. Nawaz announced, "Fatima, we have two guests for dinner. They'll be staying the night as well. Make up the guest room for them."

Fatima was irritated. Apparently, having unexpected guests is a universal pet peeve of wives everywhere. She pulled her scarf over her head, bowed subserviently and asked, "Husband, may I have a word with you in the kitchen?"

"Excuse me gentlemen. A husband's duties. You understand."

Nawaz strode into the kitchen with Fatima a couple of paces behind him. Once the door closed, Khalid and Mohammad overheard her berating her husband in Urdu. She was not happy. Nawaz was saying something about Islamabad and a possible promotion at the plant. She calmed down and Nawaz exited the kitchen with a forced smile on his face. Fatima followed with two more place settings in her hands.

After dinner, they retired to the small room that passed as Nawaz's study while Fatima did the dishes before going upstairs to prepare the guest room. Mohammad shut the door to the study and snapped on a radio sitting on a shelf. He didn't ask, he just did it. Nawaz started to protest but Al-Maadi silently waved his finger and touched his ear. Mohammad turned up the volume as Al-Maadi sidled up to their host. Nawaz got it. Sound masking. Mohammad was making sure no one or nothing was eavesdropping on their conversation.

Speaking in a low voice, Nawaz said, "I assure you, Abu Almawt, there are no bugs here. I am trusted at the plant."

"One can never be too sure. I am convinced that the only reason I'm alive is because of Mohammad's caution. Maybe if my cousin had had his own Mohammad, he'd be alive today."

"I understand. My condolences for your cousin."

Al-Maadi nodded and said, "Thank you. Now where do we stand on our project?"

Nawaz was instantly more serious. "I have access to the items you require, but we have to be extremely thoughtful as to how we secure and transport them. If we are not careful, we will be the victims, not the blasphemers."

"Understood."

"I have arranged for you to receive the isotopes in varying quantities." Nawaz explained, "I'm in charge of logging materials in the inventory system. I've been under-recording the amounts of these isotopes obtained during the last reprocessing cycle. The amounts you take must match my numbers exactly. Any more or any less and the theft will be discovered at the next inventory which is scheduled for next month when we finish reprocessing this last batch of spent fuel. Any discrepancy will point directly to me. If you need more, you cannot have it. If you need less, you have to take it all anyway and dispose of the excess yourselves. Do you understand?"

Al-Maadi nodded. "Yes, I understand. We will protect you, Nawaz. We couldn't do this without you."

"That's all I ask."

"You have the isotopes then?"

"Yes, I have two of the isotopes you requested."

Al-Maadi was taken aback. He was led to believe Nawaz got everything he wanted. "Only two?"

"The first isotope, the Iodine-131, we don't have."

"But I was told that it comes from reactors and was one of the major killers after Chernobyl."

Nawaz interjected. "Well, yes and no. Iodine-131 is produced in nuclear reactors and was emitted in the Chernobyl accident. However, it has a relatively short half-life—only eight days. By the time the spent fuel has cooled enough to be sent to us for reprocessing, it has all but dissipated completely. We recover only trace amounts. At Chernobyl, the reactor exploded while it was in operation so it was making Iodine-131 right up to the moment it blew up."

Al-Maadi nodded and said, "I understand. I was misinformed." In truth, Al-Maadi came up with his list of isotopes from an internet article on the Chernobyl disaster. He didn't really understand the physics or how plutonium reprocessing actually worked.

Nawaz continued, "I don't know the details of what you have planned, but I assumed you had three separate targets so I gave you enough of the other two isotopes to make up for the missing Iodine-131. Don't worry, they are sufficiently dangerous."

Al-Maadi smiled and said, "I appreciate your willingness to adjust the plan as needed. I understand they're dangerous but explain it to Mohammad so he can protect himself in the event I am not around." In truth, Khalid needed to know too. Nuclear chemistry was not his forte but he didn't want to appear ignorant in front of Mohammad.

Turning to Mohammad, Nawaz said, "The first isotope is Cesium-137 in the form of solid pellets of cesium chloride salt that will readily dissolve in water. It undergoes beta and gamma decay.

Mohammad asked, "Decay?"

"It's complicated, but the type of decay determines the type of radiation emitted. Alpha decay is the safest. Alpha particles are slow and heavy and don't penetrate well. They are stopped by clothing or even a piece of paper. Beta particles have more energy and penetrate the skin. Gamma radiation is the most dangerous. It is a ray, like an X-ray or a radio signal. It penetrates almost anything. You need something very dense to stop it."

Mohammad nodded. "Like lead?"

"Exactly. If ingested in very small amounts, the Cesium-137 will spread throughout the soft tissue but causes pancreatic cancer. It has a high mortality rate depending on the amount ingested. Just carrying a couple of grams of the material unshielded will quickly kill you, so you will need to be extremely careful."

Al-Maadi replied, "Yes, I understand."

"The second is Strontium-90. It is also in the form of a salt. It is a beta emitter. Not as dangerous as the cesium but it will still kill you if you're not careful. What makes it dangerous is that it is what they call a 'bone seeker.' It's in the same family in the periodic table as calcium and accumulates in the bones where it causes cancer of the bone and marrow. Once present in the bones, it is very difficult to remove."

Khalid nodded. "I'm familiar with some of these from my time at university. If they need to be shielded with lead, how are we to transport them?"

"I had suitable containers fabricated; metal cans lined with a thick layer of lead. They are very heavy and impossible to explain so if you are caught..."

"I understand. What shape and dimensions?"

"They are cylinders; twelve centimeters in diameter and twenty-five tall." Nawaz added, "There's another problem. The government has radiation sensors installed along all the highways at random locations. They use them to monitor the movement of the country's nuclear weapons. They are very, very sensitive. Even shielded, our materials will set them off."

Al-Maadi leaned back in his chair and threw his hands in the air. "Well how the hell are we to move them then?"

Nawaz grinned. "I know where the sensors are placed. The military moves the nuclear weapons in large, heavily armed convoys. Because of this, they only use the major roads. All the sensors are on these major roads. I have prepared a map with routes from here to Karachi that will allow you to avoid the sensors. It will take longer, but you should arrive unmolested."

Khalid smiled and clapped Zaman on the back. "Brother Nawaz, I should never have doubted you."

"You must follow the route exactly. They also have mobile sensors. If you travel even a mile on a major highway, you risk being detected."

"Understood. When do we get the isotopes?"

"I'll bring them tomorrow. As soon as I give them to you, you must leave. I don't want that stuff near my family."

Mohammad had been standing quietly this whole time. Nawaz's last statement got his attention. *He doesn't want it around his family for more than a few minutes. That doesn't bode well for us.*

The next morning, Khalid Al-Maadi and his bodyguard rose with the sun. Nawaz was already up and getting ready to go to the plant. Al-Maadi asked in a low voice, "What is the plan?"

"I'll go to work as usual. I'll tell them I have to go to town to take some equipment for repair. I must leave exactly at eight o'clock."

"Why?"

"We have sensors at the plant exit to prevent exactly what I am about to do. Since I'm in charge of those sensors, I'll initiate a system backup during which the sensors won't be functional. It takes about ten minutes. Plenty of time for me to slip out. We transfer the isotopes to your car and go our separate ways."

Al-Maadi took a deep breath. "We will await your return, brother."

Nawaz Zaman went to work like he did every day. He parked his old Toyota in his usual spot. He went to his office, logged onto his computer, and sent a short email to his supervisor informing him that he was taking some diagnostic equipment to the dealer in town for repair. He checked out a van from the motor pool and drove it to the loading dock. The guards were familiar with him, of course; he'd worked there for years. Speaking to the guard, he said, "Hi Gamal. I've got to take some equipment into town for repair. I'll be back in a second."

"Okay, Mr. Zaman."

A few minutes later, Nawaz returned with a cart loaded with three metal boxes; cubes about half a meter on a side. Each had two handles and a hinged lid secured by a heavy clasp. "Give me a hand with these, will you?"

"I need to inspect them. You know the protocols."

Nawaz chuckled and replied, "Yeah, I wrote them."

The guard was a little embarrassed. "Oh yeah, right. But still."

"Of course." Nawaz had anticipated the inspection and purposely put the chest with the less volatile Strontium-90 on top. He only hoped the guard would be satisfied with inspecting only one of the cases. Nawaz opened the lid of the top metal chest. Inside were four gray metal cylinders roughly the size of a two-liter bottle with two wires attached. "Ion detectors.

The material inside needs to be replaced periodically. The stuff is toxic so we make the manufacturer do it."

The guard chuckled, "Better them than us, right?" With the guard's help, he swung the three cases into the back of the van.

Nawaz checked his watch. It was 7:55—he needed to go. "Well, I'm off. Back in a little while." The guard just gave him a casual salute and returned to his tiny office. The most nerve-racking time was when he actually exited the compound. If his system reboot didn't work, his trip would be very short. He sat nervously as he approached the guard. This one was much more serious. Nawaz showed him his checkout slip for the van and his ID badge. The guard made a quick notation on his clipboard and waved him through.

To Nawaz, every eye in Pakistan was on him as he drove the thirty minutes back to his home in Kundian. As he pulled up to his house, the gate to his courtyard swung open. Mohammad had been waiting for him. He stopped the van next to the blue Mercedes and opened the rear doors. Al-Maadi asked, "Which is which?"

Nawaz replied, "Just below the clasp is a small letter; two have a C for Cesium and the other an S for Strontium." He opened one of the chests to reveal the cans. "The isotopes are inside. The wires are just for show. I told the guard they were detectors being returned for service. Their tops screw off. The cans are lined with lead so you should be safe in the car."

Mohammad shot back, "*Should* be?!"

"Yes. Like I said they are lined with lead. Put the Strontium-90 in first; it's the safest. Then the two containing the Cesium-137. It's the most dangerous isotope, so its canisters have more lead and are heavier. They don't hold as much material, but you have twice as many. Keep them to the back and as far away from you as possible."

Al-Maadi asked, "So we should be safe in the passenger compartment?"

"Yes." Nawaz replied before adding sheepishly, "But I wouldn't sit in the back seat. Just in case."

Mohammad and Nawaz muscled the chests out of the van and onto the ground before loading them into the Mercedes's ample trunk in the order Nawaz recommended. Nawaz reached under the front seat of the van and retrieved a small package. Removing a paper map, he handed it to Mohammad. "This map contains the route that will get you around the Ministry of Defense highway sensors. Do not deviate from it or we risk being discovered."

Mohammad nodded. "Understood."

Nawaz removed from the package what appeared to be an oven mitt and handed it to Al-Maadi. It was unusually heavy. "Abu Almawt, this is a lead glove. There are two. If for any reason you have to open one of the canisters or when you're ready to deploy the isotopes, use these. They will offer some protection, but you must minimize your exposure as much as possible."

"Thank you, Nawaz. You've thought of everything."

"Okay, I need to get back to the plant."

Mohammad said, "You leave first. We'll wait a few minutes and follow. We don't want your neighbors seeing our vehicles together."

"Good thinking."

Mohammad asked, "What of your wife?"

"She thinks you're from the PAEC, uh that's the Pakistan Atomic Energy Commission. I told her you were going to visit the plant today before returning to Islamabad. She expects you to leave soon anyway. I don't tell her about my work."

"Good." Mohammad checked the time. "You need to get moving. We have a long drive ahead of us and we cannot start until you leave."

Nawaz actually choked up a bit. "Abu Almawt, I just wanted to tell you how much I admire you and how happy I am to play a role in your struggle."

Al-Maadi smiled, gave him a hug, and kissed him on both cheeks. "We all have our part to play. Now go, before they miss you."

Nawaz backed the van onto the street as Muhammad closed the gate behind him. He took one last glance over his shoulder before speeding away.

Mohammad returned to the Mercedes and was surprised to find Khalid opening a chest containing Cesium-137. "What are you doing?"

Khalid was wearing the lead mittens and had a pair of kitchen tongs. "Tying up a loose end." He unscrewed the top of one of the canisters. The white pellets inside gave off an eerie purple glow. "Stand back." Khalid grabbed one of the pellets with the tongs and set it on the ground before quickly resealing the canister and closing the chest.

"What are you going to do with that?"

"Making sure Nawaz doesn't talk. I don't like the idea of sacrificing him, but we cannot have any loose ends. You go distract his wife. Thank her for her hospitality or something while I put this in Nawaz's study."

"Yes, sir." Mohammad was uneasy. Khalid hadn't told him about this. *Am I a loose end too?*

Mohammad did as he was told. He entered the house and called out for Fatima. She came shuffling out from the kitchen. "Yes, may I help you gentlemen?"

"I just wanted to thank you for your gracious hospitality. I realize you weren't expecting visitors last night and we appreciate everything you did…"

As Mohammad talked, Khalid slipped into the study. Draped over the back of Nawaz's chair was a well-worn sport jacket. Khalid pulled back the left lapel and dropped the pellet of Cesium-137 into the inside breast pocket. Whether Nawaz wore the jacket or sat with it on the back of the chair, the radioactive pellet would be right next to his heart. He'd be dead within twenty-four hours; forty-eight at the most. His murderous task completed, Al-Maadi returned the lead mittens to the car. Fatima and Mohammad were walking out as he closed the trunk. Al-Maadi walked around the car and gave Fatima a little bow. "Thank you, madam, for your hospitality. We foresee great things for your husband and it's clear you are responsible for much of it." Fatima blushed like a schoolgirl and only nodded. "Now, we must be going. They're expecting us at the plant."

As Mohammad backed the Mercedes out onto the street, Khalid gave Fatima a brief wave while she closed the gate behind them. Mohammad took a quick glance at Nawaz's map, pointed the car east on Kundian Street and drove toward the morning sun.

* * *

Analyzing the take from Al-Maadi's office in the safe house was a much more tedious task. It didn't involve hacking or computers—mostly old-fashioned paperwork. The documents taken were in a mix of languages; Arabic, Urdu, and English. During the raid, Lon grabbed whatever he found and shoved it into pillow cases. There was no order to the mess. As with the take from Kotov's Syrian compound, they simply spread the papers out on the floor in the gym and started sifting. They were hoping to find a copy of Al-Maadi's master plan. They didn't.

Rusty and Gunny checked how it was going. Gunny asked, "Any luck yet?"

Lon stood and stretched his back. "Not really. There are a lot of hand written financial documents about money coming in from one hawala and going out through another."

Rusty asked, "Hawalas? Those are those informal banking networks, right?"

Lon replied, "Yes. They're a way of transferring money around the world without money physically changing hands or going through the banking system."

Gunny chuckled. "Not unlike our Federal Reserve. All electrons, smoke, and mirrors."

Lon explained, "A hawala works on trust, not contracts. If I want to send my mother a thousand dollars, I contact my local hawala broker and give him the money, my mom's name, the city where she lives, and a password. He finds another broker in her city and asks him to give her the thousand bucks. All she has to do is show up, give her name and the password, and he gives her the cash—minus a small commission. It may be done in a day or two, or even a few hours."

"How does the second guy get his money?"

"They keep track of who is owed what and settle up about once a year. Payment may be cash, property, gold, or even favors. Since money flows in both directions, none of the guys are ever out of pocket too much."

Rusty quipped, "Unless one of the guys welches."

Lon shook his head. "That rarely happens. If you fail to pay, you're kicked out. It is considered a severe breach of trust and honor. Not only are you kicked out of the system forever, you bring shame on yourself and your family. It sounds crazy but the system has been working for over a thousand years."

Rusty laughed, "Makes too much sense to be legal. How does the government get its slice?"

"Yeah, they worried about that too. It's regulated in most countries but not all. It's completely legal in Dubai. Others, like India and Pakistan have passed laws to control it under the 'anti-money laundering' rubric, but it still goes on. Expat workers throughout Asia use it to send money home without having to worry about taxes."

"Well, if we have the names and the cities, we track them that way, right?"

"Nope. The names don't have to be real. No one asks for ID. You just say, "I'm John Smith, I'm here to pick up five hundred bucks. The password is 'Frito bandito.' That's all there is too it."

Rusty shook his head. "Well shit."

Lon grinned. "It ain't all bad news. We've got other stuff to exploit."

"These hawala transactions…how much money are we talking about?"

"Millions."

"Well, that's not good."

"I need to borrow Hans or Sarah. They have the best Arabic and we have a bunch of documents."

Gunny nodded. "Sure. Steve has his shit under control. I'll send one of them over."

"Thanks."

As Lon returned to his pile of papers, John shouted out. "I got something weird here. Some handwritten notes in a couple of languages. Chemistry stuff, I think."

Alen was sitting next to him on the floor and slid over. "Yeah. It's chemistry. Nothing scary though. It's talking about potassium, chlorine, and magnesium. Potassium chloride is a common salt. It's not table salt but is used in medicine to treat low blood pressure. Magnesium is a dietary supplement."

John asked, "Why would he have this shit?"

Alen shrugged. "Well, he was a doctor before he was a terrorist. Maybe he is using it on himself. I have no idea, but you'd be hard-pressed to kill a shitload of people with this stuff."

John looked at the paper intently as if he was willing more information to spring from the page. "I recall enough from high school science to know the Cl, K, and Mg are the symbols for chlorine, potassium, and magnesium, but what are these little numbers about?"

"What little numbers?"

"Each has a 'plus two' superscript after it. What does that mean?"

Alen scratched his head. "Good question. An isotope is marked by a superscript indicating the atomic mass, but it comes before the symbol, not after it. Besides, the only thing with an atomic mass of two is deuterium, an isotope of hydrogen. These chemicals are ten to twenty times heavier."

Alen studied the paper. "There's some other stuff here, but I'm not familiar with it. I was a biology guy. This other stuff is a mix of English, Cyrillic, and maybe Greek. There's also a reference to 'mev' and I have no clue what that means."

Rusty interjected, "I'm not sure what this means either, but the most wanted terrorist in the world had a paper on it in his safe house. I'm thinking it might be important. Let's dig into it."

John handed the paper to Alen and said, "Yes sir, Rusty. Alen's on it."

The big Serb glared at him and growled, "Thanks a lot, asshole."

John laughed, "That's what ya get for being smart."

Lon quipped, "No one ever accused John of that. I guarantee it."

John smirked, "And see how well it's working out for me."

Alen turned to Rusty and Gunny. "Uh, I know a guy who can probably help me with this, but he's in Serbia."

Rusty asked, "Who is he?"

"A friend of my parents. He's the smartest man I've ever met. I've known him since I was a kid and I trust him with my life. Mind if I give him a call?"

Gunny replied, "Yes, I do mind—unless you're going to talk to him over an encrypted link."

"Well, he's a retired college professor. Pretty sure he doesn't have access to the American president's red phone."

Rusty said, "Go meet him in person. Take the jet. It's a short flight."

Alen was embarrassed. "I'm not comfortable with that. It's a little over the top for one person."

Rusty shook his head. "Nonsense. That's what it's for. If it makes you happy, take one of these other worthless mopes with you. How long will it take?"

"Not long. Overnight. Two days at the longest."

"Okay, call your guy. If he's available, I'll call Gil and tell him to file a flight plan for Belgrade. Take Kernan with you as back up, just in case. And don't fret about the plane. The jet is just a tool that happens to cost more than most."

Alen was still not accustomed to the amount of trust Rusty and Gunny put in him. "Aren't you going to ask me who he is or if he's trustworthy?"

Gunny shrugged. "You said you trust him so…"

Alen was still uneasy. Rusty asked, "Okay, what's his name?"

"Dr. Ivan Pretrukhin."

"Russian?"

Alen replied, "He is. He was a dissident back in the 1970s. He pissed off Brezhnev and had to move to Yugoslavia. Will that be a problem?"

Rusty shook his head, "Nope. Sounds like my kind of guy."

"I'll only tell him what I must."

"I assumed as much. Now get going."

* * *

The evening after Khalid Al-Maadi and his bodyguard, Mohammad, departed Kundian, Nawaz Zaman returned home late from work at the plutonium reprocessing plant. As he walked in, Fatima said, "So, are you getting a promotion? Is Mr. Khalid going to put in a good word for you with Islamabad?"

Nawaz smiled, "I hope so. Today went well. But either way, I am destined to do great things, if Allah wills it."

"I am sure of it too. Well, your dinner is ready. I've already eaten."

Nawaz kissed her on the forehead and said, "Sorry I'm late. I have a lot of reading to do tonight. Do you mind if I eat in my study?"

She smiled. "Not at all. I have work in the kitchen. I'll bring your plate."

Nawaz settled into his office chair and removed a couple of technical journals from his briefcase. He wanted to brush up on the latest nuclear papers. He planned to casually mention them in front of the inspection team from the Pakistan Atomic Energy Agency to impress upon them that he was keeping up on the technology.

As he finished his food, Fatima came in to remove his plate. Nawaz picked up a copy of Nuclear News and sat in his chair to read about high-level nuclear waste handling procedures. He leaned back. His old sport jacket was still draped over the chair. Inside the left interior breast pocket was the small pellet of Cesium-137. It was only a few centimeters from his heart.

After reading for a couple of hours, Nawaz went to bed but didn't sleep. He had a strange burning sensation on his back and he grew nauseous. After getting up just after midnight to throw up, he returned to bed and drifted off. The next morning, he refused breakfast. Fatima was concerned, but he assured her it was nothing. He must have eaten something that disagreed with him.

Upon arriving at work, Nawaz logged onto his computer to check his emails. The audit was still on schedule and he had a lot of work to do. Hoping a little tea would settle his stomach, Nawaz walked to the small kitchen in the corner of the office. As he was pouring the hot water over the tea leaves, he was overcome with another wave of nausea. He ran to the bathroom fighting the urge to vomit. Just as he opened the lavatory door, he was hit with pangs of violent diarrhea. He rushed into the first stall, ripping off his trousers as he went, but he had already soiled himself. As he tried to sit on the toilet he swooned. He struggled to maintain his balance. The room began to spin and he vomited violently all down the front of his shirt. His head slammed into the wall and he collapsed unconscious onto the floor, half-naked and bathed in vomit, feces, and sweat.

The commotion caused one of his coworkers to investigate. Finding Nawaz splayed out on the floor, he immediately called for the on-site paramedics. They arrived a few minutes later. The room smelled so badly of vomit and diarrhea, one of the medics puked in the sink before helping his partner deal with Nawaz. They dragged him from the stall and stretched him out on the tile floor and checked his vitals. His pulse was weak. They cleared his mouth and airway of vomit.

The paramedics had handled industrial accidents before but had never witnessed what was happening to Nawaz. They cut off his vomit covered shirt to examined his body for wounds. Finding none on his chest, they rolled him onto his right side. It was then they discovered the large festering burn on his back to the left of his spine. It was bright red and about eight inches in diameter with a large, liquid filled boil in the middle. As they tried to maneuver his body into a more stable posture, one of the medics ruptured the boil. Pinkish clear liquid splashed onto the floor and the skin peeled away to reveal a raw, red burn. His heart was only a couple centimeters away and the bloody, burned flesh pulsed with every beat.

The senior paramedic yelled out, "Call an ambulance! Immediately! And keep everyone back." He was beginning to understand this was not an injury or disease. This was something much, much more.

Before the ambulance showed up, the plant's medical safety officer arrived from his office in the main administration building. He was a doctor but hadn't actually treated a patient in some time. His day consisted of filing reports and making sure the technicians properly logged data from the workers' dosimeters. The real dirty work of spent fuel reprocessing was performed by robotic arms behind thick, concrete walls. Once he examined Nawaz's back, he identified what it was. "This is a severe radiation burn! Keep everyone out of here." He had brought with him a Geiger counter. He snapped on the machine and was surprised when it registered only normal background radiation. "Where does this man sit? Where is his desk?"

The man who had first found Nawaz in the bathroom stepped forward. "I'm Amal. Mr. Zaman sat over here. I'll show you." He led the doctor to Nawaz's desk but stopped several meters short and pointed. *He did say radiation, right?* "That one there."

The doctor again turned on his Geiger counter. As before, there was nothing above background. Turning to his escort, he asked, "Amal, did any of your area gamma detectors go off?"

"No, of course not. I wouldn't be here if they had. Is it alpha or beta radiation?"

"No, they would have registered on my counter." The ambulance had arrived and EMTs wheeled in a stretcher. The doctor shouted to them, "The victim is in the toilet. We need to get him to the hospital immediately. Make sure they isolate him and take all precautions for a radiation accident." Turning back to Amal, he said, "Evacuate this area immediately. Everyone out. Everything stays here until we find the radiation source, do you understand?"

"Yes, sir."

Nawaz Zaman died on the way to the hospital. A rapid reaction team from the plant was dispatched to his house where they found Fatima sick. The team quickly located the pellet of Cesium-137 in the pocket of his sport jacket. What they didn't understand is how it got there. While Nawaz was one of the few people with physical access to such material, he also understood what it would do to him. Nothing made sense. They reported the incident to the PAEC in Islamabad, but that was as far as it went. The International Atomic Energy Agency was not informed. The plutonium reprocessing plant did not fall under their safeguards and the PAEC wasn't about to invite them in now. They'd do their own investigation and as quietly as possible.

CHAPTER SEVEN
PANDORA'S BOX

The Bombardier Global 8000 rolled down the runway of the Larnaca airport and lifted gracefully into the air, bound for Belgrade. Alen sat back in his seat reviewing the notes he'd made before leaving the villa. John Kernan had no anxiety about appearing smart in front of the man they were to visit, so he helped himself to a glass of Rusty's finest bourbon. "I do love how rich people travel."

Gil walked back from the cockpit as John sipped the bourbon and said, "I'm telling dad."

John dramatically took a big gulp. "Go ahead. See if I care, ya bitch." Gil remained stone-faced. Suddenly nervous, John asked, "You're not gonna, are you?"

Gil chuckled. "No, your secret is safe with me." Turning to Alen, he quipped, "Well, at least one of you is earning his keep. We'll be on the ground in an hour and a half. Donny and I will stay at the Frankenstein. I assume you guys are downtown?"

John perked up. "The Frankenstein?"

Alen laughed, "That's the Frankensteiner Hotel. Nice choice, Gil."

"It's a short ride to the airport. Less traffic."

"We're at the Belgrade City Hotel. It's close to our guy's apartment."

"How long you planning to stay in town?"

"If all goes well, we'll be done by tomorrow afternoon. That okay with you?"

Gil shrugged. "Doesn't matter to me. I'm on salary." He turned to walk back to the cockpit and added, "Just call me when you're ready to head out. We'll meet you at the airport with the motor running."

"Okay, great."

After Gil left, John asked, "Alen, who is this guy we're going to meet?"

"Dr. Ivan Pretrukhin. He was a professor at the University of Belgrade. He's retired now. He was good friends with my parents. He's kind of like an uncle to me. He's a brilliant guy. Hans fancies himself as a renaissance man but Pretrukhin really is one. He is a doctor specializing in nuclear medicine, a physicist, and a scientific ethicist. He is also a historian—reads and writes several ancient languages including Latin, Phoenician, and ancient Egyptian. He's from a small village in Russia but ended up at Moscow State University."

"Sounds like an overachiever to me. What is a scientific ethicist?"

Alen replied with a chuckle, "Someone who doesn't ask if we *can* do something but rather if we *should*. That's what got him in trouble with the Soviet regime. In the late 70s, he went public with allegations that they were killing a lot of people in their nuclear program in the name of keeping up with the West. After his Soviet bosses ignored him, he aired his concerns to the European scientific community. Needless to say, the Kremlin was none too happy with him. He lost his job at the university but wouldn't back down. He was sent to the gulags for over a year. Western scientific organizations threatened to stop cooperating with the Soviet Union if they didn't cut him loose. The Soviets needed western technology, so they relented and he was exiled. The Soviets cut a deal for Yugoslavia to take in Dr. Pretrukhin with the stipulation that he not be allowed to leave to the West. He became a faculty member at the university. He worked with my parents and they became best friends. His wife refused to leave Moscow, so they divorced. They never had kids; he kind of adopted me as a surrogate son."

John asked, "So you trust this guy?"

Alen replied seriously, "With my life. He'll help us, no questions asked."

"If you trust him, I trust him."

Alen asked, "So, John, tell me. Why did you join the Praetorians?"

John took a swig of bourbon. "Not much to tell, really. I joined the Navy right out of high school. Always wanted to be a SEAL, so I went for it. It was a shitload harder than I thought, I gotta tell ya, but I made it through. After a few years I was selected for DEVGRU, assigned to Blue Squadron, and eventually made it to Master Chief. Anyway, I loved it, but I'd been in twenty years and was maxed out. They were going to send me to SOCOM. I didn't want to be a pencil pusher, so I put in my papers and retired. I was kicking around Florida trying to figure out what to do next when Gunny showed up at my door. I'd heard of him, of course. The guy is a legend. I even met him on a couple of deployments. He'd show up in places no one was supposed to be, let alone right when we were. That's when I learned he was Agency. Anyway, he told me about a new antiterrorism outfit they were organizing. No military hierarchy. Privately funded. Best of everything. No rules, just results. I was sold. He signed me up the same day. I was the second guy they recruited. Lon was the first. He and Gunny go way back. Anyway, been here ever since."

Alen asked, "Any family?"

"I got an ex-wife." He laughed, "Hell, every SEAL has at least one of those. They issue you one as soon as you finish BUD/S. That's Basic Underwater Demolition/SEAL training."

"No kids?"

"Nope. Dodged that bullet. Personally, I think it's due to all that time on submarines, all that radiation causes a low sperm count. How about you? Wife? Kids?"

Alen smiled, "Same as you. Ex-wife and no kids."

John grinned, "I guess all special forces are pretty much the same. It is definitely a single man's gig."

After they landed in Belgrade, Alen and John immediately headed for immigration and caught a taxi into the city while Gil and Donnie dealt with the plane. John had never been to Belgrade and spent the taxi ride taking in his surroundings. Because of the driver, they didn't discuss anything operational. Alen gazed out at the city he used to call home. It was both familiar and foreign at the same time. He hadn't been back since the day he left with Lon to join the Praetorians. He gave up his apartment after about six months, deciding to live full time in the villa. He gave it and all its contents to one of his old army buddies. Clean breaks are the easiest.

After checking into their hotel, Alen called Dr. Pretrukhin to set up a meeting for the next morning. Ivan insisted, however, that they meet that night for dinner to discuss old times before getting down to business. Alen glanced at John who was finishing off a beer and belching. "Are you sure? I have a friend with me and he is…"

Ivan laughed, "Alen, my boy, any friend of yours is a friend of mine. I'll meet you at eight o'clock at that restaurant just down the street from my apartment. You remember it?"

"You mean Mali Pariz?"

The old man laughed, "You do remember! Ah, to have a young mind."

"Until then." Alen ended the call and turned to John. "No more beer for you. I don't want you embarrassing me in front of this man."

"Yeah, yeah, yeah. Whatever."

Alen and John conducted a surveillance detection route (SDR) to determine if they were being followed. After the fiasco with Nura Ostergaard nee Al-Doghmush in Cairo, Sarah gave the team basic surveillance and SDR training to avoid a repeat performance. They had no reason to believe anyone was paying attention to them, but the city afforded a good opportunity for some practice.

As planned, they arrived early to case the area. Alen had been to the restaurant many times but never really assessed it with an operational eye. It was on the corner of Birčaninova and Svetozara Markoviča on the ground floor of a three-story residential building. The front door faced the corner but there was also a back door accessing an alley that winded its way among three other building before exiting on Svetozara about a hundred meters to the northeast. A number of high windows faced the street and there were a few tables along the sidewalk for al fresco dining. Tactically, it was less than ideal, but they weren't expecting trouble. Despite this, both men were armed. Old habits die hard.

They arrived early to assess the room and select a discreet table only to find Dr. Pretrukhin was already there. He'd picked a quiet table in a corner where no one easily eavesdropped on them. When he espied Alen, the old Russian jumped up and strode over to meet him. Pretrukhin was a distinguished man in his seventies. He had a thick head of gray hair and wore an old tweed jacket with patches on the elbows, the international uniform of old professors everywhere. Though a little stooped with age, his gray eyes were bright and energetic. He gave Alen a big hug before shaking John's hand. "Alen, my boy, it has been too long. What's it been? Two years?"

"Something like that."

"I dropped by your apartment a year or so ago and found a strange man living there."

"Yeah, that's Vladi. He's an old army buddy of mine. He took over my apartment when I left."

They sat down and the waiter came over with water. John was unable to read the menu so he let Alen and Dr. Pretrukhin order for him. After the waiter left, Alen said, "Dr. Pretrukhin, I'm glad you agreed to meet with us."

"Alen, we have known each other too long. Call me Ivan."

Alen blushed a bit, "Okay but it's just that dad would never allow me to be so familiar. Uh, this is my friend, John."

"We're too old to abide such formality." Ivan addressed John, "So, do you work together?"

Alen interjected, "What makes you say that?"

Ivan was a little perturbed. "Please. You're both clearly military from your bearing, haircuts, and demeanor. I saw you both scope out the restaurant as you entered. John is not Serbian. American, right? He may not have been Special Brigade with you, but he's clearly military."

"Uh, we're both retired. Just old habits."

The old Russian smirked. "You're both very fit for old retired people."

Alen wasn't going to put one over on Ivan. "We keep active. We're both retired from the military but involved in other things now."

Pleased with his little victory, Ivan smiled and nodded. "Clearly, based on the pistols you both are trying to hide. I don't need details. One cannot accidentally betray what one doesn't know about in the first place." That was the last mention of Alen or John's former or current employment. The rest of the dinner was spent discussing happier times with Alen and his parents. By eleven o'clock and after four bottles of wine, the restaurant was about to close, so they adjourned with a plan to meet at Ivan's apartment in the morning.

The next morning Alen and John walked from their hotel to Dr. Pretrukhin's apartment. Like the night before, they did not take a direct route but rather departed their hotel in the opposite direction and then conducted an SDR to determine if they were being tailed. Confident they were in the clear, they proceeded to the apartment.

Pretrukhin lived in a small, two-bedroom flat on the second floor of an old residential building not far from the restaurant. It was his first home upon arriving from the Soviet Union and he had no reason to leave it. It looked like an old professor lived there. The place smelled of pipe tobacco and dust. The kitchen was small but tidy with no modern appliances save a coffee machine. "Gentlemen, please come in. Have a seat in the living room while I get us some coffee."

The small living room contained furniture that was rather old and tattered but functional. The walls were adorned with artwork. Some original oils and some copies of the masters. The coffee table was covered with magazines on art, nuclear medicine, and anthropology. The wall space not occupied by art was home to shelves crammed with books with titles in Serbian, Russian, English, French, and German. Perusing them, John discovered a leather-bound copy of Plato's Republic, numerous books on the Russian Revolution, European history, and ancient Greece, Rome, and Egypt. Also present were the complete works of H. G. Wells and Jules Verne as well as a few books by Zane Grey. As Pretrukhin came in with the coffee on a tray, John said, "Quite an eclectic collection of books. Couldn't help but notice you have some Zane Grey."

Ivan smiled broadly. "Yes, I love his stories of the American West. My favorite is *Riders of the Purple Sage*. Have you read it?"

"Of course! I'm from the west."

Alen interjected. "Uh, Ivan. The reason I came was to get your opinion on something."

"Well, I'm no military expert unless you're talking about the Peloponnesian Wars. I doubt you are, so is it medicine or physics that brings you here?"

"That's just it; we're not sure. We obtained some information from some…let's just say bad people."

"How bad?"

"Bad enough that I flew all the way to Belgrade to figure it out. We have it on good authority that he wants to kill a bunch of people and these notes might tell us how he plans to do it."

"Okay. What do you have?"

Alen removed copies of the papers taken from Al-Maadi's safe house from an envelope and handed them to Ivan. He glanced over them and said, "Let's go to my study. My technical volumes are there." He led them to the room he converted from a bedroom to a study. The walls were completely covered with bookshelves crammed with hundreds and hundreds of academic books. In front of the window was a battered old desk and leather chair. Opposite was an ancient leather couch. "Please, sit."

John sat but Alen moved over Ivan's shoulder. Pointing to the papers, Alen said, "Here he is referring to kilograms of chlorine, magnesium, and potassium but I don't know what the 'plus 2' superscript means. Also, there are some notations in Cyrillic or Greek I couldn't decipher."

Ivan picked up a large magnifying glass and studied the pages intently.

"The superscripts make no sense. That usually denotes the atomic mass of an ion but none of the atoms have atomic masses even close to that. Whoever wrote this may have had his own notation system. Now, this beta is Greek; not Russian. In chemistry and physics, it is used to denote the type of decay for radioisotopes. For example, this ß⁻ means negative beta emission. But again, this doesn't make sense. Magnesium has three naturally occurring isotopes, but they're all stable; no radioactive decay. The man-made ones only last seconds, hours at the most."

John asked, "Man-made ones?"

"Yes, you make isotopes by bombarding atoms with subatomic particles. This is done commonly to make radioisotopes for chemotherapy or industrial tracers. Chlorine has only two naturally occurring isotopes and both are stable. I'm not sure about potassium. Let me check." He removed a thick, heavy book from the bottom shelf near his desk. "This is the Handbook of Chemistry and Physics. It has all the information you never thought you'd need." He opened the dusty book and flipped through the pages. "Here we go. Potassium has three naturally occurring isotopes. Two are completely stable."

Alen asked, "And the third?"

"It has a half-life of 1.28 million years. While that isn't technically stable, it's pretty damn stable. Besides, it's so rare, getting enough of it to do anything bad would be next to impossible."

"How rare?"

Ivan replied, "According to the book, it makes up 0.000118% of potassium atoms. That's pretty damn rare. Not very dangerous anyway."

Alen rubbed his chin. "What about the beta thing?"

Ivan peered again at the pages. "Whoever wrote this included decay energies. The 'mev' he wrote stands for millielectronvolt which is pretty low energy. Not really useful for much."

John quipped, "Maybe he's talking about some other isotopes. Just go through your book until you match the number of those electronvolt thingies to the right isotope. Easy peasy!"

Alen scoffed. "You're no help. There are thousands of different isotopes." He mumbled under his breath. "Moron."

"I heard that!"

Alen replied, "Don't care."

Ivan said, "Your moronic friend may be on to something."

John blurted out, "Hey!"

Ignoring him, Ivan continued. "These decay numbers clearly don't belong to chlorine, potassium, or magnesium. I'll try to determine what they correspond to, but it's going to take time. I can't look at it today. I'm leaving this afternoon for Niš. I'm lecturing at the Faculty of Medicine tomorrow, but I'll be back tomorrow night. Let me take pictures of your paper and I'll research it on the train."

"Okay. I guess that'll be okay. We have to get back. Contact me if you find anything."

Ivan nodded. "Of course, I'll call you with my results. Whatever you are into Alen, be careful."

* * *

Khalid Al-Maadi and Mohammad took their time getting back to Karachi. The route Nawaz had designed for them purposely avoided all the major highways to steer clear of the Pakistani military's system of static radiation detection stations it used to track its nuclear weapons as they were transported around the country. The Pakistani Atomic Energy Commission, the PAEC, also operated a number of mobile detectors that worked in conjunction with the military system to monitor and track its own shipments of spent fuel, fission products, and enriched uranium. Having worked at the plutonium reprocessing plant for several years, Nawaz was familiar with the locations of all the major nuclear facilities and the logical routes between them. While he wasn't sure of the exact location of any of the mobile detectors at any given time, he made a very educated guess as to where they would, and more importantly, would *not* be.

Most of Pakistan's nuclear facilities were north and east of Chashma, but he also had to take into account military bases where the nuclear weapons were stored. Nawaz's map took them south of Kundian on dirt roads until they crossed south over the canal and then east via farm roads toward the barrage. Crossing the Indus River was the time they were most at risk. The Indus was a wide river with few crossings. If they were to encounter a mobile detector, this was the most likely place. Khalid and Mohammad held their breaths as they drove onto the Chashma Barrage. Immediately after crossing, they turned left onto another dirt road and continued south. Their first choke point was successfully navigated.

Traveling this way was nerve-wracking. The roads were rough and dusty. The blue Mercedes traveling on roads used primarily by farm equipment and donkey carts drew a lot of unwanted attention. The constant navigation on unmarked roads and inevitable wrong turns only added to their frustration and stress. They stopped for the night at the small town of Nutkani. It was only some 200 kilometers from their starting point. Had they been able to take the highway, it would have been a four-hour drive. By Nawaz's map, it had taken more than nine. This was going to be a long trip.

The next morning, they rose with the sun and after a quick breakfast, continued their trek to the ocean. Their next obstacle lay some 135 kilometers to the south; the uranium mines near Dera Ghazi Khan. The yellow cake uranium ore the mines produced was not nearly as radioactive as what they had in their trunk, but it was valuable nonetheless. Both the Pakistani weapons and electric generation programs considered it a vital state asset, so the chances of encountering a mobile detector were not negligible. The area was crossed by two major highways—the N70 and the N55—both of which were used for transporting nuclear materials. Nawaz's map had them cross the N70 midway between Dera Ghazi Khan and the Indus River before continuing south. They reached the area around noon. Mohammad wasted no time slipping across the highway and into the relative safety of the farmland beyond. As before, the rural tracks made for slow going. The large trucks and heavy farm equipment traversing the area left the road rutted and cratered with potholes. Was it fair to even call them roads? Mohammad doubted they had been touched by a grader's blade since the British left. With every bone-rattling drop into a bottomless pothole, the Mercedes shook and vibrated. After Mohammad hit a particularly bad one, Khalid nearly bounced out of his seat. "Brother Mohammad, you may want to drive like in Afghanistan and try aiming for the smaller ones."

Mohammad turned to him and replied, "That *was* the smaller one."

Khalid chuckled, "Well then, let's hope the Germans are as good at building cars as they think they are."

Mohammad smiled, "The car will make it, but it won't be worth a lot once we arrive."

The constant jarring took a toll on their bodies and they drove only as far as their backs would allow. They stopped for the night at a remote farming village just east of Kot Chutta where they took a room at a modest inn. There was a conundrum over where to park the Mercedes. They feared that it might get stolen. Normally, they'd park close to their door and sleep with the window cracked so as to be alerted if anyone tried to break into it. However, with a trunk full of highly radioactive materials, they didn't relish the idea of spending all night in close proximity after riding with it all day. Al-Maadi rubbed his chin. "Well, one of us could sleep in the car?"

Mohammad recognized what "one of us" meant and it certainly wasn't Dr. Khalid ibn Mahfous Al-Maadi. "Abu Almawt, if you want to sleep in the car, I won't argue with you."

"That's not what I was suggesting."

"Well, I don't want to sleep next to that poison either."

"So, what do you suggest? It's far too valuable to leave unprotected and we can't bring it into the room. I don't care what Nawaz said about it being safe."

Mohammad snorted, "Right. So safe he didn't want it in his house for even a few minutes. So safe that he suggested we not sit in the back seat."

"So, any ideas?"

"Well, if some thief is looking at the car, he is looking for a Mercedes, not the stuff in the trunk. He'll want to hot-wire the car and get away as fast as possible. I'll remove the fuel pump relay. No one will start it."

"Okay. That makes sense." Al-Maadi added nervously, "But park it further away before you do."

The next morning, they paid the bill and returned to the car to find a rather disheveled young man standing next to it. He was in his mid-twenties, wearing dirty clothes, and a greasy red keffiyeh. His filthy hair and patchy skin were indications of abject poverty, drug use, or both. As they neared the car, Mohammad discovered the driver's window had been smashed with a rock. Glass was strewn across the seat and floorboard. Speaking to the young man, Mohammad asked, "Did you see who did this?"

The man smiled exposing his brown, rotten teeth. "Is there a reward if I tell you?"

As he neared the man, Mohammad turned his face to avoid the stench of the man's breath. "No, but there will be hell to pay if you don't." He peeked into the car; the ignition had been damaged as well. He reached in to pop the hood before walking around to the front of the car, lifting the hood and replacing the fuel pump relay.

The vagrant was irritated. "If I had known that, you'd still have a window." His tone turned menacing. "Give me a thousand rupees and I'll let you go."

Mohammad chuckled, "And if I don't?"

The man pulled a large, rusty knife from his pocket and pointed it at Mohammad's chest. Al-Maadi had been standing back, content to let Mohammad handle the situation. Now he interjected. "No need for all this. We'll pay you. Just put down the knife."

Mohammad growled, "No, we won't. We won't give this piece of trash a single rupee."

The young man lunged at Mohammad who parried his thrust, grabbed the wrist holding the knife, spun the man around and slammed his face onto the roof of the car. The vagrant dropped the knife and Mohammad slammed his face repeatedly on the roof until it was a bloody mess. The man dropped to the ground unconscious.

Al-Maadi was shocked. "Why did you do that? I said we would pay him and leave in peace!"

"This man deserves nothing. He's filth." Mohammad pulled up the man's sleeve to reveal needle tracks running from his wrist to beyond his elbow. "He's a junkie. A heroin addict. Human trash."

"Yeah, but now what? We can't leave him lying in the dirt, beaten to a pulp. The innkeeper will call the police!"

Mohammad opened the back door and threw the man into the backseat. "Let's go. We'll dispose of him later. Get in."

Al-Maadi wasn't used to taking orders and certainly not from a servant. "I am in charge, Mohammad. Don't you forget it."

"Abu Almawt, when it comes to fighting the infidels and traitors, you're in charge. But, when it comes to keeping us alive, I am. Get in."

Mohammad was obviously irritated and Al-Maadi opted not to push the issue. "So be it."

The bodyguard brushed the glass off the seat and started the car. "With the window broken, the air conditioner will be all but useless. It's going to be dusty."

They drove a few kilometers south before turning east on a crude track leading to a pasture surrounded by trees. There was no one around. Mohammad stopped the car and said, "Wait here." He opened the back door and dragged the unconscious junkie from the car into some tall grass. He took out his 9mm pistol and shot the man in the back of the head.

Al-Maadi was taken aback. "Why did you do that?"

"Tying up a loose end, just like you with Nawaz, only my way is faster."

* * *

When the jet touched down in Larnaca, Lon was there to pick up Alen and John. Encountering the scruffy Texan, Alen quipped, "I would've preferred Sarah."

Lon snorted, "With that ugly mug, I'm the best you can hope for. What'd you learn?"

"Not much. It didn't make sense to him either but he's going to dig into it. If there is anything there, Ivan will find it."

Lon said, "Well, let him work. We have plenty of other stuff to do. We need to find that Novichok."

* * *

Khalid and Mohammad were growing frustrated by their slow progress. In two days, they had covered only a few hundred kilometers. The rough, dusty roads made for miserable conditions. They would inevitably get stuck behind some slow-moving truck which kicked up a cloud of thick dust that Al-Maadi was convinced was actually about 95% animal dung.

Finally, midway through the third day, their situation changed. Nawaz's map directed them to cross Highway N55 just north of Jampur and continue west to the Dera Ghazi Khan Canal. The canal started at the Taunsa Barrage on the Indus River some ninety kilometers north and followed the arid western edge of the Indus River Valley south for several hundred kilometers. Running alongside the canal was a dirt road. Not only was this route much more direct, the road was maintained by the canal authority, so they made much better time. The area around the canal was mostly desert, which guaranteed plenty of dust, but there were few farm trucks. Except for a detour around Rajanpur Air Force Base, for the next two days they were able to follow the canal road south for 650 kilometers until it reached Manchar Lake some hundred kilometers northeast of Hyderabad.

Back on farm roads, they drove to the Kotri Barrage which diverts water into the Karachi Canal. They followed the canal to the rich farm lands southeast of Karachi. The map guided them past Port Qasim and abruptly stopped. Mohammad stopped the Mercedes, got out and stretched. "Now what?"

"Good question. This is as far as the map goes. I guess we're on our own. I need to call Zihad."

"Zihad? Back on the ocean?" Mohammad found it irritating that Al-Maadi provided details of his plan in a piecemeal fashion. He understood the need for security, but he had been with Al-Maadi since shortly after he arrived in Pakistan. He had earned more trust.

Al-Maadi retrieved a new burner from the glovebox and dialed a number scribbled on a piece of paper in his pocket. "Zihad, we are here. We are north of Port Qasim, not far from the steel mills. Where do we meet you?"

"Good to hear your voice, Abu Almawt. I have access to a private dock on Korangi Creek where we'll transfer the material. I will send you the address. It will take me some time to get there, at least an hour or so. Do you have an issue with waiting?"

"No. We're okay. We'll get close and wait for your call." Moments later, a chime indicated he'd received a text. Turning to Mohammad, he said, "It's the address of an ice depot on Korangi Creek."

"I've been to the area. It's maybe twenty kilometers from here. We need to get moving. If we get there before him, we should buy some new clothes. Mine smell like a goat has lived in them."

Al-Maadi laughed, "I'm afraid to smell mine." Placing his hand on Mohammad's shoulder, he smiled and said, "We are near the end, my friend."

Mohammad nodded. "Then, let's go."

* * *

Two days after Alen and John returned to Cyprus, Dr. Pretrukhin called early in the morning. "Alen, my son. I found something last night while on the train back from Niš and it is...disconcerting."

Gunny was in the room, so Alen put the call on speaker. "Ivan, I have you on speaker with a colleague. Is that okay?"

"Yes. Of course. Well, I think I determined what your bad man may be up to. I think..."

Gunny interrupted, "Excuse me Doctor, but this may not be something we want to discuss on an open telephone line."

There was a long pause. "Alen, your friend may be right. If what I found is correct, this may be something for the authorities."

Gunny said, "Doctor, we *are* the authorities. Are you available to meet today?"

"Yes, but I understand Alen is…living abroad, shall we say. It might be better if we…"

Gunny interrupted again. "It's a little after 8 a.m. We can be at your home by noon. Is that okay?"

"But that is less than four hours! How can you…"

"We have a jet."

"Uh, okay. Noon it is."

Gunny replied, "Goodbye, Doctor. I have calls to make." He turned on his heal and left.

Alen chuckled, "See you at noon Ivan. My colleague is a little abrupt but you'll like him."

Gil and Donnie had the engines on the Bombardier spinning by the time they got to the airport. As Alen and Gunny piled on, Gil asked, "Any idea on duration?"

Gunny replied, "Quick trip. Back this afternoon."

"You're the boss."

The airplane landed in Belgrade a little after 10:45 a.m. Gil had called ahead and a hired Audi was waiting for them as soon as they cleared customs. They arrived at Dr. Pretrukhin's flat just before noon. Alen knocked and a surprised Pretrukhin answered the door. He checked his pocket watch in disbelief. "You weren't kidding about noon, were you."

Gunny pushed past Alen and stuck out his hand. "We weren't kidding about the jet either. Hi, I'm Juan Medina. We spoke on the phone."

Pretrukhin shook his hand and studied the battle-hardened old man. Though he was wearing a suit, the eye patch and scar slashing down his face made him resemble a pirate more than a businessman. "Welcome to my home Mr. Medina."

"Please, call me Gunny. Everyone does."

"Okay…Gunny. May I offer you a coffee?"

"Absolutely."

"Cream or sugar?"

Gunny replied, "Black."

Alen smiled, "Likewise."

The three men took their coffees and walked into the living room. "Mr. Medina, I had a chance to closely examine the information Alen provided me the other day and what I found was disturbing."

"Not surprising. These men are terrorists." The bluntness set Ivan aback. Gunny withdrew an envelope from his jacket pocket. It held the original papers they found in Al-Maadi's safe house. Smoothing them out on the coffee table, Gunny asked, "Well, Doctor, what did you find?"

Ivan pointed to figures on the paper. "These radioactive decay numbers don't belong to chlorine, potassium, or magnesium. They simply can't. Then I remembered the 'plus two' superscript. If this man is a…terrorist, I thought maybe it was a code." His thick Handbook of Chemistry and Physics was on the table. He flipped open the front of the book to a periodic table of elements. "Okay, chlorine is in column seven, row three. There is no column nine, so I looked at row five. That's Iodine. It definitely has radioactive isotopes." Pointing again to the paper, he explained, "We originally assumed the 'mev' was millielectronvolts, but we misinterpreted the man's handwriting. The M and V are actually capitalized. That would mean Megaelectronvolts."

Gunny said, "I take it that's a lot more?"

Ivan said, "Yes. A billion times more. The decay energy of 0.970 MeV your bad guy wrote down corresponds to Iodine-131. Very radioactive, but its half-life is only eight days. Too short to be much use as a weapon unless you're standing next to the reactor. Okay, the next one is potassium; column one, row four. Row six is…cesium. This really isn't good." Ivan had bookmarked a couple of pages in the Table of Isotopes and found the entries for cesium. "Alen, what was the beta decay number given for potassium?"

He scanned the paper and said, "Uh, that would be 1.176 MeV."

Pointing to a line on the page, Ivan said, "Mr. Medina, that corresponds to cesium-137. This is a very, very dangerous radioisotope with a half-life over thirty years. Okay, last one, magnesium is column two, row three. Row five is…strontium." He flipped to the other bookmarked page. "The decay number he gave for magnesium was 1.176 MeV which corresponds to strontium-90; another dangerous radioisotope with a half-life of twenty-eight years. It mimics calcium when ingested and settles in the bones."

Ivan picked up the original paper and started studying it up and down. He flipped it over. "Ah, here it is. See this?"

Gunny picked out a faded word in Russian, Припять. "It says Pripyat."

Alen peered at the word. "What's Pripyat?"

Gunny replied, "It's not a what, it's a where. It's a city in Ukraine just outside Chernobyl."

"Exactly."

Alen turned pale. "Oh shit."

Ivan stared at the page in silence for several seconds. "I assess your bad guy has been doing research on a dirty bomb and using the Chernobyl accident as a guide. That's why he included Iodine-131. It was a major contaminate released into the air. The soil in that part of Ukraine is iodine deficient. The people and animals absorbed the radioactive iodine which then settled in their thyroid glands giving them cancer. It was a major factor in the post-accident lethality. However, iodine is not particularly good for a dirty bomb because of its short half-life. It comes from spent nuclear fuel but dissipates quickly once the fuel is put in a cooling pond; but the other two, the cesium and strontium, they're persistent."

Gunny leaned back, absorbing what he had just learned.

Alen pointed to a smudged phrase penciled along the bottom of the page. "Ivan, do you know what this means?"

Ivan studied it with his magnifying glass and copied it to a sheet of paper. He double-checked the original writing and edited his copy. "It's Latin."

Gunny was surprised. "Latin? Are you sure?"

Ivan smirked. "You were expecting something else? Like maybe Arabic?"

Gunny's initial silence told Ivan he was right. "What does it say?"

Ivan read the message aloud. "Qui tradit fratres suos, a Deo punietur. Et ego gladius dei sum."

Gunny sighed. "Doc, in English if you please? I haven't heard Latin since I was a kid in church."

Ivan translated, "He who betrays his brothers will be punished by God. And I am God's sword."

In unison, Alen and Gunny said. "Fuck."

Ivan understood they were onto something very serious. "Gentlemen, if the man you are pursuing releases kilograms of these materials without warning, he could kill thousands of people and contaminate an entire city."

Gunny said, "Hold on, Doc, this is just scribbles on a piece of paper. We have no confirmation that he has any of this stuff."

Ivan said coldly, "I suggest you find out." Turning to Markovic, Ivan said, "Alen, you are like a son to me. Your parents were disappointed when you gave up your studies to join the army. They didn't understand it then, but I do now. God chose you and your friends to be the protectors of mankind; archangels if you will. You must stop this madman before he obtains this material and opens Pandora's Box."

* * *

It took Khalid Al-Maadi and his bodyguard, Mohammad, less than an hour to locate the ice depot Zihad had chosen for a rendezvous point. It was in a working-class neighborhood near the docks. They were early and took the opportunity to buy some new clothes at a local outdoor market. While Al-Maadi bought some simple trousers and a few shirts, Mohammad nervously guarded the car. Even as filthy as it was, the big Mercedes was out of place in the poor neighborhood and drew unwanted attention. As Al-Maadi returned, Mohammad motioned for him to get into the car. "We need to move."

"Why?"

Nodding to a group of men some thirty meters away, Mohammad explained, "That group of men over there; they've been eyeing our car since we arrived. Two of them just moved off to the right. They're trying to get behind us." He had his hand on the 9mm pistol tucked into his belt. "It would be best for all involved if we were no longer here when they do." Khalid threw his parcels into the backseat and quickly jumped in. The Mercedes roared away just as the two prospective thieves emerged from the crowd behind them. The two thugs only narrowly escaped death, if not by the driver of the car, then by its cargo.

They drove around the area for about half an hour before the phone finally rang. It was Zahid. "I'm approaching the dock by the ice depot now. Are you nearby?"

Al-Maadi replied, "Only a few minutes away. We will meet you there."

"Okay." The line went dead. They were one step closer to executing their plan.

When the Mercedes screeched to a stop on the dock, Al-Maadi was irritated not to find the *Sailfish* waiting for them. The pier was deserted except for a blue trawler with the distinctive side booms of a purse seiner. A man was lashing the boat to the dock. Al-Maadi was surprised to recognize the sailor. It was Hamid, Zihad's trusted deckhand. Moments later Zihad appeared from the bridge, waved and jumped to the pier. As Al-Maadi neared the vessel, he recognized it as their home for all those weeks at sea. In the week since they had stepped off the venerable *Sailfish*, it had completely changed—new paint, new side booms and net hoists, and a new name—*Qirsh, Shark* in Arabic.

Al-Maadi reached out to shake Zihad's hand. "It's like a whole new boat?" Glancing back at the vessel, Zihad smiled, "We've been busy since you left us."

"I like it, but why?"

Zihad said, "I deemed it necessary since we encountered that drone off the coast of Yemen. Whoever it was definitely got a good look at the trawler. I assumed it best if we change her name and appearance. If anyone is searching, they'll be searching for the *Sailfish*, not the *Qirsh*."

Mohammad approached with the bags of clothing that constituted their luggage. Tossing them to Hamid he said, "*Shark*. I like it. We're warriors and warriors should have an apt name and there is none better." Turning to Zihad, he added, "Smart move with the changes. Good tactical thinking on your part."

Zihad almost blushed at the comment. Coming from a hardened Al-Qaeda warrior, it was the greatest compliment. "It seemed the logical thing to do. Now about our cargo. I assume it's in the car?"

Al-Maadi replied, "Yes, in the trunk. Three metal cases. The weapon materials are inside. They are…dangerous, so precautions will need to be taken."

"Show me."

Al-Maadi and Zihad walked to the back of the car and popped the trunk. Al-Maadi slid the closest case to the edge and, with Zihad's help, swung it out and onto the ground. He opened the case to reveal the four canisters inside. "This stuff is very dangerous, but these canisters are lined with lead so they are safe to handle…for limited duration. Probably don't want them inside the boat."

"Lead, huh? Radioactive?" Al-Maadi nodded. Zihad studied the canisters. "Hmm. Appear to be what? Ten centimeters in diameter?"

"Twelve," Al-Maadi corrected, "And twenty-five centimeters tall."

Zihad smiled, "I can work with that. How many canisters in total?" "Twelve."

"Okay, I have an idea." He walked over to Hamid and said, "Your telephone, please." Hamid handed it to him without a word. Zihad flipped it open and dialed. He held a brief conversation in Urdu before handing the phone back to Hamid. "That should do it. We should load the cases and leave. What do you want to do with the car?"

Al-Maadi said, "Leave it."

Zihad laughed. "A Mercedes abandoned in this neighborhood? It will be gone by morning."

"That's what I'm counting on."

* * *

Gunny and Alen returned to Cyprus immediately after meeting with Dr. Pretrukhin. Gunny was on the encrypted satphone as soon as their wheels were up. Lon was waiting for them at the airport in Larnaca. "How'd it go? What did Alen's guy find out?"

Gunny growled, "Nothing good."

Lon groaned, "Why is it always bad news?"

As soon as they got back to the villa, an all-hands meeting was convened in the conference room. When all were seated, Rusty asked, "What did you find out?"

Alen said, "I didn't understand it all. Nuclear stuff isn't my strong suit."

Rusty was taken aback. "Nuclear? I thought it was chemical shit."

Gunny said, "It turns out it was in a sort of code. Dr. Pretrukhin figured it out. He's one smart cookie. When Al-Maadi mentioned a chemical, he really meant a different chemical in the same column but two rows further down on the periodic table of elements. Chlorine was iodine. Potassium was cesium. Magnesium was strontium."

"How the hell did he figure that out?"

Alen explained, "First there were those 'plus two' superscripts. They didn't make sense. And those other numbers with the 'mev' after them? Turns out the 'm' and 'v' were capitalized. MeV stands for Megaelectronvolt and refers to the decay of radioisotopes. He matched the decay numbers with the different isotopes. Like Gunny said, Ivan is a really smart guy. Bottom line is Al-Maadi was researching a dirty bomb."

Rusty groaned, "Oh great. Just what we need, a dirty bomb to go along with the nerve agent. Wait, *was* or *is*?"

"Don't know. Dr. Pretrukhin also found a word in Cyrillic—Pripyat. It's a city near Chernobyl. Pretrukhin thinks Al-Maadi used the Chernobyl disaster as a sort of blueprint. He was researching radioactive isotopes released; specifically, cesium-137, strontium-90, and iodine-131. However, Ivan said the iodine isn't workable. Its half-life is too short to be useful. Spent fuel has to go from the reactor to a pond to cool down before you work with it. Most of the iodine-131 decays while the spent fuel is cooling, so it's not recovered during reprocessing. It was a serious factor in the Chernobyl disaster because it came directly from the reactor during the explosion."

Hans asked, "Then why is our guy interested?"

Alen replied, "Ivan said it was an indicator that Al-Maadi really doesn't understand all the science behind this. That said, if he got the other two isotopes, he can definitely make it work. Whoever he gets it from would understand that the iodine is a nonstarter."

Rusty asked, "Where would he get this crap? It's gotta be hard to come by."

"It is. The radioactive cesium and strontium really only come from reprocessing spent fuel."

Hans asked, "Who still reprocesses these days? America stopped decades ago."

"I researched that on the flight back. France is the biggest, followed by Russia, China, India, Pakistan, and North Korea." Alen turned to Sarah and added, "Israel does too, but I don't think they'd hand it over to Al-Maadi. Japan has reprocessed in the past and plans to in the future, but the new plant is still under construction."

Rusty said, "My money is on Pakistan or North Korea."

Lon added, "We can't dismiss Russia either. After all, where'd he get the nerve agent?"

"Good point."

Sarah volunteered, "Pakistan is the only Islamic state on the list and we actually found the information in Pakistan. I'd say that's a clue. Besides, when we lost Al-Maadi, he was heading north into Pakistan." Turning to Alen, she asked, "Where are all the Paki nuke facilities relative to Karachi?"

"North. But then you knew that already." Sarah just smiled.

Magne interjected, "Need I point out we have zero evidence that Al-Maadi has actually acquired this stuff? For all we know, this was his Plan A and when it proved impossible to obtain, he went with Plan B, the nerve agent."

Rusty mulled this over. "That's possible, of course, but we can't afford to be wrong about this. We must assume he's at least pursuing the dirty bomb." The group grumbled, but in the end all nodded in agreement. Rusty leaned forward. "Okay folks, we now have a second potential threat. We aren't sure if Al-Maadi even has this crap, but we have to assume he does or will soon. How much does he need?"

Alen replied, "Unknown, sir."

"Any idea as to his target?"

"Not really. Nothing solid."

Rusty quipped, "Anything squishy?"

Gunny took a deep breath and glanced at Alen. "There was another thing Dr. Pretrukhin, found. There was a handwritten passage in Latin."

"Latin? Are you kidding me?"

Alen said, "No. Dr. Pretrukhin noticed it. He reads several ancient languages—Latin, ancient Greek, Egyptian, Phoenician. He's a bit of a renaissance man."

"What did it say?"

Alen opened his notepad and read, "Qui tradit fratres suos, a Deo punietur. Et ego gladius dei sum."

"Which means?"

Hans answered, "He who betrays his brothers will be punished by God. And I am God's sword."

Alen nodded to Hans, "What he said."

Rusty leaned back and stared at the ceiling. "Well, that doesn't sound friendly. But who is he talking about? Israel? Jordan for chasing him out of the region? Egypt for screwing with his family after the mess in the West Bank?"

Sarah chimed in. "I don't think he is referring to Israel this time. They always refer to them as Zionist scum and stuff like that. Probably not the West either. They are usually just infidels. He talked of betrayal, like it was a fellow Muslim."

"What about the Iranians?" Lon suggested.

Sarah pondered this for a moment. "Maybe, but they're usually called blasphemers or heretics because of the whole Sunni/Shia thing. I'm thinking it's an Arab."

Magne said, "An Arab who betrayed Islam? That would certainly justify a harsh judgement."

Sarah shook her head. "No. They'd be heretics. Traitor sounds almost…"

"Political?" It was Nigel. He'd been listening in silence. "You're a traitor to your country, or your comrades."

Sarah nodded. "I think Nigel may be right."

Gunny piped up. "All this from one word in Latin? Jesus Christ, this is thin. I mean one-ply, gas station toilet paper thin."

Rusty shrugged. "Well, what else do we have to go on?" Turning to Lon, he asked, "Did you pull anything more out of those financial records you snagged? That hawala shit?"

"Nothing specific. Just a bunch of money transfers to unknown people in unknown cities. They used burner phones for all transactions. We ran all the numbers we found, but they were randomly assigned—only functional for a few days or weeks—and none are still working."

"Unknown cities and unknown people but what countries? If I run an illegal hawala, I'm going to change my phone regularly. But ya know what isn't getting changed? The ground I'm standing on. If I buy a burner in Yemen and activate it in Yemen, my phone number is going to be Yemeni. In the US, you can request a phone number for almost any state, but the country code will still be one."

Lon nodded. "That's right. Most cellphone companies aren't allowed to issue phone numbers for other countries."

Hans added, "We may not determine *who* is receiving the money, but we can figure out *where* it's going, at least in broad terms."

Rusty asked Lon, "You have that info?"

"Not on me but give me a few minutes." Lon jumped up from the table and ran to the basement where he and the others had been combing through the take from the Karachi safe house. After a few minutes he returned. "Okay, give me a sec." He flipped through his notebook. "Alright, we have two transactions to country code 93."

Sarah took out her laptop and pulled up a list of country codes from the internet. "That's Afghanistan. Makes sense. Next one."

"Uh, eight to country code 92."

"Pakistan."

Lon continued, "One to country code 966."

John interjected, "That is Saudi. I was assigned there."

Lon scanned down his list. "Three to 968."

Sarah said, "That's Oman."

"Okay last two have the most. We have seventeen calls to country code 971 and twenty-two to 973."

Sarah scanned her list. "Okay, 971 is the UAE. Given that one of the Al-

Rashid guys works there, that makes sense. The last one, 973, is…Bahrain? Why Bahrain?"

Steve Chang spoke for the first time. "The Abraham Accords."

Lon asked, "The what?"

"Don't you read the news? The Abraham Accords were a diplomatic effort that resulted in the normalization of relations between Israel, the UAE, and Bahrain."

Rusty let out a long whistle. "If you're a radical terrorist whose whole purpose in life is to destroy the State of Israel and return it to Arab control, any Arab countries normalizing relations with Israel would probably fit your definition of traitor."

Sarah quipped, "I would say so."

Gunny said, "Interesting theory. Now all we have do is prove it and then figure out Al-Maadi's plan and foil it without getting everyone killed. No problem."

Rusty said, "He already has the nerve agent, so we need to zero in on those isotopes. Where would Al-Maadi get them and how would he transport them without getting nuked like a microwave burrito?"

Hans motioned to Steve and Sarah, "We'll get right on it."

Lon added, "Now that we know what to look for, we'll rescrub the safe house take."

Speaking to Alen, Rusty said, "You and Hans do some research on this stuff. How dangerous is it? How do you transport it? How much do you need for an attack? How would you deploy it?"

"I'm not a physicist, sir," Alen protested.

Rusty smiled, "You're as close as we've got. Just do your best. The rest of you work on locating the mopes who picked up the Novichok in Yemen." Rusty rose to leave. "I have to make some unpleasant phone calls. Praetorians, you have your orders."

* * *

After loading the three metal cases onto the newly rechristened *Qirsh*, Mohammad pulled Khalid Al-Maadi aside. "I have to say I'm impressed with Zihad's forward thinking. He was smart to change the name and appearance of the boat. That may be very helpful if the people flying that drone near Yemen are searching for us."

"Yes, he has proved to be quite clever. When our mission is successful, we'll owe him a great debt." He eyed Mohammad with a degree of suspicion. "You aren't one to freely give compliments. What do you really mean to say?"

"It is not my place to question you, of course, it's just that…Nawaz…"

Al-Maadi smiled. "I get it. You don't agree with eliminating Nawaz and you don't want the same fate to befall Zihad."

"I didn't see the need in sacrificing someone so well-placed with access to materials we may need again in the future."

"I understand, but I had to consider the long term good of Shams Sawda. The movement is more important than any one man; be that Nawaz, Zihad, you, or even me. I didn't make the decision lightly. Yes, Nawaz had unique access but after our attack, his access would have certainly disappeared. The Americans would quickly determine where the isotopes came from. Nawaz said as much. He said the Americans can tell which reactor it came from and even when it was made. After we strike, there will be immense pressure brought to bear by the West, the Saudis, the Bharanians, and even the Chinese. The Pakistanis will be forced to cooperate. They'd quickly determine that Nawaz was the man on the inside. He was brilliant but weak. He would've cracked and revealed all that he knew and, Mohammad, that was a lot. He would've given up me, you, and a large part of our Pakistani network. It had to be done."

"I didn't know, Abu Almawt. Forgive me for questioning you."

"Mohammad, since the death of my cousin, you are my most loyal and trusted friend. Understand that I only do what has to be done. As for Zihad, he is smart and strong but has only been told just enough to do his job. I have no plans to eliminate him because there is no need to do so."

The *Qirsh* did not head to sea but motored into Karachi harbor to Baba Island where Zihad Haq lived. Baba Island was quite small—only about thirteen hectares—but densely populated by over 10,000 people, mostly ethnic Kutchi fishermen. It was almost dark when they tied up at the Baba Jetty on the extreme eastern tip of the island. Leaving Mohammad and Hamid to protect the boat and its valuable cargo, Zihad and Al-Maadi struck out into the crowded, densely packed town. Their destination was a boat building and repair yard some two hundred meters to the west on the north shore of the island. It was home to a number of workshops, but they were interested in one in particular; the machine shop.

Zihad was greeted warmly by the man who ran the shop. "Brother! It is good to see you again."

"You as well, cousin." Motioning to Al-Maadi, he added. "This is a friend of mine, Khalid."

"He is most welcome."

Zihad asked, "Did you find the buoys I called about?"

"Of course." Pointing across the shop he added, "They're over there. My workers are gone for the day. You have the place to yourself. You know your way around."

Zihad shoved a thick wad of rupees into the man's hand. "This should cover the cost of the buoys and anything else we use."

The man stared at the money and smiled, "Praise be to Allah, but this is too much."

"Nonsense. It's for your inconvenience. This was on very short notice." Zihad smiled slyly, "Besides, I expect this to be a profitable venture."

The man shoved the money in his pocket. "Just lock up when you leave."

After he departed, Al-Maadi asked, "Profitable venture?"

"He assumes I am involved in smuggling; a common side business for us Kutchi. Illegal enough for him to keep his mouth shut but not dangerous enough to rat us out to the police."

"Good plan."

The shop was equipped with drills, saws, welding equipment, lathes, and any other tools one might need to build or repair a boat. Zihad really only needed two—a bandsaw and a large drill press. The buoys he requested were nothing special. They were solid foam cylinders, thirty centimeters in diameter and sixty centimeters long with a hole maybe five centimeters wide running lengthwise down the middle. The exterior was covered in hard, red plastic.

Zihad took one of the buoys and sliced it in half with the bandsaw. He then took each half and, using a fifteen-centimeter auger bit, he drilled into the foam until he had hollowed out a cavity to a depth of fifteen centimeters. "You said the canisters are twenty-five centimeters long, right?"

"Yes."

"A canister should easily fit inside." He found a spool of thin stainless-steel cable and cut off a meter-long length. He then used a cable crimp to make a loop at one end and slid a large rubber grommet down to the loop. He fished the cable through the two halves of the buoy matching the cut ends in the middle. He then slid a grommet over the cable extending out the opposite side and fashioned another loop on the other end.

Al-Maadi asked, "What do we do with these?"

Zihad disassembled the buoy and found an empty two-liter bottle in the trash to demonstrate. "Pretend this is our canister." He put the bottle inside the hollowed-out section of one half before sliding the other half of the buoy over it, fishing the cable through as he did. "We will use epoxy glue to seal the two halves together with the canister inside. We pull the cable tight, slide another grommet on before fashioning another loop and crimping it tight. Voila. We then paint over the cut and attach it to the nets between the real buoys. If we encounter a patrol ship, we simply drop the nets into the water like any other fisherman. Even if they board us, our contraband is in the water. You said those canisters were lined with lead. If they inspect the nets, these buoys will be underwater."

Al-Maadi beamed. "Captain Haq, you're a genius!"

Zihad smiled. "Now all we have to do is make eleven more of these."

* * *

The Praetorians needed to narrow their search for a supplier of radioisotopes. The political ramifications of supplying a terrorist organization were too serious for most of the countries on their list. The most logical sources were Pakistan and North Korea. They assessed that the North Koreans would have no real qualms about supplying the ingredients for a dirty bomb but they were motivated by money and would expect rich compensation. Did Al-Maadi have the financial wherewithal to come up with that kind of cash? Delivery was far from assured either. North Korean ships suspected of breaking international embargoes risked getting stopped and boarded. High flux radioisotopes were detectable from airborne platforms making them difficult to transport covertly on the open seas. While North Korea was an option, their first target would be Pakistan. It had an advanced nuclear program which included plutonium reprocessing, was closer to the assumed targets, and was a Muslim state. The likelihood of finding an ideological ally there was much greater.

Unfortunately for the Praetorians, the Pakistani Atomic Energy Commission was not an easy hack. Hans and Steve worked tirelessly to identify the systems they needed to access. They found networks for the power reactors, equipment suppliers, subcontractors, and even the uranium mining entities. However, when it came to the plutonium reprocessing programs, they came up empty. It wasn't that they couldn't hack into those networks; those networks didn't exist. Nothing on the plutonium production reactors, the spent fuel storage, fuel chopping, chemical separation plants, or waste disposal. Even though the world was fully aware that Pakistan had all of these things, as far as the PAEC networks were concerned, they didn't exist.

Steve gave Rusty the bad news. "We're sorry boss, but we can't hack their reprocessing program. Hell, we can't even find the networks to hack. I suspect it's completely air-gapped; no outside connectivity at all."

"Really? That is a pretty huge program to hide. It has to be connected somewhere, I mean HR, health insurance, public affairs, something."

"We mapped all of PAEC's network. I got into every nuclear power station, every mine, their fuel fabrication plants, personnel records, even their headquarters network in Islamabad. I searched for open nodes, closed nodes, dormant servers, unused domains, everything that might indicate another networked isolated from the main net. We got nothing."

Sarah had walked in on the last part of the conversation. "Boss, if you don't mind, let me reach out to some of my former colleagues. Maybe they have some insights on how to get in. They were into A. Q. Khan's knickers ages ago."

Steve asked, "Who's A. Q. Khan?"

"He was the father of the Pakistani nuclear weapons program. He was a metallurgist who worked for URENCO, a Dutch-German uranium enrichment consortium. In the 70s, Khan stole the plans for the centrifuges the Europeans used to enrich uranium for their power reactors and gave it to the Pakistani government. While the Europeans used it for electricity, the Pakis used it for atomic bombs. Khan got away and was sentenced to four years in prison in absentia. In Pakistan, he was a hero and they gave him his own lab, the Khan Research Lab."

Rusty pondered this. "Can you make contact on the sly? Unofficial?"

"Yes, I think so."

"Go ahead."

* * *

Sarah Rabin grabbed a Range Rover and drove into Nicosia. After spending two hours making sure she wasn't being followed, she stopped in a popular tourist area and turned on her burner cellphone. She snapped a few photos and uploaded them to a photo-sharing site to generate innocuous traffic for the phone before opening the Signal encrypted communications app and dialing the number for her Mossad contact, Daniel Charon.

The phone rang six times before a familiar voice came on the line. "Hello, pretty lady. To what do I owe the honor?"

"I was checking in on my little sister to make sure she hasn't been too much of a pain in the ass."

Daniel laughed, "She's doing great work, like her sister, and is very much a pain in my ass, also like her sister. Both traits must be genetic. Why did you really call?"

"I need some historical information pertaining to the British Raj."

It took Charon a couple of seconds to get her meaning. "Oh? The western part I assume?"

"Correct. My associates are trying to reach out to an old friend, Abdul Qadeer, but can't find his email address."

"Ah, I know the place you are seeking and you won't find their address anywhere online, and I mean *anywhere* on the internet or even secure government networks."

"Are you sure?"

"Yes, after they received...*junk mail* from us, Paris, New Delhi, and Langley, they got wise and canceled their accounts. Moved all their billing to the post. I believe the kids call it 'snail mail.' Everything is transmitted in writing or on removable, encrypted drives."

"Sounds incredibly inefficient."

"Yes, but also incredibly secure. Everything is sent by courier; multiple couriers actually. To get access to the data, you need to intercept them en route. To do it undetected would require you recruit both and since they are, as best we can tell, assigned randomly, you would have to wait for both to be on the same trip."

Sarah sighed. "Damn. We don't have that kind of time."

"Was this useful?"

"Only in that we now know not to waste our time."

Charon's voice took a more serious tone. "Does this have to do with the subject of our previous conversation?"

"Afraid so. My boss has already informed the steering committee.

We don't have anything definitive yet, but we're assuming the worst and proceeding accordingly."

"With that man, assuming the worst is a wise plan. Good luck and if you need anything from us, don't hesitate to reach out. What is this about, anyway?"

"Radioisotopes, and not the good kind."

"Are there any good kind?"

Sarah returned to the villa with the bad news. She sat down the team and explained, "The Pakistanis have been the target of multiple cyberattacks in the past. They'd been penetrated by the French, Israelis, Indians, US intelligence services, and God knows who else. They learned from these attacks and eventually decided the best way to safeguard their most secret data was to not have them transmitted via the internet at all. Their most vital secrets are kept on stand-alone computers not connected to the internet or even isolated, government controlled encrypted networks. To move data from one place to another, they used removable encrypted drives carried by military couriers. This is not going to be a matter of Steve dialing in and hacking their fire wall."

Rusty growled, "Well, shit! We need to find out if Al-Maadi has access to their isotopes."

Steve chimed in, "I might be able to dig up something…indirect."

"How?"

"I'm into the PAEC's network but there is no reprocessing info there. However, I have access to Human Resources, so I review job descriptions and educational backgrounds. I cross reference this with similar data from the old US program to determine who might be working on reprocessing based on their job description and background. For example, there is no reactor at a reprocessing plant so you wouldn't need a reactor operator. Reprocessing is a fairly straight forward industrial process that's been around for eighty years, so you wouldn't need a theoretical physicist either. I mean, it's no easy task in a large organization full of people with very technical backgrounds, but it's better than nothing. Once we figure out who works there, we look for terrorist connections."

"Okay, better than nothing. Get on it." Rusty turned to Gunny and said, "I need a drink."

* * *

On Baba Island, Al-Maadi and Zihad were able to turn out the twelve buoy concealment devices for the canisters before the night was over. They took enough grommets and crimps to complete them back on the boat. This required them taking a crimping tool from the machine shop. As they were about to leave, Al-Maadi gave Zihad a wad of rupees. "What's this for?"

"Your cousin."

"I already paid him."

"This is to compensate him for the tools. Leave it for him in his office with a note."

Zihad shook his head. "Not necessary. I'll return the tools tomorrow after we're done."

"No. We're going to leave as soon as we get back to the boat. We're on a schedule. Our brothers in Oman have strict orders and will proceed without us. We'll finish the buoys once we are at sea. Take whatever else we might need."

"Yes, Abu Almawt. In that case, I will take extra crimps and grommets."

"Don't forget the glue and the paint. They need to pass a visual inspection."

"Of course."

Zihad and Al-Maadi gathered up everything they needed from the shop. They loaded them and the hollow buoys into a large crate and placed it on a wheeled cart they found in the yard. Before they left, Zihad put the extra money in an envelope along with a note to tell his cousin where to retrieve his cart. It was late at night before they returned to the boat. The streets of the crowded island were mostly deserted save the odd dog or stray cat, and the metal wheels of the simple cart made a loud and consistent clamor as they pulled it down the rough alleys that passed as roads on Baba Island. Al-Maadi was nervous, fearing the noise would draw unwanted attention. Zihad was unconcerned. "We're just fishermen getting ready to put to sea. No one will care." He was right. What few people they encountered ignored them.

Back at the boat, Mohammad waited impatiently. He'd been up all night. He was not privy to what they were doing or how long it would take so every passing minute was torture for him. His job was to protect Abu Almawt, the leader of Shams Sawda, but to do that, he had to be with him. The stillness of the night made it all the more unnerving.

The clatter of the approaching cart broke the silence. When Al-Maadi and Zihad emerged from the gloom, Mohammad's relief was palpable. "Praise be to Allah, you are safe."

Khalid laughed, "Why wouldn't we be?" As he said this, Zihad hopped aboard the *Qirsh* and moved to the bridge to get Hamid.

Mohammad whispered, "There are countless eyes around here and you are a wanted man. Any of these people would give you up in a second for a mere fraction of the reward on your head. I don't trust Pakistanis, well, except maybe for Zihad. I had too many bad experiences with them in Afghanistan."

Al-Maadi clapped him on the shoulder. "Your fears might be warranted, but we will soon be back at sea. Now help me get this crate on board."

"I never thought I would be so happy to leave dry land again."

They quickly muscled the awkward crate onto the boat. Hamid pushed the cart next to the closest building before trotting back and casting off the lines securing the boat to the dock. As Zihad fired up the engines, Hamid jumped on board and using a long pole, pushed the vessel from the dock. Within a few minutes, they were motoring east down the channel toward the breakwater and the open seas beyond.

* * *

Steve Chang understood what Sarah said about the PAEC network security, but he initially refused to accept it. Penetrating the system was a gauntlet thrown, a personal challenge. He worked half the night trying to find access to the weapons side somewhere on the network, but the more he dug without success, the more he came to accept Mossad was right. The entire Pakistani nuclear weapons program was air-gapped.

That didn't mean he didn't find something useful. With Hans and Alen helping, he dove into the personnel files. They started by excluding the obvious. Anyone with access to the dangerous radioisotopes would need to be an educated technical professional. No janitors, no secretaries, no business managers. They wanted engineers or technicians. Open-source information about the old US program helped identify job descriptions and educational backgrounds that might apply to a modern-day program. Nuclear engineering was obvious but also physics, radiochemistry, inorganic chemistry, nuclear medicine, robotics, chemical engineering, mechanical engineering, electrical engineering, and hazardous waste handling. The wide range of skills that applied to plutonium reprocessing also applied equally to other aspects of a well-developed civilian nuclear energy program like Pakistan's. This wasn't going to be easy.

The men worked tirelessly. The PAEC Human Resources database didn't list specific positions or locations but did provide other data like home addresses and educational backgrounds. They zeroed in on home addresses near Pakistan's two reprocessing facilities. If you worked at a plant, you probably lived nearby. When they identified a possible candidate, they then pulled school records, academic papers published, conferences attended, or anything else that might give a clue as to what they really did for a living. One of the problems they ran into was that the larger plutonium reprocessing facility was right next to the huge Chashma Nuclear Power Plant (CNPP), a facility that employed hundreds of technicians and engineers who all had similar educations and backgrounds as the people they were targeting. CNPP was the haystack in which their needles were hiding.

Steve Chang pushed back from his computer, stretched his back, and rubbed his eyes. "Jesus Christ, this is tedious. If I have to read one more resumé of some guy named Khan, I'm going to shoot myself."

Alen laughed, "Yeah, they all start to run together, don't they?"

Hans interjected, "I consider myself a renaissance man but this nuclear shit reads like stereo instructions."

Chang sighed, "We have to keep at it. Who do we have next?"

Alen said, "Employee number one million and seven—Nawaz Zaman. Bachelors in Chemical engineering from the University of Peshawar. Masters from the National University of Sciences and Technology."

Hans asked, "Any particular focus for his Masters?"

"Just says 'Industrial Processes' which could mean anything."

"Any papers? Publish or perish, right?"

Alen shrugged, "A couple, but I can't tell what they're about. I only speak bio-geek, not chemist-geek."

Hans asked, "What's the most recent one?"

"Something about phosphates and metal."

"Title?"

"Uh, it's a study on phosphate separation of tetravalent metal ions or something like that. No clue what that means."

Hans asked, "Does it mention plutonium reprocessing?"

Alen did a quick keyword search on the paper. "Nope. Zero hits on 'plutonium' or 'reprocessing.'"

"Another dead end," Steve said before asking, "What's a tetravalent metal, anyway?"

Alen threw up his hands, "How the hell should I know?"

"You're supposed to be the brainiac. Jesus, I'll google it myself." Steve returned to his computer and started typing. "Okay, tetravalent means it has four valence states. And before you ask, I'm looking up what valence means. Alright, according to this website, the valence of an atom of an element is that property which is measured by the number of hydrogen atoms or its equivalent that one atom of the element can hold in combination if negative, or displace in reaction if positive."

Hans grunted, "Well, that's clear as mud."

Alen leaned forward in his chair. "I actually recall a little of this from my high school chemistry class. Hydrogen is plus one or minus one. Chlorine is minus one. Carbon is plus four. Something like that."

Steve had dug a little deeper. "The big oaf is right; at least partially. Carbon can be plus two, plus four, or minus four."

Alen said, "Correct. It has three valence states. That makes it trivalent."

Hans asked, "So what metals are tetravalent?"

Steve replied, "Good question. Let me see." He pulled up a periodic table of elements from the internet and ran his finger across the first few rows. "Okay, here we go. The first one is Mn."

Alen added, "That's manganese. What else?"

Steve continued to scan the rows. "Nothing else. Oh wait, there are these two extra rows. Here we go…oh shit."

Hans asked, "What?"

"There are three more; U, Np, and Pu."

Alen said, "That would be uranium, neptunium, and plutonium. You need to separate plutonium from the uranium in spent fuel to make a bomb."

Hans mused, "Why do I suspect that phosphates are somehow involved? Mr. Zaman belongs on the 'probable' list. Where does he live?"

Steve navigated back to the personnel database. "He lives near Chashma in a town called Kundian. Oh, strike that. He did."

"Moved?"

Steve replied, "Dead."

Hans smirked, "Well, I guess he has the perfect alibi. Okay, who's next?"

CHAPTER EIGHT
AND THE HORSE YOU RODE IN ON

On Cyprus, the Praetorians were trying to determine what to do next. There were possibly two plots afoot. But which do they prioritize? The chemical weapon or the radiological one? While there was a debate among the team, to Rusty and Gunny it was clear. Gunny announced, "We're gonna focus on the Novichok first."

Steve asked, "What about the dirty bomb?"

Rusty replied, "It's not like we're going to ignore it, but they definitely have the nerve agent. The dirty bomb is still a big 'maybe.' You worry more about the enemy you *are* facing than the one you might be."

"I understand that, Rusty, but the more I find out about this dead guy, Zaman, the more I'm convinced he was dirty. I pulled his cellphone records. Lots of calls to unregistered burners. Three that never showed up on the network again; one and done. The first call was the evening of the safe house raid. It came from Gambat."

Gunny asked, "What time was the call?"

"About seven hours after we hit the safe house."

"How long does it take to drive from the safe house to Gambat?"

"According to Google Maps, six and a half hours."

Gunny groaned, "Of course it does."

Addressing the group, Steve continued, "There was another call the next day from outside Multan, and a third later the same day from near Chashma. In each case, the burners made only one call to Zaman, and then dropped off the network permanently. If you plot them on a map, it's the most direct route from Karachi to Kundian where our dead guy lived. I worked on Zaman's history too. He's from Peshawar. 'Indian country', according to Gunny. He has no record of criminal or extremist activity, but he has an uncle who was AQ. His mom's brother, Hakim Wazir."

Nigel chimed in. "Wazir? That's a Pashtun name. From eastern Afghanistan and northern Pakistan."

Rusty asked Steve, "How do you know this?"

"Uncle Hakim was a guest of General Abdul Rashid Dostum, one of our preferred Afghan warlords after 9/11. The uncle was picked up in Mazar-i-Sharif after it fell in November 2001. He spent the next year or so locked up in Sherbeghan along with a shitload of other Pakistani Al-Qaeda fighters left behind when the Arab Al-Qaeda leadership abandoned them. FBI photographed and fingerprinted him in 2002. He was released a year later and returned to live with his sister in Peshawar. Since Zaman's father died when he was a baby, I think Uncle Hakim was his father figure, at least until Hakim died of tuberculosis in 2008."

Rusty was impressed. "That's amazing work, Steve. While it doesn't prove Al-Maadi was the one talking to him or that the guy provided the ingredients for a dirty bomb, if I was a betting man, I'd put my money on this Zaman guy being tied up in this mess. That said, we still have to go with what is certain. We're going to focus on the Novichok first." Turning to Alen, he said, "Markovic, grab whoever you need and keep digging on the dirty bomb stuff. Assume the worst, that Al-Maadi has the radioisotopes, and go from there. How would they transport it without being detected? How would they deploy it? Where would they use it for maximum impact? Reach out to your doctor friend if you need to. While no terrorist group has every used a dirty bomb, there's been a lot of analysis on the hypothetical. See what the experts have said. We need an idea of where to start."

Alen nodded and replied, "Yes, sir. I'll get on it."

"In the meantime, we need to find the mopes that met the dhow in Yemen. Find them and we most likely find the Novichok."

"I'll tell the steering committee what's going on. While we're focusing on the Novichok, maybe they can keep the radioactive shit from getting out of Pakistan or at least away from their intended targets."

Magne asked, "How will they move it?"

Rusty shrugged. "Beats me. I'm making this up as I go along."

* * *

S teve Chang and Hans Koenig worked to locate Aziz Uddin and Odai Safi, the two Al-Rashid Engineering employees who picked up the Novichok in Yemen. It was a fairly straightforward process. Their company vehicles had trackers on them and they had already hacked into the monitoring software. In addition, both men were "on call" technicians and were issued company cellphones, so their managers could reach out to them 24/7. Their telephone numbers were listed in the company directory. The company phones were all Samsung models running Android. The Android Operating System, unlike Apple's iOS, was based on a Linux kernel and other open-source software which made it much easier to hack. Steve made equally short work of the Omani and UAE cellular networks. He accessed a non-public service channel used by field technicians and radio frequency engineers. Within minutes of inputting their telephone numbers, he located both men to within a few feet.

Hans was amazed. "Well, that was easy."

"Not really that easy. I'd already mapped the Al-Rashid network from before. I expected we'd need access to the cell nets so I hacked them a few days ago. I put in a backdoor and left it open."

Hans laughed. "You shouldn't have told me. I would've assumed you were a hacking stud."

Steve smiled, "Oh, don't worry. I still am. I'm searching for other associated cellphones. Since Al-Rashid tracks their vehicles, these guys must assume the company tracks their phones as well and has access to their geolocation information. In addition, they should assume the company reads every text or email sent to or from a company phone. These guys aren't stupid. If they're going to coordinate a terrorist plot, they're not going to use their work phones."

Hans asked, "Have you checked the local cell company records for personal cells?"

"Yes. And nothing shows up which means either they trust their company with details of every call they make or..."

"Burners."

"Bingo."

Hans leaned back in his chair. "Well, that sucks. How are we going to find them?" Steve just grinned. "You've already figured that out, haven't you."

"Yeah. Joe Terrorist has a day job working for Al-Rashid which gives him a cellphone, so he's reachable anytime, day or night. He also has to be available to his terrorist boss, so he has a separate burner. He never knows when either boss is going to call so…"

Hans replied, "He keeps both on him."

"Exactly. A professional technician carrying two phones is not unusual, one for work and one for the family."

Hans asked, "If the personal phone is a burner, how do we find it?"

"Correlation. I have a program that will collect the Electronic Serial Numbers of any cellphone within close proximity to the target phone, kind of like what we used in Cairo to find that relay on the bus. It was developed to identify suspect terrorists. A known bad guy meets with a bunch of unknown bad guys. By determining what phones are near the known bad guy, we identify the phones of the other bad guys. You then do the same with those bad guys and so on. You map a whole network that way. It worked great until they figured out they shouldn't take cellphones to terrorist meetings. Our two technicians may not have that luxury. They have to be reachable. If we put their Al-Rashid numbers in the program, the telephones within close proximity for a majority of the time, especially when the Al-Rashid phone is moving, should be our burners."

Steve and Hans set up the program, entered Uddin's and Safi's work cellphones and went to get some lunch. After eating, they checked on the computer program. Safi was static at an office building in Dubai with three other cellphones nearby. By six o'clock, two of the phones split off and moved away. Safi's work phone and the other third unidentified phone moved together toward Sharjah. It had to be his burner. Uddin had been in Oman driving north most of the day. His company phone and another unidentified phone were in lock step the entire trip. Either it was his burner or he had a passenger.

Steve peered at the numbers on the screen. "Okay, I think Safi is heading home. He works out of Sharjah, right?" Hans nodded. "Those other two phones must have belonged to other technicians working on the same job. They split up and are pinging in Dubai, one at an apartment out by the airport, and the other in a working-class neighborhood in Al Awir, west of the city."

Hans noted the time. "Yeah, that makes sense. It's after six there. Uddin still on the road?"

"Last time I checked. He has a huge service area." Steve highlighted the two numbers on his computer. "These two numbers with Uddin and Safi have to be our burners. Let's check again tomorrow morning to confirm it after our guys go to work."

"Agreed. We should keep the correlation program running in case they toss their phones for new burners."

Steve nodded. "Good idea. It also should help us identify other members of the cell. I doubt these two are working alone. Hell, they'd need muscle for security if nothing else. I'll set the program to start ranking all associated cellphones. I'll start tracking both work phones and both burners. I'll also get into the network archives to map out where these guys have been traveling over the last couple of months. Being that these guys are essentially traveling salesmen, I'm not sure what that will tell us, but it can't hurt."

Hans asked, "Can you pull up their old texts? Kids these days just love to text."

Steve smiled, "Does the Pope shit in the woods?"

The German was suddenly confused. "What?"

"I'll explain later."

* * *

The *Qirsh* cleared the breakwater, extending out from Fort Qasim at the mouth of Karachi harbor steering south like the other trawlers toward the fishing grounds of the Arabian Sea. Unlike the others, however, it motored south for only an hour before turning west toward the Gulf of Oman.

Zihad piloted the small craft across the smooth seas while Hamid slept in anticipation of taking the helm later that evening. This gave the others the opportunity to load the canisters into the hollowed-out buoys that were to be their hiding places. The first thing they did was waterproof the canisters by brushing on a thick layer of marine paint along the seam of the lids. Nawaz never said the canisters were watertight and they weren't willing to risk it.

While the paint was drying, they prepared the buoys. They laid them out on the deck along with a rubber grommet and cable crimp for each. Once the paint on the canisters was somewhat dry, Zihad placed a canister inside the buoy half with the looped cable and fished the other end of the cable through the other half of the buoy. He slid the cable through a grommet and then one side of a cable crimp. He then passed the cable back through the other side of the cable crimp to fashion a loop. Placing the assembly on the deck, he had Mohammad hold it while he grabbed the heavy crimping tool they took from the workshop. The tool resembled a large bolt cutter but instead of cutting, it mashed the crimp tight.

Zihad showed them how to blend the two components of the epoxy, the resin and hardener, into a milky paste. There was enough slack in the cable to separate the two buoy halves a few centimeters. Using a flat stick, he smeared the epoxy liberally on the cut edges of the buoy and smashed them together tightly. Finally, he wrapped the seam with duct tape to hold the two halves in place while the glue hardened.

As he gingerly placed the reassembled buoy in the crate, he said, "Okay, you need to do this for the other eleven while I steer the boat. Can you manage?"

Mohammad nodded. "We'll be fine. I've used epoxy before to make roadside bombs in Afghanistan."

Zihad laughed, "Well, this is not that dangerous."

Al-Maadi smirked, "Don't be so sure."

It took them a couple of hours but Al-Maadi and Mohammad securely sealed the other eleven lead canisters inside the buoys. Once they were finished, Al-Maadi walked to the bridge. "Captain Haq, we're done. When do we finish?"

"We need to make sure the epoxy sets firmly. It will take several hours. Then we need to sand off any epoxy that oozed out and paint them. You have time to clean up and rest."

Al-Maadi wasn't used to any kind of physical labor. His hands were dirty and sticky from the epoxy. "How do you get this stuff off your hands? It really stinks."

Zihad chuckled and replied, "It doesn't come off very easily. The easiest method is to wash your hands in diesel but then, instead of smelling like epoxy, you smell like diesel."

Al-Maadi scowled. "Well, at least I won't be sticky."

The buoys were left to harden overnight. Hamid had been asleep during the assembly process and was none the wiser. The fewer people who knew, the better. About eight o'clock in the morning, Zihad relieved Hamid at the helm. By nine o'clock, Hamid had eaten and retired to his bunk for some much-needed sleep. Once Hamid was contentedly snoring, they set about to finish. They removed a buoy and stripped off the duct tape. Using a rasp, Zihad ground off any burrs of hardened epoxy on the exterior before sanding the seam. He then took a can of red spray paint to cover the seam. Al-Maadi was amazed. Aside from its weight, it was like any other buoy. "Now, do the other eleven."

It took them less than an hour to finish the other eleven concealments. An hour after that and the paint was dry. Zihad returned from the bridge to check on their progress. Picking up one of the buoys and inspecting it, he declared it acceptable. "We're ready for the last step."

With Mohammad's help, he dragged a large section of fishing net out onto the deck. The net was made of thin but very strong nylon mesh. Along the top edge ran a heavy, braided nylon rope. This provided the real strength of the net. Attached to the rope at regular intervals were red plastic buoys almost identical to those they had just prepared. Each was attached to the rope by two large threaded, chain quick links. Zihad unscrewed the links, disconnected a buoy and connected their new buoy in its place. "Can you tell the difference?"

Mohammad shook his head. "It's just like the others."

"That was the plan. Now, we need to replace every third buoy on each side of the top rope starting with the ones closest to the two ends. The ones we just made won't float; we need to space them out or they'll be obvious when in the water. Once we do this, we're done, at least until we reach our destination."

* * *

The next morning, Steve and Hans checked on the two Al-Rashid technicians. Safi's cellphone had him in Sharjah with his suspect burner phone in the same location. Uddin's situation was a little unclear. His suspect burner was with him, but he wasn't at home. He was in a hotel in Ibri, a city west of Muscat. Hans asked, "He lives in Salalah, doesn't he?"

Steve nodded. "Yeah, way down south, near Yemen. What is he doing all the way up here?"

"Meeting a customer?"

"That doesn't make sense. This location is way closer to the home office in Muscat."

Hans mused, "Maybe he's heading back to the home office for a meeting or something?"

"I don't think so." Steve zoomed out on the map. "If he was driving from

Salalah to Muscat, he'd stay on Highway 31. Ibri is two hundred miles west. Let me check something." Steve opened another screen on his computer and accessed the vehicle tracking program Al-Rashid used. "Okay, his company van is still in Salalah. He must be in his personal vehicle."

Hans asked, "Is he on holiday?"

"Let's find out." Steve accessed Al-Rashid's personnel network and pulled up Uddin's file. "Yep. Says here he is on personal leave for a week starting yesterday. Notes indicate he's going to Dubai."

"Safi is right next door in Sharjah." Hans pondered this for a moment and posited, "Why wouldn't he fly? I mean, that has to be like a twelve-hour drive through the desert. Why not a two-hour flight instead?"

Steve turned to face Hans and snapped his fingers. "Airport security. He doesn't want to go through security."

"Because he's carrying something he doesn't want anyone to find."

"Makes sense. Not actually proof of anything, but it makes sense. You keep tracking him and I'll tell Gunny."

Gunny came down a few minutes later. Steve and Hans went over what they knew and what they suspected. Gunny was stoic. "Good work guys. Where is this Uddin asshole now?"

Steve replied, "He just got back on Highway 21 moving west."

"And what about the other one, Safi?"

Steve pulled up the map of Sharjah. "He's still at home. He's two hours ahead of us; he should be at work." He checked Safi's personnel file. "Well, guess who else is on vacation this week?"

Gunny asked, "How long before Uddin gets to Dubai?"

"Four hours, give or take."

"Okay, keep tracking them. They're up to no good. We need to find out if they're the ones going to use the Novichok or just middlemen. Also, check out other cellphones near them. How many have subscribers and how many are burners. If they're meeting with other bad guys, they'll probably have burners too. Let's identify their circle of friends, or at least their cellphones, and then track them backwards if possible. I doubt Safi would keep the Novichok at his house. We need to pinpoint any locations Safi and his contacts congregated at after he returned from Yemen. One of those places must be where they stashed it."

"Already on it, boss. We started collecting raw data on associated cellular phones yesterday. Already gained access to the text messages on their company phones. I'll pull it off the Omani and UAE telephone company servers for the burners too, now that we've identified them. We just need to separate the wheat from the chaff."

"Good, I'll tell the boss. Be prepared to move out. I suspect we're going to Dubai soon."

Hans smiled, "I always liked that town."

* * *

As the Praetorians loaded their gear aboard the Bombardier 8000, the mood was unusually somber. Missing was the usual joking and repartee they used to hide their stress. They were accustomed to going into battle, but this was somehow different. None of them doubted their ability to best an opponent in anything close to a fair fight. They were almost always outnumbered and always won. In the raid on the Libyan Black Sun cell, they were outnumbered twenty-three to six. At Kotov's compound in Syria, it was eighteen to six. Aboard the *Amuratu*, twenty-one to eight. While there had been a couple of injuries, they hadn't lost a member of the team. But it wasn't men with weapons they were worried about, it was the Novichok; a silent killer you couldn't out-fight, out-shoot, or out-think. For the first time since the Praetorians were organized, they were packing gas masks.

Novichok was an advanced nerve agent and, like it's less sophisticated predecessors, was an organophosphate acetylcholinesterase inhibitor. It killed by stopping the natural breakdown of acetylcholinesterase, a neurotransmitter. This caused all the muscles in the body to contract involuntarily, resulting in respiratory and cardiac arrest. Unlike its predecessors, Novichok was initially designed in the 1970s to be undetectable to the standard NATO chemical detectors of the day and to defeat NATO chemical protective equipment. The standard reaction to nerve agent exposure was injection with atropine followed by decontamination, but it was not totally clear if that would work with the Russian agent. He was the unseen enemy that, by the time you recognized you were fighting him, he had already killed you.

The Praetorians did have one advantage—Novichok was binary— two components that when mixed produced the weapon. While each precursor was dangerous, it wasn't deadly. If they got to the precursors before the terrorists mixed them, they'd thwart the attack.

Nigel was the first to ask the obvious question. "When we get this shit, what do we do with it? It's not like we flush it down the loo."

Gunny mulled this over for a minute. "That's a good point. I sure as hell don't want it on the jet and we can't exactly leave it lying around either."

Sarah posited, "Why not leave it to the Emiratis? It's their country and their people we're saving. The least they can do is clean up the mess."

"Maybe. I see the attraction of dropping it in their laps and walking away, but they won't know what to do with it. That might be as dangerous as leaving it with the terrorists."

Alen Markovic raised his hand and said, "Uh, sir? I have been doing some research on Novichok like you asked. One of the things I researched was how to destroy it. Since we didn't find it on the *Amuratu*, I didn't see any reason to mention it before."

"Well, mention it now."

"In the 1990s, the US and Russia agreed to destroy all the old chemical weapons."

Lon quipped, "Well, obviously not all of them."

Alen continued, "Apparently not. Anyway, the Russians built several plants for the chemical destruction of chemical agents. They wanted to recycle the components into useful products such as pesticides, rubber, fertilizer, etc. They used solvents like monoethanolamine, ethylene glycol, and orthophosphoric acid to chemically transform and neutralize the agents."

John said, "Gee, let me check my rucksack. I may just have a bottle of the orthophospho shit in there."

Alen glared at him. "I'm just telling you what I found out, dumbass."

Rusty leaned forward. "That was the Russians. What did the US do with theirs?"

Alen smiled, "That was what I was about to get to before I was interrupted by a moron." John flipped him off and Alen continued. "The US opted for incineration at very high heat. Essentially broke the chemicals down to their elements which then recombined randomly and harmlessly in the exhaust stream. Water, nitrogen, and other gasses were added to direct this recombination toward more benign chemicals."

Rusty said, "That's good and all, but we no more have a high heat industrial furnace than we have some of that orthophospho crap. Is there an actual practical solution in all this talk?"

"Yes, sir. Gas turbines."

"Turbines?"

Alen explained. "Gas turbines are used throughout the world for electricity generation in peaking plants. They spin up quickly to provide lots of power during peak demand, hence the name. The Middle East is awash in cheap natural gas, so they tend to use them for everyday generation more than we do in the west. A power turbine combustion chamber runs at about 1100 degrees Celsius. That's over 2000 degrees Fahrenheit. That is more than hot enough to chemically destroy the precursors. All we need to do is inject them into the fuel stream."

"How do we do that?"

Nigel volunteered. "It's not that difficult. Navy ships have been using gas turbines for years. The name is deceptive. Gas turbine refers to hot gases spinning a turbine blade, not the fuel. Navy ships run on liquid, petroleum-based fuels."

Alen patted Nigel on the shoulder. "My big Scottish friend is right. These turbines run on natural gas, refined oil, or both. All we need to do is identify two peaking plants running on liquid fuel and add our precursors to the fuel stream."

Rusty asked, "Two?"

"Well, yeah. We don't want the precursors to accidentally mix in the fuel tank."

"Good point. Have you located two such plants?"

"Uh, not yet. Not sure where to start."

Rusty yelled behind him, "Steve?"

"I'm on it. I'll find a couple."

Gunny snorted, "I'm so glad we figured out what to do with the shit afterwards. All we have to do is find it, take it, and kill the bad guys before they use it."

* * *

Aziz Uddin expected it would take about five hours to drive his rented van the 290 kilometers from Ibri to Dubai. He wasn't in any particular hurry and he didn't want to draw the attention of the police on either side of the border. When he got to the Mezyad Border Post just inside the UAE, his vehicle was stopped for inspection. He provided his Pakistani passport and opened it to his Omani resident permit. On the opposite page was the UAE visa from a previous work trip. The inspector studied his passport before asking. "What's your business in the UAE?"

Uddin handed the inspector his company ID and a folded piece of paper. It was a work order on Al-Rashid letterhead. "I work for the Al-Rashid company. I'm carrying a new dehumidifier and canisters of air conditioning refrigerant for the new stadium. Apparently, the Sheik's private box was too muggy for his wife. The Sheik's wife gets what she wants."

The inspector chuckled. "Like wives everywhere, I suppose." He tapped on the side of the van. "This is not an Al-Rashid van."

"No, it's a rental. The transmission in my company van went out on the way here. This is a priority job, so my boss told me to rent a van. Had a hell of a time moving the dehumidifier. Had to borrow a forklift from a nearby warehouse. I have the rental contract if you want it."

"Not necessary. Open the van."

"Yes, sir." Uddin jumped out of the van and scurried to the back. He opened the two doors to reveal a large piece of equipment on a pallet. "Here it is. Just a big air conditioner really. Those boxes contain canisters of refrigerant and respirators. The way this thing works is…"

The inspector waived him off. "I don't care." He placed an entry stamp in Uddin's passport. "You may go."

"Thanks. Have a good one." By the time he said this, the inspector was already moving toward the next vehicle in line.

As Uddin pulled back onto the highway, he dialed his phone. "Safi, it's me. I'm through. I'm about two hours out. We need to go over things when I arrive."

"Understood. I will tell the others." The line went dead. They were entering the final stages of what they hoped would be the deadliest terrorist attack in history. They didn't know the half of it.

* * *

Using the Bombardier's satellite link, Steve Chang was able to hack into the Dubai power authority's network fairly quickly. Once inside, he turned over to Hans and Nigel the tasks of navigating the network and identifying two liquid fueled peaking plants. Hans asked, "What are we looking for?"

"Their SCADA System."

"A what system?"

"SCADA. That stands for Supervisory Control and Data Acquisition. It controls their entire power grid from generation to the outlet. There will be a system schematic that will list all the generation sources and tell you which are online, which are offline, and which are scheduled to be fired up or wound down. We want turbine units currently running on liquid fuel."

Hans asked, "How do we find these turbines on the schematic?"

Nigel answered, "They'll be isosceles trapezoids."

Hans replied, "One, what is that? And two, how do you know that?"

Nigel chuckled and drew a picture of an isosceles trapezoid on a piece of paper. "It's a triangle with the top chopped off and laying on its side. There may be two; one for the compressor and a mirror image for the turbine. I know it from serving on a Type 45 destroyer. They're turbine powered. The engineering control system is similar to this SCADA thing Steve was talking about."

Steve smiled and said, "And with that, I leave you in Nigel's capable hands."

Hans asked sarcastically, "What are you going to be doing while we're working?"

"I've got bigger fish to fry. I have to find the terrorists and identify their cell."

"Oh."

To collect the Electronic Serial Numbers of cellphones in proximity to Uddin and Safi, Steve's computer program had been running on his laptop continuously for a couple of days. He now ran them through the two major UAE telecommunications companies' subscriber databases to separate the phones with subscriber data from the burners. Legitimate co-workers or customers would most likely be using company phones or personally subscribed cellular phones. The Shams Sawda members would most likely be using burners. Next, he reviewed the call records of Uddin's and Safi's burners. They deleted their call logs on their phones regularly, but he was able to retrieve the information from the phone companies in UAE and Oman. He cross-referenced the calls to and from their burners with the cellphones the program had identified based on proximity to Uddin and Safi. It quickly came up with eight suspect numbers. All eight were pinging on the network in Dubai. All eight suspect phones were purchased and registered in Dubai within the last five weeks. What convinced Steve he was onto something was the fact that all of the eight phones had only placed calls to Uddin's burner, Safi's burner, and each other; ten phones that only contacted each other. "Well damn if this isn't a textbook terrorist cell."

* * *

As Aziz Uddin entered the outskirts of Dubai, his cellphone chirped. He had a text. The message contained only an address in the Alsajaa industrial area east of the Sharjah International Airport. When he arrived at the address, he found a small, shabby building with a faded sign above the door reading "Jazaan Mechanical." As he slowed, the front door opened. It was Odai Safi. "Go around back and park inside the shop."

Uddin drove the van behind the building. The garage door was already open. As soon as he pulled in, Safi closed it behind him. As Uddin got out of the van and stretched, Safi walked up and gave him a big hug before kissing him on both cheeks. "I am so happy to see you, my brother."

"And I you. What is this place?"

"It was a small mechanical repair shop. I was acquainted with the owner, Mr. Jazaan. He was a good man. He died a few months ago. I rented this place from his son last month."

"Is the son going to be a problem?" Uddin asked with concern.

Safi laughed. "Him? No. He works at one of the fancy hotels on the coast. He refused to follow in his father's footsteps. He's a dandy who doesn't like to get his hands dirty, that one. I paid three months in advance. He won't be back until the money runs out."

"Good. But we won't need it that long. Just a few days more, inshallah."

Safi asked, "Have you heard from Abu Almawt?"

"No, but then, we aren't supposed to. Everything is going according to plan." Uddin surveyed the place. There was a small office/lobby in the front. Except for a thick layer of dust, the simple metal desk was unchanged from when the previous owner died; invoices and paperwork in neat piles, a green lamp, an ancient stapler, a tea-stained cup, and a small wooden pencil holder with an assortment of random pens. In the back was the shop. On one side was a large metal work bench with vises, a grinder, and several plastic bins with nuts, bolts, screws, etc. On the opposite wall were metal shelves holding a myriad of hand tools, spare parts, and a number of small appliances in varying states of disassembly. Uddin reflected on the man who had made his livelihood from this simple space which allowed him to raise a son with little or no appreciation of hard work. *Maybe the little ingrate will be at the stadium.*

Safi interrupted his daydream. "Any problem with the bottles?"

"Uh, no. No problem." They walked to the back of the van. Uddin took out one of the boxes. Inside was a standard green, eleven-kilogram industrial refrigerant tank.

Safi picked it up and inspected it. "This is it? It looks like every tank out there."

Uddin laughed, "It's supposed to, you idiot."

"I'm afraid I'll mistake it for a real one."

"Well, don't. These have been modified. The top screws off to pour in the two ingredients. The have an extra tube to make sure it draws from the bottom of the tank. Before we connect them, we'll pressurize them with air or freon so the chemical is forced out." He reached into another box in the van. "I also brought these."

"Respirators? We already have some of those."

Uddin explained, "Our Al-Rashid respirators are designed for ammonia and halon. This is a military gas mask designed for nerve gas. We need to wear them when we transfer the precursors into the tanks."

"I thought the precursors weren't dangerous?"

"Not as dangerous as the Novichok, but do you want to breathe that shit?"

Safi shook his head. "No, you're right."

"When do we meet the men?"

"Tonight. I have one of the precursors stored here. The other is at my shop."

Uddin was taken aback. "Your shop! Is that safe?"

"Yes. My work partner, Abdul, is on a job in Abu Dhabi. He won't be back for a week."

"Well, let's get started with the half that's here."

Uddin and Safi donned hazmat suits that covered them from head to toe. The suits were made of chemical resistant polyethylene-coated Tyvek and included heavy duty neoprene gloves. Rather than the face shields, they wore the gas masks Uddin brought. Safi retrieved a funnel with a long rubber hose attached as Uddin unscrewed the top of a green refrigerant tank. The precursor was in a large, heavy steel cylinder about twice the size of their green tank and required both men to muscle it into position. It had a tapered neck with a screw top about eight centimeters in diameter. There were no markings on the gray cylinder except for "Компонент А" (Component A).

They set the heavy gray cylinder on a crate and removed the top. They placed the end of the rubber hose into the empty refrigerant tank on the floor. Safi started to slowly tip the cylinder as Uddin positioned the funnel to catch the milky liquid as it poured out. The men were sweating and flinched with every drop of the toxic elixir that splashed on their suits. It took them several minutes to transfer about half of the precursor into the green tank. Uddin sealed the green tank and replaced it with another. They then repeated the process. It took less than twenty minutes but both men were exhausted—mentally more than physically.

Safi said, "We need to mark them somehow to distinguish them from the others."

"I considered that. I have some stickers. We'll label these as R-22 and the other as R-32. To anyone else, they're like any other tank. If it makes you feel better, we'll put a red dot on them or something."

"Good idea. We need to wash these off. Some spilled."

"I was told to use ethylene glycol to clean out the Russian bottle. I guess it would work on these too."

"Ethylene glycol? Antifreeze?"

"Yes. I don't suppose we have any."

Safi pointed to the van. "There's some in the radiator."

Uddin shrugged. "Good point. I guess we could siphon some out. Do you have a hose?"

"There's the one on the funnel."

"Do you want to suck on that?"

Safi snapped back, "Hell no! I'll look around. There has to be something."

While Safi searched for a hose, Uddin raised the hood on the van. He immediately spotted the radiator overflow tank. It was about a third full of coolant. He shouted, "Never mind. I've got it." He disconnected the small hose leading from the radiator to the overflow tank. The tank was wedged into a slot held on only by friction and gravity. With one big tug, he was able to dislodge it. He poured some of the neon yellow liquid into a plastic bucket he found on a work bench. He scrounged up a relatively clean shop towel and dipped it in the liquid. He used it to wipe down the two green refrigerant tanks they had just filled. He then put the lid on the Russian cylinder before wiping down the exterior.

Safi said, "Do we need to rinse that out?"

"Why? I don't care what happens to it. I just don't want to get any of that shit on me. Is there somewhere we can dump it?"

"Sure. There's a scrap yard a block or so away. I'll toss it over the fence when it gets dark." Uddin started to strip off his hazmat suit and stuff it in a large trash barrel. "Aren't we going to need that again?"

"No, I brought extras." Uddin reinstalled the overflow tank in the van and shut the back doors. "We need to get going. We have the other precursor to deal with."

* * *

The Bombardier 8000 landed at Sharjah International Airport about the time Uddin and Safi were finishing filling the first green refrigerant tank. Gil routinely used Sharjah instead of the larger Dubai International because it was much easier to get in and out of. He'd been doing this for years and the local customs and immigration officials were familiar with him. This meant a cursory inspection if any inspection at all. As Donnie spun down the engines, Gil lowered the stairs to meet the inspector. "Hey, Hamid. I see they haven't fired you yet."

Hamid chuckled. "It's all but impossible to fire me. I am a native Emirati and a civil servant. I am what you would call 'bulletproof,' no?"

Gil laughed, "I guess you are at that."

"Who do we have today? Mr. Wyatt?"

"Yes. Him and a bunch of others. It's a full flight, twelve with Donnie and me."

Hamid leaned in and whispered, "Is *she* on board?" Hamid had glimpsed Sarah a year or so earlier and she had made an impression.

Gil glanced around conspiratorially and whispered back, "Yes, but you didn't hear it from me."

Rusty deplaned, followed by Gunny and Sarah. Walking down the stairs, he reached out to shake Hamid's hand. "It's Hamid, right? How ya been?"

Hamid was unaccustomed to being treated respectfully by the rich people who used his airport and he appreciated it. "Yes, Mr. Wyatt. I've been fine."

"Please call me Rusty." Motioning to Gunny and Sarah, he said, "You remember Mr. Medina, my chief of security and my personal assistant."

"Of course, sir. Welcome back to Sharjah." He was talking to Rusty but staring at Sarah. "Please, right this way." As he led Rusty, Gunny, and Sarah to immigration, the rest of the team piled off the plane.

Lon shook his head and smiled. "With her around, why do we even bother with passports. We might as well be furniture."

John said, "Hey, fine by me. The less hassle the better."

Magne walked past him and quipped, "If the Emiratis employed female customs agents, you'd all be thanking me."

Nigel shoulder-checked the Norwegian as he walked by, adding, "You are so full of shit, you dandy twit."

"Jealousy doesn't suit you."

As expected, immigration and customs were cursory. Rusty Wyatt was a billionaire with multiple business interests and a residence in the country. The Emiratis were nothing if not pro-business. Gil and Donnie saw that all the luggage and equipment was loaded onto a truck and taken to Rusty's home on Hussain Al-Shaali Road. His house was in the upscale Meshairef neighborhood north of Sharjah proper. It wasn't the largest house on the street but was set back from the road, shrouded by thick trees and had access to the harbor beyond. Its relative proximity to the sheik's palace also meant there was ample security. Rusty was confident leaving the home unattended for months and returning to find all was as he left it.

Steve Chang had been monitoring Uddin and Safi's cellphones continuously since they left Cyprus. As he piled into a rented Mercedes SUV with Gunny, Rusty, and Hans, he opened his laptop and used a cellular modem to access the internet. "Okay, I got them. They're in an industrial park east of the Sharjah airport. Hell, we should have dropped a bomb on them and gone home."

Rusty asked, "That Safi guy works there? Is it his office?"

"Negative. His office is in Ajman which is only a couple of miles from your house. Their phones are pinging further east. Let me pull up a map." A few seconds later, Steve said, "Okay, Safi and Uddin—or at least their phones—are registering inside the Alsajaa industrial area."

Gunny asked, "You got an exact location?"

"Neither burner is GPS enabled but Uddin's company phone is. Let me zero in." He navigated through the local phone network until he found the page he wanted. Typing in Uddin's number, the system came back with geocoordinates. He copied the location data and dropped it into his mapping software. It gave him an address. A quick search on the address yielded a hit. "Okay, our guys are currently at a place called Jazaan Mechanical. It's a small business. No more that 1200 square feet." He continued digging. "Jazaan Mechanical is owned by Ali Jazaan, age 67. He is listed as the owner/operator; no additional employees. Let's see what there is on him." A few moments later he added, "Well, this is a dead end, quite literally. Mr. Jazaan died three months ago. According to his obituary, he is survived by his wife and one son, Kamal."

Gunny asked, "What about the kid? Any terrorist connections?"

"He's on LinkedIn. Not typical for a terrorist. Uh, says here he works as a manager at the Four Seasons Dubai at Jumeirah Beach. Very high-end place. Went to college locally. Undergrad in Hospitality Management and an MBA. Married. One kid. Doesn't read like a terrorist but then Al-Maadi is a doctor so..."

"Not one to take over daddy's repair shop either," Rusty noted.

Hans said, "Maybe he rented it out or lets a friend use it?"

Gunny mulled it over. "That makes more sense. Let's get unpacked. We'll do some recon tonight. Meanwhile, keep an eye on these mopes."

"Yes, sir."

* * *

Leaving the canisters with Component A at the rented repair shop, Safi drove his car to his Al-Rashid facility while Uddin followed in the van. The Al-Rashid shop was large, orderly and well-equipped. Uddin drove the van into the shop and the two repeated the process with the Novichok Component B. They were still nervous but accomplished their task more quickly this time. Like before, they used coolant from the van to wipe down the two modified green refrigerant tanks and the Russian cylinder that had held the Component B.

Safi asked, "You ready to meet with the others?"

"Yes, we need to go over the plan. Have they been told the target?"

"Of course not. It is as Abu Almawt ordered. I will contact them. They're expecting your arrival. We have a rented a house close to the camel race track in Lahbab. The track provides good cover for strangers being in the area. I'll text them to meet tonight at eight o'clock." Safi opened his burner and typed, "Meeting tonight at 8:00 at house."

Lahbab was a farming community an hour south of Sharjah. Rather than take the van, they drove Safi's personal car, a nondescript Kia sedan, to the simple farmhouse south of the race track. Uddin surveyed the area. The farmhouse was a simple, concrete block structure. There were no lights on, no car in the driveway, no children's toys in the yard, no sign of human activity. "What is the story behind this place?"

"The farmer who owns it retired and moved in with his daughter in Al Dhaid. He leased the farmland to a neighbor. We rent the house, ostensibly as a place to sleep after the camel races. It is an ideal location, lots of privacy. No other houses within five hundred meters. The trees around the house provide screening. Any cars are not visible from the road."

Uddin nodded. "Good. When will the others be here?"

"They should arrive in the next ten minutes or so."

The inside of the house was dark and musty. All the windows had their blinds drawn and curtains shut to keep out prying eyes. Entering through the front door, the kitchen was directly ahead along with a door leading to the backyard. The kitchen was furnished with a small table and four chairs. The cabinets had curtains instead of doors. The appliances consisted of an ancient refrigerator and a stove that he assessed would sooner explode than light up. To the right of the front door was a living room with a couple of dirty, threadbare couches, a few cheap plastic patio chairs, and an old television. To the left was a narrow hallway. Down the hall was a bedroom with a small window overlooking the front yard. Across the hall was a pantry/laundry room and in the back corner of the house, the lone bathroom.

After a few minutes, the first car arrived with four passengers. Within a minute, an old van followed by a taxi squealed to a stop. Uddin was concerned until Safi reassured him. "The taxi belongs to Imran. It might as well be invisible."

The men walked into the house; there was little chatter. What they were there to discuss was very, very serious business. It had been sold to them as an attack to eclipse 9/11. They were all hardened extremists and relished the opportunity to strike a blow against the traitors who chose Jews and infidels over their Islamic brothers. They were the Shams Sawda cell in Dubai.

* * *

Gunny chose Lon, Alen, John, and Hans to reconnoiter the rented shop in Alsajaa. The area was laid out in a grid of commercial lots. Most of the lots had an office or warehouse with an adjacent yard to store vehicles, bulk materials, or equipment. The businesses were extremely varied. There were machine shops, stone masons, scaffolding companies, excavating companies, crane rentals, and wholesale grocery suppliers. It was ideal for the terrorists. No one kept track of who belonged there and who didn't. This made it ideal for the Praetorians as well.

The four men drove east on highway E88 to Alsajaa. They were concerned the big Mercedes would be conspicuous, but this was Dubai. Mercedes SUVs were a dime a dozen. It took them some time to find their target. Compared to the other commercial businesses, it was tiny. They drove by it twice in the dark before someone finally read the faded sign above the door. They drove another block before turning onto another street. They didn't want their vehicle within visual range of Jazaan Mechanical in case there was trouble. Lon and Hans walked back to the store front. The street was quiet. Almost all the nearby businesses were closed for the day. There was no apparent activity at the business so Hans cupped his hands, pressed them to the dirty glass, and peered in.

"That's a real good way to get shot, dummkopf."

Hans replied, "Stop worrying, mother. This place is abandoned. I'd bet nothing has been touched since Mr. Jazaan died. See for yourself."

Lon strained to peer inside the dark office, but it only confirmed Hans' assessment. "You may be right. This place is abandoned." All the men were wearing their standard communications gear. Lon keyed his mic and said, "Alpha Two, this is Alpha One. Front is clear. There's a small office or lobby up front. It's been deserted for a while. What's the status out back?"

John replied, "Alpha One this is Alpha Two. Rear access is via a garage door. It's secure. No way to open it from the outside. There are fresh vehicle tracks back here." He clicked on a small flashlight with a red filter. He knelt down and studied the tracks. "One vehicle entered and exited. Judging by the tire width and tread pattern, it was a truck or delivery van. Too wide to be a passenger car."

Lon nudged Hans and pointed to the door knob. "Roger that. We'll enter through the front. Be alert to anyone exiting the back as we go in."

John removed his Sig 9mm pistol from his jacket pocket and screwed on a suppressor. "Copy that. We've got the back."

Lon drew his own weapon while Hans knelt down to pick the lock on the front door. It took him only a few seconds and they were in. As Lon moved in to clear the space, Hans closed and locked the door, drew his own weapon and followed. After passing through the small office, they crept into the shop behind. It was one room save a toilet in the corner behind the office. It only took seconds to clear; there was no place for anyone to hide. "Alpha Two, this is Alpha One. We're secure. Is the alley clear?"

John replied, "Copy. No activity."

"Roger. I'll let you in."

Lon rolled up the garage door just enough for John and Alen to dart in. Once they were inside, Hans shut the door to the office and turned on the lights. "Well shit. This shouldn't take long."

Alen scanned the area and immediately snapped his fingers. "Got something over here."

"What?"

Alen pointed to the heavy, steel canister that originally held the precursor. "This is out of place. No markings on it except in Russian."

"What does it say?"

"Component A."

Hans walked over and retrieved a CW detector from his coat. The minute he snapped it on, it started chirping. He walked over to the trash barrel and using a stick, picked up one of the yellow hazmat suits. "Bingo. This is it."

Using a shop rag, Alen picked up the canister. "It's empty. They must have transferred it into some other container. Damn it! We missed it!"

Hans surveyed the shop. "Not necessarily. Judging by the spare parts and cannibalized appliances, I'd say this guy repaired appliances, electric motors, pumps, and stuff like that."

Lon shrugged, "So?"

Hans pointed to the two green refrigerant tanks in the corner. "None of that requires freon." Those tanks are labeled R-22. That is the stuff they put in air conditioning units."

John added, "The same kind of shit Al-Rashid Engineering is known for."

Alen walked over and picked up one of the tanks. "This is full." He set it back down a couple of feet from the other one.

Hans waved his CW detector near the first tank and then the other.

Both times the detector chirped loudly. "Gentlemen, we found what we came for. Let's grab it and get out of here."

Lon paused. "Let's not rush things. If we take them, they'll know we're on to them. They'll dump their phones and disappear. I'd really like to zip these guys up."

Hans said, "We can't leave this stuff behind as bait. It's too dangerous."

"Agreed. We need to take the stuff without them realizing it's gone." Lon took out his phone and snapped a picture of the tanks and sent it to Gunny and Steve with the caption "Please ID."

A couple minutes later Steve called him. "That's a standard AC refrigerant bottle. They're everywhere."

Lon asked, "Any around here?"

"I don't copy."

"Are there any AC companies around here who might have the same bottle? I'm thinking of a little bait and switch action."

Steve chuckled, "I gotcha. Give me a second." After a couple of minutes, he came back on the line. "There's an AC outfit three streets north of your location. I'm texting you the name and address. They should have some. Oh, and I just intercepted a text from Safi to the others. They're meeting tonight at 'the house,' wherever that is."

"Copy that. So long as they ain't here." Turning to his comrades, Lon asked, "Feel like doing some shopping?"

They left Jazaan Engineering and set out in search of their new objective. Within two minutes they'd found it, a refrigeration supply wholesaler. They made quick work of the lock on the back door and slipped in. An alarm started beeping. Hans immediately ran toward the source of the noise. "On it." He disappeared into the darkness and within a few seconds, the beeping stopped. As he trotted back, he whispered, "Piece of cake. Even Kernan could have done it. Well, maybe not."

John softly snapped, "Fuck you, douche bag. Why am I always the butt of your jokes?"

Lon replied, "Because he's lazy and you're an easy target. Let's go."

They quickly cleared the warehouse to ensure they were alone. No one working late, no night watchman. They quickly found where the refrigerant was stored inside a locked, chain link cage. Hans picked the lock and they entered. Lon pulled up the picture of the green tank to show the others. "We're looking for this." It only took a couple of minutes to find the right tank.

Alen called out, "Over here."

Lon compared Alen's tank to his photo. "That's definitely it. Grab two."

Hans stopped him. "They may have used the same thing for Component B. We should take four, just in case."

"Good idea." They each grabbed a tank and locked the cage behind them. Hans reset the alarm and trotted to the backdoor where the others were waiting outside.

Back at Jazaan Engineering, they brought in two of the purloined tanks. Setting one next to a tank of precursor, Lon asked, "Okay, what's different?"

Hans picked up their stolen tank and then the Component A tank. "Weight is about right."

Alen pointed to their stolen tank. "The label is wrong. It says R134a. Theirs says R-22."

Hans added, "There is also that red sticker."

Lon took out a knife and started to peel the sticker off the precursor tank. Because Uddin and Safi had wiped it down with anti-freeze, the label didn't adhere completely. It came off intact too. He carefully placed the R-22 label over the R134a label on the stolen tank and gently pressed it on. "Voila!"

John stared at it intently. "It'd fool me."

After repeating the process with the other stolen tank, they stacked their replacement tanks just as they had found the originals. The terrorists would never figure out they'd been there. Alen and John grabbed the two tanks of precursor and slipped out the back. Hans closed the door behind them and secured it before slipping out with Lon through the front. Once out on the street, Hans asked, "What are we going to do with the precursor?"

Lon replied, "How the fuck should I know? I'm making this up as I go along."

* * *

In Lahbab, Uddin and Safi called their meeting to order. Safi said, "Men, we're about to execute a plan that will put Shams Sawda on the lips of every true believer in the world. Abu Almawt has been planning this operation for over a year and you've been chosen by Allah to carry it out. I am humbled to be in your presence."

Uddin stepped forward. "You're all curious about the target, but we had to keep it from you for security reasons. I myself, only just found out a few weeks ago. I am happy to share it with you tonight."

Imran, the taxi driver, was the first to speak out. "I don't care what it is. Just tell me and I will attack it."

"I appreciate your enthusiasm."

"So, what is it?"

Uddin paused for effect. "It is the Rashid bin Saeed Al Maktoum Stadium in Dubai." The men sat stone-faced. Imran's cockiness disappeared. "You're shocked? We need a great target if we are to make a great impact."

Another of the men, Salah, spoke up. "How exactly are we to attack a facility that big with just ten men? Any event held there will have hundreds of security guards. It was designed to host the World Cup. Not like they're going to leave a door open or something."

Uddin smiled. "I appreciate the scope of the mission. The more difficult the target, the greater the weapon needed to attack it."

Salah quipped, "Do you have a nuclear weapon or something?" As soon as he said this, he didn't want the answer.

Safi answered, "A nuclear weapon? No. However we have the next best thing. We have a chemical weapon. A nerve gas of horrific power courtesy of the Russian infidels."

Imran blurted, "Nerve gas! Allah has provided most generously."

Salah asked, "You have told us *what* the target is but not *who*. As far as I am aware, there are no major sporting events scheduled for the stadium. There might be some small, local match but that won't garner the attention you crave."

"Ah but there is. It's not a football match or even cricket. We're going to attack the sheik's equestrian event. There is to be a dressage contest and horse show in three days' time. This is our target."

Imran chuckled. "Not exactly the World Cup. How many are expected to attend?"

Safi answered, "Approximately 11,000 people."

Salah snorted, "Eleven thousand is a fair number, but I assumed we'd pick something more…grandiose. How many do we expect to kill? Even with this nerve gas, the stadium is huge. It is unlikely to kill everyone. In my experience, ten percent would be a great outcome for us."

Uddin explained, "This nerve gas is probably the deadliest chemical weapon ever developed. A tiny drop anywhere on your skin is fatal and we have more than enough to kill everyone. More importantly, we have a method to expose all 11,000 people at the same time; including all of the security officials as well. But just as important as the number of the targets are their identities. Those who own such animals are among the wealthiest and most powerful people in the Emirates, even the world. This is the stadium's inaugural event. No politician would pass up such an opportunity."

Salah was convinced Uddin was exaggerating. "Oh? Like who?"

"Sheikh Mohammed bin Rashid Al Maktoum, the Prime Minister and ruler of Dubai. Sheikh Mohamed bin Zayed Al Nahyan, the President of the UAE and ruler of Abu Dhabi. And my favorite, Sheikh Abdullah bin Zayed bin Sultan Al Nahyan, the president's brother and Foreign Minister—the man who betrayed Islam by signing the Abraham Accords on behalf of the United Arab Emirates. Are those significant enough for you?"

Salah gulped. "I am sorry for questioning you. Please forgive me."

Uddin walked over and placed his hand on the man's shoulder. "Just do your job and all will be forgiven."

Safi interjected. "We have tasks for every one of you. Now, let's go over them."

* * *

As John drove them back, Lon called Gunny. "Hey boss. Mission accomplished. There was a change of plan, though."

"Yeah, Steve told me about your bait and switch. Good job. What did you do with the precursor?"

"It's with us."

There was a long pause from Gunny. "Well, I'm not thrilled at the concept, but I guess you don't put it in a locker at the train station."

"Alen is holding onto the tanks in the back seat to make sure they don't bang together. I figure we'll put them in the garage or something."

"Jesus, why don't you just put them under my bed?" Lon ignored the comment. "Get back here ASAP. Steve may have located the other stash site."

Lon replied sarcastically, "I guess that's good news?"

It took a little less than an hour to navigate Sharjah's evening traffic. John turned off the headlights as he pulled into Rusty's estate. The massive trees on either side grew together forming a thick canopy over the driveway, completely enveloping the Mercedes in darkness. Beneath and behind the trees were thick, tall bushes that completely obscured the three-meter security wall behind them. From the street, the property was a giant maw with an asphalt tongue. Gunny had the vehicle gate open and was waiting for them when they pulled into the garage.

Shutting the door behind them, he waited for the men to pile out. "Where is this shit?"

Alen exited the back holding a green refrigerant tank in each hand. "This would be the shit. Where do you want it?"

"If I had my druthers, anywhere but here, but that's not really an option. There's a storage closet in the corner. In there is as good as anyplace, I suppose." Alen took the tanks and placed them in the closet.

Hans asked, "What's the word on this other place."

"Head inside, grab a soda, and go to the conference room."

"I was gonna get a beer."

Gunny shook his head. "Sorry Hans, no booze, not yet anyway. You guys aren't done for the night. Steve tracked these guys to another location east of here, an Al-Rashid Engineering site. It's Safi's work place."

"Would he really risk storing this crap at work? I mean, why risk it being discovered by someone who'd ask questions, being misplaced, or even accidentally thrown away?"

"We figured the same thing, so Steve dove back into the Al-Rashid computer network. Safi has only one co-worker assigned to this facility and he's in Abu Dhabi helping on a job there. He'll be gone for a week."

"Well, okay then. Just point us in the right direction."

Gunny laughed, "We'll do ya one better. Steve has pulled up the alarm codes for the place and the PIN for the remote entry access keypad."

"That'll make this a lot easier."

"Yeah, you owe the kid a beer."

Hans replied, "Several."

* * *

Uddin and Safi detailed the plan. They were going to inject the nerve agent into the stadium's air handling system. It was more than just air conditioning; it was a total environmental control system, one of the most advanced in the world. It not only controlled temperature and humidity, it had advanced filtration systems to remove dust and odors. For the VIP sections, it even included High Efficiency Particulate Air (HEPA) filters to remove airborne bacteria, viruses, and spores. While the air conditioning system dried the air as it chilled it, a humidity control system maintained the desired moisture level of the air by adding water vapor as needed. In addition, this system remotely added fragrance or disinfectants to the air inside the stadium if desired. It was this last feature they were going to exploit for their nefarious goals.

Uddin said, "The system is divided into two sectors, east and west. Warm air is drawn into registers above the upper tier. It is cooled and humidified in the environmental engineering spaces above the second concourse before blowing back over the stands via air ducts throughout the stadium. The sheikh's personal suite is on the east side and his minions have ordered that fragrance be added to the environment during the horse show. Apparently, the sheikh likes to own and admire his horses but not smell them. We'll inject the nerve gas at the humidifiers just after the chillers. The fragrance injection system is operated remotely. We'll replace their perfume with something a bit more potent."

Safi added, "I help maintain this system, so I'm very familiar with it. We'll work in two five-man teams, one for each sector. I'll lead one, Uddin the other. We'll give you all Al-Rashid engineering uniforms. Our cover will be that we are installing upgraded filtration units, hence the extra men."

One of the men, Hashir, asked, "What if they question us? We know nothing about these systems?"

"You are laborers, only there for your back. Uddin brought with him two new air filter assemblies, so you will have something to push. I've already told the stadium's maintenance managers that we're installing an upgraded system for the sheikh's grand opening. They're expecting us. The nerve agent and our weapons will be hidden inside the assemblies."

Imran queried, "Weapons? I thought..."

Uddin cut him off. "They're only a precaution. This is routine maintenance. They won't ask questions. Once we get to the second concourse, three of you will stand guard while pretending to install the air filter assemblies. The other will help me or Safi remove the fragrance canisters and replace them with the precursor tanks. When the fragrance system is activated on the day of the horse show, the precursors will mix in the line. By the time they reach the spray nozzles, they will be nerve gas."

Salah asked, "What if they don't activate the fragrance or activate it too soon? Then what?"

Safi replied, "The sheikh is scheduled to address the crowd at eleven o'clock. It will be aired live on television. I have full access to the environmental system's computerized control system and have programmed it not to activate before that time. When the nerve agent begins to flow, everyone and everything inside that stadium will die in front of the whole world. Even when they figure out something is wrong, this nerve agent, this Novichok, works too fast to do anything about it. By the time you discover it's there, you're already dead."

One of the men in the back, Umar, asked, "What about the horses. Will it kill them too?"

"Yes, every living thing in the stadium will be killed. In addition, the stadium will be unusable. It will be impossible to decontaminate a building of that size."

Umar added, "I don't care about the people or the building, but I like horses. Sad they must be sacrificed."

Uddin was surprised by the man's priorities and just shook his head. Safi tried to assure the man. "Well, Umar, it is unavoidable."

Imran asked, "When do we do it?"

Uddin replied, "The horse show is in three days. Since tomorrow is the sabbath, a large work crew would be out of place. Safi and I will go to the stadium for a final recon and to remind the guards we'll be installing new equipment the next morning. Saturday morning you meet us at the Al-Rashid warehouse at eight o'clock to get your uniforms. Half of us will go in my rented van with me, the others will ride with Safi in his Al-Rashid van. Once we reach the stadium, we'll check in with security, unload the air filter assemblies and split up. Does everyone understand?" The men nodded.

A man who, up until now had been silent, raised his hand. Safi said, "Yes, Mohsin, what is it."

"When do we martyr ourselves?"

Safi laughed, "If all goes well, you won't have to. We'll be long gone when the nerve gas is released. However, I wouldn't recommend being downwind."

The man was visibly disappointed. "I assumed we would..."

Uddin placed his hand on the man's back and said, "Brother, there will always be opportunities for you to martyr yourself for the cause but right now Shams Sawda needs you alive. There is still much to do. Brother Osama led Al Qaeda for many years before he was taken to heaven."

* * *

After grabbing a quick bite to eat, the Praetorians set out for their next target. The Al-Rashid Engineering service facility was in Ajman, a commercial neighborhood less than two miles from Rusty's house. Ajman was a more established and expensive commercial area. Where Alsajaa was home to lower-end, dirtier businesses; Ajman was much more high-end. It housed warehouses, offices, and shops belonging to multinational companies like Siemens, Boeing, and Samsung as well as local trading companies, wholesale suppliers, and small manufacturers. It was a mixed bag for the Praetorians. While their Mercedes wouldn't stand out, there were more people around to see it. Many of the companies provided services to the local airports and hotels. That meant being available 24/7, so many of the nearby buildings were open and occupied. Thank God Steve found those codes.

John dropped Lon and Hans off near the front of the Al-Rashid building and then parked the SUV around the corner. The streets here were well lit. Kneeling down to pick a lock would not go unnoticed. Thankfully, the Al-Rashid building included a small foyer. The outer door was secured by a cypher lock, the inner door by a key. Lon punched in the code Steve had provided and there was a reassuring "click" as the magnetic bolt retracted. Once inside the darkened foyer, they had some privacy. Hans inspected the lock. It was a commercial Medco lock. "Shit. This is a good lock."

Lon asked warily, "You can pick it, right?"

The German grinned. "Of course. It'll just take a little longer." Hans took out his lock pick set, selected a couple tools, and went to work while holding a small, red LED flashlight in his mouth. Less than a minute later, he pulled on the handle and opened the door. "Never in doubt." Immediately, an alarm pad beeped.

Entering the small lobby, Lon whispered, "No post-game celebrations in the third quarter. Bad form."

Hans walked over to the panel on the far wall and punched in the number Steve had provided. The beeping stopped. "Now may I pop the champagne?"

"Not until we get back to the house." Lon keyed his mic and whispered. "Alpha Two, this is Alpha One. We're in, alarm is off. Repeat, the alarm is off. No one visible. Beginning to clear from the front."

John replied, "Alpha Two copies. The back is clear. We're coming in. Don't shoot us."

"No promises."

John punched in the same code as the front cypher lock and pushed down on the handle. He and Alen slipped in with weapons drawn and began to clear the building from the rear. The space was much bigger than Jazaan Mechanical. There was a large bay in the back which held two vans and had room for at least one more. Alen placed his hand on the hood of the van in Al-Rashid livery. It was cold. The other, a plain white sprinter van, was still warm. The Al-Rashid van was empty, but the other had some equipment in the back. Alen opened the door to make sure no one was hiding inside before continuing. With weapons raised, John and Alen swept through the garage area. It was well kept and organized. It was dimly lit by a couple of small fluorescent lights high on the ceiling.

Lon and Hans swept in from the front. The lobby was connected to the rear shop area by a long hallway with two doors near the lobby. The door on the right led to an office with two desks, computers, and several filing cabinets. It was unoccupied. The other was a bathroom with a sink, a toilet, and a shower. Aside from a metal supply cabinet and large first-aid kit, it too was empty. They emerged into the garage area just as John and Alen had finished their initial sweep.

Either side of the hallway were sets of double steel doors. Two more rooms to clear. Communicating using only hand signals, Lon indicated that he and Hans would clear the room to their right. John covered their entry while Alen actively swept the area around the vans. Lon entered to find a large open workshop with metal benches, machine tools, and a large air compressor. The far wall was dominated by a huge pegboard holding a myriad of hand tools, tubing, and equipment. Metal storage cabinets lined the walls. After a quick inspection, they backed out and gave the "all clear" sign. John and Alen then entered the other room while Lon and Hans provided cover. It was a supply room. The far half was dominated by heavy steel shelves filled with boxes, various refrigerant tanks, and parts. The front housed larger equipment on pallets, gas bottles of various sizes chained loosely to the wall, and a couple of pallet jacks. In one corner was a refrigerator with a case of Coke Zero sitting on top. They stalked up and down the aisles between the shelves scrutinizing any gap or space. The room was clear.

Lon said, "Okay, we're clear. Hans, get out the CW detector. Let's see if that crap is here."

Hans removed the handheld device from his jacket pocket. It almost immediately began to register. "Got a hit." He walked slowly around the garage area with the device out in front of him. "I'm getting a signal, but it's weak. I'm going to try the other rooms." As soon as he entered the storage room, the device began chirping. "It's gotta be in here." He walked slowly ahead sweeping the device from right to left as he went. As he neared the bottles along the wall, the chirping increased. "Over here!"

Alen walked past him with a flashlight. Tucked behind three tall tanks of nitrogen, oxygen, and acetylene, he found two green eleven-kilogram refrigerant tanks. "Why aren't these on the shelves with the others?" Using a rag, he pulled one of the tanks out. "These are labeled R-32. Weren't the others R-22?"

Lon nodded, "Yeah, that's right. I guess they need to tell them apart too."

Hans moved his detector near the two bottles and it started singing. "I say this is what we're searching for."

John interjected, "Uh, where's the big Russian bottle?"

Alen replied, "That's a good question. We need to see if it's here." After a quick search, they found the Russian tank in the bottom of a large metal trash barrel under two yellow Tyvek suits. "Just like at the other place."

Lon said, "Okay, leave it."

"We probably shouldn't. We're going to take the green tanks but there is likely some residual precursor in this and the other one. It didn't dawn on me at the time, but we should've decontaminated the Component A tank before we left the other place. If they mixed even a few drops from these two canisters, it would be enough to kill a lot of people."

John asked, "Well, how are we supposed to decontaminate this thing?"

Alen pondered this for a minute. "Okay, one of the chemicals the Russians used to destroy their stocks was orthophosphoric acid."

Lon shot back, "It's not like we have a bunch of that laying around, now do we? This is an air conditioning repair shop, not a chemical weapons destruction plant."

Alen walked over to the refrigerator and took a can of Coke Zero from the case sitting on top. He clicked on his flashlight and read the label. A big grin spread over his face. He tossed the can to Lon and said, "Read the ingredients."

Lon read aloud, "Water, caramel color, phosphoric acid...well, holy shit!"

Alen said, "It's a food additive. It's what gives Coke its bite. Pour a can or two inside the bottle and swish it around. It should render any residual precursor inert."

John shook his head in disbelief. "Dr. Science strikes again." The others started chuckling.

Lon refocused them. "Back to work, gentlemen. John, go get those two other bottles out of the SUV. Alen, get the labels off of their tanks."

"On it." Alen was able to gently tease the label from the first tank. Like before, the anti-freeze the terrorists used to wipe down the tanks after filling them kept them from adhering properly. Within a minute, John was back with the green tanks they had stolen in Alsajaa. They carefully placed the R-32 sticker over the original R134a sticker and smoothed it flat. They repeated the process with the second tank and placed the harmless tanks back behind the tall bottles where they'd found them.

Eyeballing the two plain green tanks filled with Novichok precursor, Lon said, "These look just like the other ones, and not in a good way. How are *we* supposed to tell them apart?"

Hans went to the shop and took a roll of blue electrical tape off the peg board. He pulled off two lengths and wrapped them around the handles of the tanks. "There ya go. Keep the plain tanks and the ones with blue tape away from each other and we should be good to go."

John added, "Let's just hope the damn tape stays on."

* * *

Aziz Uddin spent Thursday night at Odai Safi's apartment. Safi lived in a one-bedroom flat not far from his work and his friend crashed on his couch. The next day was Friday, the Muslim sabbath, the day of worship. Dubai was a more international and cosmopolitan city with a large percentage of international residents. Like New York, Dubai never slept and only loosely enforced the restrictions of the sabbath. Sharjah, however, was more traditional and geared toward families. Most businesses closed on Friday as they expected their customers and employees to attend mosque. Of course, this was not strictly adhered to in either Emirate, but of the two, Sharjah was definitely the more conservative.

Unable to sleep, Aziz rose early to take a shower. His stress induced sweat from the night before and the grime from two days on the road, combined to form a gritty paste coating his entire body. The warm water cascading over him was invigorating; he was a new man. When he got out of the shower, the smell of fresh coffee hit his nostrils. He dressed and walked into the small kitchen to find Odai drinking a cup of thick, sweet Arab coffee and munching on a croissant. "Feel better? You were in there long enough. I warmed up a croissant for you and there's coffee on the stove. We need to go to the stadium. I want to show you around."

Uddin dropped four sugar cubes into a cup and dissolved them with the hot black coffee. A quick stir and he slurped half down at once. The flaky French croissant was great. He took a bite from one end and then stuffed in some butter before squeezing in a generous portion of honey. Complex carbs, sugar, and caffeine. What more did he need?

They donned their Al-Rashid shirts and drove to the shop. Everything was as they left it. Odai retrieved a clipboard from the office and slid behind the wheel of the Al-Rashid service van. It took forty-five minutes to drive to the new stadium located just south of the Dubai Hills Golf Club. Uddin was impressed. Rising from the desert was an immense structure that was completely foreign to the landscape. Dubai prided itself on erecting structures with architectural significance. The Burg Al Arab hotel resembles a billowing sail, an homage to the area's seafaring history. The artificial land of the Palm Jumeirah, when viewed from the sky, are like the spreading fronds of a desert palm tree. Some claimed the huge stadium was based on the shape of a sleeping camel, but in truth the physical realities of building a space capable of comfortably enclosing 110,000 people in the middle of one of the hottest deserts in the world dictated the design. Despite being a massive structure, fully half of the stadium was below ground level to take advantage of the cooler ambient ground temperatures. As far as Sham Sawda was concerned, this was a plus. The Novichok was heavier than the surrounding air and would sink to the depths of the stadium where the field and VIP seating were located, assuring a high and impactful casualty rate.

As they approached the stadium, Safi guided his van to the service entrance. He pulled up to the gate, rolled down his window and showed the guard his ID. The guard checked the ID; it was on the list. "Mr. Safi, right? Why are you here on the sabbath? You're not scheduled to be here until tomorrow."

"I know. This is my boss. He is in from Muscat. He wants to go over the installation before the equipment comes tomorrow. This is for the sheikh and we want to make sure everything is done right. You understand."

The guard said, "Sure. Open the van. I need to inspect it."

"Really? Never had to do that before."

"Never had the sheikh coming here before either. Now open up."

"Sure." Safi jumped out and opened the rear doors. The van was empty. "See. Nothing here." He whispered to the guard with a smile, "My only cargo is my boss. Do you mind if I leave him here with you and I go home?"

The guard chuckled. "No. I have enough problems. Go ahead."

Safi and Uddin drove through the gate. Safi said, "The perimeter has the strictest security. Once you get to the stadium, you can pretty much go where you want, except for the VIP areas of course. We park at the service and employee parking lot just south of the stadium." When they arrived, they were surprised that the large lot was filled with scores of semi-trucks and custom trailers. Uddin asked, "What's all this?"

"They're horse trailers. Makes sense given the equestrian event starts on Sunday." They drove slowly past the trailers; all had air conditioners built into them. Most of the trucks and their trailers had matching paint schemes. These were dedicated horse carriers.

Uddin exclaimed, "Each one of these things must cost at least a quarter of a million dollars!"

Safi said, "Probably more." They stopped as a groom led a beautiful Arab stallion from a gold trailer across the road in front of them. The horse reared up and pulled against the rope as the groom tried to calm him down. "Can you imagine having so much money that you spend millions on horses you probably never ride?"

Uddin growled, "Oil money paid by Jews and infidels. Money spent by sheikhs and emirs on horses while their people struggle to buy food." He smirked and added, "They will be punished soon enough. Let's go."

Safi parked his van in an area reserved for contractors. He and Uddin walked in unmolested. Safi and Uddin took the freight elevator to the environmental engineering spaces above the second concourse. As the doors opened, they were met by the din of the massive refrigeration units whirring away in an effort to keep the huge structure cool. Near the elevator hanging from pegs on the wall were a score of hearing protection ear muffs. Safi put on a pair, handed another to Uddin and shouted, "Put these on or you'll be deaf by morning." Safi led him to the huge humidifier unit. He opened the massive device and pointed out the major components. He then unlocked a panel to reveal a number of purple eleven-kilogram tanks similar to their green refrigerant tanks. "These contain the concentrated fragrance they use to scent the air. This is where we will connect our bottles. I have fabricated a connector that will allow us to hook our precursor tanks to the fragrance dispensers. On Sunday morning, when the sheikh is giving his speech, we will trigger the devices and flood this stadium with Novichok."

Uddin nodded. "I understand. This is pretty straight forward."

"The Prime Minister, the President, the Minister of Foreign Affairs, and all the other dignitaries present will die."

"When it happens, Abu Almawt will release his statement announcing that Sham Sawda was responsible and punished the traitors for choosing Israel over their fellow Muslims. The other Arab leaders in love with Western money will pay the price for their treason."

* * *

The Praetorians were monitoring the location of Uddin, Safi, and the other cell members, even if they didn't know who those other members actually were. They were alarmed when Uddin and Safi's burners went offline. Their Al-Rashid phones, however, moved together from Safi's apartment to the Al-Rashid shop and then to the stadium. There was no event scheduled that day, so they were confident no attack was eminent. They were comforted by the fact that none of the other cell members' phones were headed in that direction. Most were stationary and far from the stadium. Two others were on the move but moving in different directions. Convinced nothing would happen that day, they used the time to dispose of the precursors.

Steve was drinking coffee when Gunny walked into the kitchen. "What's the word on these Shams Sawda fucks?"

"As of five minutes ago, Uddin and Safi were at the stadium…alone. Six of the others were stationary in residential apartment blocks. One was at Dubai International. He's in the taxi waiting area. Given how much he moves and how random his movements, he's probably a cabbie."

"Well, that's smart. He can go anywhere without drawing attention. And the other one?"

"He's at a mosque in north Sharjah."

"Good work. Now what about finding a power plant where we can get rid of this shit?"

Steve took a sip of coffee. "UAE has a decentralized generation network."

"What does that mean for us?"

"We have lots of choices. Personally, I would opt for the Wasit Power Station. They have nine gas turbines to choose from and it's close."

Gunny asked, "How close?"

"Practically walking distance; three clicks, nine if you drive."

"How do we get in?"

"At least four of the turbines are GE Frame 9E models. GE's local service rep has a maintenance contract. The guys enter the place and steal some uniforms while I dummy up some IDs. The power plant is owned by the Sharjah Electricity and Water Authority. I'll hack into their network and schedule a maintenance visit."

"Will that work?"

Steve shrugged, "If it's on the computer, it must be true, right?"

"Okay, if we get in and get access to the turbine, how do we get rid of the precursor?"

"The fuel input system has a filter to ensure no foreign material in the fuel fouls the injectors, not unlike a car. Since these turbines need to run 24/7, there are actually two filters in parallel. If one needs to be replaced, you shunt the fuel through Filter B while you replace Filter A. When Filter B needs to be replaced, you reverse the process. All we have to do is open the canister for the unused filter, pour in our precursor, seal it back up and switch the fuel flow. The precursor will be taken up by the fuel and burned by the turbine at 2000 degrees."

"Will that clog up the turbine and make it shut down?"

"It shouldn't. We're only talking about a couple of gallons in a system that burns a hell of a lot of fuel. Besides, the precursors are organic chemicals and should burn on their own. It'd be like putting a drop of diesel in your gas tank."

"Let's get on it. Who should we send?"

Steve suggested, "I'd definitely send Nigel. He's the only one who has any experience with turbines. GE manufactured these turbines in France so maybe Magne doing his best haughty French engineer impersonation."

"That wouldn't be a stretch. Who else?"

"Sarah for the distraction and me."

"You? Why you?"

"If there's any problem with the online work order, I can fix it. Plus, I'm getting bored. I haven't seen any action since Karachi."

Gunny chuckled, "Fair enough."

"What if the local technicians interfere or ask what you're doing?"

"We will tell them it is some sort of fancy injection cleaner or something. Actually, I'll add that to the work order. If it's on the computer…"

Gunny interrupted him. "I know, it must be true."

"If they screw with us, I'll have Sarah beat the shit out of them."

Gunny chuckled. "She'd love that."

Lon, Hans, and Alen were tasked with breaking into the GE service office. It was in an industrial park not far from the airport. It turned out to be pretty straightforward. It was closed for the Muslin sabbath and the locks and alarms were mediocre at best. There really wasn't anything worth stealing anyway. They were in and out in less than fifteen minutes with four sets of coveralls replete with the GE logo and ID lanyards. Nigel asked the entry team to take inspection tags, hard hats, hearing protection, neoprene gloves, and a couple of small tool bags to complete the disguise. "You never do anything on a power plant without adding a new tag."

Back at the house, Steve scanned one of the IDs and quickly created duplicates with appropriate aliases, job titles, and photos for Sarah, Nigel, Magne, and himself. Steve had also printed out details of each turbine and their layout on fake GE letterhead. As they got ready to leave, Nigel gathered them together. "We may have to access all four turbines. They were all installed under the same contract so it doesn't make sense to service only two. It'll take a little longer but it will appear more normal."

Steve said, "Good to know. I'll amend the online work order on the way over."

They didn't drive straight to the power plant but conducted an SDR through Sharjah. They had no reason to believe anyone was aware of who they were or what they were up to, but they didn't take any chances. After about an hour and a half, they arrived at the Wasit Power Station on the Ajman Ring Road. Since it was Friday, there was only a skeleton crew. When they arrived, Magne was driving with Sarah in the passenger seat. He put on a thick French accent and announced to the guard, "We are here to service zee turbines."

The guard was surprised. "What turbines?"

Magne acted perturbed, checked a paper in front of him and replied, "Turbines GT 1-1, GT 1-2, GT 2-1 and GT 3-1, of course. This has been scheduled for weeks. We have several other plants to visit while we're here. We need to start as soon as possible."

Sarah assessed the man's English comprehension was cursory at best and Magne's accent only made it worse. In perfect Arabic, she said, "You'll have to forgive my French colleague, he is, well, French. If you check your computer, you'll find our visit on your schedule. We really need to get started. We have to visit the Layyah Power Plant after this."

As she spoke, the guard focused on her and how beautiful she was. She passed him her GE ID lanyard to inspect. "Uh, madam, this is most unusual on the sabbath."

She smiled and said, "I understand, but this is warranty work and it must be completed per the contract or the company pays a penalty. Sadly, these westerners have little appreciation for the sabbath—theirs or ours."

"So, I see. Let me check." The guard returned to his shack and flipped through papers on a clipboard. He then turned to his computer. After a couple of minutes, he came back. "You weren't on the clipboard, but I found it on the computer. Apparently, they updated it late." He handed them four bright orange badges. "These must be worn at all times. You have hard hats and hearing protection, right?"

Nigel leaned forward between the two front seats to show the guard his hard hat and ear protection. "Yes, we do sir."

The guard nodded. "Okay, turn left and park on the left side of the road. The units you want are in the first two buildings. I'll call the on-call engineer to help you."

Sarah said, "Don't bother. We'll be done before he gets here."

"Do you know your way around?"

Magne chirped, "My good man, who do you think built this plant?"

They parked across from the first building. According to Steve's research, this housed turbines GT 1-1 and GT 1-2. They got out of the Mercedes and put on their hard hats and hearing protection. Steve and Sarah grabbed the tool kits as Nigel and Magne each picked up a tank of precursor. Magne said, "Make sure we both have the same precursor. I don't want to accidentally mix this shit and kill everyone in the neighborhood."

Nigel laughed, "We only put in one tank per turbine."

"Still."

They entered the turbine hall and while it was loud, it wasn't deafening. Magne had expected it to be like standing next to a jet engine running at full power. It would've been, but the exhaust was directed upwards through a series of large sound baffles and out through the smokestack. Nigel pointed to the turbine and pointed out its components. "This over here is the compressor. It takes in fresh air, compresses it and sends it into this section, the combustion chamber. There the fuel is injected and ignited. The hot gasses spin the turbine which drives the generator." He studied the machine before pointing out two large cylinders. "There they are. Those are the filters."

The fuel line feeding the filters split into two identical branches. Each branch led to a valve, then the filter, and then another valve before the lines merged on the other side to feed the turbine. Nigel checked the valves on one branch and then pointed to its filter. "This one is not in use. Both of its valves are closed. It's isolated. This is our guy."

The top of the filter was made of thick steel and held on with six large bolts. Magne reached into one of the tool kits for a wrench but Nigel stopped him. On the wall next to the filter was a large wrench. Since changing the filters was routine, they kept the wrench close by. It took them about ten minutes to remove the bolts and the lid. Inside was a new filter waiting its turn. Nigel said, "Get the tank and give me some gloves." Magne put the tank on the ground and inspected it. "How the hell do you open this thing?" This was the one thing they hadn't considered.

Steve stepped up. "These tanks are for freon but at room temperature and pressure, freon is a gas. The Novichok precursors are liquid. How did they get the precursor in this thing, especially in that shitty little workshop in Alsajaa? Pushing it through that valve would have taken a while. This thing must be modified."

As they carefully inspected the tank, Magne noticed a thin line under the valve assembly. "This whole top screws off. Nigel, I'll hold while you turn."

Nigel nodded. He took a pipe wrench from the tool kit, attached it to the nozzle and turned. The whole top of the tank began to turn. In a few seconds it was off. They set it on the ground, picked up the tank and gently poured its contents into the filter assembly. They put the top back on the filter and tightened the bolts.

Sarah asked, "What about the tank? It still has that shit in it."

Nigel motioned to the other tool kit. "Reach in and grab me a Coke."

"A Coke? Now?"

Nigel grinned. "Trust me." She handed him the Coke which he opened and poured into the tank. He then screwed the top back on the tank and swirled it around. He then took the few drops of Coke left in the can and poured it on the tank making sure to rub it all around the seam. "Alen told me about this. Coke contains phosphoric acid which neutralizes the shit in the tank."

Sarah blanched. "No wonder my mom wouldn't let me drink that stuff."

Nigel smiled. "But it sure goes well with rum." Nigel opened the valve on the fuel line leading to the filter. He then slowly opened the valve after the filter. The fuel began filling the filter assembly and forcing the air out. "This is the tricky part. You don't want to bleed off the air too quickly or you cause the turbine to burp." After a couple of minutes, the gurgling emanating from the filter stopped. When it did, Nigel opened the second valve wide open. He then closed the valve feeding the other filter. All the fuel for the turbine was now flowing through the filter assembly with their Novichok. The precursor, along with the fuel, was burning up inside the combustion chamber at 2000 degrees Fahrenheit. They let it run for a few minutes more to make sure the precursor was gone and then set the valve configuration back to the way they had found it. One down, three to go. For the last two, they switched who opened the tanks and poured the contents into the filter assembly. They wouldn't risk a stray droplet of Component A accidentally coming in contact with a droplet of Component B.

As with anything, the more you do something, the faster you get. While the first turbine had taken over half an hour, the fourth took only about fifteen minutes. Before getting into the Mercedes, they stripped off their coveralls and stuffed them into trash bags. Even though they had been wearing gloves, they washed their hands with Coke. On the way back to the house, they disposed of their coveralls and the four empty tanks in various dumpsters throughout Sharjah. All of them were uncomfortable handling the Novichok precursors and the all took long hot showers upon their return to the house.

That evening, the Praetorians celebrated. They finally had a victory. After two failed attempts, one in Syria and one on the Indian Ocean, they were finally able to recover the Novichok and destroy it. No one would die as a result of that poison. Rusty opened a bottle of Pappy Van Winkle bourbon and poured out generous glasses for everyone. Nigel took a long pull and said, "I am a Scotch whiskey man, of course, but goddamn that is good."

Rusty stood and raised his glass. "A toast to the Praetorians. The best damn fighting force in the world. We have done with a dozen warriors what most countries couldn't accomplish with a thousand. And with no loss of innocent life!"

John chuckled, "There was the loss of not-so-innocent life."

Lon took a swig of his bourbon. "Yeah, but not enough. Fuckin' Al-Maadi is still out there somewhere and the assholes who were going to use this shit still need to be zipped up."

Gunny nodded. "The week ain't over yet. The good news is these motherfuckers are going to understand they failed before we kill them."

Sarah asked, "Do you think one of those other burners is Al-Maadi? I would relish the idea of slipping a knife between his ribs and whispering Nura's name in his ear as I watch him bleed out."

Magne snorted, "Remind me never to piss *you* off."

Rusty took a sip and said, "Lady and gentlemen, drink up but not too much. Tomorrow, we're back to work. We still need to take out this cell, find Al-Maadi and figure out for sure if he ever got his hands on the radioactive stuff he was researching. Then we celebrate properly."

* * *

Getting up at 4:30 a.m. on Saturday morning, Steve Chang monitored the program tracking the terrorists' burners to make sure the members of the cell were still in pocket. Before dawn, Hans Koenig and Alen Markovic were in a beige Toyota sedan parked on the street near Safi's apartment building sipping strong coffee and waiting for him and Uddin to leave. At about seven o'clock, Steve called them. "We've got activity. Our tangos are on the move."

Hans replied, "Copy. He drives a red Nissan, right?"

"According to the motor vehicles department but they might be in a rental car or a taxi. I think one of the other guys is a cabbie. I'll keep you updated on their location."

Alen was studying the parking garage exit with binoculars and pointed to a car leaving the building. "Red Nissan." The vehicle turned toward them and drove past within a few feet. "That's definitely them. I recognize them from the drone video."

Hans nodded. "I'm on it." He let the Nissan move further down the street before making a U-turn and following. "Alpha Eight, he just passed us and is turning west."

"Yeah, that's him Alpha Three. Alpha Two and I are already mobile. We'll set up at the front of the shop. You cover the rear."

"Roger."

As the ten members of the Shams Sawda Dubai cell drove to the Al-Rashid Engineering facility in Sharjah, none of them paid any attention to the black Mercedes SUV parked down the street as they drove past. Steve Chang and John Kernan sat behind the dark tinted glass using a telephoto lens to snap pictures of everyone entering or exiting through the front door. Just off the alley in the back, the beige Toyota sedan was on the street with a clear line of sight to the rear vehicle entrance.

A taxi approached and stopped. Rather than dropping off its fares, it parked on the street right behind the red Nissan and the driver along with the two men in back got out and entered the Al-Rashid building. Moments later an old van drove past and parked half a block beyond the office. Three more men exited the van and started walking back to the Al-Rashid facility. As they did, a blue sedan approached from behind them and parked on the street. Two men got out of the car and followed about twenty meters behind the other three. One of the three men was nervous. He scanned all around them. One of the others elbowed him in the ribs and scolded him. The three men entered the Al-Rashid facility followed shortly after by the last two. Steve checked his computer. "All ten burners are pinging at the Al-Rashid address. They're having a Boy Scout meeting."

The Praetorians waited patiently, studying the building for any sign of activity. Finally, after about half an hour, the rear garage door opened. Hans keyed his mic and said, "Action at the rear. Door is open. They're getting ready to leave. I got tail lights on both vans. There are a couple guys in Al-Rashid coveralls putting something in the back of the vans. Our green tanks. Two in each van."

Alen asked, "Any blue tape on the handles?"

Hans paused as he pressed his binoculars to his eyes. "Uh, yeah. One blue tape in each vehicle."

Alen said, "That means they think they have one of each precursor in each van; that each van has a complete weapon. They gotta be going to deploy it or at least getting ready to."

Steve got on and said, "You guys tail them. I want to beacon their vehicles after they leave. We'll catch up in a minute."

Hans replied, "Copy that. We've got the eye."

The two vans backed out of the garage and drove onto the street with the Al-Rashid van in the lead. After the second van turned the next corner, Hans and Alen pulled out to follow. Since Steve was tracking all their cellphones, they kept a discreet distance.

Once the vans were out of sight, Steve and John jumped out of the Mercedes. John attached magnetic beacons under the bumpers of the taxi and the red Nissan. Steve walked briskly down the street and did the same to the other two vehicles. John pulled up in the Mercedes and Steve jumped in while it was still rolling. "Tally ho, my good man. The hunt is on!"

The two vans drove the thirty kilometers to the stadium casually. They stayed under the speed limit and took the most direct route using major roads. Either they were not trying to detect surveillance or wanted to appear as boring as possible. Either way, Hans and Alen easily tailed them from a comfortable distance. When they turned onto the service road for the stadium, Hans drove on past. "They're entering the stadium grounds. They were stopping at the guard gate when we passed."

John replied, "Copy that. We're about a click behind you. We'll pass them in a minute."

Steve peered at the vans through his binoculars as they drove by. "Damn. The first van is already through. We'll meet by the golf course."

Hans and Alen were out of their car when the Mercedes pulled up. Steve had moved to the back seat where he had two laptops running. Hans slid in the back seat with him. Steve gave him one of the laptops. "Here, you keep an eye on their cellphones."

"What are you going to do?"

"Hack into the stadium's security cameras so we see what they do inside."

"Nice."

Steve had already mapped the stadium's security network the night before to kill time. It only took him a few seconds to pull up the security cameras. There must have been fifty camera feeds and they were mere thumbnails on the laptop's screen. "Shit. I didn't take this into consideration. There are a lot of people here, and horses too. We may lose them in all this clutter."

Hans said, "Well, the phone company has a bunch of nano cells in this place, so I'm getting pretty good granularity on their location. They're currently at the west loading dock."

Steve pulled up the cameras for that area as the two vans backed up to the dock and opened their doors. Five men climbed out of each van. The only men they recognized were Uddin and Safi. "Any decent pics of their faces?" Hans asked.

"Not sure. I'm recording everything, just in case. We'll check back at the house. I don't want to miss what they're doing right now." The men removed pallet jacks from the backs of the vans and parked them on the dock as the men muscled two large metal cabinets wrapped in plastic out of the vans and onto the dock. They then slipped a pallet jack under each, pumped the handle to lower the wheels, and pulled the load toward a large freight elevator.

Alen snapped, "Shit, we're going to lose them!"

"No, we're not. There are cameras in the elevator. Hey? Where are the green tanks?" He pulled up another view from inside the elevator as the terrorists pushed the equipment inside. Steve zoomed in on the panel. "Okay, he pushed the button for the second floor. Gonna flip to that camera now. Still no green tanks by the way." A couple of keystrokes and a view appeared of the second concourse. The elevator doors were in the distance. As they opened, the men pushed out their cargo. "There they are…oh shit! They're splitting up! One pallet to the right, the other to the left."

Hans said, "Pick one and I'll track the other via their phones."

"Gotcha. I'm going with the guys on the right." They headed toward the west side of the area. The men pushed the piece of equipment around the concourse until they were near the middle. "They've stopped. What's that door? Is that another elevator?"

Alen leaned in to study the grainy image. "Yeah. They pushed the 'up' button. That's another freight elevator. What's above this concourse?"

Steve pulled up the stadium schematics he had downloaded earlier. "Uh, that would be admin spaces. Specifically, environmental engineering. Great place to launch a CW attack."

"Are there cameras up there?"

"Yeah." A few seconds later a view of the space came on the computer screen. The men wrestled with the heavy piece of equipment. "Hans, where are the other guys?"

"The same place but on the other side of the stadium."

"That makes sense. The two sides are essentially mirror images of each other." The camera did not provide a very close view and they struggled to make sense of what was on the screen.

John asked, "Are they opening that piece of equipment?"

Steve replied, "It would seem so. Hey are those weapons?" One of the terrorists had opened a panel on the equipment and pulled out three AKs and handed them to three of his comrades. He then reached in and retrieved two green refrigerant tanks. "There's our shit. They must have stashed them inside that big cabinet thing en route."

The terrorists abandoned the cabinet, took the tanks, and moved toward a machine connected to the massive ductwork. The Praetorians couldn't determine what the men were doing, but three were working while two stood guard with the AKs. Alen asked, "What's that thing they're messing with?"

Steve replied, "Not sure, but they don't want anyone interfering. Let me pull up the engineering schematics." He typed furiously for about thirty seconds before a blueprint popped up on his screen. He toggled back and forth between the schematic and the security camera feed. Tapping the schematic, he said, "That's this thing, right? That is an air scent modification unit. That's a fancy way of saying perfume dispenser."

John asked, "A giant Febreze plug-in?"

"Essentially. They adjust the smell inside the stadium. They make it smell like fresh cut grass for a soccer game or..."

John interjected, "Or pot for a Grateful Dead concert?"

Steve chuckled, "Sure, why not. The horse jumping show starts tomorrow. What scent would you use for that?"

Hans quipped, "Horseshit?"

Alen said, "It'll already smell like that. I imagine they'd want anything *but* horseshit. We can't see what these guys are doing so switch over to the other group."

Steve pulled up a camera feed in the opposite engineering spaces. "Check this out. They're working on the same gizmo on the other side."

Hans said, "So, that's their plan; substitute nerve agent for the fancy perfume in the air conditioners. Instead of smelling roses, you choke to death."

Alen quipped, "Pretty smart, if you think about it." The others stared at him blankly. He quickly added, "In an evil motherfucker sort of way. All I'm saying is that this Al-Maadi asshole tends to think outside the box, that's all. First the bioweapon and now the Novichok. No simple car bombs for him. All the more reason we need to kill his ass."

John asked, "They believe it is nerve gas, but it's really just freon. The question is, is the freon dangerous? If it is, we need to either remove it ourselves or warn the locals. That might spook our targets and cause them they to bail on us."

Steve searched on "R-22 health risks." "It says here that R-22 is not dangerous except when it displaces enough oxygen to affect you. The remedy, believe it or not, is to take deep breaths."

Alen shrugged and said, "We're talking about forty-four kilograms of R-22 and R-23 released inside one of the largest enclosed spaces in the world. We'll be okay."

"Yeah, I'd say so."

They continued to observe the terrorists. When they were done connecting the freon tanks, they put their weapons and the fragrance tanks they removed inside the equipment cabinet and rolled it back into the elevator. Hans laughed, "They're taking it back! It was just a Trojan Horse."

John shook his head. "Big enough to hold their crap but also big enough to justify having five guys to man-handle it. Clever. If anyone questions them, they just claim it didn't fit or something. I doubt anyone will ask anyway."

The Praetorians tracked the terrorists back to the Al-Rashid facility where they got in their cars and split up. They were convinced they were about to initiate the deadliest terror attack in history. They would learn the real truth soon enough.

* * *

"You're sure that freon is not going to hurt anyone, right?" Rusty asked.

Alen responded, "Yes, sir. We researched it. Freon isn't toxic to begin with and in a facility that large, it's insignificant. It has a volume of just over four million cubic meters. That works out to eleven milligrams per cubic meter. You get ten times more than that using canned air to clean your keyboard. It'll be completely benign."

Rusty was reassured. "Good. What about the Shams Sawda cell? We need to clean them up."

Gunny interjected. "That's the next order of business. We're tracking them via their burners but if they have half a brain, they'll be dumping those soon. If not before the planned attack, definitely after. We need to hit them before the event tomorrow."

"How are they going to trigger the device? They won't risk simply waiting for them to activate this scent dispenser thing. They'll want maximum impact which means killing VIPs. If it gets triggered too soon, most of the people won't have arrived yet. Trigger it too late and risk missing the VIPs who may not stick around for the whole show."

Sarah said, "I checked the official website of the equestrian show. The ruler of Dubai is going to officially open the stadium tomorrow. He dedicates it to his father at eleven o'clock. If I was Al-Maadi, that's when I'd do it. The dedication is to be televised. Talk about maximum impact!"

Gunny seconded her opinion. "Rabin's right. That would be the bang for their buck. While you could just set a timer for 11:00, I wouldn't risk it if I were them. Things get delayed. Besides, who's going to tell the sheikh he's late."

Rusty mulled this over. "This would point to remote release. They watch the dedication on TV and hit the button as the sheikh takes the podium. They'd need to have a guy willing to martyr themselves in the stadium to push the button."

"Two guys, actually," Hans noted. "There are two different locations on opposite sides of the stadium. No one person could trigger the first and then get to the second without getting gassed."

Steve interjected, "Not necessarily."

Hans shook his head. "Even you can't run that fast, especially in a gas mask."

"No, you miss my point. Everything in that stadium is automated—I mean *everything*. The dispenser is part of the environmental engineering system. Uddin or Safi can trigger it remotely. Given Al-Rashid's maintenance contract, they'd have access to the computer. I bet they'll be watching on TV and trigger the CW as soon as the sheikh shows up."

Alen broke in. "This is all hypothetical, guys. There is no CW. We burned it up yesterday. We just need to find these assholes and wax 'em."

Nigel huffed, "The man has a point. The stadium is a nonissue. Let's just kill them and go home."

Rusty said, "We can pick them off one at a time but that increases the risk of civilian entanglements. I'd like to get them all together somewhere like the Al-Rashid office but it's in the middle of a busy neighborhood." As the boss was talking, there was an audible ping from Steve's laptop. "What's that?"

Steve opened his laptop and said, "A text from Safi's burner!"

Sarah asked, "To whom?"

He pulled up the other addressees. "The rest of the cell. Well, everyone but Uddin."

Lon said, "They were together already. What does the text say?"

Steve grinned wildly and turned to Rusty. "Ask and ye shall receive." He turned the laptop around to face the others. "It says to meet at the house tomorrow at 10 a.m."

Magne asked, "The house?"

"That's where they met Thursday night. It's that place east of here in Lahbab. I have the geocoords."

Rusty asked, "Could they trigger the gas from there?"

"Sure. They could trigger it from anywhere. All they need is an internet connection. He could trigger it with his phone."

Lon smiled, "I bet they're going to watch the event on TV together. It'd be like an Oscar party for terrorists. No better place to hit them."

Sarah glared directly at Gunny. "I'm going on this one. I'm going to be the first one through the door. If Al-Maadi is there, I get to kill him." She wasn't asking; she was telling. Sarah gave the men in the room a sneer that would make a charging tiger reconsider. "Anyone else kills that bastard, he answers to me. Do you understand?"

The rest of the Praetorian team just nodded. No one dared to smile or crack a joke. She was deadly serious. After a long awkward pause, Rusty finally said, "You need to lighten up, Rabin. You can kill the son of a bitch if he's there, but Jesus, I think Hans wet himself."

The guys finally started to chuckle, but she remained dead serious.

* * *

The men of the Shams Sawda cell in Dubai arrived at the house in Lahbab acting like soccer fans at the World Cup. They were giddy with anticipation. They were going to be famous, like Mohammad Atta and the other 9/11 hijackers. People would sing their praises for years to come and, unlike the 9/11 hijackers, they might even live long enough to enjoy the glory.

The other eight members of the cell were already at the house when Uddin and Safi arrived. It was a warm, sunny day in Lahbab. There were no camel races scheduled so the dusty town resembled any other farming community. Uddin was driving his rented white van and Safi in his red Nissan. The others had come in the taxi, the old van, and the blue sedan they'd driven the day before. The men were in front of the TV and surprised when both Safi and Uddin walked in carrying armloads of AK-47s.

Imran, suddenly concerned, asked, "What's with the guns? Are we expecting trouble?"

Uddin explained, "Not right away. Everyone needs to take one for your protection during your escape. The authorities will figure out that Al-Rashid Engineering passes were used to gain entry to the stadium and that Safi was involved. We expect them to raid his apartment; maybe as early as this evening. The stadium has CCTV, so it's very likely they'll have all of our faces on camera. There will be a lot of confusion, at least initially, and we need to take advantage of that to make our escape. It will only be a matter of time before we are recognized. You were all instructed to make escape plans, right?" The men nodded. "Everyone, take out your burners and destroy them. After it is done, do not return to your homes or contact anyone for any reason. Tell no one of your escape plan, including the men in this room. That way, if they're captured, they cannot betray you."

Salah was offended. "I would never betray a brother and none of my brothers would betray me!"

Uddin replied calmly, "That was not an insult. No one intends to betray his brother, but everyone breaks under torture eventually. That is just a fact. Even the great Khalid Sheikh Mohammad talked. If you know nothing, you reveal nothing. Understand?"

A humbled Salah hung his head. "I understand." It was as if the seriousness of their endeavor had finally occurred to him.

The members of the cell opened soft drinks and gathered around the television. Uddin and Safi were convinced their plot remained undiscovered. They hadn't bothered to place a guard. If they had, he might have picked out the small drone circling high above the house.

* * *

The Praetorians were positioned north of the farmhouse near the race track. They'd been there since before dawn. With Lon Oden and John Kernan up front, Hans and Magne sat in the back seat of their SUV to control the small, battery-powered drone they had launched to monitor the farm from above. Around seven o'clock, an older man in a white Toyota pickup drove to the farm. He didn't enter the farmhouse but rather walked into the small field behind it. He knelt down and pulled a plant from the ground, inspected it and put it in a bag. He repeated this in three additional locations in the same field before returning to his truck and driving away. They followed him with the drone as he drove to another small farm just down the road. At this one, a plump, middle-aged woman was outside the farmhouse feeding chickens. As the man pulled up, a couple of goats scurried out of his way only to continue grazing after he drove past. The contrast between the two farms was obvious. The second was clearly someone's residence while the first showed no sign of habitation.

They observed the arrival of the eight members of the Shams Sawda cell whose identities were as yet unknown. A little after ten o'clock, Uddin and Safi drove up. Hans keyed his mic and said, "This is Alpha Four. Last two tangos are arriving now. Parking on the east side with the other vehicles."

Gunny replied, "Copy. That makes all ten. Any civilians in the area?" He and Rusty were in a Range Rover a couple of miles west to block the road if any of the cell members made a break for Dubai.

Hans replied, "Affirmative. We have a kid with a donkey cart on the road but he's at least two hundred meters and moving away."

"We're in no hurry. Let him clear the area."

"Copy that, Bravo Two." Something on the monitor caught his attention. "Uh oh. The last two tangos, Safi and Uddin, are packing." The two removed assault rifles from the trunk of Safi's red Nissan. Hans reported, "Eight to ten AKs in the trunk of the red vehicle. They're carrying them into the house. Entering through the front door on the south side. Well, so much for our turkey shoot. Car Two confirm."

Sarah was sitting in the passenger seat of the other Mercedes. Nigel was driving with Steve and Alen in the back. "Car Two copies."

Gunny chirped, "Not that anyone asked, but Car Three copies too."

Hans said, "Sorry, Bravo Car. We forgot about you for a second."

"Bravo stands for boss, remember?"

"I thought it stood for backup or bench players. Thanks for the clarification. Car One is moving to our deployment point."

Nigel keyed his mic and said, "Car Two doing likewise."

Car One drove east from the race course about half a kilometer and then dropped south and then west to approach the farm from the southeast. Car Two drove west, turned south on Highway 44 and went through the roundabout before angling southeast to approach the farm from the northwest. It was about this time that Steve chimed in. "Uh, all the bad guys' burners just went off the network."

Lon asked, "Just now? At once?"

"Yes. All within a minute. I'd say they're getting ready to bail."

Sarah asked, "Has Sheikh Maktoum started his speech?"

Gunny chimed in. "No, we're monitoring the ceremony via live feed. He hasn't started."

"They won't leave before the attack. If you're not going to watch it live, why come all the way out here to meet up? They'd have just skipped town yesterday. They want to witness their handiwork together."

Lon interjected, "Like I said, it's a fuckin' terrorist Oscar party. I'm going to love shooting these assholes."

Sarah stressed, "Remember, Al-Maadi is mine."

Lon turned to John and said, "I don't care what she says. If I see that fucker, I'm dropping him."

"Amen to that brother."

Gunny asked, "Alpha Four, what's the status of our kid on the donkey cart?"

"Still moving away...slowly."

"Copy. Alpha Team, move into attack position."

* * *

Inside the farmhouse, the Sham Sawda fighters waited anxiously. Uddin checked his watch repeatedly even though the actual time didn't matter.

Nothing would happen until the sheikh walked onto that platform. There was a commotion on the TV screen. The camera panned to the left and focused on a distinguished man in his mid-seventies making his way through the crowd. He had a neatly trimmed black beard and mustache and was wearing glasses. His keffiyeh was pure white and held on by a black aqel cord made of dyed camel hair. His shirt was a pale blue and over his shoulders was a cape of gold silk. It was the sheikh.

Uddin blurted out excitedly, "There he is!"

Safi said, "That one behind him. That's the Foreign Minister. That's the bastard who signed that damn accord with the Israelis. They are all there. It is time to act." Safi retrieved his Al-Rashid Engineering cellphone and opened his web browser. He had the page for the environmental engineering program for the stadium already running in the background. He tapped on the initiation icon, took one last glance at Uddin and the other cell members, and pushed the button. "It is done!"

They all stared at the television waiting for the first signs of exposure. After a couple of minutes, nothing had happened. Salah asked, "What's wrong? No one is dying!"

A confused Safi turned to Uddin. "Don't worry, Odai. It is a huge facility. It will take time for the weapon to pass through all the ducts and drift down to the stadium floor."

After another five minutes, there was still nothing. The sheikh started his speech dedicating the new stadium to the memory of his late father. There was no coughing, no panic, not even mild concern. Safi pulled up the environmental control program again and checked its status. "The computer says the scent dispensers are activated and functioning properly. It indicates that it is at maximum dispersal rate and that eighteen kilograms have been expelled from each unit. Something is seriously wrong. They should all be dead!"

Panic started to wash over Uddin. What went wrong? Did he screw up somewhere? If so, where? They did exactly as they were told. They followed all the instructions. His conclusion? There was no chemical weapon from the start. He growled to Safi, "Kotov, that Russian son of a whore, screwed us over. He took Abu Almawt's money and delivered nothing! This has all been for nothing!"

Imran was the first to point out the obvious. "If the attack has failed, are they even searching for us? I mean, if they had learned of our attack and disrupted it, would they have let the sheikh even enter the stadium at all? Would they have let us install the tanks and leave unmolested? No. We're in the clear. We don't have to leave. In fact, we should probably go about our lives as normal. We will figure another way to strike at the leaders for their treachery."

Safi said to Uddin, "He has a point. We did our part and it would've worked if they had given us the Novichok as promised. Our cell is intact. We'll regroup and fight another day."

Uddin ruminated on this for a couple of minutes. "I need to speak to Abu Almawt. He'll know what to do."

Like the others, Uddin had already trashed his burner. Desperate times call for desperate measures. He turned on his Al-Rashid cellphone, took a scrap of paper from his wallet, and dialed the telephone number scribbled on it. After a few rings, it went to voicemail. "Abu Almawt, it is Aziz. I know you said not to contact you, but there is a problem. The plan was executed as designed but nothing happened. We think the...chemical was false. The man who provided it, Alnamir, has cheated us. Our group is intact. Please contact me with instructions on what to do next."

Uddin addressed the group. "Brothers, it's clear our attack has failed. It wasn't through any fault of ours, or of Abu Almawt. The infidel who we paid for the Novichok has clearly cheated us. We will deal with him harshly. I have asked Abu Almawt for guidance on what to do next. It will be a day or two before he contacts us. Everyone go home. Act as if nothing has happened. We'll meet back here in three days' time, on Wednesday night at eight o'clock. Do you understand?"

The men nodded. Salah asked, "What about the rifles?"

Safi said, "Keep them. We may need them."

Imran said to his comrades. "Well, I guess there is no reason to stick around. I'm going to go back to the city. If anyone investigates me, I want to appear as normal as possible. I'm going to pick up a shift at work." He grabbed his AK and headed for the door.

Salah quipped, "Don't leave that in the trunk when you head to the airport."

Imran opened the door but turned back to Salah. "I'm not stupid, you asshole."

* * *

Outside the house, the Praetorians moved into their assault positions. Everyone was armed with a fully suppressed MP-5 9mm submachine gun except Magne and Alen. They were armed with suppressed M-4 5.56mm assault weapons to provide cover at a distance. They didn't like the idea of making a daylight assault, but they had little choice. They wouldn't have time to clean up the scene afterwards, so they opted for weapons of common calibers to make the post incident investigation all the more difficult.

They weren't sure who was in there, but the drone overhead gave no indication of innocent bystanders in the area. The same growth of trees that made the house and the terrorists' vehicles difficult to surveil from the road or adjacent fields also provided the Praetorians with concealment as they approached. From the east, Lon, John, and Magne crept along an overgrown fence line. Hans was a few meters behind them monitoring the feed from the drone via the controller around his neck. West of them, Sarah, Nigel, Alen, and Steve worked their way along the edge of an alfalfa field toward the farmhouse. For both groups, the last twenty meters or so would be over open ground.

Lon motioned for Magne to move to his right. "Alpha Five, find a spot where you can cover our approach."

Magne moved silently to his right and, in a crouch, trotted up to a clump of bushes near the driveway. He crawled on his belly under the growth and aimed his weapon at the front door of the farmhouse. "Alpha Five in position. I have visual of the front door and the windows either side of it. No windows on the east side where the vehicles are parked." From his pack, Magne took out what appeared to be a spotting scope but with a small screen instead of an eye piece. It was a wall penetrating radar system. With it he saw through the walls of the farmhouse. The device was tuned to the thermal frequency of humans. Magne counted the images on his screen as he panned from one end of the house to the other. Magne keyed his microphone and said, "I've scanned the house. I count ten signatures; all in the living room on the east side of the house nearest the vehicles."

On the other side of the farm, Alen maneuvered into position. From his vantage point, he covered the back door. There was only one small, high window immediately to the right of the back door with two larger windows to the left. Beyond that was the graveled area where the cars were parked. "Alpha Seven in position. I have the back covered. No windows on the west wall. Copy ten tangos east side interior."

From the west, Sarah led Nigel and Steve toward the house. On the east, Lon led John and Hans. Just as they slipped behind a large tree, Hans said. "We've got movement. The front door is opening."

Magne replied, "I see it. There's someone standing in the doorway. He's still mostly inside. I don't have a shot yet."

Lon peeked out from behind his tree. He was about fifteen meters from the house; the man standing in the doorway was holding an AK. "He's armed."

Sarah, Nigel and Steve had moved up to the house and were next to the back door. She said, "We're in position. Ready when you are."

Lon said, "Copy that. Going hot." Just as the man turned around and stepped through the door, Lon hit him with a six-round burst. The terrorists in the house were oblivious to the shots and were shocked when Imran staggered back into the house and collapsed on the floor.

Safi gaped at Imran's bloodied body splayed out on the floor; the expression of shock permanent on his dead face. "What the fuck?"

Uddin was the first to react. He picked up an AK and chambered a round. He yelled, "Grab your guns and get down!" The others grabbed their weapons and dove to the floor as a fusillade of small arms fire blasted through the open door and windows on the front of the house perforating the curtains.

Salah crawled toward the front door and tried to close it, but Imran's foot was in the way. Another of the terrorists, Umar, got up to grab Imran and drag his corpse away from the door. He moved him enough for Salah to slam the door but caught three rounds in the chest from John's MP-5 for his trouble. Uddin and Safi pushed one of the couches over to block the front door.

Outside, Lon reported, "Two tangos down. Front door is closed. They're bottled up. Alpha Six, expect action in the back."

No sooner than he said this, three terrorists, running away from the fire, bolted out the back door as someone inside slammed the door behind them. They sprinted to their right, along the side of the house toward their vehicles. They never even saw Sarah, Steve, and Nigel crouched alongside the building to their left. Sarah let them get a few meters away before she dropped all three. Turning to Nigel, she said, "Cover the door. I'm going to make sure they're out of action." That was only partially true. She wanted to determine if one of them was Al-Maadi. Making sure to stay below the windows, she crept up to the downed men and rolled them over. All were too young to be her quarry. "Damn it!" She put an extra round into each man's skull to make sure he was dead before returning to the door. She keyed her mic and said, "This is Alpha Six. Scratch three more tangos."

Lon replied, "Copy that Six. Good shooting, Tex. By my calculations, that leaves five alive inside."

Magne replied, "Radar confirms movement times five."

In the house, panic was setting in. The terrorists were armed but had nothing to shoot at. One of the men, Ali, crept over to the window next to the front door. The tattered blinds and curtains were still drawn; no one could see in or out. He raised his AK and gently slid the muzzle through the crack in the curtains as Hans was running up to take a position on the opposite side of the front door. Before he put his finger on the trigger, a single round from Magne's 5.56 hit him in the center of his forehead. He dropped in a heap on the floor as blood quickly pooled around his head.

Magne said, "This is Alpha Five. Scratch one more."

Lon replied, "I don't know Five, you might have missed."

Magne snorted, "I never miss."

The four remaining members of the cell, were freaking out. Six of their comrades had been killed in less than a minute. Uddin whispered, "Who are these people? I haven't heard a single gunshot."

Safi was pointing his weapon at the front door waiting for any sign of motion. "These cannot be regular police. They must be the Police Special Unit, the counterterrorism guys. They're trained by the British SAS."

"But why the silencers? Why would they care about making noise. It's not like we haven't figured out they're here. I'd expect them to blow this place apart by now."

Safi replied, "None of this makes sense."

Outside, Lon said to John. "Time to smoke 'em out."

The former SEAL grinned. "I'll smoke 'em, you skin 'em."

Lon keyed his mic and said, "Alpha Six, get ready, we're going to hit them with tear gas."

"Copy." She glanced to where Alen was set up behind a pile of cinderblocks some thirty meters away. Turning back to Nigel and Steve, she said, "You two move toward their vehicles. If any get out through the windows, that's probably where they'll go. Alen and I will cover the back door. They nodded and crept off toward the opposite end of the house where the cars were parked. Sarah keyed her mic, "Seven, you and I have the back."

Alen replied, "Copy."

A few seconds later, John's CS grenade crashed through a window. Uddin and Safi retreated down the hall to the bathroom where they took off their shirts, soaked them in water and tied them across their faces in an attempt to mitigate the effects of the tear gas. In the corner of the bathroom, was a water heater. Low on the wall next to it was a thin plywood panel a little under a meter square. Uddin kicked the panel and it cracked. Two more kicks and it split. He tugged on the shattered wood and pealed the plywood back. Behind it was a hole in the west wall of the house covered by a metal screen. Safi asked, "What's that?"

"A vent in case of gas leaks. The screen is to keep out snakes and mice. Help me with it."

They easily kicked through the old, rusted screen. Uddin cautiously stuck his head out. None of their attackers were in sight. "Follow me." Grabbing his AK, he shimmied through the hole. They were on the windowless west side of the house. Safi crept along the wall to the south and peeked around the corner toward the front. Espying Lon, John, and Hans by the front door, he rolled back to safety. He eased up to Uddin. "There are at least three men up front with submachine guns. They are Westerners!"

"Are you sure?"

"Yes, they look British or American. What would they be doing here?"

"Whoever they are, they've been onto us long before today. Who else would have a reason to target us like that?"

Uddin said coldly, "The Israelis."

Safi blanched. "We need to get out of here." Uddin and Safi moved to the opposite corner to assess the situation at the rear of the house. They had some bushes for cover and stared as Nigel and Steve moved toward the cars. Sarah was alone by the back door. They missed Alen tucked in behind the pile of old cinderblocks. Uddin was in front. He slowly raised his AK and pointed it at Sarah. A second later, there was a loud crash. The two remaining terrorists were making a run for it. They came blasting through the back door and ran toward the cars. Steve spun on his heal to fire but hesitated as Sarah was directly behind the running terrorists. Encountering Steve, the men veered to their left, sprinting for the weeds at the edge of the backyard. When they did, Steve's sight line was clear and he dropped the first one while Sarah shot the other.

As Sarah rose from her crouch, Uddin prepared to fire. Just before he pulled the trigger, Alen's 5.56 round entered his head just behind and below his left ear. It destroyed his medulla oblongata killing him instantly. The "splat" of the bullet as it smashed into his head, drew Sarah's attention. She spun around to find Safi peeking around the corner. She fired a burst from her MP-5 and dropped him on the spot. She turned to Alen who was still on his weapon behind the blocks. She gave him a two-finger salute. It signaled, "Thanks" and his nod acknowledged it.

Sarah keyed her mic and said, "Four more tangos down in back. That should be it. Moving to clear the structure."

The Praetorians quickly cleared the small farmhouse. They searched for exploitable intel but there was none. Sarah and Hans took photos of the dead terrorists to try to identify them later. The mission had gone about as good as possible. All the terrorists dead and no friendly casualties. Lon called Gunny. "Bravo Two. We're done here. No obvious intel. Collecting phones and wallets. What do you want us to do with the bodies and the weapons?"

"Good work One. What's your current security status?"

"The scene is secure. The tangos didn't even get a shot off. The loudest noise was the CS grenade going off in the house, but someone has to come around eventually."

"Okay, stow the tangos and their weapons in the house."

"Copy that. We'll be mobile in five minutes. See you back home."

CHAPTER NINE
INVISIBLE ENEMIES

After the operation in Lahbab, the Praetorians conducted an after-action review back at Rusty's house in Sharjah. The encounter had gone off flawlessly. The entire cell had been neutralized in a matter of minutes. Except for Safi and Uddin climbing out through the vent on the west side of the house, they were able to discretely corral the terrorists inside the house, concentrate their fire on a relatively small area, and eliminate them efficiently. All agreed that a good part of this was luck. These were not battle-hardened jihadis but rather tyros new to combat. They had placed no sentries outside the farmhouse. They didn't even have weapons until Safi and Uddin arrived. When the shooting started, they panicked. Rather than mount a concerted defense, they broke and ran right into the teeth of their attackers without getting a single shot off. They even carried their wallets with them making identifying their corpses relatively simple. The Praetorians had gotten lucky.

Sarah ran photos of the dead Shams Sawda fighters through the Wise Owl visual recognition system. Where there were matches, it showed their true names matched their wallets. Almost all were Pakistani save a lone Indian Muslim in the group. Only two had police records. Imran and Salah had been arrested as youths in Pakistan for rioting in connection with a Tehrik-i-Taliban protest. As they were minors at the time, the charges were later dropped.

Gunny was the first to make a connection. "Tehrik-i-Taliban? Isn't that the same group the trawler captain was connected to?"

Sarah nodded and said, "Mad Dog is right. The boat captain, Zihad Haq, was arrested in connection with a Tehrik-i-Taliban riot too. I wonder if at least some of the others were connected as well? Was Al-Maadi using this group as a recruiting ground? It makes sense. He gets access to young, radicalized Muslims who either don't have police records or were too young at the time of their arrests to have adult records that would alert law enforcement."

Rusty snorted, "I hate that this Al-Maadi asshole is so creative."

John said, "All the more reason to kill him."

Nigel added, "Aye, my wee SEAL is correct…for a change."

Gunny brought everyone back on topic. "Okay, so we had a cell of inexperienced yet motivated jihadis that, except for a couple, had been operating completely in the shadows. While it made them easy targets, it begs another, more disturbing question—how many more of them are out there?"

Lon said, "That's the upside of using rookies; no one knows who they are, even if they're standing right in front of you."

Sarah asked, "Aside from when they picked up the Novichok, has there been any direct contact with Al-Maadi?"

Steve replied, "We were up on Safi and Uddin's Al-Rashid Engineering phones since the day we identified them. Same for the others' burners once we ID'd them. There was nothing indicative of contact with Al-Maadi during that time. However, there was one thing yesterday. Just before we hit them, all their burners went dead."

Sarah added, "Yeah, a little before the Sheikh gave his speech."

"Inside the house, we recovered twelve broken phones and the two Al-Rashid Engineering cellphones, both of which were still on. Safi's phone was still on the internet. It was logged onto a remote access portal for the stadium's environmental control system."

Alen said, "That must have been how they triggered the release of the Novichok—well, the fake Novichok anyway."

Steve smiled. "Yes, it was. However, there was one outgoing call on Uddin's company phone. It was to a burner, of course, registered in Lahore five weeks ago. It hasn't been online since it was registered on the network. The call was placed at 11:15 a.m., about fifteen minutes after the sheikh started talking."

Alen interjected, "That would be about the time they figured out their attack was a bust. So, who'd he call?"

Sarah answered. "Al-Maadi. He was calling Al-Maadi to report that the attack had failed."

Lon added, "And to probably ask what to do next. Did the call go through?"

Steve shook his head. "No. Went to voice mail."

Gunny asked, "You have the number of the burner. Can you recover the voice mail?"

Steve smiled, "Oh, hell yeah. I need some time to crack back into the Paki cell system but give me a few minutes."

The group kicked back while Steve typed furiously on his laptop computer. After about ten minutes he leaned back. "Okay, I got it." Everyone gathered around as he played the message.

Uddin's voice came on the speakers, "Abu Almawt, it is Aziz. I know you said not to contact you but there is a problem. The plan was executed as you designed but nothing happened. We think the...chemical was false. The man who provided it, Alnamir, has cheated us. Our group is intact. Please contact me with instructions on what to do next."

Rusty leaned forward on his elbows. "Well, I'll be goddamned. Who is Alnamir?"

Sarah answered, "That has to be Kotov. Kotov means 'cat' in Russian. Alnamir means 'tiger' in Arabic; his nom de guerre."

John added, "The Arabic word for cat is actually 'qita' but I guess tiger sounds more intimidating." Turning to Alen he asked, "Did it work? Were you intimidated when you shot him in the head?" Alen didn't answer.

Gunny asked, "Where is this mystery burner now?"

Steve shrugged. "I don't know. It hasn't been on the network again. I guess, he'll have to check his voice mail eventually but until he does, we're blind."

"Monitor it and tell us if it comes up on the network again." Steve nodded. "In the meantime, I need a drink."

Rusty slapped his hand on the table. "Mad Dog is right. We have a major victory to celebrate." They retired to the living room where Rusty broke out another bottle of Pappy Van Winkle. After pouring a glass for everyone, he proposed a toast. "Here's to another successful Praetorian mission. The Novichok is destroyed and the assholes who were going to use it are dead. The entire country of the United Arab Emirates owes you guys a huge thanks, they just don't know it."

Lon added, "And here's to them never finding out."

The group drank well into the evening. Lon and John played pool while Hans, Nigel, Alen, and Steve threw darts. Sarah and Magne put on some music and danced a tango. Rusty and Gunny drank bourbon, recounted the events of the day, and admired what was undoubtedly the best counterterrorism team on the planet.

As the evening wound down, the party started to break up. Rusty and Gunny slipped out first and others slowly followed. The luxurious house was big but didn't have ten bedrooms. Rusty had the guest rooms furnished with twin beds in anticipation of this exact situation. Rusty got the master bedroom, of course. Sarah also had the luxury of her own room, being the lone female member. Gunny and Lon bunked together as did Hans and Magne, Steve and John, and Nigel and Alen. A drunken Nigel, it turns out, snored…loudly. Really loudly. After an hour, Alen gave up. He grabbed his pillow and blanket, and retreated to the pool house.

Making a bed on one of the couches, Alen stripped to his shorts and laid down to catch at least a few hours of sleep before the morning sun woke him. He'd been prone for all of ten minutes when there was a splash. He mumbled to himself. "Jesus Christ! Are you fucking kidding me?" Expecting to find one of his drunken comrades had fallen into the pool, he was shocked by what he encountered. It was Sarah—casually swimming laps. And she was completely nude.

Alen just stared at her as she swam the length of the pool. While she was most assuredly beautiful and sexy, he was staring not out of lust but admiration. It was like a Greek statue had come to life. Her body was lithe and perfectly proportioned. She was muscular, graceful, and extremely feminine. She was the perfect physical specimen.

When she turned to swim back, she spotted him. She said nothing but continued to swim. After a couple of laps, she stopped, climbed up the steps and retrieved her robe from a chaise lounge. Slipping it on, she loosely tied it at her waist before picking up a nearby towel to dry her hair. "Are you just going to stare at me?"

"I'm sorry. I was just surprised. I didn't mean to…"

She chuckled, "You're cute when you're embarrassed. Why are you down here?"

"Nigel snores. Like a lot."

"I know; but only when he drinks. We all know. That's why everyone picked roommates before you did."

"So, why are you down here? Little late for a swim, isn't it?"

Sarah slinked over to him. Standing mere inches from his face, she said, "There's no gym here and I was too keyed up to sleep."

Alen was nervous. "Sure. Makes sense. Sorry to, uh, interrupt."

Sarah opened her robe exposing her breasts. "I can think of other ways to release some stress. Can't you?"

"Absolutely."

Sarah pushed him through the flowing curtains of the pool house, shoving him backwards onto the couch. Alen stared up at her. He didn't believe what was happening. She shook out her wet hair before slipping off her robe. Sliding on top of him she said, "This doesn't mean we're going steady. I just need to fuck."

"Yes, ma'am. Fine by me, but I assumed you and Magne…"

She laughed. "I refuse to sleep with a man who thinks he's prettier than me."

"No one is prettier than you."

"That's the right answer. Now get naked."

The big Serb grinned. "Yes, ma'am."

* * *

The day after the failed attack in Dubai, Khalid Al-Maadi and his bodyguard, Mohammad woke up on board the *Qirsh* to find Captain Zihad Haq and his deckhand, Hamid, feeding the net over the stern of the boat. Al-Maadi asked, "What's going on? We're not actually supposed to be fishing." He meant it as a joke but Haq wasn't laughing.

"Other nearby ships have been on the radio. The UAE Coast Guard has been boarding ships for inspection. We need to appear like any other fishing boat and that means having nets in the water."

Mohammad was taken aback. "Aren't we in international waters?"

"Yes."

"By what authority do they stop us?"

"By the authority that they have a bigger boat with a deck gun." Haq paused and tried to reassure his guests. "We are in international waters, but they'll simply say they are ensuring that international fishing limits are being adhered to and they may actually be doing that this time. In reality, they are probably hunting for smugglers; Iranians running guns to Yemen. If we cooperate, they should move on quickly."

Al-Maadi was not convinced. "We are carrying contraband. And if they find it?"

Haq took a deep breath. "They're after larger cargo than a few net buoys. I've been stopped and boarded several times over the years. No one has ever ripped apart buoys. That is exactly why I used them. If we all keep our wits about us, it'll be fine."

Khalid steeled himself. There was nothing to do about it now. "Okay, how can we help?"

Zihad replied, "Help us get this net in the water. Even if they board us, I doubt they'd pull in the net. If Coast Guard officers liked the smell of fish, they'd be fishermen."

It took the four of them about fifteen minutes to finish deploying the net. They had to slowly move the boat forward while playing out the net, making sure to keep it away from the boat's props. They then started to trawl westward, toward Bahrain.

After an hour and a half, Zihad spotted an Al-Saber-class patrol boat approaching from the south. He shouted out to the others. "Look smart! UAE Coast Guard vessel on the port side."

Five minutes later, the patrol boat pulled alongside, being careful to avoid their nets, as Haq throttled back his engines. Via a bull horn, a man called out. "Fishing vessel *Qirsh*. Heel to and prepare to be boarded." Haq waved and smiled, as Hamid hurried to hang inflatable bumpers over the side. Hamid tossed a line to a crewman on the ship and he tied it off, lashing the two vessels together.

Two other crewmen were armed with assault rifles. Whispering to Haq, Al-Maadi said, "That isn't good."

Haq smiled, "Standard operating procedure. They assume every encounter is dangerous until it's not. We will give them no reason to think we are anything other than humble fishermen."

The boarding party consisted of a junior officer and two sailors. They climbed down a short rope ladder and jumped onto the *Qirsh*. "I am Lieutenant Nazim. Who is the captain?"

Haq stepped forward. "I am Captain Haq. This is my vessel." He handed the officer a copy of his registration and fishing license.

The officer inspected them and commented, "Pakistani? What brings you so far from home?"

"The famous Persian Gulf flying fish. They fetch a premium in the market in Karachi."

"There are strict limits on how many you're allowed to harvest."

"Yes, Lieutenant, I'm aware."

"How many do you have in your tanks?"

"Sadly, none as yet. We only just arrived in the fishing grounds, but we hope Allah will fill our nets."

"Show me." Haq walked amidship and opened the lids to the catch tanks. The officer peered into the inky water but the tanks were clearly empty.

Haq pointed to the net in the water and quipped, "I hope by tomorrow, we'll have something worth inspecting."

The Lieutenant motioned for his men to search the boat. With a gaff pole, they probed the empty catch tanks for submerged items before moving on to the rest of the small vessel. They opened every hatch and cabinet but found nothing until one of the men returned to the deck and said, "A weapon, sir." The man held up an ancient .455 caliber Webley revolver.

Haq shrugged. "For sharks. If you don't kill them quickly, they thrash around and ruin your nets."

The Lieutenant inspected the rusty gun. He broke it open and ejected the rounds in the cylinder. Their lead bullets were white with oxidation from the salty sea air. It hadn't been fired in ages. He snapped it shut and handed the gun and ammunition to Haq. "You should take better care of that weapon. It needs to be cleaned and lubricated if you want it to work when you need it."

Haq gave the man a little bow, "You are absolutely right, sir. To be honest I forgot it was even there. It belonged to my uncle. I inherited the boat from him. But I will take your advice."

The Lieutenant nodded. "A man should take care of his tools. Alright, everything appears to be in order. Good luck with your fishing but no more than a thousand kilos of flying fish or there will be very stiff fines."

"Yes, Lieutenant. We'll be careful."

The young officer and his men scrambled up the rope ladder and a seaman on the patrol boat untied the line and threw it back to Hamid. Using a long pole, another crewman pushed the *Qirsh* away as the patrol boat moved slowly forward. Once clear of the trawler, the ship motored off in search of its next victim.

Once he was sure it was gone, Al-Maadi gave a big sigh of relief. "I was really worried when they found that pistol. Why did you keep something like that on board? It's inviting trouble."

Haq didn't like being chastised but responded calmly. "Abu Almawt, you are a great leader and warrior but you don't understand fishermen. It would've been more suspicious if we did *not* have a gun on board."

Al-Maadi was a bit embarrassed. "I'm sorry, Zihad. I shouldn't question you."

"Abu Almawt, my job is to get you, Mohammad, and those containers to Bahrain and that's what I'm going to do. We'll leave the nets out for a little while. I would actually like to have some fish in the tanks in case we are boarded again."

Khalid gave him a modest bow. "You are the expert. I defer to your judgement."

* * *

Flying high and invisible to the *Qirsh* and the Emirati Coast Guard vessel was a twin turboprop aircraft. It was owned and operated by the United States Government, specifically the National Nuclear Security Agency (NNSA). The action arm of the NNSA was the Nuclear Emergency Support Team, or NEST. The aircraft was a key component of NEST's Aerial Measurement System. It was crammed full of extremely sensitive technical equipment used to sniff out and collect airborne particles indicative of a clandestine nuclear program. It also detected radiation signatures from miles away. It was flying out of Kuwait under cover as a maritime patrol aircraft. What it was actually doing was ferreting out information on Iran's nuclear program. The airplane routinely flew up and down the Persian Gulf. While it stayed in international airspace, it did tend to stay to the north; the Iranian side of the gulf.

As the airplane droned eastward, the men inside were bored. While their mission was certainly important, it was anything but exciting. The technician in the back had almost fallen asleep when he got an audible alarm in his headset. He perked up immediately and focused on his computer screen. He called to the pilot, "I got a gamma hit."

"Bearing and distance?"

He checked his screen. "Okay, this is weird. Bearing is 95 degrees. That's almost due south of us."

The pilot replied, "Nah, probably oilfield equipment. They use it for diagnostics in wells, refineries, and the like. Probably a commercial cobalt-60 source."

The technician adjusted his equipment and took another reading. "Nope. This is only two or three miles from us. We're nearly ninety nautical miles from shore. It's gotta be right below us."

"Maybe something on a cargo ship."

The airplane was equipped with multiple cameras and the technician pulled up the view of what was directly below them. "The only things below us are fishing boats. I make out a patrol vessel but nothing over thirty meters. No factory ships or anything. This is a weird place for this kind of signal."

The pilot wanted any reason to break his tedium so he suggested, "How about we circle back around and make a couple of passes over the same stretch of water."

The technician laughed, "You just want to play."

"Well, what's the point of having a fine airplane like this if you drive it like your grandma's station wagon."

"Hey, it's your call." The tech anticipated what the pilot would do, so he cinched his seatbelt tight. As expected, the airplane banked hard to the right and went into a dive.

"We'll get ya little closer so we can clean up this contact." The NEST plane dropped a couple thousand feet in altitude as it completed its U-turn. "Okay, we should be approaching it now."

The technician focused on his instruments. He quickly reacquired the signal and was able to train his ultra-sensitive radiation detector on it. "That's definitely a gamma source. The signal is a bit fuzzy. It might be submerged or shielded. Is the Navy running attack boats in our pond right now?"

"There's a Los Angeles Class boat, but it's up by Bahrain. Too far for us to detect. We have to come back around to get back on track anyway. I'll get a little closer. Make sure the cameras are recording."

"Yes, sir."

The pilot flew west a few more miles before banking to the left and lining up on their previous path. As he did, he bled more altitude until they were about 5,000 feet off the waves. The tech set his gamma collector on auto-track as they flew over the fishing boats below. After a couple of minutes, they'd passed the last of them. The pilot said, "We have to get back on our planned heading or it'll be my ass. Did you get what you need?"

"Yes." He reviewed the data on his screen. "These readings are odd, though. The electron energy corresponds to cesium-137 and strontium-90 but there is no use for them on a fishing boat. The readings also correspond to high concentrations of material but that much would kill you if you got near it."

The pilot replied, "But didn't you say the signal was fuzzy; like it was shielded or underwater?"

"Yes, I did."

"Well, run a tape and let the eggheads back at the base figure it out. We have Iranians to snoop on." The pilot returned the airplane to its original heading and they slipped back into their boring routine.

* * *

Ibrahim Safra was the working alias of deep cover Mossad agent Saman Kashani, who worked on the docks in Karachi. Saman was a very busy man. In addition to using his myriad of commercial connections to monitor the comings and goings of cargo of interest to the State of Israel, he also handled spies—real spies within the Pakistani Government. Israel was a small country with limited resources so its agents were often assigned double, even triple duties.

Saman took time away from the port to meet one of his agents, Tafaar Rind, a computer forensics specialist at the Karachi Nuclear Power Complex. Rind's family was from Balochistan, just across the border from where Saman's Iranian ancestors had lived. Saman took on a Baloch alias surname, Kalpar, when targeting Rind and they hit it off immediately. Over the course of a year, Saman became Rind's friend and confident. When Saman recruited Rind, it was not to work for the Israelis. Rind was a devout Sunni Muslim so Saman recruited him under what is called a "false flag." Saman told Rind that he was working for the Saudis. He explained that the Saudis were interested in Pakistani nuclear technology so they might defend the Holy Sites against the Iranians and Israelis. This would require Rind to apply for a job at a plutonium reprocessing or uranium enrichment facility. Due to his sense of loyalty to Sunni Islam and the money Saman provided, Rind proved an eager asset but was as yet unsuccessful in obtaining a transfer to one of the desired facilities.

Saman and Rind met for a late lunch at a small café in northeast Karachi that catered to local workers and shopkeepers. It was far from both the nuclear plant and the docks. The restaurant was nearly deserted when the men got down to business. Saman passed Rind a folded newspaper. Inside was a thick envelope full of rupees and a handwritten receipt. Rind scrawled an illegible signature on the receipt and slid the envelope into his lap. Saman cautioned him. "Do not deposit the money into your bank account. The PAEC will audit your accounts as part of your routine security reinvestigation. Any money that is unaccounted for..."

"I know, I know. It'll trigger a deeper investigation."

"So, what are you going to do with this?"

"I'm using a hawala to send it to my cousin in Abu Dhabi. He has opened an account for me at a European bank."

"Good. If you spend any of it, spend only cash and on things that are not reoccurring expenses. Go to dinner or the cinema, but don't pay your rent or electric bill with it. Those you always pay by check or direct account debit. You want the security people to see your income and spending are aligned."

Tafaar let out an exasperated sigh. "We go over this every time."

Saman reached over and patted his hand. "And we will continue to. I need to make sure you are always safe. What you are doing for the Kingdom is a great thing but your safety is of more interest to me."

"I know. I'm sorry. You're only looking out for me. You're the big brother I never had."

"So, any news on the transfer?"

"Yes and no." Saman's expression begged details. Tafaar said, "I was assigned to the plutonium reprocessing plant at Chashma but it was only temporary."

"Temporary? Why?"

"They needed a forensic specialist. Since I had put in for a transfer and my security clearances were up to date, I was selected."

"What was going on? Why did they need you?"

Tafaar explained, "They had an incident at the plant. A guy died. It has been very hush-hush. Not in the papers."

"What happened?"

"A chemical engineer named Nawaz Zaman in the reprocessing waste department died at work of severe radiation poisoning. I read the inspection report. It's awful. I made a copy of the report for you." As he said this, he slid a Micro-SD card across the table under his index finger.

"Well, that happens on occasion, doesn't it?"

"Not like this. He was killed by cesium-137 which they found at his house! His wife was sickened too but she's expected to survive. The dead guy, this Zaman, was also in charge of the security protocols which were obviously circumvented. The radiation detection system at the front gate was deactivated for a system reboot the day before, right when he was leaving to take some equipment for repairs."

Saman shrugged. "Coincidence."

"No way! Besides, it turns out no equipment was to be repaired. He lied to the security guards."

Saman was eager for more but didn't want to show Tafaar how eager. "Tragic, but how does waste material affect the plutonium?"

"It doesn't. Not directly anyway. They ordered me to do a deep dive. I pulled all the registers and backup files. I found where he installed a subroutine two days earlier that allows him to initiate a complete system reboot with three keystrokes. I also found where he deleted it the day of the reboot which was the day before he died. He turned off the radiation detectors. That only means one thing."

"That he was stealing something radioactive."

"Exactly. They immediately feared it was plutonium but it was all accounted for. I was ordered to conduct a full audit. This guy may have been a good chemist but his computer skills were shit. I found it right away. The fucking amateur."

Saman was now fully engrossed. "Found what?"

"He'd been skimming."

Saman was suddenly confused. "Skimming? What, money?"

"Radioisotopes. He'd been underreporting the amounts of cesium-137 and strontium-90 for months and apparently hiding it away. He skimmed kilos of the stuff."

"How much, exactly?"

"I'm not sure. I didn't have access to the whole system. Just what I needed to do the audit. They were bringing people in from Islamabad."

"Where is it? The stuff he skimmed?"

"No one knows and it's freaking them out. The national network of roadside detectors is on high alert. The mobile detection unit at my power plant was activated and sent away."

"Where were they sent?"

"I don't know, just outside the plant. Apparently, they're not worried this radioactive stuff will show up at our plant. The same thing is happening with the teams from other facilities. The PAEC is really trying to recover the stuff but without the public ever finding out it was missing. Nothing has been in the press and nothing will be, unless of course someone has a death wish."

"Is there any way to get access to the system again?"

"No. It's completely air-gapped. It doesn't show up on the network anywhere. I never knew it even existed. They gave me access while I was there and deleted my temporary account when I left. Even if I was in the plant, I couldn't log back on. So, is this the kind of information the Saudis need?"

Saman downplayed the importance of what he'd just learned. "Well, not exactly. I mean it's fascinating background but if it doesn't detail the plutonium or enriched uranium production…"

Tafaar was a little downtrodden. "Oh. I just thought…"

"My friend, we're almost there. If they called you in for this forensic investigation, then they trust you. You have to be at the top of the list. I'm confident that the next job opening will be yours. In the meantime, I'll get you a big fat bonus. This is really great news Tafaar." He checked his watch. "Damn, I have to get going. The guys in Riyadh will want to hear about this right away."

Saman stood to leave and threw money on the table to cover the meal. Tafaar stood and shook his hand. "Until next time."

Saman cautioned, "Now remember, wait at least…"

"Yeah, yeah. Wait at least ten minutes before I leave."

* * *

The next morning, Alen woke up in the pool house alone. Sarah had slipped away while he was sleeping. Did their encounter even really happen? Or was it just a vivid dream? No, he was naked and he never slept naked. A habit born of living in combat zones. *You don't want to be naked if the enemy attacks.* He got dressed and walked back to the main house. Several of the Praetorians were already there getting coffee and making breakfast. Magne walked over to refill his mug and quipped, "Jesus, Markovic, you look like shit. No sleep last night?"

Several others chuckled at Magne's comment as Alen sipped his coffee. *Did they know something?* "It was a bit of a rough night."

John Kernan snorted. "That Nigel is a great bunkmate." The others laughed as if in on an inside joke.

Alen said, "Yeah, Nigel is not the quietest of mice, is he."

Nigel walked in as Alen said this and roared, "Fuck all of you! It isn't my fault I have sleep apnea."

Magne shot back, "Sleep apnea, my ass. You have whiskey apnea, you drunken bastard. A week at sea aboard *Mother Goose* and not as much as a peep out of you. One night of drinking and you sound like an elephant in heat." Nigel grumbled but said nothing.

Alen quipped, "So nice of all of you to saddle me with him has a roommate, by the way. I ended up having to sleep in the pool house. I won't forget it and I always get even." The others just laughed and returned to their meals. Moments later, Sarah sauntered into the room. Alen was standing by the coffee maker as she approached. Trying to be nonchalant, he said, "Good morning, Sarah. I hope you slept well."

Avoiding eye contact, she poured a cup of coffee. "Well enough. Nigel certainly wasn't my roommate." She glanced up at the big Serb and gave him just a hint of a smile before grabbing a Danish and taking a seat at the table. Alen took two for himself and followed.

After a few minutes, Nigel, Magne, and John left the room leaving Alen alone with Sarah. In a hushed voice, Alen said, "Uh, about last night…"

She cut him off. "Alen, last night was fun but that's all it was. I wanted sex, you wanted sex so…we had sex. Don't make a big deal of it. I don't expect you to give me your letterman sweater."

"My what?"

"Sorry, I've been hanging around Americans too long. What I'm saying is this doesn't mean we're a couple. We are just colleagues who happened to fuck once. This isn't going to be awkward now, is it?"

Alen was taken aback. He wasn't sure what he expected but this wasn't it. "No. Not at all. I was just going to say I haven't told anyone about…ya know, and I'm not going to."

"Good, because neither am I. It was a fun little diversion. Let's not overcomplicate it."

Alen's mind was racing. It had definitely meant something to him. She was the woman of his dreams. He had been enamored with her since the first moment he met her. She was extremely independent—the fastest way to push her away was to try to pull her closer. "No. You're right. I was going to say the same thing. We have to work together and we shouldn't let our little tryst impact our professional relationship. I'm good if you are."

Sarah glanced at him with a bit of a jaundiced eye. He obviously had a thing for her. Hell, all the guys probably did at one time or another. She was not one of those pretty women who insists she's unattractive. She was beautiful and she knew it. She had to have that kind of confidence to do her job. Put a beautiful woman among seven virile men in a close environment, it would be stupid to assume there wouldn't be attractions. "Well, I'm definitely good."

"Then we won't mention it again." What Alen was really hoping was, if he successfully downplayed the entire incident, the next time she wanted sex, she would knock on his door first.

A second later, Sarah's cellphone chimed. It wasn't a telephone call; it was a text on an encrypted app. It simply read, "Call me. D." It was Daniel Charon, her contact within Mossad. Sarah got up immediately and ran to get dressed.

Sarah found Rusty and Gunny and told them about the message. She grabbed the keys to one of the Range Rovers and sped off. Her first stop was the local suq where she bought a new burner phone. She drove to a local McDonalds near University City to activate the phone and download the Signal App. She then walked to the University Hospital, found a waiting room and called Daniel.

"It's me."

"I have something you need to know about. From our man in K."

"What is it?"

"Our friends over there have a serious problem. Some nasty material has gone missing. C-137 and S-90. I'm sending you a copy of a report. It details what happened to the man who stole it. You need to be aware of what you're up against." They talked for a few more minutes before Daniel said, "Sarah. Be careful. This stuff is extremely dangerous."

"Understood. I'm always careful." Daniel just snorted in disbelief. "Shut up. Say 'hi' to my sister for me."

Sarah fought the urge to drive right back to the house. Instead, she conducted an SDR to make sure no one was following her. She assessed it was unlikely but was not going to risk the safety of the others. After a couple of hours, she returned to the house. Walking through the door, she called out. "All hands meeting in the kitchen! Now! Steve, bring your laptop."

Sarah rarely called meetings, so everyone responded immediately. This had to be important. Steve plopped down at the table and fired up his computer. Sarah handed him her burner. "There is one downloaded file. Pull it up."

"You got it."

Rusty and Gunny were the last to arrive. Gunny was in a robe and toweling his hair dry. "Do you always have to do that when I'm in the damn shower?"

Ignoring his carping, Sarah explained. "I got a call from one of my old Mossad contacts. One of their agents in Pakistan reported that radioactive materials have gone missing from one of their reprocessing plants."

Rusty asked, "Plutonium?"

"No. Cesium and strontium."

Alen reacted. "Oh shit."

Gunny asked, "That's what your buddy, Dr. Pretrukhin, was talking about, isn't it?" The big Serb only nodded.

Sarah continued, "The man who apparently took it died of acute radiation poisoning. Daniel sent me a copy of the incident report. Steve?"

"On it." It took Steve a few seconds to open the file. When he did, he let out a long whistle. "He died at work. Cause of death: acute radiation poisoning. Source was cesium-137. Sound familiar? Says a team recovered a sample from his home! Wife is also sick, hospitalized in serious condition but expected to survive. Says here there is to be no press release, state secret."

Alen asked, "When did this happen?"

"Several days ago, on the seventh."

Hans asked, "That was what? Four days after we lost Al-Maadi heading north out of Karachi?"

Hans asked, "Who was this guy? The dead one."

Steve scrolled up. "His name was Nawaz Zaman."

Hans winced. "Zaman? We were looking at that guy. Right Alen?"

"Yes, he was the one with the paper on tetravalent metal ions." The others reacted as if Alen was speaking in tongues. "Uh, that is a discreet way to refer to plutonium and uranium without actually saying plutonium and uranium."

Steve said, "He's right. I kept a copy of the paper and his resumé.So,

Zaman, is a PAEC chemist who wrote a paper about plutonium reprocessing without mentioning the words 'plutonium' or 'reprocessing' anywhere in it and he just happened to live near a top-secret plutonium reprocessing plant. Shortly after Al-Maadi escapes, Zaman dies of acute radiation poisoning from the same shit Al-Maadi was researching. The radioactive shit was found in his home meaning he, or someone, apparently got it out of a high security plant undetected."

Sarah said, "Daniel told me that Zaman had compromised the nuclear detection system at the plant the day before he died. Their asset said the PAEC was on high alert but also keeping things very hush-hush. Normally, this type of thing would be a huge public health problem but PAEC declares it a state secret and sweeps it under the rug. Coincidence?"

Alen replied, "I don't believe in coincidences."

"Me neither."

* * *

Slowly pulling its nets west in the Persian Gulf, the *Qirsh* moved steadily toward Bahrain. As it approached the northern tip of Qatar, Khalid Al-Maadi wanted to touch base with his cell in Bahrain. They'd heard nothing about the attack in Dubai. There'd been no news on the maritime radio channels but then they were supposed to be used for commercial communications only. *Still, someone would mention an attack of that magnitude.*

As they got within twenty miles of the Qatari coast, Al-Maadi finally got a signal. A red circle indicated he had an unheard voice mail. It was from an Omani telephone number. The Caller ID said "Al-Rashid Engineering." Protocol dictated that you never access a message from an unknown caller but his curiosity got the better of him. He played the message and instantly recognized Aziz Uddin's voice.

"Abu Almawt, it is Aziz. I know you said not to contact you but there is a problem. The plan was executed as you designed but nothing happened. We think the...chemical was false. The man who provided it, Alnamir, has cheated us. Our group is intact. Please contact me with instructions on what to do next."

"Shit!" Al-Maadi said this to no one in particular but his bodyguard, Mohammad, overheard him.

"What's the problem, Abu Almawt?"

Al-Maadi barely controlled his anger. "The attack in Dubai failed. Listen." He played the message again.

Mohammad was shocked. "What happened?"

"You know just as much as I do. You heard him, he said the operation went according to plan but the chemical was false."

"Or maybe Aziz was lying to you to cover his own error—or cowardice?"

"As to the former, there were redundancies. Odai and Aziz planted the chemical in separate systems. Even if one had failed, the other would have worked and killed thousands."

Mohammad asked cautiously, "And the latter?"

"No, I don't think so. There were redundancies there too. If one had lost his nerve, the other would've still carried out his mission. And don't forget there were eight other loyal jihadis involved. At the very least, one of them would have reported any cowardice."

"Unless a single coward betrayed the entire cell to government authorities."

"I don't want to believe that possible but, even if it were, something like that would make the news. What Aziz said is the most likely explanation— we were betrayed by that Russian bastard in Syria. He promised, didn't deliver, but took our money anyway. We'll deal with him later; for now, we need to focus on the second phase."

Mohammad asked, "What about the cell in Dubai? What do we do about them?"

"I hope they had the sense to either return to their normal lives or execute their escape plans. Either way, there is nothing we can do to help them. Aziz was calling from his work number which would suggest he and the others already destroyed their burners. Even if we wanted to contact them, how would we?"

"If they were arrested, Phase Two may already be compromised!"

"No. None of them knew anything about Phase Two. They were unaware that there was a Phase Two just like those involved in Phase Two are unaware of Phase One. It was planned that way from the start. We must proceed. If the Dubai cell has been compromised, or heaven forbid, eliminated, they deserve that their sacrifice not be in vain."

Zihad Haq walked down from the bridge. He asked, "Any news?"

Al-Maadi replied grimly, "The Dubai attack has failed."

Haq's mood went from jubilant to somber. "What happened?"

"The leader of the cell only said that the chemical was false."

"Chemical?" Haq wasn't privy to the details either.

"Yes, the material we picked up from the *Amuratu*. It was a binary nerve agent, or at least it was supposed to be. We purchased it from a Russian arms dealer in Syria; it now appears we have been cheated."

Haq flashed red with anger. "Then we need to slaughter the infidel!"

"Yes, yes. In due time. But now we need to focus on the other phase of our attack."

"Just tell me what to do, Abu Almawt."

"Get us and our cargo to Bahrain."

* * *

After being briefed on what Sarah had learned from Mossad, Rusty contacted the steering committee. In an ideal world, they'd receive the same information, but ideal worlds don't have cumbersome bureaucracies and the right people rarely get key information in a timely manner. While they were disturbed by what Rusty told them, he was equally disturbed by what the steering committee told him. The day before, a Nuclear Emergency Support Team (NEST) surveillance aircraft had detected a powerful, unknown gamma source in the middle of the Persian Gulf where no such source should be. They had scant details but promised him more information as soon as they received it.

As Rusty hung up the handset on his secure communication system, Steve barged in. "Boss, we got something."

"Yeah, me too. Gather the team."

Steve darted away just as a secure fax started to come in. *Fax? No one uses faxes anymore.* Rusty pulled the paper from the printer and studied it. "Jesus Tap Dancing Christ."

In the kitchen, the team was waiting. Lon asked, "Okay, what now?"

Steve turned to Rusty. "You or me?" Rusty motioned for Steve to proceed "Okay, just before the raid, Aziz's Al-Rashid company cellphone called a burner registered in Lahore that is probably Al-Maadi. He left a voice mail which we intercepted. Well, that burner just came back up on the network. It retrieved Aziz's message."

Lon said, "So, now he's aware that the attack failed."

Gunny added, "If he wasn't already."

Steve continued. "He made a number of calls to other burners. Now they're from various countries—Pakistan, Iran, UAE—but they were all pinging off of Bahraini cell towers."

Rusty asked, "Did you get the conversations?"

"No. They were going through a network I haven't hacked yet."

"What network?"

Steve replied somberly, "Qatar. The phone was not GPS enabled, so I don't have an exact location; it was pinging off a tower near Al Ruwais on the northern tip of the country."

Rusty shook his head. "Well, that's just fuckin' dandy and is a great segue to my news. I just talked to the steering committee. A NEST plane flying over the gulf to keep tabs on the Iranian nuclear program got a hit yesterday. A powerful gamma source out in the middle of the ocean. Nothing below them but fishing boats. The pilot flew back over the area to confirm the hit. He got a speed and heading, and this." Rusty threw the fax onto the table. It was a somewhat grainy color photo of a fishing boat. "Look familiar?"

Steve peered at the photo. "If it weren't for the color, I'd say it was the same boat Al-Maadi was on when they picked up the Novichok from the *Amuratu*; the *Sailfish* if memory serves. But the *Sailfish* was white."

Nigel studied the photo intently. "It's the same boat, alright. They painted her blue and changed her rigging a bit, but it's her. The aft deck planking was rather unusual and distinctive, like she'd been repaired using different kinds of wood. And that plaque above the wheel house. That ain't standard. Someone is trying to make her look different, though."

Rusty smiled. "Good eye for a drunken Scotsman. The CIA came to the same conclusion. They changed her name too. She's now the *Qirsh*."

Sarah chimed in, "That's Arabic for shark."

Lon asked, "Where were they and where were they headed?"

Rusty said, "They were ninety miles north of Dubai on a bearing of 300° and headed west northwest."

"West, as in toward Qatar?"

"And Bahrain. Folks, saddle up. We're going to Manama."

* * *

The Kingdom of Bahrain is a small, island nation in the Persian Gulf east of the Saudi oil city of Dhahran, where Saudi Aramco is headquartered. The country has been officially ruled by the House of Khalifa for over two hundred years though it was administered and protected by the British from 1860 until its formal independence in 1971. Like many countries in the region, Bahrain had once been oil rich but as its reserves declined over time, it repositioned itself to be a regional financial center with a much more liberal, cosmopolitan society than many of its neighbors. It welcomed western businesses with open arms and even the US Navy's Fifth Fleet. Bahrain still had its share of troubles, however. While its king is a Sunni Muslim, over half the population are Shia Muslims. Iran had been fighting for influence over the Shia population since the time of the shahs and Iranian meddling led to periodic strife in the country including a failed coup in 1981. It was this inter-factional tension on which Al-Maadi's plan relied.

* * *

While the team prepared to reposition to Bahrain, Gunny pulled Rusty aside. "Boss, we need to call our stateside contacts and update them on what Steve found."

"Oh? Why is that? You don't think we can handle this?"

"I do, its just…"

"What. Talk to me Gunny Medina."

"We don't have exactly what we need for this operation."

Rusty was incredulous. "And what are we missing, exactly?"

"A navy. This material is extremely dangerous. If we intercept it as they bring it to shore, a stray bullet or one crazy terrorist willing to martyr himself and we have radiological mess on our hands. The best place to interdict them is at sea. They have no escape options and if they opt to go out in a blaze of glory and release the radioisotopes, you just sink the boat and the let the shit be diluted in a few trillion gallons of sea water."

"But we can do this!" Rusty was almost pleading.

"Boss, but does it make sense? We can't let our egos make our decisions. It's like when they got Zawahiri. They could have sent in a team and captured or killed him but it made more sense to dispatch a drone with that Flying Ginsu missile. Maybe not as satisfying, but he is just as dead and we didn't lose any soldiers. I suspect the steering committee will agree. The

Fifth Fleet is right there to do it. We still go to Manama. If Steve and Hans locate the locals involved, we take them out while the Navy does what it does best—blow shit out of the water."

Rusty sighed. Deep down inside, he understood Gunny was right. He nodded. "You're right. Let's make the call."

As soon as they told their CIA contact what they'd put together, they immediately brought in the military. Their assessment of the situation was in lockstep with Gunny's. Stop them at sea and contain any radioactive materials far from shore. Shortly after, they called the Praetorians together to break the news. All were disappointed that they would not be in on the kill. Sarah carped, "If they kill Al-Maadi before I do…"

Nigel chimed in, "I'm with ya darlin' but Gunny has a point. We don't have the assets to interdict them at sea. If only we'd kept *Mother Goose* in theater."

Rusty accepted blame. "That was my decision. I sent her back to Cyprus. I really assumed we wouldn't be needing her anymore. Regardless, *Mother Goose* is no destroyer. I'd love to be the ones to wax these guys, but it makes more sense for the Navy to do it."

John asked, "What about the Bahrainis? Are they going to be involved?"

Gunny answered, "Not sure. Maybe. It's their country after all. But if it were me, the answer would be *no*. Al-Maadi has coopted people all over the place. I'd keep this one a very close hold. I'd use the SEALs to take down the vessel, but it ain't my call."

Lon asked, "What about us? What do we do? Just sit on our hands?"

Rusty replied, "No. We're still going to Bahrain. Al-Maadi wasn't going to release this crap all by himself. He has to have one or more cells in country to deploy it. Those were the people he was talking to yesterday. Even if the Navy gets Al-Maadi, the others might cause a lot of trouble on their own. We're going to find them and take them out."

Magne grinned, "Now you're talking. Let the Navy deal with the radioactive shit. I'd rather take out the terrorists…personally."

Alen added, "I'm with Magne on this one."

Hans turned to Steve and asked, "Can you hack into the Bahraini cell system and locate these assholes?"

Steve grinned. "Oh, hell yeah. I'm all over it. I'll find those fuckers before we hit the ground."

Gunny interjected, "Not to piss on your parade, but we need to figure out how to get weapons into the country. Gil's contacts there are limited at best. Any ideas?"

John Kernan raised his hand. "I've got a couple of buddies in the Fifth Fleet. Let me make a call."

"All right. Everyone, get packed. We're airborne as soon as Gil files a flight plan."

* * *

K halid Al-Maadi had been diligent when devising his plan. He had kept the two groups completely separate without as much of a whisper to one cell about the other's existence. While all members of the Dubai cell had been Pakistani Sunnis, the Manama cell was recruited from militant pro-Iranian factions within the local Shia community. They were only too happy to punish their government for its recognition of Israel.

What made them even more attractive to Al-Maadi was their social status. The government didn't really trust the Shia community, especially after their failed coup. As a result, they were excluded from most high-level or even modest managerial positions within the government. They were relegated to more menial, physical jobs in the trades, construction, and public works. They were exactly the types of people Al-Maadi needed if his plan was to work.

Aboard the *Qirsh*, Al-Maadi snapped closed his cheap burner phone and waved to Haq. "Zihad, I have our destination."

Haq climbed down from the bridge to where Al-Maadi and Mohammad were standing at the stern of the boat. "Where are we going?"

Al-Maadi tore a piece of paper out of the small notebook. "These are the coordinates. Can you find it?"

Haq glanced at the paper and shrugged. "So long as this is in the ocean, I'll find it. If you don't mind me asking, what is your plan, Abu Almawt? I've been helpful, have I not? I have risked my boat, my crew, my livelihood, and my life for you. I just want to know if it has been..."

Al-Maadi smiled slightly. "Worth it?"

"Well, yes. I don't know what you had planned in Dubai, but I do know it didn't work. I want to help you as much as possible. I can't if you don't tell me what you need."

Al-Maadi took a deep breath. He turned to Mohammad who stood stone-faced. His trusted bodyguard would advise against telling anyone anything more than what was absolutely necessary, but Mohammad would ultimately defer to him. Al-Maadi made his decision to reward Zihad for his loyalty; also to assuage his own ego. *Why come up with such a brilliant plan if you won't take credit for it? Shouldn't people appreciate how brilliant I am?* "Okay, Zihad, I'll tell you since we are so close to the end. The stuff we have hidden in the buoys is deadly radioactive material called cesium and strontium. Just being near it will kill you." Haq blanched. "Oh, don't worry. The containers are made of lead and keep it from harming us."

Zihad let out a sigh of relief. "Well, that's good. What are you...we... going to do with it?"

"We have brothers in Bahrain who are going to inject it secretly and slowly into the Bahraini water system. The strontium will attach to the calcium scale inside the pipes. They won't be able to simply flush it from the system. They will have to dig up and replace every water main, every pipe, and every faucet. The sewers, too, will be contaminated. People who drink the water, bathe in it, wash their clothes in it, or cook with it will become sickened. Thousands will die.

"But the people..."

Haq was clearly uncomfortable and Al-Maadi now regretted telling him at all. He tried to reassure the captain. "We are only going to inject it into the pipes that service the government offices, the King's palace, and the American navy base. Sadly, there will be some innocent deaths. Civilian casualties are an unavoidable aspect of war, but my plan limits them to the traitors and the infidels," he lied. "Don't be fooled, Zihad, we are most definitely in a war. The UAE and Bahrain betrayed all Muslims when they normalized relations with Israel. They must be punished. We don't want equally weak Muslim leaders following in their footsteps."

Zihad Haq stood straight like a soldier. "I understand, Abu Almawt. I will do whatever is needed of me."

"We need to get this material to our brothers so they can strike a blow for Islam."

The Bahraini water system relied on a series of large desalinization plants to turn seawater into potable water for the population. These were large, modern facilities in multiple locations along the coast. An integral part of the water supply were the chlorination systems which added calcium hypochlorite to disinfect the water by killing bacteria, viruses or fungi. In these plants, this process was controlled by computers that monitored the purity of the water and adjusted the amount of chlorine as necessary. Instead of calcium hypochlorite, Al-Maadi's plan would allow him to release the radioactive isotopes into the water at the desalination plants and other key points in the system at the same time with a phone call. By the time the Bahrainis even detected the attack, their entire system would be contaminated.

* * *

The Bombardier 8000 gracefully lifted off from the runway in Sharjah International before banking west toward Bahrain. At only 500 kilometers, it would be a short flight with no time to relax. Steve Chang was working furiously to access the Bahraini cellular network. Once he did, he entered the numbers of all the burners Al-Maadi had contacted the day before while at sea north of Qatar. While a couple were offline, the rest were on and pinging the network.

Behind Steve, John Kernan was working on their logistics problem. They didn't have their full accompaniment of weapons on board; what they did have would have to stay in the cargo compartment until they found a way to get them through or around customs. Gil was of little help on this one. He had only flown into Manama a couple of times and that was years ago. He had no connections there. Thankfully, John did.

John was on a satellite phone talking to one of his old SEAL teammates. "Mike, were you able to help me out?"

"Yeah, but you fuckin' owe me big for this."

"Don't worry, bro. We'll take care of ya."

"You'd better. What airport you landing at?"

"Bahrain International, like you said. Nothing more…discreet?"

"What, like Isa Air Base where the F-16s are or Shakhir Air Base next to the king's palace?"

"Okay, I got ya."

"Taxi to the cargo area at the west end of the airport. Head for the yellow DHL airplanes. That's where the command's non-military cargo comes in. I'll meet you there. I have a Customs tag. It won't be in the system, but I'll tell them you're carrying a present for the king from a wealthy American defense contractor."

Steve was listening to their conversation and volunteered, "If he gets me the particulars, I'll log it into their Custom's database. If it's in the computer, it's gotta be true."

John said, "Hey Mike, did you hear that? That was our computer guy."

"Is he that good?"

John smiled, "Yeah, but don't tell him I said so."

"Okay, I'll text you the details."

When the Praetorians' plane arrived, Gil taxied to the cargo area. He wasn't exactly sure where to go. John squeezed in between Gil and Donny in the cockpit and spotted Mike standing on the tarmac. "That big dumb-looking guy is him."

They parked where Mike indicated and spun down the engines. Walking down the stairs, John greeted his old friend warmly. "Hey ya old goat, you look good for a man of your advanced years."

"Because I don't go drinking with you anymore." Motioning to the $75 million aircraft, he said. "Well, you sure landed on your feet."

"Yeah, it doesn't suck. Maybe when you get tired of eating MREs, you'll consider a career change?" As he said this, Sarah and the rest of the group walked down the stairs.

Staring at Sarah, Mike replied, "Yeah, maybe I will."

Donny approached Mike and asked, "How long before we need to move her to a different part of the apron?"

Mike replied, "You're good for a few days. These three spots belong to the Command and we have nothing coming in until next week."

Gunny walked up to Mike and put out his hand. "Master Chief Mike Forester, if my memory serves. I'm Juan Medina."

"I remember you, Gunny. You approached me about a job a few years back."

Gunny laughed, "And you turned me down."

"But if I had known then what I know now…"

"Why is a SEAL on cargo duty?"

"Wrenched my knee. I'm stuck on shore until the docs clear me."

"Well, thanks for your help." Motioning to Rusty, he added, "This is our boss, Rusty Travis."

Rusty shook his hand. "We appreciate your help, son."

"No problem. I owe John, big time. Least I could do." He handed Rusty an envelope. "Here's your Customs tag. You'd better use it before they get here."

Rusty handed it to Steve who went back on the aircraft and attached it to a large pelican case. A few minutes later, the Customs officer arrived. He scanned the QR code on the tag with his cellphone. A second later there was a chime and the screen turned green. He turned to Gil and said, "You're good to go. Immigration is over there. Enjoy your stay."

Immigration was perfunctory. A $75 million private jet and a US military escort doesn't exactly scream "I'm a terrorist." They reserved four SUVs which were waiting for them at the airport. Given the short-fused nature of their trip, they didn't have time to rent a villa but instead opted for a hotel. Rusty picked the Ritz-Carlton. All because you're working, doesn't mean you have to be uncomfortable.

Mike accompanied them to their hotel. Gunny pulled John aside and said, "Read Mike in. He deserves to know."

"Copy that, Gunny."

Mike was in John's room as the porter delivered his luggage along with the large pelican case. After the man left, Mike asked, "What are you guys doing here?"

"Security work."

"Bullshit. Legit security work doesn't need my help getting stuff into the country. Also, Gunny Medina doing security work? No fuckin' way. Whatever you're into, I admire your style. Five-star hotel. Fancy jet. Smoking hot stewardess."

John replied, "She's not a stewardess."

Mike grinned, "Oh, the boss's personal assistant?"

"Hardly. She's an operator. One of the best I've ever worked with and that includes the teams."

Mike scoffed. "That hot piece of ass is an operator? I gotta call bullshit."

"You'd better not let her hear you say that. You'd be on your hands and knees trying to find your balls. That 'hot piece of ass' has killed more men than cancer. She took out four guys two days ago and three or four more in Karachi last week." John was stone-faced.

Mike laughed nervously. "You're fuckin' with me, right?"

"No, I am not. Sarah is Israeli; former deep cover operative with the Mista'avrim counterterrorist unit. Our guys are the best in the world and she can take any one of them in hand-to-hand."

"How do you know that?"

John replied coldly, "Because she has. I have the bruises to prove it."

"Holy shit! What are you guys into?"

"Like I said, security work."

"Yeah, right. What's in the pelican case?"

John asked, "Do you really want to know?"

"Yeah, I do."

"When Gunny approached you about a job, what did he say you'd be doing?"

Mike shrugged. "He didn't; not really. Just that it was a private venture and I'd be doing the same work but with better pay and less rules. I thought he had gone merc, so I turned him down." Mike was suddenly very serious. "What the fuck do you do, John?"

John removed the customs tag and opened the case. On top was a piece of dark foam with some high-tech electronic equipment nestled into cut out spaces in the foam. He lifted this layer out to reveal eight Heckler and Koch MP-7 machine pistols chambered for the 4.6x30mm round and several extra magazines. In addition, there were eight Sig 9mm pistols. "We're a private concern. We work for a consortium of Western intel agencies. We get operational freedom and they get results, plausible deniability, and no prisoners...ever."

Mike was taken aback. "Jesus Christ, John, who are you after?"

"You remember those assholes who tried to attack Israel with a biological weapon a while back?"

"Shams Sawda. The guys the Israelis whacked in the West Bank." John didn't respond but just smirked. Mike gulped. "Why do I suddenly get the feeling that it wasn't the Israelis at all."

John shrugged. "No, they helped. They killed two of them with a drone."

"But none of the others."

"Nope."

"So, this is what Medina was trying to hire me to do. I wish he'd told me. I'd probably would've said yes."

"Ya snooze, ya lose. Anyway, we're after the same terrorist group. They tried to pull off a CW attack in Dubai a couple of days ago."

"CW? Like mustard gas?"

"No. Fourth Gen nerve agent. Russian Novichok."

Mike was confused. "I've seen no intel on that."

"And you won't."

"You guys stopped them?"

"Yes, but these assholes aren't done. We took out ten of them and destroyed the CW but that was just one cell. We're convinced they're planning to attack Bahrain with a radiological weapon. Our Navy has been tapped to stop them bringing it ashore. When you get briefed on it, act surprised."

"Yeah, sure. Why Bahrain, of all places?"

"The Abraham Accords. They want to punish Bahrain for making nice with Israel."

"Well, if the Navy is going to interdict them, what are you guys doing here armed to the teeth?"

"We're going to take out the local cell. Want to join us? Should be fun."

Mike demurred. "Uh, no man, I'll pass. I'm too close to my pension."

"Suit yourself."

Admiring the hotel room, Mike said. "Best digs, best weapons, best airplane. You guys definitely travel in style."

"If we have an opening, ya interested? After you collect your creaky knee pension, I mean."

Mike handed him a card. "Put me on the standby list."

"Will do." Handing his own card to his friend, John said, "Call me when you drop your retirement papers. Now you need to put some distance between you and us in case the shit hits the fan."

"You mean *when* the shit hits the fan. I've known you too long to think otherwise. Good hunting."

* * *

At 2100 hours, the Pakistani trawler *Qirsh* was motoring slowly to the southwest in the Gulf of Bahrain. She was running dark, but the dim glow from the instruments on the vessel's bridge were visible through the night vision goggles of the SEALs approaching through the gloom in an 11-meter-long Naval Special Warfare Rigid Hull Inflatable Boat more commonly referred to as a Zodiac. As they neared, they slowed to match their target's speed. While there was a drone flying silently above them, the team leader wanted to make some first-hand observations of his own. Attacking this early was not ideal. He preferred the early morning; 0300 to 0400 hours when those on the night watch were tired and the rest of the crew was deep asleep. They didn't have that luxury this time. Intel indicated this boat was carrying very dangerous stuff and the brass wanted to keep it as far from shore as possible, so they moved up the timetable. He radioed back to the LPD 17 amphibious transport dock they had launched from. "This is Charlie One. Any update from the bird?"

A voice replied. "Negative changes. We still have only two bogeys topside, both on the bridge. No others visible. You are free to engage."

"Copy that. Executing now." The Zodiac surged ahead. It slipped in behind the *Qirsh* while staying to starboard. The drone feed showed her nets piled on the deck or hanging from the outriggers. That said, they had no guarantee there weren't other nets or a stray line in the water so they'd come in at an angle to close the distance quickly while making sure not to get their props fowled. The Zodiac's twin engines were muffled to make its approach silent except for the slap of its hull on the waves.

The critical point was when they were close enough to be seen from the *Qirsh* but not close enough to board her. With any luck, by the time the crew of the trawler even discovered the team was there, it would be too late.

Captain Zihad Haq was at the helm of the trawler peering into the inky blackness ahead of him. He was just starting to make out the dim lights from Bahrain. Distant channel markers and navigation lights of other ships dotted the horizon. Pointing to a flashing light far ahead on the starboard side he said, "That must be the Bin Salman Causeway beacon. We need to stay well to the south. Due west of the causeway is the US Navy Base and the Bahraini Coast Guard."

Hamid replied, "Yes, let's avoid them at all cost."

"We may want to set the nets again so we look like any other active trawler."

"Aye, captain." Hamid turned to leave the bridge when he made out something that terrified him; an amphibious attack boat approaching their starboard side. As he stared, a maritime commando dressed in black threw a grappling hook onto the *Qirsh* and quickly pulled the two vessels together. As he did this, four more dark figures leapt aboard with weapons drawn. "Captain! We're being attacked!"

Haq spun to find the four men running toward the front of the trawler. "Arm yourself!" Hamid grabbed an AK-47 leaning in the corner. As he spun to fire at the mysterious assailants, he was hit in the chest by a three-round burst of automatic weapons fire and crumpled onto the deck in a bloody heap. Abandoning the helm, Zihad Haq snatched up the AK-47 and dove through the open hatchway into his cabin below. As he lay on the floor, the door leading to the deck flew open and the man standing there fired a burst. The man expected Haq to be standing and the rounds flew harmlessly over him and lodged into the bulkhead beyond. Haq managed to slew his weapon toward the threat and fire randomly at the intruder. While most of the bullets lodged into the wall, one hit home and the dark figure staggered back, retreating from the door.

Above him, another assailant had reached the bridge. He checked on Hamid, and after confirming he was dead, pointed his weapon through the open hatch and fired into the gloom below. One of his rounds struck Haq in the thigh. Haq returned fire but hit nothing. Seconds later, a flash-bang grenade exploded. The tight quarters of the cabin only amplified the deleterious effects. Haq was completely stunned. He was blinded by the intense flash and his ears were ringing painfully. There was muffled shouting from outside the door and above him, but he couldn't make out what they were saying. He groped around on the floor feeling for the AK. When he found it, he fired wildly. He wasn't sure what he was firing at but hoped it would keep his tormentors at bay long enough for him to collect his wits.

As his ears recovered, a voice was shouting at him in Arabic; telling him to throw out his weapon and surrender. The voice was accented. It was from an American or maybe a Brit. His vision was starting to return. He made out the shape of the doorway leading to the deck. His wounded leg was throbbing. Unable to stand, he dragged himself deeper into the cabin so as not to be visible from above. With his back against the far wall, he fired his AK toward the door. He emptied his entire magazine, hitting nothing. There was an eerie silence for several seconds when the voice returned. "Give yourself up and I promise you will not be hurt. You're out of ammunition and you've been hit. Surrender and you'll receive medical attention."

Haq fumbled in the dark. *Where's that other magazine?* Then it hit him. It was on the bridge in a map cubby next to the wheel. *Damn it!* He removed the AK's magazine and checked it in the dim light of the cabin. It was empty. He pulled back the bolt but the chamber was empty as well. They were right. He was out of ammo. Then it hit him, the old Webley! He pulled himself to his knees and ran his hands under the bunk's mattress. There it was. His ancient revolver, the same one the Emirati coast guard had found. He now appreciated that he had taken the man's advice and cleaned and oiled the gun. With the pistol in his hand, he slunk back into his corner and called out. "Okay, I surrender."

"Move to the door. Crawl out on your belly with your hands in front of you."

"I can't. I've been shot."

"Alright. When I open the door, toss your weapon out." The door was kicked open but no one was there. Haq tossed the AK, but it landed just inside the doorway. When a hand reached over to grab the butt of the rifle, Haq fired three shots from the revolver. He was immediately met with return fire from both above and in front of him. He was hit twice more, in the left arm and the gut. He let out a pained groan.

The man above him called out. "I have him. If he twitches, I'll waste him."

The man outside the door now said, "Captain Haq, we know who's on your boat and what you're carrying. The weapon will not be delivered. Abu Almawt has been stopped. You can still save yourself."

Haq replied, "Only Allah can save me. Long live Shams Sawda!" He pressed the Webley to his temple and pulled the trigger.

"Tango is down, repeat tango is down. Search the rest of the ship." The SEALs systematically went through the vessel. It was not a big boat and there were limited places for someone to hide.

"The boat's clean, sir. Just the two dead tangos."

"There were supposed to be two others."

The sailor replied, "Yes sir, but there's no one else on board."

"Okay, find the radioisotopes. They're very dangerous, so use the radiation detectors. If you find something, tag it but don't touch it."

The SEALs combed the Qirsh but found nothing. Finally, one of the men pointed to the net winch and a large puddle of water on the deck. "Their nets were recently in the water. If I was hauling something that nasty, I'd want it as far away from me as possible."

The Lieutenant nodded. "Check them."

The SEALs combed through the large pile of nets. Aside from a few random fish, there was nothing. The Lieutenant was getting frustrated. One of his men had suffered a wound, albeit a minor one, and for what? Then one of his men pointed out that several buoys were removed. The lines fastening them to the net had been sloppily cut. "This ain't right, sir."

From behind, another SEAL called out. "Found something weird over here." They walked over to find the man holding the pieces of an orange net buoy. "This thing was ripped apart. There's a hollow space in the middle and a steel cable passing through it. Whatever they were smuggling was hidden inside this buoy."

The Lieutenant asked, "Anything from the radiation detector?"

"Yeah, ionizing radiation consistent with a gamma source."

Turning to the other SEAL, the Lieutenant asked, "How many buoys have been removed?"

Two of the SEALs stretched out the top line of the net. "Ten. Maybe twelve."

"Goddamnit. We're too late."

* * *

From his hotel room in Manama, Steve Chang monitored the location of the burner phones Al-Maadi had contacted while off the Qatari coast. There were six originally, but he noted that, in the interim, those six had contacted seven other cellphones. None of these new phones had subscriber information. More burners. About the time the SEALs launched their attack on the *Qirsh*, Steve briefed the others on what he'd found. "Okay, all these new burners, like the others, were registered on multiple foreign cell networks in Iran, Iraq, Qatar, and Kuwait. The Bahraini network call registry shows that, aside from the contact with Al-Maadi's burner, these thirteen phones have only talked to each other. No other calls at all."

Magne said, "Sure looks like a terrorist cell, doesn't it?"

Alen replied, "Yeah and not a very smart one at that. They should've generated an innocuous call pattern in case anyone was paying attention. This makes it too easy."

Gunny chimed in, "If they have the same profile as the Dubai cell, they'll have clean criminal records but no operational experience. Ya gotta take the bad with the good. Where are they now?"

"They've been scattered throughout the island all day. I mapped the locations where the phones have been located in the last 24-hours. During the work day, they travel in pairs and spend their time at various infrastructure locations."

Lon asked, "What kind of infrastructure?"

"Municipal water. Desalination plants, water storage towers, and distribution facilities."

Alen groaned, "Jesus Christ. They were going to put that shit in the water supply! Do you realize how many people they would've killed?"

Nigel added, "And it would have contaminated not just the water but all the equipment, pipes, everything. They'd have to rebuild the entire system. It would cost billions."

Lon asked, "Exactly what infrastructure? Which facilities?"

Steve turned to his computer. "I dropped pins at their houses and the places they traveled to. Let me check." After a few seconds, he said, "Okay, they were at the Al-Hidd Desalination Plant south of the airport, the Ras Abu Jarjur Desalination plant about midway down the island on the east coast, and the Al Dur Plant."

"Where is that one?"

"Further south on the east coast. Just north of the Isa Air Base."

Alen commented, "The desalination plants supply most of the water to the island. They're a logical target if you want maximum damage. What were the other facilities?"

Steve turned his computer screen toward the others. "They're all water distribution stations. Basically, large water tanks with an associated water tower to maintain pressure. One in the north, one near the harbor, and one further south in the middle."

Nigel pointed to the northernmost one and asked. "Where is this one?"

"Uh, on Enterprise Avenue."

"What's around that area?"

Steve zoomed in. "The diplomatic section and government offices."

John pointed to the next one. "And that one. What's that to the south of it?"

Steve replied with a gulp. "That would be our Fifth Fleet base."

Rusty quipped, "I see a trend developing. And the last one?"

Steve scrolled down the map. "That's the Hamid Town distribution center. Everything to the west is residential."

Rusty pointed to the right of the screen. "What's that to the east?"

Steve zoomed in. "Oh shit. That's the King's royal palace. Just south of it is Sakhir Airbase."

"In addition to the entire country's water supply, they're going after government buildings, diplomatic quarters, our fleet, and the king specifically."

Gunny got everyone back on point. "Okay, okay. Focus people. John, when is the navy planning to take down the *Sailfish*, or *Qirsh* or whatever they're calling it today?"

"Well, according to Mike, it should be happening as we speak."

"The SEALs will take out the boat easily. That means the radioisotopes will never make it to shore, so their target list is a moot point. Communications jamming is part of SEAL standard operating procedure. The tangos on the boat won't have a chance to warn the cell members on shore. They'll still be expecting Al-Maadi or one of his people to deliver the radioisotopes. It makes more sense to bring the cell together to one location and distribute the radioisotopes."

Lon nodded. "Agreed. That's where we should hit them, when they're all together in one place. They'll be expecting Al-Maadi but get us instead."

"Anyone disagree?" Gunny tacitly polled the group, receiving nods of agreement. "Lon has more urban warfare experience, so he's the lead. We have four vehicles— two shooters per ride. Steve, you and Hans track them on two different computers in two different vehicles. No single point of failure. I don't want to lose these guys because you get t-boned by a drunk Saudi. Rusty and I will tag along to maintain coms during the action. Once we find out where they land, we set up a perimeter, lock them down, and take them out. It's sort of half-assed, but we don't have a choice. Once they figure out Al-Maadi ain't showing, they'll scatter like cockroaches. We need to get them before they do. Any questions?" There were none. "Okay, Lon, how do you want to pair up?"

Lon rubbed his chin. "Anyone have a problem with one-two, three-four, five-six, seven-eight?" Nobody objected. "Okay then, that's it. Rusty, you ride with Nigel and Hans, and Gunny, you ride with Alen and Steve. They'll need extra sets of eyes since Hans and Steve will be on computer duty. Comms are going to be cellular push-to-talk through the encrypted app, channel three. Clear?"

Nigel shot back, "Crystal."

Steve glanced up from his computer. "We have activity. A group text just went out. Now I have two together and moving east. The others are on the move as well. It appears coordinated."

Gunny loomed over Steve's shoulder to peer at the screen. "Where are they going?"

"Undetermined. The two traveling together are headed east on Salman Highway toward the airport. One is near the fishing harbor east of the coast guard base, but he isn't moving; at least not yet. As for the others, I can't tell yet."

"Okay folks, time to saddle up."

* * *

In the dark of night, a black, high-performance racing boat rounded the northern tip of the island of Bahrain. It had been running at over a hundred kilometers per hour before throttling back to enter the Bay of Bahrain. It moved gracefully through the water as it passed through the breakwater and under the Salman Causeway Bridge. Even in the well-lit city, its matte black finish made it very difficult to spot. Its twin inboard engines were barely idling but still emitted a low, throaty rumble as it slid beneath the Shaikh Hamad Causeway bridge and into the Bay of Arad. It steered east past the coast guard station before slipping into the fisherman's port just beyond.

The man driving the speedboat peered northeast. He was waiting for a signal. A second later, there it was. A green light flashed twice, then three times, then twice again. He flashed his running lights twice and then turned them off. He guided the sleek boat toward the easternmost jetty. As he eased up to the dock, the bearded man next to him jumped from the cockpit to the dock with a line in his hand. He stopped the boat and tied the line to the nearest cleat. The captain said, "Mohammad, no need to tie it off. We won't be here very long. I want that stuff off my boat as soon as possible."

"No, he needs my help." Mohammad approached the man on shore who had signaled them. "You Barbad?" The man nodded. "Do you have a wagon or a cart?"

Barbad pointed to a three-wheeled, motorized cart. It had one seat in front of a small cargo box between two spoked wheels. "I was told it was not that much."

"They aren't that large, but they're heavier than they look. I'll hand them over to you." Mohammad clambered back onto the speedboat, grabbed a line buoy off the floor, and handed it to the man on shore.

Placing it in his cart, Barbad commented, "These are heavy. You weren't kidding."

"The material is packed in lead. You'll appreciate that since it is all that is keeping any of us alive."

Mohammad and Barbad quickly moved ten additional line buoys to the cart. Mohammad had the last canister in his hand as he jumped off the boat. Handing it to Barbad, he said, "This one broke apart while we were recovering it from the water. Don't worry, the canister is still intact."

Barbad gingerly placed it in the cart with the others. As Mohammad untied the mooring line, Barbad motioned to the speedboat where a third man had been overseeing. He asked meekly, "Is that him? Is that Abu Almawt?"

"Yes." Mohammad pushed the boat from the dock and jumped onboard. From the cockpit, Khalid Al-Maadi had been observing in silence. As the boat's pilot reversed the engines to pull away from the dock, Al-Maadi said in a firm voice, "Barbad, you and your people are in tactical command of the mission now. Its success, the defense of our faith, and the punishment of those who would betray Islam are in your capable hands."

Barbad stood erect, like a soldier. "We will not disappoint you, Abu Almawt."

* * *

As the Praetorians moved out into the city, Steve and Hans tracked the cell members via their phones. Steve updated the other cars via their encrypted comms. "This is Alpha Eight with your terrorist traffic report. Two tangos are still headed toward the airport. I assess the one by the harbor is the leader. He's the one Al-Maadi called first and almost all calls within the cell originate from him." A few minutes later, he gave them an update. "This is Alpha Eight again. A couple of the other members of the cell have stopped at some sort of industrial area. Wait a sec and I'll zoom in." There was a pause. "Okay, it's the East Isa Town Water Distribution Station. The water theme continues. It covers an entire city block. Two big storage tanks to the north and two water towers to the west and south. Cellular triangulation has them in the building on the south side. The building has two parts—a one-story section in the front and a two-story section in the back. The roof of the one-story section is covered with AC equipment and ductwork. The roof of the two-story section is clear which, along with the large rolling vehicle door on the west side, would suggest it's most likely an open high bay; interior layout unknown. The whole compound is surrounded by a wall, maybe three meters high, topped with razor wire. Vehicle gate on south with a guard shack or something just inside the gate to the east. No visible pedestrian entrances. It's at the corner of Road 3431 and Avenue 36; two klicks east of the Bahrain National Stadium. Be advised, there are a number of residential apartment blocks in the area. Would've been nice if they picked somewhere more discreet."

Lon came on the radio, "Alpha One copies. What's the status on the others?"

"They're generally headed in that direction but a few are pretty far out. It'll be a while before they get there."

"Copy. We'll take the west. Alpha Three, you guys take the east. Alpha Five go the south and Alpha Seven north. Keep your distance until we have them in pocket. I don't want to accidentally spook them. Copy?" The other cars copied in order.

Steve came back on. "Aspect change in the target. The pair headed to the airport crossed the bridge but turned south toward the harbor. He is not, repeat not, headed to the airport. He's now on the access road between the highway and the water headed toward the leader. I guess they're his Uber."

"Meeting the *Qirsh* at the fish harbor makes sense." Lon chuckled and added, "They're going to be disappointed."

* * *

Barbad watched the sleek, black speedboat turn around and make its way out of the harbor and into the open water of the Bay of Arad. As it moved out of sight, its twin engines revved and pushed it into the night. *There goes the greatest warrior since Sulieman.*

Barbad refocused on the task at hand. He started the engine on his little cart, motored off the dock, and around the perimeter of the little harbor to Road 1655. He pulled the little vehicle into the shadows where he sent a text. "Ready." He then lit a cigarette and waited.

His phone chimed. "5 min."

He waited nervously. The area was deserted which caused him both comfort and unease. No one to see him but were anyone to happen by, he had no excuse for being there. His anxiety eased when the lights of an approaching vehicle proved to be a familiar white van. He stepped out of the shadows to flag it down. It pulled up next to him and screeched to a halt. The side door slid open immediately. Barbad started handing buoys to the man inside. "What are these?"

"The material is hidden inside. We need to take them apart. It won't take long." He then handed the man the one naked canister. "This is what's inside. This is the prize. When we deploy this weapon, the King will die and his government will fall. We Shia will then take control of the country as Allah wills it."

They transferred the buoys into the van in a matter of seconds. Barbad jumped in and was still trying to close the door as the driver sped away. In less than thirty seconds, they were back on the road to meet their colleagues. Steve's estimation of the number of terrorists was spot on. There were thirteen members of Shams Sawda's Bahrain cell. It would prove an unlucky number for somebody.

* * *

Steve Chang studied the dots on his computer screen. He was unsure what to expect. How long would they be willing to wait before it dawned on them that Al-Maadi and the radioisotopes weren't coming? An hour? Two hours? Four? Then something unexpected happened. He keyed his mic and said, "Uh, something is weird here. Our Tango Uber car rolled past the Bahraini Coast Guard facility and into the Al-Muharraq Port fishing docks where the leader is. It was there a less than a minute and rolled right back out again."

Lon broke in. "This is Alpha One. Did it stop?"

"Unsure. The refresh rate on this is erratic. If it stopped, it wasn't for very long. The leader is with the Uber now. I have three phones moving together."

"Could they have learned that the *Qirsh* was interdicted and bailed?"

"I don't think so. No calls in or out. Maybe he has a second burner."

Lon mulled this over for a few seconds. "Alpha Eight, stay on the leader. Alpha Four, keep your eyes on the others and tell us if their burners go offline or they move out. If they find out Al-Maadi is toast, they'll bolt."

Hans replied, "Copy that. No action from them yet. A couple of stragglers are still heading to East Isa. Traveling together."

Steve broke in. "The leader's vehicle has reversed course. He's west on the Sheikh Hamad Causeway and now...turning south on Al Fatih Highway."

Lon asked, "How's his speed? Is he spooked?"

Steve replied, "I'd say it's...casual."

For the next twenty minutes, they tracked the three terrorists as they navigated Bahraini traffic. As they neared the site where their comrades were waiting, they turned into a neighborhood to the north. They drove aggressively down streets, drove in circles, reversed their route, and stopped on the street for a few minutes before moving on. Steve asked Gunny, "What they hell is this all about?"

Gunny snorted. "He's trying to run a surveillance detection route. He is being overly aggressive to make sure no one is tailing him before he meets the others."

"Kind of a smart move."

"It would be if he wasn't carrying his damned cellphone with him. A little knowledge is a dangerous thing." He keyed his mic and asked, "Alpha Four, what's the status on our stragglers?"

"Still straggling. I'd say they're ten or fifteen minutes out. He's approaching from the southwest."

Lon broke in. "Copy that. When he arrives, we'll move in."

* * *

John was waiting impatiently for the action to start. This was the part he hated most; it was when he had the least amount of control. He wanted to ask for another update on the stragglers, but Hans had just provided one less than thirty seconds before. Then his phone vibrated. It was Mike Forester calling via an encrypted app.

"Uh, Mike. We're kind of in the middle of something. Can I call ya back?"

"No. If you're in the middle of what I think you are, you need to hear this. That boat, the *Qirsh*? We took it down tonight. No bad shit and no bad guys."

"Wait, what? There were no tangos on board?"

"Well, there were two—the captain, Zihad Haq, and his mate, Hamid somebody. No sign of the guy you're after and no radioactive shit."

John was stunned. "That makes no sense."

"Unless they rendezvoused with someone before we hit them. We found indications the shit had been there hidden inside line buoys. We had gamma radiation residuals but it was gone. Also, we found out the Emirati

Coasties boarded her a couple days ago on a fishery check. Reported they searched and found one weapon on board, an old Webley revolver. When we hit it tonight, they opened fire with an AK. It had to have come from somewhere. Haq offed himself with the Webley so we got the right boat. Also, they were moving southeast, away from Bahrain like they'd already made their delivery."

"Any idea how many buoys?"

"Guys estimate ten to twelve."

"Shit." His mind turning to his former SEAL colleagues, John instinctively asked, "Any friendly casualties?"

Mike replied, "One. Pretty minor. He'll be fine. Thanks for asking. Anyway, this Al-Maadi fuck is in the wind and so is that radioactive shit. I suspect your undercard bout just got moved up to the main event."

"You may be right. Anything else?"

"Nope."

"Thanks for the intel."

"Be safe brudda. And remember, you didn't hear it from me." The line went dead.

Lon had been listening. "Well, that sucks. You'd better break the bad news to the rest of the team. Al-Maadi is getting irritating and we keep underestimating him."

"How you figure?"

"He did the same damn thing with the Novichok. He met the *Amuratu* in the middle of the fucking Indian Ocean rather than wait for her to make port. He just did the same thing with the *Qirsh*. We should've seen it coming."

John said, "There is only one remedy."

"Kill him?"

"Damn skippy."

The news about the *Qirsh* only increased the anxiety of the Praetorians. No one was thrilled about having to deal with multiple radioactive dirty bombs. They were reconciled to fighting men with machine guns and hand grenades; they had a modicum of control. But they had none when it came to cesium-137 or strontium-90. They couldn't smell it, hear it, taste it, or kill it. It was an invisible enemy who killed from a distance and through walls with them none the wiser until the terminal radiation sickness kicked in. The only one happy about the development was Sarah. The SEALs missing Al-Maadi meant she still had the chance to kill him...personally.

Lon addressed the team. "This is Alpha One. Our mission has not changed but the rules of engagement have. We cannot risk damaging one of the canisters, not with so many people living nearby. That means headshots. If one of the cans gets ruptured, stay the fuck away from it. This also means one hundred percent containment. No one escapes—no matter what."

Steve interjected. "Our fearless terrorist leader has arrived. Approaching south side of the facility from the east. Alpha Three and Alpha Five, look sharp."

* * *

The van carrying Barbad and the radioisotopes rolled slowly south down Road 3410 toward the East Isa Town water distribution station. The driver killed his lights as he turned west onto Avenue 36 driving the final block in darkness. The neighborhood was quiet. Due to the late hour, the streets were deserted, but the lights in the windows of the surrounding apartment buildings meant people were most definitely still awake. The van passed the next street and then stopped at the gate leading into the distribution station. The passenger jumped out of the van and opened the gate. After the van entered, he closed the gate and trotted toward the building.

The van drove to the vehicle entrance on the west side of the building. The overhead door leading to the dark interior bay was already open. The van drove in and the door immediately closed behind it. As soon as the door closed, the men inside turned on the lights. Standing in a group were most of the Sham Sawda Bahraini cell. Barbad opened the door and climbed out of the van. "Niaz, is everyone here?"

Niaz was the number two man of the cell. "No. Ali and Reza are on the way. They got held up due to road construction but should be here in a few minutes."

"Unload the buoys from the van."

"Buoys?"

Barbad explained, "Yes, the material is hidden inside them. We need to find some tools to open them. They are made of foam so it shouldn't be difficult."

Niaz pointed at two of the men. "Go to the shop and get something to open these." The two men trotted off without a word while the rest of the cell members unloaded the buoys. When the two men returned with saws and pry bars, they started extricating the canisters from the orange foam buoys.

Barbad took the first two canisters and handed them to one of the men. "Issa, we're not waiting for Ali and Reza, you and Mahdi take these and go to the Al Dur Desalinization Plant. It's the furthest away and you need to get on the road immediately."

"Yes, sir." Issa handed one of the heavy canisters to Mahdi and walked to the door leading outside.

The next two canisters were now available. Barbad handed them to another man. "Javad, you and Ebrahim take these to Hamid Town. It is imperative that this gets into the water supply for the palace." The men took them and followed their comrades outside. "Mirza and Khashav, you take the next two to the Al Hidd Desalinization Plant."

Outside, Issa and Mahid got into Issa's white Toyota sedan. Behind them Javad and Ebrahim placed their canisters in the back of Javad's truck before sliding into the cab. As the Toyota reached the perimeter wall, Mahid jumped out, opened the gate and jumped back in as the car rolled by. The dirty gray pickup followed. With another car right behind them, they didn't bother to close the gate.

* * *

Hans refreshed the screen on his computer. "Heads up! Last two stragglers are just a few minutes out. With the eleven inside, that should be all thirteen tangos."

Lon replied, "Copy that, Four. As soon as they get here, we move. Start moving into position."

Magne and Sarah were in an apartment building parking lot south of the compound to keep eyes on the gate. They were waiting for the arrival of the stragglers and would enter the compound right behind them. On the west side, Lon and John got out of their vehicle and started moving quietly down to the southwest corner of the compound where there were trees they'd use to get over the wall.

Alen and Steve were to the north parked in an alley right next to the compound wall. Steve had already climbed on top of their Range Rover and cut the wire. The two large water tanks would screen them as they climbed over the wall. On the east side, Nigel, Hans, and Rusty were stuck next to an apartment building with lots of potential eyes and no screening. They'd stay in their Land Cruiser and follow Sarah and Magne through the gate.

Everything was in place. Lon and John slid into the shadows under the trees at the southwest corner of the compound. Lon braced himself against the wall as John clambered up to stand on his shoulders. He made quick work of the concertina wire. After opening a six-foot gap, he climbed up and straddled the wall. He grabbed Lon's left arm and pulled him up after him. As Lon reached the top, John slid down to the ground below. Lon quickly followed and they ran over to the base of the nearest water tower for cover.

Hans called out, "Stragglers maybe a minute out." Sarah and Magne were about to exit their vehicle when, to their surprise, the gate swung open and a vehicle departed the compound turning east. Sarah keyed her mic and said, "They didn't wait for the stragglers. We have a white, Toyota Yaris exiting to the east toward Road 3410." The car drove past the apartment building and turned right. "Tangos are southbound on 3410, repeat southbound on 3410." Magne tapped her arm and pointed back to the gate. Another vehicle was departing. "Shit. A second departure. Gray extended cab pickup. Maybe a Nissan Navara. They are also eastbound." The truck approached Road 3410 and turned left. "Second vehicle is northbound on 3410, repeat northbound on 3410."

Lon keyed his mic. "Shit. Alpha Three go after the southbound tango. Alpha Seven, are you over the wall yet?"

Alen replied, "Alpha Eight just went over. I'm still outside."

Lon shot back, "You and Bravo Two go after the northbound tango. Alpha Eight, you link up with me and Alpha Two. We're behind the west water tower."

Steve Chang replied. "Eight copies. Moving your way now."

Gunny got on and said, "This is Bravo Two. We're moving to intercept the tango to the north." He laughed, "His cellphone is still pinging. It shouldn't be but a second."

Lon breathed a sigh of relief. "Five and Six, shut the door so no more get out."

Magne replied, "We're on it. See you inside." Sarah and Magne got out of their vehicle and trotted over to the gate. It was still wide open, so they slipped in. Sarah closed the gate before ducking behind what they initially assessed was a guard shack. It wasn't a guard shack at all, just a small, windowless utility building. Magne was focused on the building where the terrorists were congregating. He keyed his mic and whispered. "Some noise from the west side of the building. No visual from my angle. East side quiet."

Lon replied, "Copy. We have two tangos getting in a blue VW hatchback. They're moving your way."

"We're on it." Magne moved back behind the shack with Sarah.

The blue car pulled up to the gate and stopped. As the passenger, Khashav, got out and approached the gate, Magne slipped in behind the car and crept along the passenger side. When Khashav started to open the gate, Magne stood and put three rounds from his suppressed MP-7 into the man's head. Inside the vehicle, Mirza's sat dumbfounded as his friend collapsed. There were no audible gunshots, so he didn't grasp what was happening. He yelled out, "Khashav!" Before he reacted further, Sarah appeared at his window and put two rounds into the side of his head. Magne dragged Khashav's lifeless body away from the gate and into the shadows. Sarah pushed the driver into the passenger seat and climbed behind the wheel of the hatchback. She put it in reverse and backed it away from the gate. It would provide cover should the men in the building open fire on them. She peeked in the back to find two canisters laying casually on the seat. She slung her MP-7 over her shoulder, grabbed the two canisters and tucked them in a dark corner behind the shed.

Magne keyed his mic. "Two Tangos down. Repeat, two tangos down. Two packages secured."

Lon replied, "Good work, you guys."

Hans broke in. "We're in pursuit of the first vehicle. Have a visual south on Estiqlal Highway. He's headed south so were going to back off and wait until he's away from civilians to engage. The last stragglers are about thirty seconds from your locale."

"Copy that. Thanks for the info, Four. Did you copy Five?"

Magne replied, "Got it. We're ready."

A few moments later, the vehicle approached the gate. Rather than open it, the driver simply honked. Sarah turned to Magne, shrugged and motioned toward the gate. Magne trotted over and opened the gate, making sure to hide behind it so the driver didn't get a good view of him. As the red Kia pulled past him, Magne shot the driver through his open window. The passenger bailed out of the other door and got maybe three paces before

Sarah dropped him with a burst of 4.6x30mm rounds. Sarah keyed her mic and said, "Scratch two more."

Lon replied, "Copy that. Hey, we have more motion over here. Any way to block the gate so no one gets away?"

Sarah replied, "No problem." Magne pulled the lifeless body of the driver from the vehicle. He parked the Kia lengthwise in front of the gate, turned it off and pocketed the keys. The terrorists were trapped inside.

Lon took a second to assess their position. Four terrorists were already dead. Four more were on the road with Praetorians in pursuit. That left five still inside. "Alpha Seven, what's your status?"

Gunny replied, "This is Bravo Two. Seven is driving. We are on the northern vehicle. He is moving west toward Shaik Salman Highway. As soon as we get him somewhere that will minimize civilian interaction, we'll take him down."

"Roger that. Concur. Uh, Alpha Five and Six, we have the garage entrance covered. You cover the door on the east side."

Sarah replied, "Copy."

One of the men inside the building peered out a window toward the gate. The red Kia was blocking the gate and the blue sedan parked haphazardly nearby. Something was wrong. He ran back to the garage and yelled to Barbad. "Something isn't right. Ali and Reza's car is here but it is blocking the gate. Mirzaz and Khashav's car is pulled off to the side but I don't see them anywhere."

"Mirzaz left five minutes ago!" Barbad ran to the window facing the front. The Kia was blocking the gate. That was intentional. As he peered into the darkness, he made out two bodies splayed out on the ground. He ran back to the garage. "Someone is here! Grab your weapons and kill the lights!"

Tahir asked, "Who is it? Did you see them? Is it the police? The army?"

Picking up two AK-47s, Barbad replied, "I didn't see anyone. I don't know who it is." He handed Tahir a rifle. "Cover the front door."

The others ran up with AKs in their hands. "What do you want us to do?"

"Niaz, you cover the west side. Shoot anything that moves. Saeed, you put the remaining canisters in the van. We must salvage what we can. Ghasen, when I give you the sign, open the garage door. The rest of you start shooting. I'll try to escape with the remaining radioisotopes."

Niaz said, "Issa and Javad got away before we were discovered. They can still complete the attack."

Barbad replied. "If they got away." He took out his cellphone and dialed. After two rings, a familiar voice answered. "Yes?"

"Issa, we're under attack. Go immediately to Al Dur. Inject the isotopes. Do not wait for Abu Almawt's signal. And turn off your phones!"

Issa's voice cracked, "Yes, sir. We will."

Barbad called Javad and gave him the same instructions. Hans and Gunny were monitoring their targets from their perspective vehicles. One of Hans' targets disappeared from his screen. "This isn't good."

From the backseat, Rusty asked, "What? What ain't good?"

"One of our tangos just turned off his phone. Shit! Now the other one has too! Nigel, hit the gas; we can't risk losing him. We have to take him immediately."

Nigel stomped on the accelerator and replied, "Aye, mate."

Hans keyed his mic. "Alpha Team this is Four. Our southbound tangos just went dark. We're moving to intercept as soon as possible."

Gunny interjected, "This is Bravo Two. Ours just went dark too. They obviously got a heads up. Moving to intercept."

* * *

Nigel floored the Land Cruiser to get within visual range of the white Yaris carrying the terrorists and their dirty weapon. The Yaris had also sped up so it was taking time to close the gap. Every second they drove without establishing visual contact, their anxiety ratcheted up. Even two canisters of the radioisotopes were capable of inflicting considerable damage and loss of life. Finally, after a minute, they spotted the taillights of a small car ahead of them driving very fast and weaving in and out of traffic as they approached a major highway interchange. Nigel said, "I got him. Up ahead, far left lane." Hans handed his laptop computer to Rusty and picked up a pair of binoculars. Peering ahead, he confirmed, "Yeah, that's him! White Yaris. Same first three digits of the tag. He's hauling ass. Stay with him through this interchange. If we miss him here, we'll never find him again."

"Copy that. He's continuing south but to where?"

Rusty was following their progress via the computer's GPS. The map included the potential targets Steve had discerned. Rusty said, "One of the places on Steve's target list is up ahead on the left; the Ras Abu Jarjur Desalination plant."

"How far?"

"About four kilometers but he's going to have to exit soon. No off ramps close by. The road to the plant is pretty open. No houses. Might be a good place to stop him."

Hans turned to the computer. "The boss is right. It'd be a good place to take them out."

After a minute or so, Nigel commented. "This guy isn't slowing down. He's not getting off the highway. What's the next target in this direction?"

Rusty replied, "Uh, that would be the Al Dur Desalination Plant."

"How far?"

"Twelve klicks but the exit he needs to take is nine."

Nigel asked, "What's the terrain between here and there?"

Rusty returned the computer to Hans who said, "Open desert. There's a town on the southeast side of the highway. The best spot is the exit itself. He'll have to slow down to cross over the highway. Nothing but sand to the west."

Nigel nodded. "Good. Let's do it there. I'll force them into the desert when they start to make their turn. Be ready." Nigel sped up to close the gap between their Highlander and the little Yaris.

A few minutes later, Hans pointed to a road sign over the highway. "Jau Al Dur. This should be his exit." Nigel's MP-7 was stuck between his seat and the center console for easy access. Hans handed the computer to Rusty and placed his weapon in his lap. Hans removed his Sig 9mm from the small of his back and handed it to Rusty. "Just in case. But stay in the car."

"Aye, you were right; our friends are taking the off ramp." Nigel turned off his headlights and followed. While the Yaris slowed, Nigel accelerated. As Issa swung his little sedan slightly to the right as he started his left turn across the overpass, the big SUV slammed into its left rear corner panel. The violence of the collision whipped Issa's head into his window shattering it. Issa was completely shocked. He hadn't spotted the blacked-out vehicle following him up the ramp.

The Yaris spun across the intersection and slid off the pavement sideways before coming to a stop on the sandy shoulder. Nigel pressed his assault. He gunned the Highlander again, rammed the driver's side door pushing the sedan until it was buried in the sand.

Issa tried to open his door but he was pinned in. As he struggled with his door, Hans leapt from the Highlander with his MP-7, aimed his weapon through the gap between the chassis and his door and fired a short burst into the Yaris. He hit Issa in the neck and shoulder but the rounds intended for the passenger lodged in the driver's headrest instead.

Mahid, the man in the passenger seat, immediately ducked down, opened his door and rolled out of the car. Keeping low, he reached back into the car groping the floor in front of his seat to retrieve his pistol, an old Browning 9mm automatic. He also grabbed one of the canisters. The other rolled under his seat and out of reach.

Mahid scampered away from the car, throwing himself over the metal guardrail a couple meters away. A thick layer of sand had accumulated below the guardrail making it a natural fortification. Issa struggled to crawl out of the car after Mahid. He was seriously wounded and his only focus was on survival. It was not to be. As he dragged himself out the passenger door, Nigel fired through the window to put him out of his misery with two rounds through his skull.

Mahid pointed his pistol over the top of the guard rail and fired blindly at his assailants. He hit nothing but caused Nigel and Hans to duck for cover. Mahid called out in Arabic. "I have a radiation bomb. Stay back or I will detonate it! You will die alongside me!" Of course, there were no explosives attached to the canister, so there was no "bomb," but his attackers didn't know that.

The first response was a burst of fire from Nigel shooting across the hood of the Yaris. He hit the guard rail, but the thick metal kept Mahid safe. Hans called out. "We know what you have and how you planned to use it. You have no bomb."

"Are you willing to risk your lives? Even if the canister ruptures, we all die."

Hans didn't want to drag this out. While their weapons were suppressed, Mahid's pistol was not. Someone probably reported the shots. He whispered to Nigel. "Let's play along, get him to stand up, then take him out." Nigel nodded in agreement. Hans shouted out, "Okay, you win. We'll let you go but only if you leave the radioactive stuff behind."

Mahid was no fool. He didn't believe them. "No. I leave with the material. You move back behind your vehicle with your hands in the air. I have my gun pointed at the canister. If you try something, I will shoot it and spread this poison all over the place!"

Nigel shouted to Hans, "We can't risk a spill. We have to do what he says." He didn't mean it, of course. He just hoped Mahid understood English.

Hans shouted out. "Okay, we're moving behind our vehicle." Hans slowly stood, held his weapon high and backed away. Nigel followed suit.

Mahid stood. His hands were in front of him, chest high. In his left hand he held a canister of cesium-137. In his right, he gripped his pistol, pressing its muzzle against the canister. "I'm going to back across the overpass toward the town. If you follow me, I shoot the canister. I am prepared to martyr myself. Are you?"

Hans shook his head, "No I'm not. This is just a job and not one worth dying for."

Mahid smiled. *I have bested the infidels!* Mahid stepped over the guardrail and edged to his right keeping the canister between him and his enemies. He glanced over his right shoulder at the overpass. It was empty. He started to shuffle backwards toward it when a shot rang out. Mahid was hit in the groin. He dropped both the canister and the pistol as he grabbed his wounded manhood with both hands. When he did, Nigel put five rounds into his chest while Hans put two into his forehead. Nigel trained his weapon on Mahid's lifeless corpse as he ran up to him and kicked his pistol away. Mahid was clearly dead but Nigel was more worried about the canister. It hit the ground pretty hard. He was relieved to find it still intact. "Tango is down. Package is secure."

Hans was confused. Their weapons were suppressed. Where did the first shot come from? Then it dawned on him—Rusty! His boss came out from behind the rear end of the Yaris. He was smiling broadly. Hans was both angry and a little impressed. "You? You shot him? I told you to stay in the car!"

"Never been good about taking orders. Probably why the Army was not a realistic career option for me. When he jumped over that guardrail, I wanted to make sure he didn't sneak away in the dark. Nigel had the left and you the middle. Someone needed to cover the right flank."

As Nigel returned with the canister, he caught Rusty's explanation. "Well, you could've fucked this whole thing up!" He then remembered he was talking to his boss. "With all due respect, sir. If he had shot that canister..."

"Why do ya think I shot him in the balls? When it comes to your junk versus anything else, a man will instinctively protect his junk."

Hans gawked at Rusty incredulously. "You meant to shoot him in the dick?" He laughed, "I just assumed you aimed for his head and missed."

"Fuck you, ya kraut eating bastard."

Hans feigned offense. "I can't believe you called me that. I don't even like sauerkraut."

Rusty snorted, "Well, you deserved it."

Nigel quipped, "Ya kinda did."

Hans smiled. "I know. But how often do you get to take a shot at the boss?"

Nigel got everyone back on point. "Okay, break's over. Rusty, find the other canister. Hans, help me drag the dead guy out of the road and then we're out of here." They quickly stashed the bodies behind the Yaris. To the casual observer, it was just a broken-down car. They piled into the Land Cruiser, crossed the overpass, and turned north toward Manama. Hans keyed his mic to report to the team. "Alpha One, this is Four. Two more tangos down. Two packages recovered."

"Good work." Lon asked, "Any injuries?"

Hans answered, "Just Bravo One's cherry."

"What?"

Hans laughed, "We'll explain later."

* * *

Unlike his comrades, Javad, the driver of the gray Nissan Navara pickup truck, kept his wits about him. He and Ebrahim turned off their burners but maintained a moderate speed and a casual driving demeanor. They didn't want to draw the attention of some random police officer on the street. This made it easier for Alen and Gunny to keep them in sight without driving aggressively. After leaving the compound, the Nissan turned north on Road 3410, made its way to 16 December Highway and moved east. After passing the Bahrain National Stadium, they turned south on Shaikh Salman Highway. Alen didn't like relying completely on technology, so he was keeping the terrorists' vehicle in sight. When their burners went offline, he had no reason to panic since he was only about 100 meters behind them in light traffic.

"Gunny, what does the area ahead look like? Anywhere to run them off the road?"

Gunny studied the map. "If they stay on this road, no. We're about to come up on a residential area with several traffic circles. It's going to be slow going. High probability of civilian entanglements."

"Well, where else then? Any of Steve's targets down this way?"

"Good question. Let me see." He zoomed out on the mapping software and several red pins appeared. "Only one. The Hamid Town Water Distribution Station. It's the one that services the King's palace and the airbase to the south. He must be headed there."

Alen asked, "What's his likely route from here to there?"

"If he heads into Riffa and then turns east on Shaikh Khalifa Avenue, it'll take him to Road 4453 which connects to the highway to the facility. Wait. Scratch that. It says those roads are restricted access." He zoomed in on the satellite imagery of the area. "The western part of Riffa is very upscale."

"How upscale?"

"Like Bahraini Beverly Hills upscale. There has to be police and private security all over this place. One false move and you'd have people sticking guns in your face in a matter of seconds."

"What's their alternative?"

Gunny checked the map. "Go west and then south on Bin Salman Highway."

Alen said, "That's a non-starter. This guy is headed south into Riffa."

"Well, shit." Gunny poured over his map. "Okay, if he continues south toward Awali and turns west on Zallaq Highway, it'll take him to Bin Salman Highway. Actually, this makes sense. The distribution station is on the east side of Bin Salman and you can't cross the median. The only access is from the south."

"Can we take them on Zallaq?"

Gunny grumbled, "Fuck no. There's another damn palace complex on Zallaq. What is with these Arabs and their palaces? From what I see, the best location may be at the target itself."

Alen took a deep breath. "We don't have much choice."

They continued to follow the pickup truck through a series of traffic circles in Riffa. They didn't want to get too close and risk alerting their prey. When the Nissan turned right on Zallaq Highway, Alen sped up to keep them in sight. When the pickup turned north on Bin Salman Highway, the climax was at hand. Gunny racked Alen's MP-7 to make sure there was a round in the chamber. The big Serb laid the weapon across his lap. Gunny had brought his own Sig Saur 9mm. Unlike Rusty, he always prepared for combat. He removed a suppresser from the thigh pocket of his pants and screwed it onto the end of the barrel. Gunny said, "Slow down. Give them time to get off the highway and open the gate. There's a neighborhood on the west side of the highway. I want to keep our rounds inside the walls of the distribution station if possible."

"Understood." Alen slowed the Range Rover. When the Nissan turned right onto the short dirt road leading to the distribution center, he pulled off onto the shoulder about three hundred meters to the south and turned off his headlights. The passenger jumped out of the truck and ran up to open the gate. Seconds later, the truck was inside.

Gunny motioned ahead, "Go." Alen pulled forward on the shoulder with his headlights off. When he reached the road, Alen stopped short by a cluster of palm trees. Gunny studied the gate some seventy-meters to his right. "Gate is partially closed, but not locked. I suspect they want a quick getaway. Let's roll."

Alen slowly eased the Range Rover up to the gate and Gunny jumped out. As Gunny pushed the gate open, Alen had his MP-7 at the ready. Some sixty meters beyond was a two-story building with the gray Nissan pickup parked outside. A vehicle door on the north end was open and there was a dim light coming from inside.

Alen drove the Range Rover closer. Gunny walked alongside keeping his Sig trained on the open overhead door. When the bumper of the Range Rover was almost in contact with the back of the truck, Alen stopped. The pickup was blocked in. He slid out and moved to the left side of the large overhead door opposite Gunny. Neither man knew what to expect. They had no idea the layout of the building. There were no other vehicles inside the distribution station. They hoped this meant there were no additional terrorists to deal with.

Using only hand signals, Alen told Gunny to cover him while he entered the building. He slipped through the door and crouched behind a heavy wooden crate. The room was some ten by fifteen meters with a number of large diameter pipes rising from the concrete floor to feed a series of valves and manifolds before diving back down again. This was some sort of control system dictating the flow of water from the huge storage tanks outside to the water mains feeding the surrounding community. Alen's eye was drawn to a dim light to his right. He moved up to some barrels to get a better view. One of the terrorists, Javad, was working on a large pipe with a wrench. Alen glanced back at Gunny and signaled for him to enter and move to the opposite side of the hall. Alen signaled that he had eyes on only one.

Javad was oblivious to the presence of the two Praetorians behind him. He was preoccupied with the two large valves in front of him that released water from one of the large tanks to the water main. In the pipe between the two valves was an access port in the form of a "T" junction. The access port was half a meter long with a thick metal flange at the end. It was sealed by a heavy, threaded steel cap that screwed into the flange and was also held in place by six large bolts. Javad had to remove the bolts before unscrewing the cap. Once opened, he would empty the canisters into the pipe, replace the cap, and open the valves, flushing the radioisotopes into the water main. He had already removed five of the large bolts and was hard at work on the sixth. At his feet were two dull gray metal canisters containing the isotopes.

Gunny was creeping up to gain a better shooting position when Ebrahim popped up from behind a large pipe with an AK-47 in his hands. Without saying a word, he fired a burst at Gunny before slewing ninety degrees to his left and sending four rounds thunking into the barrels Alen was hiding behind. Gunny dove to his left in search of better cover while Alen immediately sent a fusillade of rounds toward the terrorist. Ebrahim had already ducked and the rounds passed harmlessly over his head. Javad, meanwhile, was removing the last bolt.

Alen keyed his mic, "Well, I'd say the element of surprise is gone."

Gunny shot back, "Ya think? These two are better than the guys in Dubai. They set up a rear guard."

"More disciplined too. The shooter is just the decoy. The guy at the pipe never stopped working."

"Well, two can play that game. I'll draw the fire of the shooter. As soon as he shoots at me, he'll expect you to come at him to protect me. Shoot the other one instead."

Alen didn't like the idea of Gunny being a decoy. "What about you?"

Gunny chuckled, "Don't worry about me, I got a plan." The old man slid to his right and got down on one knee behind a large pipe coming out of the floor at a 45-degree angle. He banged on the pipe and fired a round into the air. As expected, Ebrahim sent a long burst of 7.62x39mm rounds from his

AK in Gunny's direction. When he did, Alen moved forward to put a large valve between him and Ebrahim. Javad detected the motion, picked up an AK and ducked inside a cluster of pipes two steps closer to Ebrahim but further away from the isotopes. No longer worried about hitting a canister, Alen emptied his magazine at Javad's position. Only one of the rounds hit him directly but the other rounds ricocheted off the floor and surrounding pipes peppering Javad with lead and shrapnel. He dropped his wrench and crumpled onto the floor.

Ebrahim glanced back just as his partner collapsed. Filled with rage, he fired blindly toward Alen's new position, but the huge valve deflected the rounds. Alen was in the middle of reloading and didn't immediately return fire. Gunny rolled onto the floor and, shooting under the pipe in front of him, hit Ebrahim's boot.

The terrorist let out a loud cry as he grasped his shattered ankle. He didn't drop his weapon and managed to respond by firing under the pipes with his AK just off the floor. Gunny barely escaped being the victim of his own tactic. This gave Alen all the time he needed. With a fresh magazine in his MP-7, he moved forward and was now almost directly to Ebrahim's right, expanding the arc he need to cover from 90-degrees to 135-degrees. Alen keyed his mic and said, "Are you okay?"

"Yeah, but this fucker is pretty good."

"I'm on his three o'clock. Distract him and I'll finish it."

"Copy that. On three. Three…two…one." Gunny rolled to his left and fired three rounds toward Ebrahim. When he did, Alen sent a long burst of 4.6x30mm projectiles flying toward the terrorist at 700 meters per second. Ebrahim was hit by four of the slugs and fell backwards with his weapons clattering to the ground.

Alen called out, "He's down. Double-check him while I get the other one."

Gunny moved up to Ebrahim cautiously. He didn't totally trust the MP-7 round. It was too light for his liking. When he came up on Ebrahim stretched out on the ground, the terrorist moaned softly. *Damn, still alive.* Gunny raised his Sig and put two rounds in the man's forehead. *Two 9mm are still better than four 4.6mm.*

Alen flanked Javad's position to sidle up to him using the maze of piping for cover. When he reached Javad's body, the man appeared dead but the big Serb put two into his skull, just to be sure. *There is no such thing as too dead.* Alen was studying the scene when Gunny walked over. Staring at the plate they were removing, Alen said, "All they had to do was unscrew that cap, pour that shit in the pipe, screw the cap back on, and open these valves. It would have sucked that poison right into the water main."

"Well, it's good we killed him then. Where's the crap?"

"Here it is." Alen reached down and picked up two gray canisters.

"Good. Let's get the fuck out of here." As Alen drove the Range Rover through the gate, Gunny keyed his mic and said, "Alpha One, this is Bravo Two. Two tangos down. Two packages recovered. No casualties...on our side."

* * *

Inside the East Isa Town Water Distribution Station, Barbad was having doubts about his initial plan. *If I go out there, whoever it is will kill me just like they killed Ali, Reza, Mirza, and Khashar. But are they all dead? I only saw two bodies. But both cars are out there.* Niaz snapped him back to reality. "Barbad, we're ready to cover you when you leave."

"I'm reconsidering. The gate is blocked by Ali's car. The van isn't powerful enough to push it out of the way and break through the gate."

Niaz was starting to worry. "What do we do?"

Saeed and Ghasen walked over. They too were needing guidance. Barbad tried to project confidence. "Who are we facing, really?" The men shrugged. "If it was the police, they'd have this place surrounded, there'd be a helicopter overhead, and they'd be evacuating the apartment buildings in the area. But there is no helicopter and there are no police cars, so who is out there?"

Ghasen posited, "The anti-terror squad? American navy people?"

"No. They'd have plenty of men. They could overwhelm us easily. I don't know how many people are out there, but I don't think it's very many."

Niaz asked, "If they're not with the government, why are they attacking us? How do they even know we are here?"

Barbad didn't have the answer to any of the questions but had to say something. "Maybe a rival group trying to steal our radioisotopes. ISIS. Hizballah. Hamas. Or some new group we haven't even heard of."

Saeed asked, "Where did this stuff even come from?"

"Pakistan...I think."

"Could it be them trying to get their shit back before anyone finds out?"

Niaz added coldly, "Or the Israelis? It was they who disrupted Abu Almawt's last plan, wasn't it?" The men nodded and mumbled. They too assumed the Israeli's had foiled the biological attack.

Barbad snorted, "Well, whoever it is, we go to them or make them come to us. I vote for the latter. Look around you." The interior was very similar to the facility at Hamid Town—a labyrinth of pipes, valves, and manifolds. "This place is very defensible with all these steel pipes. Our enemies have only a couple of ways in. Three of us will hold them off while the other two deploy the weapon here."

"Here? But Abu Almawt's plan was for..."

Barbad snapped back, "I'm aware what the plan was! Do things look like they're going according to plan?" The answer was only silence. Seconds later, Taher came trotting up. "I told you to cover the front."

"I saw something. No one was out front, so I checked the window facing the gate. I saw two people behind Mirza's car. I also checked the west side. There are two, maybe three men behind the base of the water tower. I've seen no one else."

Barbad processed this new information. "If there are only four or five people out there, the numbers are even; the odds are in our favor since they have to attack. In the meantime, we inject all the isotopes in the water here. If they're a rival group, once we inject the radioisotopes into the water main, there is nothing to fight over. They'd be foolish to press an attack that yields nothing except the imminent arrival of the police." Turning to Saeed, he said. "Find the injection point for this facility. Take Niaz, gather all the remaining canisters, find some tools, and start opening it. Taher, cover the front door. Ghasen and I will guard the vehicle door. It is the only other way in. Go!"

Taher ran back to the small office at the front of the building. He piled up furniture and whatever else he found to create a makeshift barricade facing the door. While he was working, Sarah trained her weapon on the front door as Magne ran toward the building. In addition to his MP-7, he carried a handheld version of the wall penetrating radar they had used so effectively in Dubai. He moved away from the windows and trained the device on the office. Through the walls, the small screen showed a man piling up chairs and computers. Keying his mic, he said, "This is Alpha Five. Radar confirms one tango directly opposite the door. Appears to be armed with an AK." He chuckled, "Junior is building a fort too."

Lon replied, "Can you eliminate him?"

Magne tapped on the side of the building. "The exterior wall is concrete block. If I had the Barrett .50 Cal, sure, but our MP-7s won't do it. There's a window on this side which would give me an angle, but it's too high."

Sarah broke in. "The front door is glass and there are two additional glass panels either side of it."

Magne replied, "Yeah, so."

"I'm thinking this place needs a drive thru. The keys are still in the Volkswagen. I'll drive it right through the front door."

Magne quipped, "He'll shoot you, ya know."

Sarah added, "Not if someone shoots him first. I'll duck down before impact. An AK won't shoot through an engine block. So long as you cap him before he gets to me…"

Lon interjected, "Okay, but give me a couple of minutes to hot-wire a truck. When you hit the front, I'll ram through that roll down vehicle door on this side. Two and Eight, enter behind me. Is that workable?"

Magne replied, "Sure. Good a plan as any. Let me move into position."

Sarah slipped into the Volkswagen through the passenger door and slid into the driver's seat. It was sticky with the congealed blood of Mirza, its recently deceased owner, but she didn't have time to be squeamish. She started the car and drove around the large water tank opposite the front door and stopped some twenty-five meters away. "Six is in position."

On the other side of the building, Lon crept up to where the terrorists had parked their vehicles. His eyes landed on an older Ford F-150 pickup truck. He just smiled. *I've been hot-wiring those since I was a kid in Laredo.* A minute later, Lon replied, "One is ready."

Sarah shot back, "That was quick. You a professional car thief or something?"

"The advantage of a misspent youth. On your cue, Six."

Sarah gripped the steering wheel. "Executing." Sarah put the car in "drive" and hit the gas. The car lurched forward and she aimed for the front door. Just before impact, she lay across the seat and braced herself. There was a huge crash as the car blew through the door and the glass panels on either side. Large pieces of the steel door frame went flying into the office. Behind his barricade, Taher was rocked back onto his butt. He struggled to get to his feet as some of the accumulated office equipment that constituted his "fort" was pushed back on top of him. He regained his footing, raised his weapon and slewed it toward the gaping hole that used to be the front door. Before he fired, three 4.6mm rounds from Magne's MP-7 hit him in the face.

Magne worked his way through the debris of the collision to Taher. He was dead. As he helped Sarah extricate herself from the Volkswagen, Magne reported, "One tango down. Front secured."

In the back half of the building, the noise of the car crashing into the office caught the other terrorists by surprise. Seconds later, the Ford pickup smashed through the overhead door of the vehicle entrance. The large sheet of articulated aluminum was ripped from its track and flopped down over the truck like a metal blanket.

Ghasen was the first to react. He raised his AK-47 and let loose a barrage of gunfire at the truck as it lurched to a stop after slamming into the back of Barbad's van. Lon ducked down in the front seat, but the overhead door laying on the vehicle protected him. A couple of the AK rounds actually penetrated the aluminum of the door but didn't retain enough energy to go through the Ford's windshield.

On either side of the truck, John Kernan and Steve Chang moved forward with their weapons at the ready. John zeroed in on Ghasen first and dropped him with four rounds in the chest. Barbad immediately retreated deeper into the building, ducking behind pipes for cover. As John searched for another target, Steve moved up to Ghasen. He was moaning as Steve put a round through his forehead. *Never leave a live enemy on your six.* Lon pushed open the driver's door of the pickup and got out. Finding Ghasen's body, he did the math. *That's two down, three to go.*

Lon, John, and Steve moved up as a team. John provided suppressing fire as Lon and Steve moved forward on the left. Once they were in a position of cover, they returned the favor as John moved up on the right. They continued to push Barbad, Niaz, and Saeed into a smaller and smaller area. A few seconds later, Magne came on the comms. "Making our way to the back. Alpha Two, we're approaching on your right. Don't shoot us."

John never took his eyes off the area in front of him. "Copy. Welcome to the party."

Lon interjected. "Five, cover our six. I want someone at the door in case these assholes called for reinforcements. Six, get somewhere where you can secure the front. I don't want anyone coming in behind you."

Magne crept back to the truck and moved to the driver's door giving him a line of fire to shoot across the hood into the building or across the bed to the driveway. Sarah held her position by the short hallway leading to the wrecked office. Most of her attention was focused on the three remaining terrorists inside. It would be next to impossible for anyone to approach through the office without making a racket.

The high bay was 30 by 15 meters. Barbad and his comrades had already been pushed into the back half. Niaz and Saeed worked feverishly to remove the six bolts securing the cap that stood between them and the water main. Unlike at the Hamid Town facility, this was never intended to be an attack point and the bolts securing the plate had not been loosened in anticipation. The rusty bolts were not cooperating.

Every burst of cover fire from the Praetorians as they inched closer was met by a short burst from Barbad. He now only had one magazine and was almost out of ammunition. Turning to his friends, he said, "Niaz, slide me a magazine. I'm almost out of bullets!"

Niaz stopped his work to retrieve another magazine. He slid it across the floor to Barbad. Then crawled on his hands and knees back to Saeed to continue working on the cap.

Barbad crawled over to retrieve the magazine but didn't consider where his enemy was. As he stretched out to grab the magazine, his right leg was briefly exposed. That was all it took. Alerted by the movement, Steve Chang squeezed off a three-round burst. One of the rounds tore into Barbad's thigh. He suppressed a scream and grabbed his bleeding leg. The wound really wasn't that bad, but he'd never been shot before. He had no frame of reference. Summoning all his strength, Barbad gritted his teeth and crawled quickly under the pipes and valves toward Niaz and Saeed leaving a blood trail.

Steve moved up cautiously. When he discovered the blood trail, he reported, "I clipped one. He's bleeding. No idea how serious; he's still mobile. Blood leads further back."

Lon replied, "Copy that. Good shooting. We need to get to them before they deploy their weapon. Move forward."

With Sarah covering his back, John Kernan moved up. The forest of pipes was both a blessing and a curse. They can't see you, but you can't see them either. To his right, several large crates were stacked near the wall. Using them as a screen, he flanked the other two terrorists. As he rounded the last crate, he peered to his left. To his horror, the metal plate was off and

Niaz was holding one of the canisters. He was starting to unscrew the cap!

There was no time to ask for covering fire. John jumped up and started pouring fire at Niaz and Saeed. Niaz was hit, fell back, and dropped the canister. Saeed rolled away, grabbed an AK and started shooting blindly in the direction of the incoming rounds. Sometimes it's better to be lucky than good. John Kernan was good but Saeed was lucky. One of his wild rounds found its target. John was hit in the left shoulder, shattering his collar bone. John rolled back behind the crate and keyed his mic. "I tapped one more tango. Not sure if he's dead. He was about to put that shit in the water. Second tango is in the wind." John took a deep breath to compose himself. "Six, you need to move up and cover this side. I caught one."

Lon asked, "How bad?"

"Not fatal but my weak side ping pong game is going to be shit for a while."

"Stay there. Six will cover east side."

Sarah interjected, "Moving up now!" Sarah quickly darted through the maze of pipes and found John. Inspecting his wound, she said, "Your collar bone is shattered. Anything else hit?"

"No. That's it. I can't believe that fucker shot me."

She scolded, "You should've asked for suppressing fire, dumbass."

"They were about to put that shit in the water. No time." Holding his MP-7 with his big right hand, John added, "Move on up. I'll cover your six." Sarah just gave him a smile before slipping off.

Saeed crawled on his belly toward the back of the high bay. He had no idea where he was going. There was no door or window. He just wanted to get as far away from his attackers as possible. His only objective was survival. He didn't care about the mission. *Whoever it is can have the damn radioisotopes!* He continued his retreat until he reached the back wall of the high bay. Nowhere left to go now. He picked up a wrench and tossed it. When it clanged noisily near the northwest corner of the room, he moved in the opposite direction. The noise of the wrench drew the attention of two of his attackers. *Might such a simple diversion work? Did they fall for it?*

They didn't. The Praetorians were nothing if not disciplined. Saeed scurried along the wall in a low crouch hunting for a way out. He was crawling on his hands and knees around a wooden crate when he encountered boots on the floor directly in front of him. He froze. He still had his AK in his hand but it was on the ground. A feminine voice said in Arabic, "I wouldn't." Now confused, Saeed peered up at a tall and stunningly beautiful woman standing over him with a submachine gun in her hand. *A woman? What the fuck?* His male ego got the better of him. He tried to jump back with his weapon. He barely moved an inch before Sarah shot him. Since she was above him, the round entered just inside his right collarbone with a downward trajectory ripping through his lung. Saeed dropped his weapon and fell back with a thud. Sarah shook her head. "Stupid men. Only learn through pain." She fired two rounds through his forehead before turning to rejoin her comrades. Keying her mic, she said, "One more tango down. No packages."

Lon replied, "Copy that Six."

Steve was still following the blood trail when he came across a discarded AK. The blood trail turned abruptly to his left and disappeared into a dark recess along the north wall. "This is Eight. My bleeder abandoned his weapon. He's holed up near the northeast corner."

Lon whispered, "Copy that Eight. Don't engage. Hold for intel." He crept a few feet further and slowly rolled around a large valve. On the other side, Niaz was lying on the ground breathing short, rapid breaths. He'd been hit in the chest and had a collapsed lung. Lon kicked Niaz's rifle away. To his right were the remaining six canisters of radioisotopes. *No need to ask this guy where they are.* Lon Oden put two more rounds in Niaz's chest and one into his skull. "This is One. Last tango is down. Six, repeat six packages recovered. Alpha Six, Eight has a survivor. See what intel he has."

Sarah replied, "With pleasure, One."

Steve and Sarah extricated Barbad from his hiding place behind a large pipe in the far corner of the high bay. After searching him, they dragged him out in the open to interrogate him. At first, he was defiant, but he was not a hardened soldier. It only took Sarah a minute or two to reach Barbad's pain threshold.

With the heal of her boot pressing into the wound in his leg, Barbad crumbled. "Okay, okay. I'll tell you. Just keep this bitch away from me!"

Lon smiled. "Now, wasn't that easier? Whose operation was this? What group?"

"Shams Sawda. Black Sun."

"Who recruited you for this operation?"

"Mohammad."

Lon asked, "Mohammad who?"

"I don't know. He's Afghani, I think. Maybe from northern Pakistan. He didn't tell me his last name."

"So, you just went to work for a stranger whose name you don't know?"

Barbad replied between breaths, "Yes, I mean no. I didn't go work for him. I went to work for his boss."

"Who is…?"

Barbad hesitated. Sarah lifted her right boot and pressed it onto his wounded leg. "Okay, okay!" There was a long pause. "Abu Almawt. The head of Shams Sawda."

Lon understood who this was, of course, but wanted to find out if Barbad did. "Abu Almawt? That's a nom de guerre. What's his real name?"

"Al-Maadi. Dr. Khalid Al-Maadi."

Sarah jumped in. "Al-Maadi. Where is he?"

Barbad was almost crying. "I don't know. I swear. May Allah strike me dead if I'm lying. I met up with him earlier tonight at the fish harbor. He was in a long black speedboat. He gave me the material and then left. I wasn't told where he was going. He didn't say and I didn't ask. We were supposed to put the radioactive stuff in the water system in six different locations."

Steve, who'd been standing silently nearby, added, "The Al Dur, Al-Hidd and Ras Abu Jarjur desalination plants and the water distribution stations serving the palace, the diplomatic section, and the US Navy base, right?"

Barbad was shocked. "How did you…?" Steve just smiled.

Lon interjected. "What role was Al-Maadi to play in all this?"

"He obtained the material. When all was in place, he was to give me the go-ahead personally."

"What time?"

"Sometime around 3 a.m. He wanted the radioisotopes to be put in the water in the middle of the night so it would have maximum spread before detection." Barbad added with a sneer, "But when you disrupted our work, I told my men to execute the plan immediately. They have certainly done so by now." He laughed, "All your efforts, all your killing was for nothing, Black Sun will still be victorious!"

Lon grinned. "I wouldn't count on that. We took out your two teams that left early."

"You're lying!" Barbad spit.

Sarah said, "Uh, hate to burst your bubble, but the white Toyota Yaris was heading to Al Dur and the gray Nissan pickup heading for Hamid Town, right? All four of your friends are dead and their radioactive poison has been recovered. Al-Maadi sacrificed you and your friends just like he sacrificed his Libyan and Palestinian cells. His own wife was sacrificed to cover his ass. How is he to contact you?"

Barbad was now completely dejected. Everything he had worked for, his friends and now his life was forfeit, and for what? "My cellphone. He's to call me on my cellphone."

Steve held up the phone he'd found on Barbad when they dragged him out. "This cellphone?" Barbad nodded. Steve turned to Lon and said, "I got no computer here. I gotta talk to Hans. We might geolocate Al-Maadi when he calls if we act fast."

"Get on it." Turning to Sarah and Magne, Lon said, "We need to get out of here. Get John in your vehicle. He needs medical attention."

Magne said, "Where? Not like we can stop by the local emergency room."

John was sitting on a crate listening. "I'll handle it. Let me call Mike."

"Okay, get going."

Sarah pointed to Barbad. "What about him? He was just about to murder a few thousand people. There's no way we just let him go."

"Agreed." Lon raised his weapon and put a single shot into Barbad's forehead.

Sarah snorted, "Well hell. I could've done that."

* * *

John called Mike and after a brief conversation, had an address. "It's a local clinic near the navy base." They sped off and were at the small building within twenty minutes. They were in the empty parking lot for five minutes when a blue Audi pulled up and rolled down its window. It was Mike Forester. "Follow me around back."

John Kernan winced with pain as he got out of the SUV. Mike briefly inspected John's shoulder and said, "You're such a pussy. This is a scratch. My ex-wife did more damage to me on a Saturday night after two margaritas."

"You got beat up by a woman and you call me a pussy?" Sarah glared at him. He quickly added, "Present company excluded."

She replied, "You're goddamned right."

Mike opened the back door of the clinic and led them in. "What is this place?" Magne asked.

"Local clinic. We have an arrangement with the owner. The guys on the teams use it when they can't go to the infirmary on base. Bar fights, falling off balconies, that kind of shit. We pay cash and he doesn't ask questions."

A tired, balding Arab man in his early fifties shuffled in. "Hello. I'm Doctor Azaad. What is it this time Mr. Forester?" Mike just pointed to John. "Oh, I haven't met you before. What's the problem?"

John pulled back his light windbreaker to reveal his damaged shoulder. Dr. Azaad's eyes got big momentarily. "Okay, hop up on the table and lie down. I'm going to have to sedate you."

"No thanks, doc. Just a local. I have shit to do and places to be."

Azaad rolled his eyes. "You Americans." He spotted Sarah for the first time. "Integrating forces I see. I must say, I approve."

Sarah smiled, "Thank you."

"Gentlemen, this may take a while. Make yourselves comfortable or go get a coffee. I won't have you poking around while I work."

Magne said, "We need to call the boss anyway. Let the man work."

Once outside, Sarah called Rusty and Gunny to fill them in on what was going on. Gunny asked for the address. "Sit tight, we're on our way."

Some twenty minutes later, Gunny and Rusty drove up in Alen's Range Rover. Magne asked, "Where's everyone else?"

"I sent them back to the hotel. Hans is monitoring phone traffic in case our friend calls. What's John's status?"

Magne replied, "Took one in the shoulder. Busted clavicle. The doc is going to clean it up and make him ambulatory. He made need surgery when we get home, but he'll be fine."

Rusty turned to Mike Forester and said, "Mike, I want to thank you for all your help tonight."

"Well, if we'd got to them before they offloaded their shit, this probably wouldn't have happened. Instead, we came up empty and John caught a round…again."

Gunny interjected, "Yeah, about that. We have something we need you to take off our hands." He walked around to the back of the SUV and opened the rear gate. Inside were a couple of heavy cardboard boxes holding a dozen, gray canisters.

Mike peered in the boxes and asked, "This isn't what I think it is, is it?"

"We recovered it tonight."

Mike was flabbergasted. "What the fuck am I supposed to do with this shit?"

Gunny replied incredulously, "Well, what the hell would you have done with it if you found it on that boat?"

"That's different! If we'd recovered it as the result of the mission…"

Rusty smiled, "Who's to say you didn't? What if your mission was a complete success? You stopped the boat, killed the bad guys and recovered the nasty stuff. You'd be heroes. All you have to do is edit your report a little bit, check this stuff in, and collect the bonuses. You'll probably get promotions. I'll bet your team would welcome the extra pay. Am I right?"

Mike mulled this over and then asked, "What about the guys you waxed tonight?"

"You let us worry about that. Hell, I'd get rid of this stuff myself, but I'd never get it through security at the airport."

Mike said, "Okay, but you have to pay the doctor. I like John, but not that much."

"Deal. We'll put them in your trunk. They're in lead canisters so they should be safe. I'd get rid of them as soon as possible—just in case."

"What the fuck. I've spent so much time on nuclear subs my nads are already fried."

As Magne and Gunny moved the boxes to the Audi's trunk, Mike just shook his head. "Who the fuck are you guys?"

A few minutes later, the door to the clinic opened and John walked out with his left arm in a sling. "Doc, great job. I owe ya one." Turning to Rusty, he said. "Hey boss. Good you're here. Pay the man."

Rusty approached Dr. Azaad. "Thanks for taking care of my man. How much do I owe ya?"

Dr. Azaad said meekly, "Uh, because of the late hour and all, it will be two thousand, US."

Rusty reached into his jacket pocket and pulled out a $10,000 bundle of $100 bills. "Here's ten grand. Don't sell yourself short. Buy something nice for your wife."

"I don't have a wife. She divorced me."

"Then buy something nice for yourself and make sure she sees it."

John slid into the backseat of Magne and Sarah's car before loudly and cheerfully declaring, "Okay, I'm ready. Let's blow this popsicle stand. I need a drink."

Dr. Azaad shrugged and said, "I gave him a pain killer. Keep his alcohol intake to a minimum."

Magne responded, "Easier said than done."

The doctor returned to his clinic shaking his head. As the door closed behind him, Mike asked Gunny, "Please tell me you guys got Al-Maadi."

"No. The son of a bitch wasn't there. We may, however, get a line on him later tonight. We don't have the resources to reach out and touch him, but you might. What kind of air assets do you guys have available?"

* * *

All the Praetorians, except for John Kernan, stayed up waiting for Khalid Al-Maadi to make the call Barbad claimed was imminent. John, as promised, had a couple of drinks from his room's minibar upon which, when mixed with Dr. Azaad's painkiller, caused him to pass out. The rest of the team gathered in Rusty's suite in nervous anticipation. They were too hopped up on stress and adrenaline to sleep anyway. Rusty ordered a couple of bottles of the hotel's finest bourbon, so the team imbibed in the interim.

Lon, Nigel, Alen, and Rusty lounged on the couches in the suite's living room talking about the night's action. They were on their third drink and angling for a fourth. Hans and Steve were at the kitchen table manning the computers, ready to geolocate Al-Maadi's cellphone if or when he called. They still had work to do and they limited themselves to one drink. Gunny paced the floor behind them. As long as Al-Maadi was unaccounted for, his mission wasn't over and he wouldn't drink until it was.

Sarah separated herself from the group, sitting alone on the kitchen counter sipping a Campari and soda. This was more personal for her. She wanted to hear Al-Maadi's voice; to talk to the man who tried to wipe out her entire country, her entire people. Her job would be to keep him on the line as long as possible while Hans and Steve zeroed in on his location. Alen entered the kitchen to add a splash of water to his bourbon. As he did, Sarah reached over, grabbed his arm and whispered, "That's your last one."

Taken aback, Alen said, "Excuse me?"

She gazed at him with her beautiful, almond eyes and gave a little smile. "I may need you later."

It suddenly dawned on him what she meant and he actually blushed a little. He poured his bourbon in the sink and smiled. "Yes, ma'am."

As the hour approached, the anticipation grew. At 0300 hours, Sarah stared at the telephone in her hand, Barbad's telephone. She hit a button and the screen lit up. *Okay, still powered on.* The men drinking in the living room checked their watches. The minutes ticked by and with each, they grew more concerned that Al-Maadi wouldn't call. Alen asked, "Did Sarah's guy warn him before she interrogated him? Or one of the others?"

Steve shook his head. "No. The computer would have registered the call."

Magne added, "Unless they used a different phone."

Sarah held up her phone. "No. The guy said he was to be called on this phone. Al-Maadi might swap phones but he'd still have to call this one to reach his crew. Or, at least I hope so."

Lon opined, "Maybe he was captured by the Bahraini police or coast guard?"

Gunny interjected, "Possible, but unlikely. News of an arrest of that magnitude would spread quickly, at least to Mike and his guys."

Steve posited, "Maybe he never intended to call at all? Maybe he was reluctant to kill fellow Arabs and just wanted to scare the Bahrainis?"

Sarah shook her head. "No way. He's shown no reluctance to send his people to their deaths before. Hell, he ordered his own wife to kill Ostergaard in Copenhagen. No, the more people dead, the bigger the impact. Consider Dubai. They definitely tried to execute that one."

Nigel added, "Yeah, but they didn't wait for Al-Maadi to give them approval either. Maybe the guy was lying. One last 'fuck you' before dying."

"No," Gunny mused, "they didn't have that luxury in Dubai. The timing was dictated by the appearance of the Emir. I'm sure Al-Maadi would have loved to push the button, but it wasn't practical. He was somewhere at sea. That cell had to have autonomy if the attack was going to work at all." As the Praetorians got into a heated discussion about who's theory was the most realistic, the phone rang. Everyone instantly froze.

Sarah let it ring twice before answering. Trying to lower her voice, she replied in Arabic, "Hello."

A voice replied, "Barbad, is that you? You sound funny."

Clearing her throat, she coughed and replied. "I, uh, inhaled some chlorine gas at Al Hibb."

"I understand." He paused for dramatic effect and said, "You and your men are authorized to deploy the weapon. This will be a glorious day for Shams Sawda and for the future Caliphate. You and your men are striking a righteous blow against the traitors of Islam and will be lionized as the modern sons of Saladin. After the wicked king and his government have been destroyed, the righteous people of Bahrain will cast out its corrupt and Jew-loving traitors and the Americans, and establish a true Islamic state worthy of Allah's blessings."

When he finished, Sarah, speaking in her true voice, said, "That's so exciting, Khalid, but how are they expected to do all that when they're dead." There was an eerie silence on the phone. "We have eliminated your cell in Manama just as we eliminated your cell in Dubai. Oh, by the way, the Novichok Kotov sold you was no phony. It was real. We just replaced it with something harmless."

Al-Maadi didn't believe it. "You're lying, whoever you are."

"Am I? We recovered the radioisotopes; the cesium and the strontium. You wanted radioactive iodine but were too ignorant to know it didn't last long enough to be obtained. I guess you're not as smart as you think you are, *Doctor* Al-Maadi."

Al-Maadi was now realizing that his plans had been thwarted...again. "I've heard enough lies."

He was about to end the call when Sarah said, "Nura."

"What did you say?"

"Nura. She's your wife, remember? Or should I say she *was* your wife. Do you want to know what happened to her?"

Al-Maadi stammered, "You can't possibly..."

"I can and I do. I was sitting at her table in Copenhagen when you told her to kill Andreas Ostergaard. I followed her through Cairo when she used herself as a decoy as you escaped. I was right behind you when you walked into that hospital in Jordan. After your attack against Israel failed, I tracked her to the mud hut in Eritrea where your Saudi friends dumped her while you fled to Pakistan. Shall I describe every door and window, the placement of every piece of furniture in her little hovel? I know all this because I was there...it's where I killed her."

"No! You're lying!"

Sarah added lightly, "She died a good death, if it matters to you. She attacked me with a knife, then I killed her with it. I laughed as the life left her eyes. The last person she saw was me, the Israeli who killed her."

Al-Maadi spit, "You Jewish whore!" Seconds later, the line went dead.

Sarah immediately turned to Steve Chang. "Did you get it?"

Steve smiled. "Yeah, we got it. I'll send the coordinates to John's friend, Mike."

* * *

"You Jewish whore!" Mohammad snatched the phone from his hand, snapped it in two, and dropped the pieces over the side of the speedboat into the inky depths of the Persian Gulf.

"Abu Almawt! They were baiting you!" He turned to the pilot of the speedboat. "Get this vessel moving immediately. Steer a course due north." The sleek black speedboat was floating silently in the middle of the Persian Gulf. The pilot stopped its engines at a point as far from Bahrain as possible while still having a cell signal for Al-Maadi.

"Due north? That's toward Iran. That wasn't part of our deal."

"Would you rather be boarded by the American navy?"

The pilot scoffed. "My boat is faster than any of theirs. And I just checked the radar. There are no vessels within several nautical miles of us. If they come after us, I'll be in Iranian waters in two minutes. They can't pursue me into Iranian waters without risking a war."

Mohammad pulled a gun from his belt and pointed it at the man's forehead. "Either you drive north or I will."

The pilot was suddenly frightened. "Okay, okay. North it is. If the Iranians stop us, I'll have to bribe them. You're paying for that."

Al-Maadi finally spoke up. "We will cover all your costs and give you an additional 5,000 Euro for your trouble. Satisfactory?"

The pilot nodded, "Yes." Gesturing toward Mohammad, he added. "You need to get a handle on your man here."

Al-Maadi was conciliatory. "We just received some bad news. You'll have to forgive him. Now please, we need to leave this area immediately."

"Understood. I need to turn on the fuel to all three engines for maximum speed. You two need to move as far forward as possible. I need more weight in the front until the boat planes out."

Mohammad put a lifejacket over his head and handed one to Al-Maadi. "Abu Almawt, take this. I don't trust this man's driving. One sharp turn and we're over the side."

Al-Maadi grabbed the life jacket but didn't put it on. "Mohammad, you worry too much."

"Whoever you were talking to just now was trying to keep you on the line to use your phone to locate you."

"You heard the pilot. We'll be in Iranian waters in a few minutes. Not even the Americans will risk a military confrontation by violating Iranian territorial waters."

The pilot opened the cover over the speedboat's three turbocharged engines. He had been running on two engines to save fuel but now speed was the priority. As he turned the valve that fed fuel to the middle engine, a faint noise got his attention. He moved back to the cockpit and checked his radar. Nothing for miles. Just as he was about to turn the key, he heard the noise again. "Did either of you hear that?"

Mohammad answered, "Hear what?"

"A noise, like a small engine, but there is nothing on radar."

He walked to the stern of the speedboat and stared up into the starry sky. He peered at the twinkling lights to determine if any were moving, a sign that one might be an airplane. He was staring south toward Bahrain when he made out a brief flash followed by a whooshing noise. A bright light moved directly toward them. It was from the motor of the AGM-114 Hellfire missile launched from a US MQ-9 Reaper drone. It had been patrolling in the area for more than an hour. Its operators had been waiting for SEAL Master Chief Mike Forester to provide the coordinates of their target.

The pilot of the speedboat had no clue what it was, but Mohammad did. He'd witnessed the Hellfire in action up close in Afghanistan. "Missile!" He pushed Khalid Al-Maadi to the deck and jumped on top of him. Seconds later there was a huge explosion and a blinding flash. This missile was the Hellfire II AGM-114K2A equipped with a nine-kilogram tandem shaped charge High Explosive Anti-Tank (HEAT) warhead augmented with an antipersonnel fragmentation sleeve.

The missile struck the middle engine at the pilot's feet. The man was practically vaporized. The shaped charge sent a jet of molten copper completely through the engine, shattering the speedboat's hull below. The back end of the boat was sheared off and it started sinking from the stern. The razor sharp, metal shards from the fragmentation sleeve flew in all directions like a thousand knives, destroying everything in front of them.

The drone began orbiting, its infrared cameras capturing the scene for its operator. Mike Forester was over the man's shoulder. "Well, Master Chief, I'd say that was a successful attack. The target is definitely destroyed."

"What about the combatants on board?"

The operator rewound the video to just before the point of explosion. "The guy in the back was obliterated. Not even a recognizable body part. The two toward the front caught the frag." He pointed to the screen. "They're stacked up here. Even if by some miracle they survived the blast, they'll bleed out or drown. This boat's going down fast." He zoomed out the camera and Mike saw he was right. The once beautiful, sleek speedboat was sinking rapidly with two-thirds of its length already underwater. Two motionless bodies floated free just as the boat slipped beneath the waves. The corpses joined the other flotsam from the wreck. Seat cushions, water bottles, life jackets, and an oil slick were the only sign that the boat ever existed.

Mike smiled. "I guess we can close the books on that chapter. Good work, sailor."

EPILOGUE

A white pickup truck pulled to a stop in front of the Pakistani Embassy on Road 1901 in the diplomatic section of Manama, Bahrain. Three clean cut, physically fit western men got out. The driver had a clipboard. The other two walked to the back of the truck, opened the tailgate and slid out a large, metal case. It had two handles on the ends with a large hasp and padlock securing the lid. The two men strained to lift the case and carry it to the front gate of the embassy. The two Pakistani guards looked on with curiosity. The driver approached them and said, "Hi. I'm Mike Finster with ASU Shipping. I have a delivery for Ambassador Raja Khan. Where do you want us to put it?"

The guard turned to his colleague as if to ask, *What the fuck?* The other guard shrugged and ducked into the guard shack. A moment later he returned with a clipboard of his own. In accented English, he said, "We have no deliveries scheduled for today."

Mike said, "I don't know about that, but I'm being paid to deliver this to Mr. Khan. There is no signature required so if he doesn't accept it, we're leaving it here. We get paid either way. If it is something he wants or is expecting, I'd suggest you guys give him a call. Hell, it might be perishable. He may have ordered Maine lobsters for all I know." He chuckled, "Being packed in ice would explain why this son of a bitch is so heavy." He added softly, as if sharing a secret, "I wouldn't want to be you if whatever this is rots out here. At least if you move it inside, it becomes someone else's problem."

The guard glanced up at the burning sun. "Okay, move it into the outer lobby to get it out of the sun. I'll call the ambassador's office to tell them something has arrived."

The two other men picked up the case and, along with Finster, followed the guard to the outer lobby. It wasn't really a lobby. It was just an open patio enclosed by two-meter walls on two sides and the front of the embassy on a third. They placed it on the ground and immediately returned to their truck. The guard asked, "Where are they going?"

Mike replied, "Back to the truck. They're just the muscle." Mike started to leave too.

"Wait! You can't just leave this here. I have no idea what's in it. It could be a bomb or something!"

"Okay, then call your boss. I'll wait."

The guard got on his walkie-talkie and spoke to someone in Urdu. "They'll be here in a minute." Mike waited patiently until a man in a suit appeared from inside the building. The guard said, "This is Mr. Farooq. Our head of security."

Mike stuck out his hand. "Hi, Mr. Farooq. I'm Mike Finster with ASU Shipping. We have a delivery for Mr. Khan."

Farooq said, "We have no record of any delivery. Take this away."

"No can do. It's yours now."

Farooq asked his guard, "What is it?"

"Seafood? Maybe? Not sure."

Mike interjected, "Actually, it's radioactive cesium-137 and strontium-90 from your not-so-secret plutonium reprocessing plant next to the Chashma Nuclear Complex. It was recently stolen. We didn't steal it, but we are returning it."

Farooq's eyes got huge. "You can't leave this here!"

"Wanna bet?"

Farooq motioned for the guard to pull his pistol. "This is illegal and against diplomatic protocol. You are on Pakistani sovereign territory. I am within my rights to detain you."

Mike smiled. "Technically, yes you are. But then you'll have to explain to the Bahrainis why three Americans delivered a chest full of Pakistani nuclear shit that was recovered from a bunch of now-dead terrorists who were going to use it to attack Bahrain, including the king. But hey, it's your choice. I'll wait while you decide."

Farooq told his guard. "Don't let him leave." He then pulled out his cellphone and made a call. Mike didn't speak Urdu but it was obvious neither party on the call was happy.

Five minutes later, a rather distinguished Pakistani man in his fifties arrived. "I am ambassador Khan. What is the meaning of this?"

Mike explained, "A week or so ago, one of your people at your plutonium reprocessing plant in Chashma stole a bunch of highly radioactive shit."

Khan blanched but quickly recovered. "I'm sure I don't know what you're talking about."

"The sweat on your forehead tells a different story but, okay. This stuff was stolen from Pakistan, given to terrorists and recently recovered in Bahrain as the result of an operation against said terrorists. Since the material is technically yours and we are sure your government knew nothing about the theft or its intended use, we're returning it to you. A simple 'thank you' would suffice." Mike removed a key from his pocket, unlocked the case and opened it. "As best we can tell, there are eight canisters of cesium-137 and four of strontium-90. The canisters apparently are made out of lead but I'd be careful just the same."

The ambassador flashed red. "You can't leave this here."

"I know. Anyway, I'll be going now. You have a nice day." As Mike turned to leave, Farooq raised his pistol as if to stop him, but the ambassador grabbed his wrist, pushed his hand down, and shook his head. Mike walked through the front gate, got in his truck and drove away.

The ambassador turned to Farooq and said, "Place this in the basement. Somewhere close to the guards' station…but not too close."

"For how long?"

"Until the PAEC retrieves it."

* * *

When the speedboat sank, the drone circled for a while and then returned to its base. After it left, Khalid Al-Maadi peeked cautiously into the morning sky. The sun was starting to rise in the east and the horizon glowed a soft yellow in anticipation. Al-Maadi was exhausted. On the surface of the water, he had been playing dead while below it, he'd been kicking his legs like mad in an effort to stay afloat without using his arms. When the drone flew away, he grabbed hold of Mohammad's body to give his aching legs a rest. Mohammad had put on his life jacket, Al-Maadi never did. *Why didn't I listen to him?*

Mohammad had been gravely injured by the shrapnel from the missile's fragmentation sleeve. His back, arms, and legs were peppered. Fortunately, his head and major organs were spared. He wore his Kevlar vest out of habit. This time it saved him. That and the life jacket he put on moments before the attack. Without that, he'd have drowned in minutes.

As Al-Maadi grabbed Mohammad in his effort to say afloat, the jostling roused his bodyguard. Mohammad was blinded by pain. Soaking his myriad of wounds in saltwater only made the pain more intense. He groaned and tried to survey his surroundings. "Where are we?"

Al-Maadi replied, "The Persian Gulf. Drifting toward Iran…I think."

"I remember…a missile. What of the boat?"

"Oh, the boat and its captain are long gone. It's just you and me, my friend."

Mohammad winced with pain. "I need a doctor…soon."

Al-Maadi chuckled. "Well, we're out of luck for the time being. I hope that an Iranian patrol boat saw the explosion and will investigate. If not, we may both be out of luck."

Mohammad sighed. "It was that phone call. They kept you on the line too long. That's how they found us. I told you to never…"

Al-Maadi never enjoyed being scolded like a child, and certainly not by an uneducated thug, but he suppressed his irritation. "Don't worry about that now, my old friend. Focus on staying alive. Someone will find us soon. I'm sure of it. It's not my destiny to die this way…or yours."

They drifted along for hours. The sun baked and blistered their skin. They had nothing for shade. They were completely at the mercy of the elements. The other flotsam from the boat had long drifted away. The only thing keeping them alive was the one medium sized, life jacket that Mohammad had thrown over his neck just before the missile hit. When Al-Maadi tried to hang on to it, it pulled Mohammad's face into the water. Mohammad instinctively reacted and pushed Khalid away from him. Khalid then panicked and grabbed the life jacket again and the process repeated itself. Finally, Al-Maadi said, "Mohammad, brother, I cannot tread water forever. We need to share the life jacket. We need to take turns."

Mohammad scowled at him in disbelief "Are you joking? You're uninjured…thanks to me. I have multiple wounds."

"What does that matter if I drown? How can I keep you alive if I'm dead? We should take turns, that's all I'm saying."

"If you had listened to me, we'd have two life jackets."

Al-Maadi was growing irritated. "What is in the past is in the past. I am talking about right now. Let me wear the life jacket for say, five minutes to rest my legs. Then you get it for the next fifty-five. That's fair."

Mohammad's expression was one of distain. "But I can't swim."

Al-Maadi was already taking the life jacket off of him. "I'll help you." Mohammad was in no condition to fight him. Al-Maadi pulled the life jacket off his bodyguard and slipped it over his own head. He found the straps, wrapped them around his body and snapped them in front. Mohammad was weakly gripping Al-Maadi's sleeve in an effort to keep his mouth and nose above water. Spitting out a mouthful of sea water, he said. "You're going to let me die, aren't you?"

"The fight must go on. And let's be honest, which of us is more critical to the cause? As a doctor, I assess that you are badly wounded and unlikely to survive, even if we were rescued in the next five minutes. It's a hard decision that must be made. If our situations were reversed, I would expect you to do the same."

"Do you? Let's not forget that my injuries were sustained saving your life from a missile attack. An attack that would never have happened if you'd just listened to me…for once. But no, your ego got in the way."

Al-Maadi pulled Mohammad's hand from his sleeve. He held it briefly before pushing it and Mohammad away. "You'll be with Allah soon where the virgins await you." When Mohammad opened his mouth to respond, he was swamped by sea water. He coughed and spit but was too weak to fight it. "Thank you for your service, old friend."

Mohammad's eyes were burning with fire. He managed to get his mouth above water long enough to spit out his final words. "See you in hell." He then slipped beneath the waves forever.

Al-Maadi drifted on for hours. He was dying of thirst. His body wanted to take a sip, just a sip, of sea water but his brain knew it was fatal. *Am I to die out here, too? What will Mohammad do to me in hell?* He even considered ending his suffering. All he had to do was ease out of the life jacket and slip away. But that required real bravery and Khalid Al-Maadi was not brave, so he lingered on.

Hours later, more than fifteen hours after he was thrown into the sea, there was a noise, a motor. He spun around until he espied it, a patrol boat of some sort. With the last of his strength, he waved his arms, slapped the water and yelled as loud as his parched throat would let him. It was enough.

Minutes later a thirty-foot fiberglass patrol boat pulled alongside him. He had no clue who was on it or where it was from. A number of hands reached down and grabbed him. They lifted him from the water and dropped him painfully onto the deck. The setting sun was in his eyes and he made out no details of his rescuers. A voice spoke to him in an unintelligible language. In Arabic, Al-Maadi replied, "I don't understand."

The voice then said in Arabic, "Ah, you speak Arabic. Who are you?"

"Who are you?"

"I am Lieutenant Merza of the Iranian Revolutionary Guard Corps Navy. I ask again, who are you?"

"Oh, praise be to Allah, I was looking for you," Khalid lied, "We were attacked by the Americans. All my comrades were killed but me. I barely escaped with my life. I am Dr. Khalid ibn Mahfous Al-Maadi, also known as Abu Almawt, the Father of Death, the head of Shams Sawda, the revolutionary group Black Sun. I demand that you take me to your commanding officer."

Lieutenant Merza and his men just laughed. "Well, Mr. Death, you are under arrest for illegally entering the territorial waters of the Islamic Republic of Iran." They flipped him over on his stomach. With his face smashed onto the deck, they cuffed his hands behind his back. Picking him up by his hands, Merza chuckled. "I'd say your Black Sun is in eclipse."

Made in the USA
Monee, IL
20 July 2025